TIME WILL TELL

The machine gave a loud ... f
smoke poured ...

"Wait!" yelled ...

Terrible pain l... body, rent asu... but soundless, sightless. He felt agony, worse than even the Londonderry bomb. There was *no thing*. He was alone, without even himself.

Skin ripped from his muscles, vessels, bones, left him white naked, bare to the void. He stared into the void, eyeless.

The void stared back . . .

"A mind-altering blend of
Arthurian, Merovingian, Masonic,
and modern-day spy suspense."

Robert Anton Wilson,
coauthor of *The Historical Illuminatus Chronicles*

Don't Miss the Concluding Volume of
ARTHUR WAR LORD
Coming Soon From AvoNova

ARTHUR WAR LORD

DAFYDD AB HUGH

AVON BOOKS • NEW YORK

ARTHUR WAR LORD is an original publication of Avon Books. This work has never before appeared in book form. This work is a novel. Any similarity to actual persons or events is purely coincidental.

AVON BOOKS
A division of
The Hearst Corporation
1350 Avenue of the Americas
New York, New York 10019

Copyright © 1994 by Dafydd ab Hugh
Published by arrangement with the author
Library of Congress Catalog Card Number: 93-90645
ISBN: 0-380-77028-8

First AvoNova Printing: March 1994

AVONOVA TRADEMARK REG. U.S. PAT. OFF. AND IN OTHER COUNTRIES, MARCA REGISTRADA, HECHO EN U.S.A.

Printed in the U.S.A.

RA   10 9 8 7 6 5 4 3 2 1

CHAPTER 1

L EVEL WITH THE SUN AND THE MOON, CAER CAMLANN, THE great fortress tower, floated upside down above an ocean of hazed and shimmering clouds, loomed like the Alban highlands, north of Emperor Hadrian's vast wall. Overhead an imperial eagle called mournfully, "flee free, flee," flapped disruptively through the palatial home of Artus *Dux Bellorum*, warlord of all the Big Island kingdoms—the last civilized Roman in Britain.

The eagle's heart burst from grief, dripped fire as red as *Her* hair. The blood royal rained upon the twin cups of Rhiannon, dispelled the reflected image of the floating Roman villa, mirrored in the clouds.

A rose grew where each spot of blood flecked the ground. The wind howled, tolled a soulless, iron chime. The music rushed from Cors Cant Ewin's harp, out of control again. Notes burst from his bowels, yanked and jerked his fingers like stick-poppet limbs.

No, not again! he raged; *I will control the music, it'll not cost me another bardic examination.*

The images flared from his harp with their own mind, animate and willful, ignoring his command. He saw a malign spirit, a black and tan crow, descend upon the dying eagle. The crow caught hold of the falling, golden bird, rode it into the ground.

"Croi!" it cawed. "Cor!" The crow hopped on dung-feet, fluttered midnight feathers, and cocked its head. It watched Cors Cant with the left eye, then the right. "Crochar!" it appended, sending a chill down the boy's spine. *Crochar* was "bier" in the Eire tongue. The bird died, fell upon its side,

1

beak wedged open. The bard's fingers froze upon the strings, silencing the doleful, portentous tune.

Cors Cant Ewin blinked, fell back into himself. He was still sitting cross-legged upon the cold, stone seat of Looking Far, Close, holding an old, chipped harp in his arms. Shaken and sweating, he brushed knotty, brown hair from his eyes.

The chime . . . had he imagined the chime? *No, by Jesus, it was the feast cymbalum!* Cors Cant jumped off the seat, long overdue home, the supper song still uncomposed. The discordant vision of eagle and crow was utterly unacceptable.

Myrddin'll kick my lazy arse from here to holy Jerusalem, thought Cors Cant. He kicked a rock, then sat hard, gripping his sandaled foot.

Cors Cant Ewin, not quite yet a bard, caught up harp and cloak and pelted down the hill toward Caer Camlann. A feast without music would not please the War-Master, *Dux Bellorum,* Artus *Pan-Draconis.*

As the boy ran, the floating castle illusion vanished. Camlann Tower rested securely on the Hill of the Talking Head, as it ought. The cloud mirage mundaned to smooth, dry fields hunkering for approaching winter.

Cors Cant watched his feet on the road, not the shops and apartments of the merchant's *insula.* He was offended by workaday bustle and even passed the half-built forum without a glance. Cors Cant focused his eyes on the inner wall of the tower, behind which the fortress itself waited like an impatient father for its prodigal bard.

The fortress and—Her.

Colors flashed past his peripheral vision. *Restless architects repainting the bloody aqueducts again,* he noted, then squinted fearfully at the last flash of the setting sun. It was dusk when he reached the Augustine mound-wall.

"Let me pass!" he cried to the legionnaire.

"Who is that?" sneered a familiar voice. "A Saxon? Yeah, must be a filthy Saxon!"

"Cacamwri, is that you?" yelled Cors Cant. "Let me in, you goat lover! The *Dux Bellorum* will just be sitting down to broth and I should be—"

"Sounds like an Æthbert? A Cuthbert? A Harald, perhaps, home from a busy day fucking swine in the mountains!"

"It's Cors Cant Ewin, you unwashed, landless lapdog!

Arawn's black balls, open the bloody gates, or by bounding Jesus I'll tell Artus about you and Cei's son in the hire barn!"

The soldiers laughed and hooted as the red-faced Centurion Cacamwri ordered the foot gate open, barely wide enough for the boy to squeeze through. *Takes an emperor of fools to trade insults with a bard,* thought Cors Cant.

He felt Cacamwri's eyes on the back of his neck all the way to the villa.

CHAPTER 2

AT THE SAME MOMENT, FIFTEEN CENTURIES LATER, TWO DARK grey Rolls Royces rolled up a long, snow-covered drive, windows tinted black against sniper fire. They paused within view of the manor house. From the second auto, Major Peter Smythe observed the property for several long moments.

He closed his eyes, numbed by tiredness; saw the flash, felt the fire—the weight pressed down and down and down. . . .

Time travel. Maybe that is *what I need, go back before the—the incident.*

He opened his eyes; Colonel Cooper watched, concerned.

"Peter, are you up to this?"

"As opposed to what? Londonderry again?"

"Or Calais. You have forty days accumulated leave. Best start using it or it goes away."

The manor was large, fifty rooms at least. Too modern, not defensible.

Windows and doors poorly placed; plenty of ground cover for a whole buggering army to crawl right up and egg the place, if they'd a mind.

"Fit as a fiddle, sir," he said in a monotone. "Never better. Bristol's only five miles thataway; I can look at the harbor."

Cooper extended his hand; Peter took it, felt the extra pressure with the ring and fourth finger and responded with the same signal. *Presto right-ho, now you're a Mason!* All it took was three weeks reading smeary-inked pamphlets in Cooper's library.

"Signal Blundell right away, Peter, but steer clear of Mason subjects. He's a fourth degree. If you try to dazzle him, he'll surely catch you."

"Your books taught me the signs all the way up through sixth degree."

Colonel Cooper snorted in amusement. "Don't flatter yourself, Peter. Those publications are mostly made-up, because of the oaths; you wouldn't fool me for longer than five minutes, for example. You've the words, but not the tune.

"Just leave Blundell the vague impression you're a brother in the craft," continued the Colonel. "Don't overplay the role. We just want him to open up about this time travel rot."

Time travel. Next they'll send me to Inverness to hunt poor Nessie.

"According to the dossiers, the only Irishman on the project is an Orangeman from a family of Orangemen. Why is the '22' involved?"

Cooper shifted uncomfortably. "Well, Roundhaven thinks—"

"That's open to debate."

"Not funny, Peter. He's an ass, but he's Minister of Defense. He takes all that American Star Track gawd-help-us seriously. Star Wars, whatever it is. Think of it as mobile desk duty, *Major.*" Peter fell silent; when Cooper resorted to rank-pulling, the conversation was ended.

"What about Selly Corwin?" Peter asked after a spell.

"A Labour whiner. Not an agitator."

"Didn't she give money to Sinn Fein once?"

Cooper shrugged. "I gave money to the Communist Party once. She's English, went to a good public school, well-to-do."

"You joined the Communist Party?"

"I'll show you my old card someday. She was seventeen, Peter. Probably buys U2 and Sinéad O'Connor albums and sings "Patriot Game" in the shower."

"Is she still a symp?"

"Well, Peter old man, we're paying you good money to find out. Aside from Blundell, they're typical scientists. Nothing interesting in their b-g's, or they wouldn't be allowed Ministry funds."

"How about the butler?"

"Rented from Servants 'R' Us."

"Backwards R?"

"Of course. University student studying Marxist political theory."

"I smell trouble belowstairs."

"Not our concern."

"So I should . . .?"

"Act officious, butter everybody up, don't make waves, keep your fly buttoned, and act like a bloody Queen's Cavalryman, not an SAS major. Give them the once-over for Republican sympathizers, write a report, and let them play H.G. Wells."

"Why a soldier? Why not a real investigator, somebody from the police, or the Yard, if they're using Ministry funds?"

Colonel Cooper turned his bulk to look Peter in the eye. "Because you're available, and you're cheap, Smythe. Keep it in the family. I'm sure those chaps have enough to do watching London Shiites and Colombian drug lords."

"Yes sir," said Smythe. The corporal opened his door and exited, exhaling steam in the cold air like a dragon. He scanned the grounds, keeping his hands inside his greatcoat, under which an Ingram Mac-10 machine pistol hid. He tried to look civilian, but failed miserably. He nodded slightly to Peter.

After a moment's breath, Smythe exited, same side.

He shivered, walked across dead, frosty grass to the front door, rang the bell. After a second ring, the surly butler finally answered, took Peter's topcoat using the dead-rat grip. As the rent-a-butler closed the massive oak door, the two SAS cars drove away, noisily crushing gravel.

A thin man with vacant eyes, close-cropped red hair, and a florid face like a pumpkin ducked under the doorjamb, approached Peter with hand extended. *Your man Mark Blundell*, thought Peter.

"Smythe, Royal Marines," said Peter, held out his hand to the pale ectomorph for a shake. The giant peered myopically through Coke-bottle glasses, dodged Peter's hand, and grabbed for the packet under his arm instead. Peter allowed Dr. Blundell to take the envelope. The physicist fumbled it open, scrutinized the papers.

What the hell does he think he's looking for? Peter thought; *I could've handed him in the Falklands Treaty and he wouldn't know the difference.* Smythe maintained a frozen smile while Blundell examined the forgeries and pronounced them genuine.

The antechamber was larger than Peter's entire flat, chilly as the out-of-doors. Octagonal, two bay windows on either side of the door—a nightmare to defend. A pair of snipers in the trees fifty yards away could catch the entire room in cross fire.

"Sorry?" Peter asked. He had missed Blundell's comment.

"I said I don't know why we need a trooper poking his nose in. It's just a research project."

"Funded by . . .?"

"Yes, well. That's irrelevant. Once we have the money you're not supposed to, you know, spy on us."

May as well stick as close to the truth as possible, Peter decided. "Just a sop to Roundhaven, I expect. He's on our case about security. You know the drill." Peter rolled his eyes.

"Rather. He's been around bothering us a lot lately. Can't hardly swing a cat . . . well, I take it you've met him?"

Peter nodded. "Large, bald, spherical gentleman with a horrible green sweater. Should wean himself from that dreadful cologne. Makes himself unpleasant at the Air Station every few weeks. Can't hardly kick out a minister, though."

Blundell returned the ersatz orders, headed for a padded-leather door. "Gang's through here, Mr. Smythe. Should I say Major Smythe?"

"Call me Peter. Incognito, you know, ha ha."

"Don't bump your head."

The physicist ducked; Peter passed with six inches to spare, wondered if the remark were a dig. *Oxford,* he remembered from the dossier; *public school—Eton?—bastard gets thirty thousand a year from his uncle, Papa the magistrate, and calls it an "allowance."*

The cavernous entry hall was tiled in red-and-black squares, reminding Peter of a chessboard. The elegance was marred by bundles of cable duct-taped to the floor, snaking over the four doorways. Peter glimpsed the gloomy, ill-lit kitchen through one arched door. Blundell brushed aside a hanging arc of wires, stepped through the opposite doorway.

Along a short corridor they found what had been the main dining room, fifty feet by thirty. Long, hardwood floorboards, stained a deep, reddish color, sprang beneath Peter's feet as he walked. Computer-generated fractals lined the walls, intricately colored line patterns that repeated endlessly.

Files and computer equipment, much of it jerry-rigged, were piled high atop an ancient, black table. The eight project scientists besides Blundell sat in the chairs not occupied by reams of fanfold paper. Peter recognized five by their pictures: project manager Dr. Henry Willks, the Reverend Dr. Knight, Jacob Hamilton, Rosenfeldt (the American), and Selly Corwin. The other three were probably the graduate student assistants, no pictures on file: Conner (the Orangeman), Zeblinski, and Faust.

Selly Corwin sat alone by the fire, sunk in an overstuffed armchair that belonged in a smoking club. She watched unblinking as he entered, hands steepled before her lips.

Blundell cleared his throat noisily. "Gentlemen—you too, Selly—this is Major Peter Smythe of the Marines. Bill Roundhaven sent him. Supposed to be our *security* man." Blundell grimaced. He introduced the seven men and Selly; Peter dutifully stumbled over names he already knew perfectly.

Selly Corwin did not react, continued to watch Peter as if waiting for him to strike a pose and demand, "What's all this then?" He flushed, uncomfortable in her frank stare.

Willks had stopped talking during the introductions, glared at Smythe. It was All His Fault. When Blundell finished, Willks pointedly began another loud, unrelated conversation with Hamilton.

"Oh get off it, Henry," snapped Blundell. Willks grew silent, glared reproachfully as the man continued; "Smythe probably doesn't like the job any better than we. Probably rather be marching, or flying an airplane, or whatever those Marine chaps do, what?"

"Yes sir," Peter said, "frankly I would rather be flying. But my alternative is flying a desk, not a Harrier." He tapped his ear. "Blew it out in the Falklands." It was a blatant bid for sympathy. In fact, Peter's ear was perfect.

"Really, sir?" said Hamilton. "I was there too. Infantry. Where were you?"

"Damned stupid war," argued Willks. "What the hell's on that island but a bunch of stupid sheep?"

"Well—I . . ." Hamilton lapsed into silence, obviously annoyed but unwilling to contradict his boss.

Peter stepped to the defense. "As a soldier, Dr. Willks, I take all wars as a personal insult. It's me they shoot at, not you. Jake Hamilton—may I call you that?—performed a dangerous, unpleasant duty for queen and country."

"Ready to lay down his life to save those sheep!" laughed Blundell. Hamilton reddened.

Peter turned the conversation slightly, avoiding interrogation about his fictitious unit in the Falklands. In fact, he had spent the microwar tracking IRA Provies in Gibraltar. "See any action, Jake?"

"Well, yes." Hamilton forced a smile. "Saw a lot of sheep too, sir. First time I ever, you know, shot a gun."

"A virgin!" marveled Blundell.

"Lot of us lost our virginity there, Jake," said Peter.

Selly raised her eyebrows, caught Peter's attention. Her voice was soft and throaty, not brassy as he expected.

"Lost your virginity? So *that's* why those sheep were so important." She spoke like a P.G. Wodehouse character from Market Snodsbury: *"sew im-PAW-tahnt."*

There was an awkward silence; finally Smythe spoke. "Lot of brave boys *died* there, Professor Corwin. Defending their country."

"No need to apologize, Major Smythe," she answered. "We English have a long tradition of hanging sheep-stealers, whatever the cost." She smiled. *"Can't* make an omelet without breaking a few eggs, what?" Her accent was so upper-class, Peter wondered if she were mocking Blundell.

Smythe scowled. On the surface, she had said nothing untoward; but the way she said it rang alarm bells. *Sheep-stealers. . . .*

"Before this gets any more ferocious," interjected Mark Blundell, "I suggest we pop down the road for a pint. Too late to fry any more circuits today, Hal?"

Willks stiffened at the familiarity, but Blundell did not notice. As the company wrapped themselves up for the short trip, Hamilton sidled up to Peter and stage-whispered in his ear so everyone could hear.

"You'll think we plotted this whole bloody conversation when you see the pub. But I swear to God it's named after the earl who used to live in this house."

They shivered and stamped their feet as they walked three

hundred yards down a narrow lane. No snow on the ground yet, but the chill pulled at Smythe like banshee fingers. They paused outside the pub.

Peter stared at the sign, chuckled. "Falkland Arms," it read. Blundell laughed aloud, pushed inside calling loudly for sherry.

CHAPTER 3

CORS CANT EWIN SLIPPED THROUGH THE OPEN GATE AROUND THE concrete, three-story palace of Artus *Dux Bellorum, Pan-Draconis,* General of the Legions and architect of the *Pax Britannicus.*

Jupiter Gate was always left open, except under siege; but using it meant the bard had to pass under the mushroom windows of Myrddin. *Pray God and his virginal mother the bastard's still sleeping off his magic at Mons Badonicus,* thought Cors Cant. The chances were good; the battle had been long and hard, with much magic needed to suppress the cantrips of Saxon witches.

Cors Cant hugged the mosaic wall beneath the purely decorative marble columns. No howl of outrage erupted from Myrddin's window, so the old Druid missed the bard's tardy return.

Cors Cant slipped into the baths, gestured a slave to bring an oiled strigil and quickly scrape the worst of the dirt from the bard. Cors Cant splashed his face and arms in the *frigidarium* to simulate a thorough cleansing.

He shook himself dry, charged across the courtyard with leine-shirt flapping, averting his eyes from the fountain of Diana and her naked, undulating nymphs, one of whom bore an uncanny resemblence to—to *Her,* his putative beloved.

He burst through the door of the feast hall, or *triclinium,* as Artus preferred it, and skidded to a halt. Senators, princes and princesses, knights, generals, their wives and husbands, all stood silent as moonlight before their couches, as did Artus himself. They stared at Cors Cant as if expecting him to grow another head.

Flushing, he slunk between tables to his couch, avoiding the gaze of the *Dux Bellorum*. Artus waited until the boy stood by his place, then asked pleasantly, "May we begin now, Bard?" Cors Cant bobbed his head, cheeks the same color as the hair of She Who Ignores.

Artus reclined on his couch. Senators, knights, and generals followed according to rank around the perfectly square banqueting hall, causing the shadows from a hundred candles to surge and leap like ghostly shades in the stirred-up air, a capering goblin army against bright mosaics and intricate tapestries. The shadows inspissated into three hundred Saxon, Irish, Nubian, and Greek slaves, each laden with a different, exotic dish to tempt the nobles of Caer Camlann.

Not a wall of Caer Camlann was allowed to stand as bare plaster, save the pure white walls of the *lararium*-chapel, where soldiers and senators paid worship to Mithras, Rhiannon, Apollo, or Jesus the Anointed. Cors Cant's head swam with the colors, every color of the rainbow and some seen only in Eastern dyes. Once again, he realized why he preferred to dine in the kitchen or his own room in Myrddin's apartments.

A wild tune tore through Cors Cant's head, too fast for him to follow or pick out the individual notes. He knew he would not sleep that night, trying to pluck the tune from head to harp. *I wish the canonical songs would spring so readily to mind,* he thought ruefully.

Within moments, the room resounded with its normal cacophony—chatter, challenge, crude jest.

Cors Cant strummed his harp, strained his memory for a feasting tune. Myrddin's absence eased the task; Artus would not mind his old favorites repeated, though the great Druid would have thrown a tantrum (and perhaps a hand axe).

Cors Cant's eyes lit on the faded tapestry of Orpheus and Eurydice, but he remembered the ancient Greek tale of Perseus instead, Gwynhwfyr's favorite.

He gave it soft voice, set it to a wonderful tune he had heard at the last *Eisteddfod* songfest. Hardly original, but the boy counted on Artus not having heard the tune before.

Artus *Dux Bellorum* wore a white Roman toga. He scorned the *braccae,* or breeches of his British kings and nobles. *Will*

he go bare-legged through another winter? wondered Cors
Cant; *he's getting old ... if he catches a chill and dies,
there'll be Saxons in every kitchen and glade, from Alban to
Eire to Cymru to Lloegr!*

Yet Cors Cant realized the War-Leader was not mocking
when he waited the entire feast for the young bard's blessing.
Artus paid honor to the ancient traditions of Britain: the
blessings of local river goddesses were called upon Roman
aqueducts; roads took sharp, angled turns to avoid faerie
mounds; and at the *Dux Bellorum's* own feast, not a soul sat,
no food was eaten until the presiding Druid or bard gave the
go-forth. With Myrddin absent, still "asleep" from the third
battle at Mons Badonicus, Cors Cant was appointed.

Roman clothes, British heart, the boy thought. He watched
the hall as he played and sang. Trouble and dissent lurked everywhere, hidden like treacherous currents beneath the thin
ice of *Pax Brittanicus.*

Cors Cant picked out the major players in the hall, wondering for the thousandth time how these strange strands wove
together into a weblike cambric shirt: Prince General Lancelot glowered at Queen Morgawse, Artus's half sister and erst-
while mistress, some said. She watched Lancelot in turn,
reptilian eyes lazy-lidded, body exuding eroticism beneath an
unadorned, grey, Eastern tunic, its Spartan-like simplicity perversely accentuating the queen's own charms.

*They say she's truly a hundred, three-score and nine years
old,* remembered the bard, shivered at her preternatural youth.
An important hostage for her husband, King Morg's behavior,
she was surrounded by her own honor guard of Sarmatian Amazons. Contrary to legend, they each had both breasts, bared out
of respect in the *triclinium.* Cors Cant quickly looked away
from the bobbing bosoms, concentrated on Lancelot during an
instrumental section of the song.

The court champion wore a rich linen shirt, dyed blue and
black, sleeve on sleeve, trimmed with otter fur and gathered
by a wide, black belt that normally supported his great-axe.
Lancelot carried a small, eagle-topped scepter to signify command of two of the *Dux Bellorum's* legions, and wore mail
armor upon his shoulders, even at the *Dux Bellorum's* feast.
He once commanded the Praetorian Guard for two years and
never let the court forget it.

His trousers were more Sicambrian than British, one leg blue, the other black, like his shirt.

Across from Cors Cant sat Brainless Bedwyr, commander of a mere two cohorts of Cei's second legion. Bedwyr would have preferred to sit on a stool at table, like a proper British warrior. Instead, he sat rigid and uncomfortable on his couch, sticking a dagger repeatedly into the wooden plank-table. Though Mons Badonicus was but a blink in his long military career, it still stirred his blood. He wanted another crack at Caedwin and his Saxons.

Prince Cei, court porter and too clever by half, spoke with Bedwyr in hushed tones, as usual. Cors Cant focused his ears as Myrddin taught and plucked out their words as he plucked the tune out of his harp.

"Indecisive? Damn your ears, Bedwyr, we had them in full rout."

"Pigshit," said Bedwyr, levering his blade from the chipped tabletop. "Caedwin withdrew to regroup. He'll be back at Badon before the snows. Mark me."

Bedwyr was the more richly clad—russet shirt and *braccae,* brass and gold rings, torcs, necklaces, thoroughly British with not a nod to civilization. Cei preferred to dress as a simple Roman general, though he controlled the *Dux Bellorum*'s treasury and privy purse and could have outdressed the Emperor Flavius himself.

The better to attract the Pan-Draconis*'s attention,* thought Cors Cant, wondering yet again at the private relationship between Artus and his porter. He slew the thought before it grew into speculation. There were some questions one could not even safely think, let alone ask.

Cors Cant's throat hurt from singing, and his wine cup was empty; no slave moved to fill it. *They would have filled Myrddin's in an instant,* he thought angrily, continuing his complicated tune.

Cutha the Saxon, Caedwin's younger son, took no part in the conversation, though he sat at the same table as "emissary" (hostage). He gazed from Cei to Bedwyr, bland smile frozen across his face. Cors Cant trusted Cutha no farther than he could kick him—mail, horse, helm, and all.

The *Dux Bellorum* himself chatted pleasantly, if vapidly, with Carolingus Mauritus, ambassador from across the Channel.

Medraut, son of Morgawse and allegedly Artus (so it was said), sat in adoring silence near Artus, as usual. Medraut's cloak was drawn tight; Cors Cant could not even see the color of his tunic.

The bard shifted concentration to Artus and his guest, eavesdropping on their conversation.

"He has a proposal," said Carolingus in Latin. "But he must tell you himself. It is a grand scheme to bring spirit and permanence to ... all this." His foppish gesture, encompassing the villa and all that lay beyond it, perfectly accented his delicate, powder blue robe and embroidered chemise.

Artus drew back on one elbow, just enough to register annoyance at the ambassador's presumption that the court had no spirit of its own.

"Sire," soothed Mauritus, eyebrows raised, "I did not intend the words to fall as they did. My tongue failed me." He bared his teeth in what could, with charity, be taken as a smile.

I hope you get the runs aboard ship going back to Sicambria, thought Cors Cant, taking far more offense at the man's unctuous declamation than did Artus.

"I am no king," said Artus, "just a simple legate. I ride with kings, as I once rode with the emperor. Please don't call me sire."

Cors Cant reached the final chords of his song. Perseus was about to hand the Gorgon's bloody head to Athena. At that moment, a cold hand gripped the boy's upper thigh.

His voice cracked an octave, and he broke a string. He continued playing rigidly, unable to breathe, as feminine fingers trailed up his leg, underneath his tunic. Artus was still engrossed in conversation with Carolingus about the imminent arrival of Merovee, the Long-Haired King of Sicambria.

Cors Cant slowly turned his head. Gwynhwfyr, wife of Artus and princess in her own right (of Cantref Dyfed), had silently materialized beside him during the song, lying on her stomach on a couch below him. She smiled innocently, strolled her hand up the boy's leg from behind to the crotch of his underbreeches.

He squirmed, deathly afraid the *Dux Bellorum* would turn around at any moment—or worse, Bedwyr! How big a running start would bardic status gain him? Despite every effort, despite what he felt for his own beloved Anlawdd, his traitorous body responded to Gwynhwfyr's touch.

He stared at her brilliant, blue tunic, embroidered with both the goldenthread eagle of Rome and the scarlet serpent of Artus, clan *Pan-Draconis*. She wore a classical, pearled crown that barely confined her cropped hair, blond nearly to white. Without conscious will, his eyes were drawn farther and father south toward an Olympian view.

Her tunic was cut low, and she wore no proper chemise beneath, just the hint of a gilt and jeweled mesh like a fisherman's net. A royal purple cope looped behind her back and fastened at her shoulder, a bold arrogance that only the empress of Rome should have worn. Beneath her tunic, from Cors Cant's angle, he viewed her breasts unobstructed; they quivered like delicate "afters" as she writhed to his music, the feminine version of the serpent *Pan-Draconis*.

He felt a pair of eyes burning into his forehead. He looked up, across the plank. General Bedwyr glared like a dire wolf across the knee-high, wooden table, clearly seeing what was going on.

Cors Cant squirmed, used his leg to push Gwynhwfyr's hand away. He gestured imploringly to her, indicated Bedwyr with his head and eyes. He struck another wrong note, but no one seemed to notice.

Gwynhwfyr laughed, still teasing. She brought her hand up to her nose and sniffed, eyes shut in mock rapture. Cors Cant squeezed as far away as he could to frustrate any future adventures of the princess's hand and finished the song a touch too soon.

"Cors Cant," she declared, "I fade to nothing from lack of food."

"I'll have a slave b-b-bring you meat," he whispered hoarsely.

"No, I couldn't possibly eat but from your own hand," breathed Gwynhwfyr. "Upon the instant, go cut me a slice of that poor, hunted boar from the platter." She smiled in delicious anticipation.

The boy stared straight ahead. He was bound to obey the wife of Artus, but—

He pressed the harp firmly against his lap and hobbled quickly to the carving table, entire body flushed with embarrassment. Every eye in the hall seemed to stare, saw *exactly* what he hid behind the instrument.

By the time he carved the slice, speared it, and carried it

back to Gwynhwfyr, Cors Cant was able to walk normally. He placed the plate before golden-haired Gwynhwfyr.

"Pig," he declared.

She scowled, looked from plate to boy. Did he spar with her? The princess tired of the tease and waved him off, pushed away her untouched plate. She began to blow silent kisses at Lancelot, who was more receptive to her advances.

Cors Cant withdrew a step, cold sweat soaking his tunic. On his way back to the bench, a meaty hand grabbed him roughly, spun him around.

"Motherless whelp," growled Bedwyr, struggling for words. "I saw the whole thing!"

"What? I didn't do anything!" *Probably running through all thirty words he knows,* thought Cors Cant.

"Well you just stay away from her, is all I say! If you know what's good for you, you . . . *insect!*" Bedwyr spit out the insult triumphantly; he had looked a long time and found it at last. "Insect insect insect! Just stay clear, you ant. She's Lance's."

"She's married to Artus."

Bedwyr, governor of Clwyd (who spent no time in Clwyd), Camlann's brewmaster as well as two-cohort general, leaned close to the boy with the cold, wild eyes of the hunt. He reeked of wine and obviously itched to kill someone. The bard was a single wrong word away from being elected.

"Next time we stand thus," said Bedwyr, "you open that hole in your face, it better be a prayer to Dagda, because on that day you die. Now *go away.*"

Bedwyr had not raised his voice; if anything, he lowered it. Yet Cors Cant felt his stomach and throat constrict. He was frozen by the giant's eyes. In his mind, he saw callused fingers circle his throat, squeezing out a dry death rattle.

With a "see-you-in-Hades" smile, Bedwyr turned away. Cors Cant ran from the hall and up the stairs, nearly forgetting his harp in his flight. As soon as he reached the first landing, he stopped and doubled over. A terrible feeling overtook him, as if he had been kicked in the groin, but without the pain.

"Damn you! I didn't *do* anything—it was her, you know what she's like!"

The rats and moths did not deign to answer, so Cors Cant sat curled on the stairs, gritting his teeth against the puckering in his groin. *I will never, ever forget you, Bedwyr,* he promised.

CHAPTER 4

I SAT IN PRINCESS GWYNHWFYR'S CRAMPED SEWING ROOM, JUST off her bed-sitter, where she always keeps the fire cold because she thinks it fades the fabrics like the noonday sun, trying to embroider a Roman eagle intertwined with a red dragon—for the *Pan-Draconis,* you understand—but really thinking about That Boy.

He was a definite problem. I knew why I came here, what I had to do. I couldn't afford distractions, and That Boy was like a puppy that you just can't help playing with, or maybe like a scab you just can't help picking. Oh, I don't know what he's like! But I knew I was spending too much time thinking of him and not enough preparing myself to ... well, to take up my dagger and do what I had to do.

I tossed the tunic aside with a curse that would have straightened the *Dux Bellorum*'s hair (but not his wife's; Gwynhwfyr swears better than anyone I know, boy or girl) and paced the room, trying to plan. The tiny, square, wood-walled sewing room was stained such a dark shade of red-brown that I felt as if I were inside a puzzle box. Great folds of fabric lined three of the walls from floor halfway to ceiling, and along the fourth wall ran a pair of shelves, the higher one coming up to my navel when I stood and too low to rest my elbows on when I sat. That shelf was the sewing table, and the one below it had the bone and steel needles and a myriad, myriad spindles of thread.

The sewing room was a wretched prison, and I couldn't leave until I'd finished the *Dux Bellorum*'s tunic. I mean, I learned to work a needle and thread as a young girl; what highborn lady didn't? But honestly, even if Gwynhwfyr didn't know who I really was, she *did* know I wasn't a slave! Yet

16

she treated her free servants worse than we treated our slaves back in Harlech.

All told, I was not a happy princess.

I stared around the dark, lamplit room, snorted, and decided to break out. There was a revel downstairs, in the *triclinium*, the first since I'd arrived in Caer Camlann, and missing it would be like staying inside reading during the first snowstorm of winter. And no, it wasn't because I wanted to see That Boy, or anything like that; I just hate being the one who misses everything because I'm up in the princess's sewing room playing seamstress.

I straightened my own tunic and chemise, very modest and proper, and stormed out of the room, head held high and auburn tresses flaring behind me like a train from beneath my turban (or so I imagined, not having a glass), striding as though I were highborn myself, which since I was, wasn't that difficult a trick.

I prowled the corridor outside Gwynhwyfr's apartment, making sure the princess (or worse, one of her other servants or slaves) wasn't hiding somewhere—mission or no mission, I would *not* submit to a beating just to maintain my cover!— then headed for the stairs. But I paused at the head of them with a little squeak, for who should you imagine was waiting on the landing but That Boy himself!

He looked like he was in pain, doubled over like an old witch-woman in a rustic village, and I almost went to him to see if he were all right. But then I noticed *where* he grabbed himself—right between his legs—and in a trice I knew exactly how he had gotten that way. He always got that way after he allowed that slinky princess to squirm and writhe on his lap, causing his member to swell like my, like my b-b-bro . . . like men do. I saw her do that once before, and he had the same reaction, bending over and hopping around like a toad!

I could have charged down and given him a piece of my mind about it, but I decided to be magnanimous, and besides, I would prove once and for all that I hadn't skipped out on my sewing task and come down to join the *ceili* just to see That Boy, so instead I just turned about and strode smartly off, fists balled at my sides. It's a good thing I *didn't* see Princess Gwynhwyfr at that moment, because I would have palmed the lead weight I carried in my belt in my fist and popped her in the mouth, probably knocking her head from her body, and Artus *Dux Bellorum,* her husband and my appointment, would have gotten upset and been on his guard.

Instead, I used the wide, marble stair at the front of the apartment building, which led onto the courtyard with the gorgeous, Greek fountain of Rhiannon and her nyads, or maybe it was Artemis and her nymphs, who knows? Artus had ordered all the lamps lit, which was the first time I'd seen the Court of Flowing Water sparkling like a faerie pond beneath a million stars, some on the heavenly sphere, others come to earth and alighted upon lantern poles. Or perhaps the lanterns looked like faeries themselves with lit torches, hovering just over the water as it shot up out of the mouth of a four-legged dolphin, cascaded over Rhiannon or Artemis, splashed among the nyads or nymphs or sylphs or elves or alternative representatives of the Good People, and flowed in all four directions along sculpted streambeds. The water flowed over shiny rocks, carefully laid in the bed to reflect the lanterns, so it appeared as if the streams were full of gold and silver, as well as tiny, golden fish.

I lingered long in the Court of Flowing Water. I decided that when I got back to Harlech, I would suggest to father that we desperately needed just such a fountain in *our* courtyard, though it wouldn't have the same impact surrounded by the crumbly fortress of Caer Harlech, designed for a siege, not a sojurn. Then I took a last breath of the clean night air, adjusted my turban so it wasn't hoodwinking me, and dived into the *triclinium.*

It took me several long moments to adjust my eyes to smoky blackness, my ears to the thunder of clumping men, and my nose to the rank odor of that peculiar, north-Mauritanian plant that Artus imported and that he insists everyone smoke, though I do admit it gives curious visions. At the moment, I didn't want a vision, however; I just wanted to enjoy the *saturnalia.*

Immediately I entered, however, I saw that pig Cutha the Saxon. He sat—yes, *sat,* not reclined—upon a couch, shoveling meat into his mouth like a starving wolf, though I knew for a fact that he had stuffed himself near noon, for I attended Gwynhwyfr as she inspected the kitchen and saw the oaf savaging a roast beast.

I sneaked as close as I dared, stared at him in horrified fascination. Again I could have sworn I'd seen him before, just as I felt earlier in the day. Something about his little, weasely eyes and snuffling nose struck a definite chord, and I knew I had seen him somewhere before I came to Camlann.

Before I could place him, however, That Boy suddenly reentered the room and I had to duck for quick cover. I divided my attention then between Cutha, Artus, and That Boy, wishing I could put one of them (at least!) out of my mind.

I noticed that That Boy had his harp, and I couldn't stop myself creeping forward to hear him play.

Why wouldn't he ever play to *me* the way he plays to the court and the *Dux Bellorum?* I bided time, waited patiently for him to need something that I could go get—but not until I first set him straight on the difference between slaves and free girls in the princess's employ. Honestly!

CHAPTER 5

ONE THOUSAND, FIVE HUNDRED AND FORTY-SEVEN AUTUMNS later, not counting the Year of No Summer, the Falkland Arms filled steadily with smoke, noise, and locals. Most of the scientists sat at the bar; Peter sat with Blundell and Willks at the table nearest Hamilton.

How the hell did the conversation turn to the Irish question? Peter wondered, swigging a mouthful of Guinness.

"Beastly," pronounced Blundell, waving a cocktail fork on which he had speared an onion, "bombing all those schools and hotels and things!"

Blundell wore a suit, even this late in the evening, while Willks had pulled a raggedy, woolen sweater over warm-up clothes. "Don't be an imperialist ass, Mark," said Willks, drinking a *screwdriver,* a strange American taste he had acquired at Princeton.

The barkeep had made their drinks as soon as they entered; they were clearly regulars.

Peter spoke quickly, trying to turn the conversation. "Where did you go to school, Mark?" Of course, it was all in the dossier.

Blundell blinked, confused by the sudden left turn. "Eton, of course. It's all in my dossier, didn't you study it?"

"Oh. Ah, of course."

The scientist raised his glass. "Here's to the dear, old sod."

"Your old school?"

"My old school headmaster." He downed a finger of gin, gasped, and thumped his chest dramatically. "I always did wonder why he insisted upon giving us the birch himself—and always bare-bummed."

"He whipped your bare bum at *Eton?*"

"No, I mean *he* was bare-bummed." Blundell honked and slapped the table.

Willks was not having a word of it. He took a long chug, continued his diatribe. "The IRA hasn't bombed a hotel for years. Just police and soldiers."

"And their bloody wives," said Blundell. "And train stations, street intersections, and Harrods."

How right you are, boy; bloody indeed after fifty pounds of Semtex. Peter drank in silence, though he secretly rooted for Blundell; the argument struck too close to home. Thinking of Semtex, the plastic explosive of choice for discriminating *connoisseurs* of terror, had opened the door for the bloody ghost of Sergeant—what was his name? MacTavish?—to waltz in and sit at Peter's table like Banquo at the banquet.

"Well," said Willks, "I admit their targets are a little um scattered, but they see it as a war, don't'cha know."

"God, I'm glad I never got sent over there," said Jake Hamilton. He turned around at the bar. "Better to face an Argie machine gun nest than a fifteen-year-old kid with a Molotov cocktail."

The barkeep mixed Selly's cocktail while Peter watched him in the mirror. She was not joking; it really *was* champagne and Guinness mixed together, a "Black Velvet" she called it. Peter shuddered.

"What does the bold 22d think of the six and the twenty-six counties?" she asked without turning round.

"What?" asked Peter, blinking. He realized he was staring at her cleavage in the mirror.

"Oh, well . . ." He puffed himself up, did a bad imitation of W.C. Fields. "On the whole, my dear, I'd rather be in Philadelphia."

Willks and Blundell were engaged in a staring contest; the old man had a distinct advantage in that he never seemed to blink anyway.

Blundell finally yielded. He swallowed his drink, leaned conspiratorially toward Peter. "It's not really time travel, you know; more like mind-transference."

"So you go out of your mind, eh?" said Peter, uneasily eyeing the table next to his, full of strangers in black suits and bowler hats. *Does the man even* know *the words "National security"?*

The joke went over Blundell's towering head. "No no, your mind goes out of your body . . . I think. Actually, nobody's tried it yet. What we hope is that consciousness will project back into the mind of somebody in the past, so one can view historical events and such. The body doesn't *go* anywhere, else we'd have to worry about the Earth's orbit, changing geographical features, and such."

He took a long pull at his gin; Peter only sipped his Guinness, hoping the physicist would mention what they planned to do with the marvelous toy, as long as he insisted upon babbling about it in public.

"Actually, it's rather a simple physical principle," said Blundell.

"Well, I think it's beyond my—"

"I really can't explain it properly to a layman."

"Good. You don't have to. I'm just curious what you plan—"

"See, we don't move through time; that's a common fallacy. Time is simply an ordering mechanism by which our brains make sense of things—events—in event-space."

Lowering his voice, Peter tried again. "So, have you thought about what you plan to *do* with the thing, once it works, I mean?"

"Events simply *are,* and we arrange them in sequence with infinite order at the beginning, infinite entropy at the end. You know, every subatomic interaction makes as much sense backwards as forwards. In a quantum sense, I mean."

"Nearly every," corrected Willks. Blundell waved his hand impatiently.

"So have you decided what you'll do with the thing?"

"The difference—" Blundell paused to drain his drink, eat his onion, and signal for another martini; ". . . is whether the reaction produces or requires energy."

An energetic waitress materialized out of nowhere with more drinks for all, vanished within the Heisenberg interval. The universe rolled on.

"Really," said Peter, plastering a fascinated smile across his face, "so you just reverse the order of perception, do you?"

Blundell stared blankly at the soldier, sipped his third gin and tonic, made a bitter face, and put it down. "We've thought of a few good uses once we perfect it, you know."

"Have you?"

"I thought of one. Willks thinks it's good."

"Does he?"

"I want to know how the Troubles started. Really started."

"Ulster?" *Wonderful. You couldn't have tried something simple, like preventing World War II?* Peter decided it would be a good time to distract Blundell with a covert "Mason" probe. "Are you really *on the level* about that?"

Mark Blundell nodded, did not seem to notice the code words. "I mean," he explained, "they really are just people. I guess. Catholics, yes, but so what? They haven't such a problem in America, you know, and there are more Catholics in New York alone than there are in all Ulster."

Peter cast his net again: "So when do you think it all started? What date *squares* with your research?"

"Hm . . . hadn't really thought about that yet," he admitted, still stubbornly oblivious to Peter's hints.

"Of course not. Silly of me even to have asked."

Blundell stared into space and stroked his chin. "The Easter uprising? When was that, the post office thing?"

"The Dublin GPO uprising, 1916. But it started long before that, Mark. Too long before."

A musical voice sang softly behind Peter's head. It was Selly, voice throaty as a London fog:

> *In 1916, did you stand up like a man,*
> *In 1920, did you fight the black and tan?*

Were you a rebel, did you fight for Ireland then,
And if you did will you stand by her once again?

"I say," said Mark, "that's rather in poor taste, don't you think?"

Peter shrugged. "Doesn't bother me. The only rebels I've fought were Cubans in the Falklands. They had tanks and AK-47s, and no support from American Catholics."

Selly smiled and slid in next to Peter. "Did Markie-poo tell you his Irish fantasy?" Despite the diminutive, her voice sounded cold, knowing.

"World peace through time travel?" Peter asked, trying to keep his face from flushing. *So close, leg pressed against mine. . . .*

"Selly!" hissed Blundell. He glared until she looked into his eyes, then shook his head, barely enough for Peter to notice. "You're not supposed to—"

"Don't you want to ask Major Smythe's opinion, a military perspective, Mark?"

Blundell looked down at his drink, face turned red as a spanked baby bottom.

Selly continued. "Mark has this idea: stop the whole thing from ever having happened. All he has to do is spend a wild night of ecstasy with Queen Liz the First, and she'll forget all about those silly Irish settlements. No Ulster, no Troubles."

Smythe cringed beneath his mask. *Sweet Jesus!* he thought; *if the Argies had used Selly instead of Cuban mercs, they'd still have the sheep, and the maps would read "Malvenas Islands."*

"Stop the whole thing from ever having happened," Peter mused. "What about—"

"The Grandfather Para Paradox?" interjected Willks's nasal voice, slurred by the vodka. He had ignored the exchange until that moment.

"Well, yes," said Peter. "If you changed history enough, you wouldn't be born, wouldn't invent the thing, wouldn't have been able to change anything in the first place. A most ingenious paradox."

"I'th . . . I thoo . . ." Willks picked up his glass, drained the screwdriver. He looked lost, and Blundell slid his half-full martini across the table to the older man.

Willks sipped it, then tossed it back. The cocktail onion

toothpick fell into his beard, where it stuck, the onion peeking out like a third eye.

"I THOUGHT about that," Willks finally managed to say. "Sci-fi writer named Fritz—Hollings, Mondale, something like that—had the answer. Law of . . . Concentration of . . . Reactionaries. Something." Willks collapsed into the seat next to Blundell, brushed the wild, grey mane of hair from his eyes.

"Law of Conservation of Reality," Blundell said, cringing fastidiously from his drunken colleague. "I haven't read this Leiber chap, but the essence of our own version is that it takes more energy to go back in time and change something than it would to change it in the present. Since it would take infinite energy to make time travel never be invented, the paradox is resolved."

"So if you shot your own grandfather—"

"You enter a parallel universe where you exist as an adult although you are never born as a baby."

"But your grandfather is dead!"

"So?"

"So who shot him?"

"Irrelevant. You have a dead body—a space-time event. Who says it has to have a cause in this universe? Or any cause at all, for that matter."

"Besides," Selly interjected, "since time travel is possible in that universe, anybody in the future can theoretically invent a machine, travel back, and off the old pederast."

Peter's head swam. "So your Irish fantasy is just a fantasy," he said.

"No, not quite. It wouldn't take much *energy* to change that problem now; everybody just stop shooting. Deport the IRA, remove the troops. It's a lack of national *will.*"

Well, we agree there, young master Blundell, Peter thought. Under the table, Selly put her hand on his thigh. He choked on his stout, but felt just large enough not to push her hand away.

Willks had faded out since his single attempt at conversation. He sat in the booth, mouth open, eyes glazed, cocktail onion still peeking from his beard.

"He always get like that?" Peter asked, voice cracking slightly. Selly slid her hand up a bit. Peter fought the urge to begin humming "God Save the Queen."

"He's nervous," said Mark. "You got here just in time, Major. We're taking the thing for the first test spin tomorrow morning."

"Tomorrow! You're a lot farther along than you've let on. You sure you're *on the level* about that?"

Blundell's eyes narrowed slightly; this time, he caught the special emphasis on the Masonic greeting. "Haven't I been playing *square* with you, Peter?"

Perfect, thought Smythe; *not quite enough for him to be sure, just the merest Masonic hint.*

"Who's going?" he asked. "Back to where?"

"Me," said Blundell, "and I think I'll witness the um coronation of Elizabeth the First. In . . . when was that, Selly?"

Selly smiled, and slid her hidden hand to midthigh.

"January, 1559. Mary died in '58, on November 17th. Elizabeth was crowned on Sunday, January 15th."

"Not for the ah reason Selly implied," added Blundell. "My hope is to um get close enough to be able to accurately describe what she wore. We can compare my description to whatever historical notes exist . . . there must be some, mustn't there?"

"I'd think so," Peter murmured, wriggling his leg away from Selly's hand. It clung like a spider. "Whose body will you jump into?" *And what am I jumping into with Selly? Is this proper? Can I use her for inside information?*

Blundell shrugged, uncomfortable. "Well we don't know, of course. Willks says into the nearest person."

"Nearest to where?"

"Nearest in *mental set* to myself."

"What happens to him? The real person, I mean?" Peter was intrigued. It might be a loony fantasy, but at least it was internally consistent.

Mark tried to drink from his gin, remembered Willks had emptied it. "Maybe he just um stays. Rather."

Selly spoke. "We think the target consciousness remains in the body as well, but is buried. Buried deep, jammed down there." She slid her hand directly between Peter's thighs. He jumped, swallowed his remaining Guinness. Under the table, he tugged at her thumb. But Selly had a death grip.

"Hey, Mark," she said, "maybe you'll find your Faerie Queen after all. The Irish question was pretty hot back then, too."

"It was?" asked Blundell, his eyebrows raising.

Selly nodded blandly. "Irish Penal Laws of 1602 made it illegal for the Irish to learn to read, own a farm or horse worth more than five pounds, have a profession, priests, mass, the sacrament, or even serve in the Irish parliament. Of course, that was in James's reign. Not Elizabeth's."

"And of course," sparred Peter, finally loosening her hand, "Bloody Mary did as bad or worse to the English Protestants."

Selly smiled, and leaned over to whisper in his ear. "You're staying in the manor? I might come visiting tonight. Leave your door unlocked."

Mark Blundell pretended he had heard nothing, but Peter saw his ears redden. Selly slowly trailed her fingers off Peter's leg. She stood, donned her cloak with a swirl, and made a grand exit.

"Right," said Blundell. "Ah, time to leave. Are you coming?"

"In a minute," said Peter, crossing his legs.

"Oh. Rather. Well, bright-eyed in the A.M., what?" Blundell stood, and Peter raised his empty glass in silent salute. Mark jabbed Willks in the ribs, finally roused the old professor to his feet, and poured him into his coat.

The quantum waitress observed Peter's upraised glass and collapsed her wave equation to the eigenstate where she produced another for his consumption.

Blundell hesitated, then awkwardly bent over the table and stuck out his hand. "In the morning, what?" he said. Peter took the hand and felt the faint pressure of the third finger and thumb.

Now what? He responded with the same Masonic sign, looking intently into the gangly giant's eyes. A faint smile crossed Blundell's lips.

"Morning, then," Peter said. They broke contact. Blundell grabbed Willks's arm and propelled him out the door.

After time and another eigenstout elapsed, Peter felt enough in control to return to the manor. The butler answered the door yawning and led him up to his room. Peter stripped, prayed for success and self-control, then climbed into bed to await his own Arabian night.

For long hours he dozed fitfully. Something was wrong, something nagged at his memory. He let his mind drift back through the conversations.

Selly. Corwin. What had she said? *Bold* ... *something*

bold. Ask our bold something, our bold 22d. What they think of the six and twenty-six counties. Smythe drifted, dreamed about the grand 22d SAS regiment, dreaming of Selly belly dancing back into his room.

An hour later, he sat bolt upright, burst out of a half-waking nightmare that involved goat-headed boys with bowlers.

Someone in the room? No, he heard no welcoming creak of boards under Selly's bare feet. It was a thought, a memory that invaded his dream.

22d.

Where did she get that number? That particular regiment, *Peter's* regiment? *I never told her my bloody damn regiment!*

A flush of realization crept along his neck, across his face. It was not a dream, not a coincidence or synchronicity.

There was only one way she could have known he was with the 22d SAS: Peter's cover was blown. And Selly Corwin was an IRA plant.

CHAPTER 6

CORS CANT EWIN SAT ON THE WOOD AND PLASTER STEPS AS THE pain between his thighs ebbed. *Damn her, why does she tease me while Artus and Bedwyr and everyone watch?* Gwynhwfyr had driven him from the hall before he could taste meat, fowl, or even the sticky pastry of Gwydden the Abstruse (fine enough for the sons of Bran).

The *chuq* of a heavy boot tread interrupted his internal dialogue. Cors Cant stood, back pressed against the wall, wondering who else would leave the feast before the main course. Then he recognized the walk: Lancelot of the Languedoc in thievish haste.

Lancelot rounded the landing, paused when he saw the bard, then fell into a credible drunkard's act. Had Cors Cant not seen him mounting stairs three at a time, he might have been fooled.

"Quo vadis, Lancelot?" he asked.

"Shtop jib—jabberering at me, infant." He spoke in an exaggerated accent. "The stairs, they are very difficult today." He gripped his head and sank to a step, swearing in his native Sicambrian tongue.

On the other hand, Cors Cant had once overheard him speaking perfect British with the faintest, romantic accent to a courtesan.

Cors Cant squeezed onto the step next to the warrior, admired his extraordinary ceremonial array. Lancelot still wore mail; but now that Cors Cant looked close, it was made of overlapping scales, like a fish.

Like a Sicambrian fish. . . .

"They say *he's* half-fish," mused Cors Cant, puckishly. He felt Lancelot's back stiffen, though no eyes but Myrddin's could have seen it on the torchlit landing.

Cors Cant continued, describing the kingly visitor whose emissary sat in the *triclinium,* crossing words with Artus: King Merovee of Sicambria, Merovius Rex, king of all the Languedoc people, former Roman governor of the region when it was called *Gallia Transalpina* . . . before Rome left Sicambria to brood and gloom alone under August's iron grey skies.

"They say *he's* invincible in battle, that he's half-god. They say his hair flows down his back and for a mile behind his horse. Has *he* arrived at last, Lancelot? Do you ride out to meet him?"

Nobody knew exactly what had happened between Lancelot and Merovee—but Lancelot of the Languedoc lived in exile, perhaps self-imposed, in Prydein-Britannia, across the Channel from his once and never-again liege.

The warrior was silent for a long moment. Then, Camlann's champion struck like a snake, iron fingers gripping the back of Cors Cant's neck, nearly squeezing his brains out his ears. Pain shot his back, God's own dart cast from the hand of Taranis Thunderer Himself! The bard was unable to squirm from Lancelot's grasp.

"He comes. He rides even now through our wood, so Bedwyr tells me. I need a favor, little one." The prince reeled him in; his foul breath near to overwhelmed the bard. "You need not betray your lord, my little one. I seek to save Artus *Pan-Draconis* from certain doom at the hands of that traitorous Christian, Merovee the Pig-King, whose father sired him in a dung heap upon a diseased Roman whore."

He relaxed his hold on Cors Cant's neck. The boy slipped and fell down a single step, scraping the small of his back.

"What do you want, Prince Lancelot?" Buttering up seemed advisable.

"Merovee is a Roman collaborator, as his father was before him, the bastard. Piglet! This I know, ah good."

"M-many served Rome." *Artus was a Roman general, you Sicambrian dolt! Haven't you noticed the court language is Latin?* But the boy said nothing else aloud.

Lancelot chuckled in the darkness. "I care nothing for titles and trappings. That long-hair fish-king goes farther, understand you? He follows the Roman Christ, spits on the old ways."

The boy crouched on the step below Lancelot, trembling as he rubbed feeling back into his muscles. He, too, had incorporated the new Roman god into his pantheon. If Lancelot suspected *him* of collaborating with the decadent remnants of the once-mighty empire . . .

"What do you wish of me, huge one?"

"Only your eyes, boy. And your ears. The tongue, you will keep it to yourself, or I shall, say, collect it for my own. Is it not true?"

Cors Cant thought for a long time. If he allowed the Sicambrian this liberty, what would Lancelot ask next?

"I'll do as you ask, Lancelot." *When pigs tell the future will you get the whole truth from me, motherless hound!*

"And in case you try to push the wool over my eyes . . . remember my Dark Maid and what she drinks." He stroked the haft of his axe, which he should not have carried at all, at all, under the roof of lief and liege, Artus *Dux Bellorum.*

Cors Cant pressed back against the wall, heart pounding. "How could I forget?"

Downstairs, tumult rose to cacophony as the feasters spotted Merovee's procession. Cacamwri howled the gates open. Half a hundred hooves broke the cobbles of Passing Bridge, followed by as many boots and more. Merovius Rex, the Long-Haired King, entered Caer Camlann—and Cors Cant, squirming on the stairs beneath Lancelot's iron-shod boots, missed the entire scene.

Lancelot cast a last, threatening grimace at Cors Cant, then rose and resumed his upward flight, a steel-scaled fish climbing a blue-plastered waterfall.

The boy sat on the step, head bowed between his legs. He was free; but fear, fanned by Prince Lancelot, bound him to his seat.

What was he like, Merovee the Half-God? Cors Cant flipped his long, brown hair to use as a cushion, leaned back against the cold steps. The wild tune from the feast still infested his mind like a hive of bees, scrambling his thoughts. Gwynhwfyr, Lancelot, Artus, Bedwyr, all merged into a single four-headed, eight-handed ogre that grabbed at his harp, tried to tear it from his grasp.

The scent of roast boar, wild pig, and wine-simmered deer flooded the stairwell, painted the walls, teased his tongue. This delicious odor finally pulled Cors Cant to his feet, dragged him belowstairs again. He stopped at the last turn, however, and watched the scene below without participating.

The hall was brilliant with more candles than stars in the summer sky. The floor undulated with a living carpet of soldiers, senators, knights, and their ladies. Merovee's men wore white tunics with red crosses, red *tablion* patches looking too Roman, an affection. Their spotless garb contrasted sharply with the ragtag blue and green, half-British, half-Roman tunics of the Camlann upper castes. Merovee's men numbered only twice twenty, but they sparkled like a cohort.

Jesus splitting Mary, thought the bard, *did they stop and change from traveling clothes just outside the gate?*

The slaves fell to their knees, heads bowed respectfully for the man who was both king and Roman governor, two titles that still eluded Artus.

The soldiers of Camlann and Sicambria squeezed past each other, each reaching out to touch the other's general, one at each end of the hall. Merovee and Artus each stood at a different focus of the mob, arms extended, touching hands that grasped and heads that bowed (like Roman priests delivering a blessing), surrounded by swirling gilt and jewels like a Greek kaleidoscope.

Armored men banged together, pots down a chimney. Cors

Cant stuffed his fingers into his ears, squinted at the painful colors.

Such contrast! Merovee had a drooping mustache and black hair long as a horse's mane, skin dark as bark, lips red as wine; Artus, smooth-cheeked and close-cropped, with alabaster skin like bleached parchment, eyes brown as thrice-brewed tea. Both dressed in white: Merovee in breeches pricked with golden thread, cross-laced boots of black calf-skin; Artus in a simple Roman governor's toga and sandals.

Cors Cant watched the revelry, cringed from participation. *Will they kill each other for a touch on the brow, brush of a hand?* He leaned his cheek against the cool, comforting plaster and felt a pair of eyes upon him.

A queer force drew his gaze to the right. Queen Morgawse watched him intently, brows lowered calculatingly. She had not risen for Merovee's entrance, still lay upon her side, goblet gripped delicately between finger and thumb.

She rose at last, regal as the Queen Mother, Arianrhod, who had died so very recently. Cors Cant's throat closed . . . she was so like the Queen Mother.

Morgawse's retinue of fighting women surrounded her, watching the boisterous men as wolves watch jackals. In theory, they held her hostage; actually, she picked them herself, and they guarded her privacy.

As a group, they swept toward the stair. Soldiers melted from their path, fog from fire.

Morgawse mounted the stairs toward Cors Cant, smiled enigmatically. He was struck dumb by her bewitching beauty. Without even knowing why, he extended his hands to her, as if in supplication.

The queen flourished her cloak. "A sweet sacrifice from the goddess of bakeries," she proclaimed. The cloth brushed across his hands, smooth as gossamer. Then she was gone, leaving only the scent of holly and mistletoe to mark her passage.

He felt a weight, looked down at his hands. A great piece of Gwydden's pastry sat sticky in his cupped hands, sweet as his beloved's laugh on Beltane. A large, ornate "CC" was carved into the crust. Morgawse's barely audible chuckle teased him from the bend in the stair.

"Th-thank you, faerie queen," he stammered. But she had

vanished. Cors Cant sat on the steps and ate his "afters," watching the tale unfold verse by verse in the hall below.

CHAPTER 7

PETER SMYTHE ROSE IN THE BLACK-DARK ROOM, INSTANTLY awake, and pulled on a pair of pants and an undershirt. He opened the door carefully. Satisfied no one waited in the corridor, he slid his 9mm into the holster at his back and ghosted by instinct down the dark hall.

22-SAS . . . she used my bloody unit name, and I was so intent upon Willks and Blundell I didn't even notice! He damned himself for a dozen kinds of fool. The Strategic Air Service, SAS, was a supposedly secret branch of the military with primary jurisdiction over IRA "incidents" and units.

Selly Corwin could not have known he was SAS, let alone division number 22, unless she had inside information . . . which, in practice, almost always meant IRA sources.

The great, marble stairs chilled his bare feet. He paused to listen after every five steps. *Mary, Mother of God, where do they keep that damned machine?* Selly Corwin had played him like an Irish harp, kept him waiting in his room for a nonexistent tryst, which gave her plenty of time to sabotage the device. Or whatever else she intended.

Damn Cooper and his bloody "intelligence"! There had been little in Corwin's dossier to raise alarm bells, apart from that one-time donation to Sinn Fein, the political branch of the IRA, when she was a teenager at university. She had no Irish ancestry. She was a churchgoing Anglican. *It's all some fantastical cover,* he reasoned; *it has to be. She knew me, knew my unit!*

Peter halted at the entry hall, the claustrophobic room with the chessboard floor. He closed his eyes, visualized the map Colonel Cooper had given him. The lab was in the basement, according to Operations. As Smythe stood, the massive front door was to his left, the kitchen straight ahead, behind it the larder with the stair. The windows hid behind iron bars like a jail, the one feeble nod to security.

He hurried across the gritty, unswept floor and stumbled across something sharp. It was two cables duct-taped together that stuck up from the floor on one of the red squares.

He crouched, bit his knuckle to hold back a yelp. He continued, sliding the kitchen doors open with no more sound than an elf on silk pillows.

Drafty kitchen, leaky faucet. Water drops filled a pot, echoed like gunshots in the cell block. Sallow, luminescent moonlight shone through a single, cracked windowpane, painting the room nightmare yellow.

Something had been left out to rot; Peter crinkled his nose as he stalked the frigid linoleum. His hands trembled slightly in excitement.

For a moment, he flashed back to Londonderry, two weeks before. *Focus,* he told himself sternly, blotted the horrific memory from his mind before he fully remembered it. *Sergeant Mac . . . MacAdoo? really spread himself that time—*

Peter twisted the knob of the basement door. Every time it creaked he hesitated, listened for response.

At last he squeezed through, crept down ancient, wooden stairs that groaned with every step. He hesitated at the light switch, chose not to turn it; the machinery itself glowed spectral blue.

It looked undamaged—not that Peter could really tell. At least there were no obviously torn wires or banged up metal bits. It hummed. The blue light glowed from a large panel.

Another possibility occurred. *Did she intend to* wreck *it, or . . . ?*

The "time machine" was a cat's cradle of plastic tubing with a MiniCray computer at one end. Surrounding the central device were eight Macintoshes, all but two of them old and battered. Cables lay in grooves along the floor, held in place with yet more duct tape.

One of the older Macs displayed a clock face in the upper left corner, set to twelve minutes past midnight. Peter checked his watch; it showed 02:35. *Time* since *some event, twelve minutes ago,* he reasoned.

Peter inched forward, stepped in a pile of cloth. He bent to examine it.

The pile consisted of a dress, the very one Selly had worn at the Falkland Arms. Scattered farther along were a bra, panties, stockings and garter belt, a pair of low-heeled shoes, all tossed haphazardly on the floor before the cat's cradle. He gingerly picked up the panties, realized they contained a dark-stained pad, and dropped them with a gasp.

Peter's gaze followed the trail of clothing. It led into the heart of the plastic tubing. The air there shimmered faintly. Light reflected from tiny dust particles, though the basement had no windows.

A shape drew his attention. He leaned closer; it was a corpse, the nude body of Selly Corwin. He sucked in a breath, alternating between staring and averting his eyes.

She was . . . dead? comatose? Her breast rose and fell, but her open eyes stared without intelligence.

Peter instantly ducked under the tubing, wriggled into the blue glow. He worked his arms beneath Selly's shoulders and knees, hoisted the deadweight.

He felt drugged, limbs shaky, though Selly could not possibly weigh more than fifty kilos.

As he wrestled her from the center of the machine, his mind became unfocused, dwelt on irrelevancies: her breasts were small, she had an appendectomy scar. He staggered, stared at the rest of her body. It settled one question: her hair was truly red. He wove back through the tubing, beginning to lose consciousness.

Drifting, far away, far beyond . . . far before, far past— what? where am I, where is . . .

He barely reached the cement floor before dropping her heavily. He shook violently, felt nauseous. His arms were bright, sunburn red, his face flushed.

Peter took two deep breaths, pulled his wits together. He slapped Selly across the face, gently at first, then sharply. She did not rouse. He pried open her lids, turned her head to face the machine, and moved his hand to alternately block and unblock the blue, glowing light. Her pupils responded slowly, unevenly. *Or is the light just too weak? Bloody hell, I'm not a doctor!* His penlight was up in his room, and he did not want to leave her alone.

He checked the rest of her vital signs, as best as he could. She had no obvious wounds or injuries. He carefully felt her entire body, told himself all the while he was not taking advantage. He felt no broken bones. She looked sunburned, but otherwise unharmed.

Belay that, he corrected; *her body is unharmed—"Selly Corwin" is dead.*

Peter rose, breath ragged. He backed into the main control panel, edged around it, and glanced at the readout: 48.851.164.817,00.

It's a big number. So what?

Selly needed a doctor, not a field dressing. She was not likely suddenly to revive and run away. He turned and mounted the stairs three at a time toward Blundell's room.

Smythe shook Blundell awake. The physicist sat up, clutched his head and fell back. "Big head," he gasped, "big big big . . ."

Peter draged Blundell into the water closet, splashed cold water on the man's face.

When Mark regained some of the composure befitting his class, he pulled on a smoking jacket and boxer shorts, limply pushed his thinning hair back with his fingers.

"Gru—greetings on all three sides of the whatsis," said Blundell.

"Sorry to rouse you at this hour, but we need a doctor. Now!"

"Anything for a brother in the You-Know." Blundell sounded as if he thought waking him at zero-two-thirty was rummy, even for a "fellow Mason."

"Mark, it's Selly."

"Selly? Who's she coshed this time?"

"Blundell, sit down."

"I *am* sitting. I'd rather be sleeping."

"Damn it, man, this is serious! She's down in the basement. Her body, at least. *We need a doctor.*"

There was a long pause. "Good God," whispered a greyfaced Mark Blundel. Then class consciousness reasserted itself, closed a mask over his features. The transformation startled Peter. "Is she . . . dead?" asked the physicist.

Peter shook his head, impatient. "Respirations and heart rate normal. Pupils respond, but unequal and sluggish. She's in some sort of a coma. Mark, snap out of it! Where's the phone? Do you have one in your room?"

Blundell lost the mask for a moment, eyes wide. "Peter," he said cautiously, "there is another possibility. Was she sitting inside the doughnut?"

"What? Yes, nude, but I don't . . ."

"The doughnut was turned on?"

"Blue glow in the air." *No. He can't possibly mean that she . . . ?*

Blundell started, knocked a glass off the nightstand. "Are you *sure?* You couldn't be mistaken?" The mask had completely vanished.

"Mark, Mark, don't tell me what you're about to tell me. It's just a coma, right? She just had a stroke or something?" Blundell said nothing. He stared, face paler with every question. "Bloody hell, she couldn't have *done it!* Could she?"

"Done it, meaning?"

"Used the machine! Gone back in the past, to Queen Elizabeth the First!"

Blundell's face spoke volumes. Peter caught the lapel of his smoking jacket, yanked him forward. "Can anyone else run that thing? Who else knows how to set it up?" Peter blinked; Blundell seemed oddly blurred, like a movie projected through an unfocused lens.

Blundell ignored Peter's rapid-fire questions. "My God," the scientist said at last, "so the old fart loses out after all."

She did it. Selly Corwin, IRA plant, has gone back in time.

"Mark! Wake up, this is *official business.* Stay in line! Can Willks operate that thing? How about you?"

"What?" Blundell suddenly noticed Peter again. "No . . . Selly was the one who knew how to set the thing. No one else, just Selly. Well, Selly and Willks, since he built it. Oh, and Hamilton, of course."

"Willks?"

"Naturally. And me, and maybe Rosenfeldt, the American chap."

"Well let's get him up! We've got to yank her back before she cocks up history! Look alive, man."

"Wake up Willks? At two-thirty, after a tear?" Blundell slumped back, unmanned by the very thought of waking the old curmudgeon.

Peter closed his eyes, took a deep breath. He let it out slowly. "Mark, if I have to, I'll drag the bugger naked down to the constable and give him the third, fifth, and tenth degrees!"

"Oh, don't get all ineffable. I'll just wake him."

Blundell trembled as he led the way along the upper balcony toward Willks's room. A snore emanated from behind the door, echoing around Peter's ears.

Blundell made Peter wait outside, crept into the room, and closed the door behind him.

The buzz-saw snore choked off in the middle, dissolved into an explosion of coughing and throat-hocking. After an angry conference, mercifully muffled by the thick walls, the door reopened and Willks appeared, clothed in a ratty dressing gown, hair escaping from his head in all unruly directions.

He blinked rapidly but seemed otherwise sober. Without a word, he elbowed past Peter and led the charge downstairs. He twisted the light switch that Peter had skipped.

Peter squinted and shielded his eyes in the sudden glare. Willks bent, stared at the control panel that still read 48.851.164.817,00. He swept a hand repeatedly through his wild, white lion's mane.

He straightened, looked at the ceiling, and appeared to calculate under his breath.

The room, Willks, Blundell were still unfocused—more than before. Peter closed and opened his eyes, noticed Mark Blundell was doing the same. Sudden blindness seemed to be contagious.

"Where did you say she'd gone?" he asked Peter.

"I didn't," Peter said, "but based on our earlier conversation, I would guess the coronation of Elizabeth the First. Now what? How do you get her back?"

Willks twisted a dial. The blue glow faded from the "doughnut." He leaned over one of the Macs, called up the "calculator," and typed in the number from the panel. He divided it a few times, squinting at the number.

Willks shook his shaggy head. "You're off by about a thousand years. You didn't go in there, did you? Not good, not good. We'd better get you to hospital."

"There's no time for that, Willks! Police business."

"Time?" croaked the old man. "Time we've got. We've got that! Any dizziness, nausea, weakness in the limbs?"

"None," he lied.

"Your skin is bright crimson."

"I burn easily. Look, we've got to get after her, drag her back before she tears history apart!"

"Smith, this dial registers seconds backward from the moment Selly stepped inside, if indeed she did. If she managed to survive, if the thing actually worked, then she's prancing around A.D. *450* even as we speak, so to speak. Or her mind is. If it wasn't simply wiped clean."

Willks shivered inside the threadbare, brown dressing gown. It made him look enormous, a grey-headed bear contemplating the comatose Goldilocks. Blundell stared at the readout, biting his knuckle.

"450 A.D.?" asked Peter. "Why go *there?* What the hell happened in 450 A.D.?"

"Well," mumbled Blundell, "the Norman conquest was 1066."

"Charlemagne?" ventured Willks. "No, he was more like the eighth century. Let's see, the Romans left at the beginning of the fifth century; fifty years after that point was . . ."

Willks turned to look at Blundell in shock; Mark stared back, eyes wide.

"What?" demanded Peter, snappishly. "What are you two thinking?"

"Well," said Blundell, "Mons Badonicus was sometimes before A.D. 500."

"If there even *was* an historical Arthur," rumbled the bear in the dressing gown.

Blundell squeezed his eyes shut, shook his head. "Oh, there was, Hank. Not like what's-his-name, Malory, but there definitely was an historical King A."

Peter's throat constricted. *Arthur?* King *Arthur? A bleedin' IRA agent at the Round Table?* "But what in God's name would she want to do in Arthurian times?"

Willks gently tugged Selly's body onto a rug. "Perhaps study the origins of British monarchy? Find something to cover her up, Blundell." Mark took a step back, looked at the ceiling, hummed something tuneless.

Peter, too, tried not to stare at the nude woman. "Well, who cares what she's doing? Bring her back!"

"Well I'm just about to, you simian twit. This business takes time to set up. Time! We don't want to lose her."

What can I say? Talk about tongue-tied!

What would the IRA want with King Arthur anyway? A suspicion formed in Peter's mind, cold sweat on the back of his neck. *Sweet Jesus,* he thought, *she wouldn't* do him . . . *would she?*

Himself as a boy, hidden in the attic. Lantern light dimly illuminates *The Boys' King Arthur, Le Morte d'Arthur,* once and future antiterrorist reads *The Once and Future King* by secret lights and wonderments. Tennyson idles by tallowlight.

Peter backed away from the feverish Willks, the fretting Blundell. He began to see faint images of trees, felt a slight breeze almost stiff upon his sweaty cheek. Mark, too, stared. Only Willks seemed unaffected.

"Mark," said Peter, "you don't, um, see trees. Do you?"

Blundell lurched, stared at Peter. "You see them too?"

"Almost . . . a forest. There, not there. I—I can't really describe it."

"Oh God. It's started. Henry, she made it. She's there. And she's . . . changing things."

"What are you two babbling about? What trees?" Willks scowled, slightly translucent.

Blundell took several deep breaths, composed his voice. "Hank, I think both Peter and I are beginning to see two different timelines. And God save me, in the other one, not a one of us is here! Jesus, what has Selly *done?*"

"Professor," said Peter, "get her back. Now. I don't give a damn if we lose her or not." He took a slow breath. Much as it struck against his nature, Peter had no choice but to tell all.

CHAPTER 8

SQUINTING AGAINST THE SUPERIMPOSED IMAGES (*IF I'M NOT ALIVE in the forest world, why can I see it?*) Peter used the kitchen phone upstairs, unconcerned whether it was monitored or not. He called Colonel Cooper's very private home number.

The phone was picked up on the third ring; "Cooper," said the voice, half-awake.

"Found the linnet, but she spotted me and flew away."

There was a long pause. "She? You mean that girl, Sally Corwin? What did she get?"

"Um, nothing. She didn't wreck anything. And it's Selly."

"Well, that's a piece, Smythe. I'll call the Yard and Interpol, we'll pick her up for a go-round."

"She . . . she didn't fly that direction, sir." Peter closed his eyes—it was easier—and explained what he understood of the project. He quickly sketched Selly's apparent temporal departure, rushing his description somewhat. Even so, he felt a total ass. He said nothing about an alternate, forest-world timeline.

The telephone was dead for so long Peter worried that the Colonel had hung up on him. "Time travel?" said Cooper at last. "Major, as one fighting man to another, that's the biggest load of mystic apples I've ever heard."

"Yes sir."

"You'd better come up with a better theory than that, soldier, and right quick. The minister is going to be hopping, I can promise you. He'll have me singing 'John Barleycorn.' *Have you ever had to sing 'John Barleycorn' for the minister?*"

"No sir," said Peter, wondering what in hell the colonel was talking about. It sounded unpleasant.

"Now how about telling me what *really* happened?"

Peter made a fast, executive decision. "I'm only telling you what our man Willks said. All I know is that she took off all her clothes, climbed into the machine, and is in some sort of coma."

"You said she was IRA. What the hell makes you think that, Major? Don't you think somebody would sing a few choruses if we let a bloody *provie* into an official defense ministry project?"

"I told you sir," said Smythe, sweat rolling slowly down his spine, "she made reference to the 22d SAS. How else could she know—"

"And then you let her kill herself!" bellowed Cooper.

"She is not dead!"

"No indeed," continued the colonel. "Tomorrow morning—or today, rather, at zero seven-thirty—I plan to be standing on the doorstep there to hear *you* sing 'John Barleycorn.'

And you had better know some verses, mister, something better than this sci-fi time travel applesauce, Major."

"Yes sir," said Peter, tugging at his damp undershirt, "0730, sir. Good-night, sir." The receiver went dead in his hand, and he replaced it on the cradle. He returned to the basement, feeling his way along the corridor and down the stairs. The full complement of project personnel was examining the machine.

Willks stared into the console, every now and again clicking the mouse button on the Macintosh. Blundell watched Peter helplessly, as well as he could with his eyes mostly closed. The rest of the project scientists tried to look busy; Jake Hamilton monitored Selly's vital signs, his face whiter than Peter's shirt.

The marching trees took on the reality of Birnam Wood to Macduff, yet Peter found them easier to ignore if he concentrated on the task at hand.

"Are you ready?" he asked, voice cracking.

Willks ignored him. Peter cleared his throat, began to repeat the question. Blundell stopped him with a raised hand.

"A moment, brother. In a moment. We're almost ready to try."

He's most upset than he lets on, thought Peter. *Shouldn't call me "brother" in mixed company.*

"Right," said Willks, clicking a final time. "Hamilton, stop fussing with the body and get her arse on the PET scan. I want to know the instant she's back."

Jacob and Conner lifted Corwin, nude again, onto the "doughnut" platform, which included an opaque, plastic tube. Peter watched curiously; he had never seen a PET scanner before. He had thought it was part of the time machine.

"Let me know when you're ready to start," ordered Peter, trying to sound official, take command of the situation.

Willks snorted. "We started a minute and a half ago, chrome-dome."

"What? *You have her?*" Smythe crowded close to Willks, stared into the screen: an intricate spiderweb filled the monitor, fuzzed and snowy on the left, defined and heavy in the lower right corner.

The old man glared sideways from under thick eyebrows. His beard bobbed up and down as he spoke. "We never lost her, Smith. As long as she's there and her body's here, we maintain a connection. Now step aside, sonny. Go back and watch her body, why don't you?"

Chastened, Peter drifted toward Hamilton. Mark Blundell was already there, watching another monitor attached to the working Cray.

"We ripped the PET screen off, attached our own," explained the physicist. He pointed at a blob that Peter recognized from pictures: a cross section of Selly's brain. But instead of the brilliant reds and blues he was used to from the television, the picture was black-and-white.

A white "teardrop" intruded into her brain like a malignant tumor.

"That's the only coherent representation of her normal personality pattern that remains," whispered Blundell. "Last piece of her soul, you might say." He removed his glasses, rubbed his eyes. At Willks's suggestion, neither Mark nor Peter had spoken of trees or timelines to the others.

The teardrop slowly grew. An invisible hand seized Peter's bowels, squeezed tight. "Mary and Joseph," he breathed, "you've got her! Bring her back." Blundell replaced his glasses, said nothing.

The monitor filled Peter's entire attention, his brain struggling to block out the forest-view, like looking through a telescope while keeping both eyes open. His world became a thousand shades of grey. The brilliant, white teardrop slowly grew, infiltrated almost three quarters of her brain.

Then, without warning, it greyed around the edges, broke into a myriad tiny whirlpools of complicated interference pattern.

"Damn you, let go!" shrieked Willks. Peter whirled to look at the scientist, just for a moment; when he turned back, the teardrop had shrunk all the way back to its original size.

Selly's body bucked and thrashed, mindlessly. "Grand mal!" yelled Hamilton, threw himself across her, just before the blue field died.

"Get something in her mouth!" Smythe shouted.

"Leads," demanded Hamilton simultaneously. Faust handed him a pair of electrodes from a mini–crash cart. Selly no longer bucked like a landed fish, but steady rolls rippled along her body.

The student called out numbers as they flickered across the LED on the cart. "One . . . one-five . . . two."

"Clear!" Hamilton held the leads to her temples.

Inside the PET scan monitor, the grey brain image turned to pure "snow" for a fraction of a second. Jacob yanked his hands away, said "leads off."

Selly Corwin lay utterly still. A slow, tartan pattern wove across the brain image. Peter held his breath, watched the snake dance.

Excruciatingly slowly, the image returned to its original state, including the tiny, white teardrop. Hamilton, Blundell, and Smythe exhaled explosively.

"Well, the CNS is back in control," said Hamilton. He noticed Peter's confusion. "Central nervous system," he explained. "Selly's got control again."

Peter turned on Willks. "What the bloody hell happened? Why didn't she come back?"

The senior scientist wiped his sweaty forehead with the sleeve of his dressing gown. "Because, you chowderhead, she didn't *want* to come back! What the blue blazes did you *say* to her, anyway?"

"How long until you can try again?"

Blundell began an answer. "Well, the machine needs two hours at least just to realign the circuits."

"A day at least, Mark," insisted Hamilton. "Twenty-four hours."

Willks nodded at the younger man. "We almost lost her this time, Smith. I mean, really lost her—lost her back in time. I don't care how much you want to torture a confession out of her, I will *not* be a party to murder! Or kidnapping, or whatever you'd call it."

A day! Peter thought of standing in the entry hall, nose-to-nose with Colonel Crapper, frantically trying to remember verses to "John Barleycorn." He swallowed hard.

"You can't bring her back?"

Willks sighed, tired and weary. "Smith, if she fought it off once, why do you think she'll come back meekly the second time? Forget it. She'll come back when she's ready, not a moment before."

When she's ready. When she's finished, *you mean.*

Peter shook his head. "No. I can't ... let her just stay there. My God, think of what she could do, to—to Arthur, to Camelot!"

Blundell spread his hands. "But if we can't bring her back . . . ?"

"Then you send someone back to *her*," said Peter, voice tiny and hollow, even in his own ears.

The silence was so sudden, he jumped. He began to hear birds and crickets, the forest denizens, still faint and distant but detectable. Then everyone began talking at once. Finally, Blundell made himself heard over the cacophony by shouting twice as loud as everyone else. "Man, we barely know where *she's* gone! The timelines don't flow linearly. God alone knows whether you'd land ahead or behind her on the time track, and by how many mouths. Or years! That is, if she went anywhere but straight to Bedlam!"

"He's *your* King Arthur as much as mine, Mark. And . . ." (he lowered his voice) "well, you and I know one other vital piece of information. Have you heard the birds, yet? Do you wonder where not only this manor, but the whole bloody village went?" Mark dropped his eyes, fell silent.

Willks spoke up, annoyed. "But why would she do anything? What is there to gain, besides being the first to time travel? Even for the IRA?"

"Professor, I've had extensive dealings with this particular organization. Let's just say it's been my professional concern for eleven years."

"Willks," interjected Blundell, worried, "if Selly really *is* IRA, and if she kills Arthur before he can set up the Round table . . ."

"Feh! The existence of Arthur does not imply a Round Table, a wizard named Merlin, or a witch who puts people to sleep for hundreds of years! What about Conservation of Reality?"

Blundell grinned sheepishly. "Well, I guess that particular symmetry doesn't seem to hold for this universe."

It took fifteen minutes hard argument to persuade the chief physicist. At last he shook his head, waved at the machine. Even Willks could see the danger.

"Glad to have you aboard," said Peter. "How long before that thing's ready?"

Willks tugged at his beard, staring at the doughnut, now suffused with blue incandescence. "As Mark said, it takes two hours to warm up. After that, any time you're ready, Major."

A terrible thought occurred to Peter. "I won't end up in outer space somewhere, will I, because of the Earth's orbit?"

Willks fluttered his hands, annoyed. "Don't be an ass! Didn't Mark go through all this? We're not projecting you *physically* back in time; just your consciousness, such as it is. You'll end up in someone's body."

"Whose?"

"Whoever's is the closest to your own personality." Willks grinned coldly. "Probably a murderer, or the royal headsman."

"So how the blue hell do I tell whose body Selly is prancing about in?"

Willks looked placid. "Why don't you ask around when you arrive?"

Peter reached behind his back, checked his 9mm automatic. He quickly inspected the rest of his gear. "Turn that damned thing on, I'm going through."

Blundell laughed. "Not like that you're not!"

"Like what?"

"You're not prudish, I hope?" asked the giant. "You have to go through naked as the day you were born."

"Naked!" No pistol . . . no rations . . . not even any pepper to trade with the natives for its weight in gold!

"Electrical fields on the skin, connected to the brain through the nervous system. Did you think Selly just wanted to give us a show? She knew what she was doing. You've got about an hour and a half; better spend it with Jake, he knows more about history than any of us." He grinned nastily. "Except for Selly, of course."

Hamilton, beginning to show the same "sunburn" blush as Peter and Selly, suggested they delay the trip until Peter could get to the library in the morning and read for the mission. Smythe shook his head.

Even if they could spare the time, the "real" world was already so tangled with the world without the manor, the village, people, the time doughnut, that Peter fretted he might go mad waiting for morning. He felt a wave of guilt lapping at his belly . . . presumably the timeline conflict would vanish when he jumped back in time to the break Selly had caused. But Mark had no such respite coming. He would have to tough it out.

"No time," said Peter. "Let's get what we can; I'll improvise the rest."

They spent as long as they could with the *Encyclopaedia Britannica*. Peter discovered that no one was even sure when Arthur existed: they "narrowed it down" to nearly an entire century!

"Selly did her own historical research," said Jake. "She must have planned this; she's not the impulsive type. If she set it for 450, I doubt she missed by much."

Peter shuffled back to the basement, heart pounding wildly. He tried to repeat back as much of the articles as he could remember.

When he entered the lab, Willks reached up and touched a Macintosh screen. The menu disappeared, and the image of an old-fashioned pocket watch appeared. The hands ran backwards.

"Like that touch?" asked Blundell. He laughed, sounding as if he were gargling with library paste, then lapsed into silence as the doughnut shimmied and sparked.

"Colonel Cooper will be here at 0730," said Peter. "Tell him the situation required initiative. If he still wants me to sing 'John Barleycorn' when I return, I'll give him ten bloody, rousing choruses." Peter smelled the strong scent of ozone. Willks pounded on the keyboard.

Blundell extended his hand, spoke so softly Peter barely caught it. "Good luck, brother. We met on the level."

"And parted on the square," responded Peter automatically. They touched hands, briefly gave the Masonic signal. Peter's stomach rolled with a flash of absurd shame, as if hoodwinking a brother in the craft. *But I'm not in the bloody craft!* he protested; his stomach did not buy into the defense.

"Mark—why only you and me? No one else sees . . . this."

Blundell shrugged. "Well, you're going back in the past. Perhaps it gives you an insight—*has* given you one, ever since we turned the corner into a universe next door where you would have to go back."

"But you see it too, the forest, the absence of people. Are you going to go back?"

Mark smiled. "Time will tell, heh heh."

Peter slowly stripped off all of his clothes. He found himself turning his back to the comatose body of Selly Corwin, as if she could see him in her condition.

Willks gestured at the tangle of wires. "Don't bump your head, Smith; they have to stay in roughly that alignment. Wish I could tell you what will happen." He seemed almost sympathetic, for a change.

The machine gave a loud pop and a trickle of smoke poured out. Under his breath, Willks muttered, "Never done that before."

"Good-bye, all of you. Carry on; it's a hell of a project." Peter saluted, half-seriously. He gritted his teeth, took a deep breath, and held it as he stepped over the first two wires, carefully ducking his head. He squatted, then Blundell gestured him to lie down next to Selly.

"Wait!" yelled Peter, suddenly panicked. "What *language* do they speak?"

"Willks!" screamed a voice behind him, so far behind . . . the sound of shouting men faded, a bad dream, sounds muffled by the water clotting the air and stuffing his ears.

Terrible pain lanced up the middle of his body, rent asunder. Peter screamed, but soundless, sightless. He felt agony, worse even than the Londonderry bomb. There was *no thing*. He was alone, without even himself.

Skin ripped from muscles, vessels, bones, left him white naked, bare to the void. He stared into the void, eyeless.

The void looked back—

The ceiling spun over his head, the floor swung straight up and smacked into his face. He tasted wood splinters and blood, dimly realized he was sprawled full length on a rough-hewn, hardwood floor.

It was not the cement basement of Willks's lab. He was not naked. He was not alone.

The room tilted alarmingly, hot as the furnace of Shadrach, Meshach, and Abednego. Already sweat-soaked, Peter pushed himself to hands and knees. He fought nausea, blinked tears away . . . but at least the ghastly double vision was gone.

Instead, two stubby, small men stared down at him. They made no move to help him to his feet.

"In the future," said the black-haired man on the left, "I fear we'll have to restrict him to goat's milk." Both men tipped their heads back and brayed like donkeys.

CHAPTER 9

PETER STOOD SLOWLY. PAIN RAZORED ALONG HIS SPINE, FORCING him to crouch again and grit his teeth. Where was he? In God's name, *who* was he?

"Leave—leave me," he wheezed. Again his stomach heaved.

"What'd he say?" asked the slightly taller man; the words sounded different than Peter's had.

"Something about a department," said black-hair. "I don't speak Sicambrian."

Peter forced his gaze up to their faces; with an effort, he fought back the agony and enunciated clearly. "Go . . . *away*. . . ."

"By Blessed Bran, you don't have to be so filthy pissed about it."

A gong tolled. "Come, Cei," said the larger man. "Leave him sleep it off."

The two walked around Peter, disappeared stage right. Peter turned his head, winced at the pain blade in his neck. A thick, black curtain swished slowly in the narrow doorway.

He gagged, overwhelmed by a flood of smells: sweat and mold, mildew, damp rot, the stink of a thousand unwashed dogs and ten thousand deceased rats. His muscles softened and again he was on his knees, trembling, stomach heaving.

He let himself heave but refused to actually vomit. At last, he felt somewhat in control. *Jesus God, I'm really here.* "Kay," he said. *Sir Kay . . . was the other one Bedivere? Percival? Galahad?*

Peter breathed deeply, tried to get used to the horrible stench, worse than the jungles of Bolivia. The pain ebbed. He still felt as if a surgeon had operated on his back without anaesthetic, but the agony faded with every breath. At last he breathed slowly and deeply, the pain but a shuddersome memory.

Peter stood, nearly stumbled again. His balance was off; he felt like a dwarf.

He staggered a few steps, waved his arms. He looked vainly about the room for a mirror: not even a shiny surface.

His hands were small, his legs bowed. He felt his head and it seemed gigantic, like a basketball or a pumpkin. He had a bristly growth of stubble, a shaved head, and more scars than normal.

Okay, he thought, *let's take stock. I know I'm much shorter, stockier—by balance, if nothing else.*

He felt himself carefully. His long, black hair was drawn back and tied with a leather strap. His cheeks were shaved, but he needed another shave soon. He sported a long, bristly mustache.

He wore a rough shirt with great, baggy, short sleeves. One arm was blue, the other greyish black; this pattern was repeated for his pants, though mirrored. Scale mail covered his arms peeked out from beneath his shirt. His boots were rawhide with wooden soles, and they felt all wrong.

He stared down at the boots. *My God,* he raged, *this dolt is so stupid he put his shoes on the wrong feet!*

He struggled the boots off, switched them. But that felt even worse. He stared at his feet. Light finally dawned.

Oh. I guess they don't have left and right shoes yet. He switched the boots back the way they were, glad no one was present to watch and hoot.

The entire room was built to scale, with tiny doorways, chairs, and a Procrustean bed over which his real feet would have hung to the calves. *No, these are my real feet now; better get used to it.*

"Short . . . they're all short. Bad nutrition, ricketts. God, I feel a hundred—wonder how old I really am? Twenty-five and middle-aged already?"

His oddly musical words had a poetic quality. *Okay,* he thought, *reason it through. They understood you, so obviously you're not speaking modern English. Not like Chaucer, either; that was much later. God, is it Old English, like Beowulf? I don't think so. . . .*

Sicambrian; the first thing I said they didn't understand, said I was speaking Sicambrian. Who the hell am I? Damn, why didn't Kay and whoever say a bleeding name?

A calfskin pouch dangled from his belt. He pulled the

strings, opened it to find a knife and shallow-bowled spoon; a handcloth; an extremely light, greyish rock; and a bit of reflective metal (for a mirror, Peter supposed); a comb; a small paring knife, perhaps for fingernails; string; a small handful of stale biscuits; mint leaves (*for breath?* he wondered); and fifteen coins of two denominations. He stared at himself in the mirror for a while, then replaced the contents, wondering a bit about the rock.

Peter paced the toy-sized room, getting the balance of his new body. It was strong and well coordinated when he did not try to force it into a "Peter Smythe" mold. Now that he was no longer trying to walk like a man of six-foot-three, he found he moved with an easy grace he almost envied.

This man's a fighter, I know that much. Peter grinned. *There'll be a whacking lot of gaping mouths when I demonstrate an inside-out kick!*

He tentatively tried a few punches and kicks, discovering his new body was quite up to the challenge. Peter launched into an aggressive, Okinawan kata. Up and down the cramped quarters he wove, lighter on his feet than ever before.

His strength was extraordinary. He picked up a well-made, wooden table and pulled it apart with ease. His grip could easily break a neck; a punch or kick might dent heavy armor, if they had any.

I think I'm going to like this assignment, he decided.

Peter prowled his room for a half hour, then exited through the same curtain that Kay and the other man had used. It led to a landing and a great stair, six feet wide leading down, narrow going up. The roar of laughter, many voices sounded below. He went down, following the noise of revelry.

About two hundred men and perhaps fifty women were lost in a drunken bacchanal belowstairs. Peter clapped hands over ears, sagged back against a wall. His eyes stung from thick torch smoke.

Most of the guests reclined on long couches, but a number wandered between the knee-high tables, pushing and wrestling with each other. They wore leather, fur, wool, linen, and a powerful lot of metal. Most wore armor, more decorative than functional. *Badges of rank?* Peter wondered. He chewed his lip. The motley crew bore little resemblance to his vision of King Arthur's noble knights.

A bunch of nearly nude boys and girls surrounded the hall. He stared uneasily, wondering who they were, why they stood so shamelessly naked in the midst of such finery.

Then a hilarious blond darted past, pursued by a drunken . . . something. Barefoot and topless, she made no move to cover herself. Peter stared, shocked for a moment, before his training reasserted itself. He stared straight ahead until she was gone.

All he could think, absurdly enough, was *isn't she bleedin' cold?* A freezing wind cut the hall like a hundred razors. It took Peter a few moments to realize that one entire end of the banquet hall had no roof, was open to stars and the night wind. Most of the banqueters huddled around the central, roofed part of the hall, near the torches and braziers that provided some warmth.

As his eyes adjusted to the dimness, he began to pick out details—fabulous mosaics, men and women dancing like whirling dervishes, smoking from water pipes on the tables. He sniffed the air, choked on the unmistakable odor of hashish. *Where the hell did they get* hash? *This isn't Morocco!* He pulled a piece of shirt up from under his mail and breathed through it, fought his way away from the landing and through the crowd toward a group that seemed the focus of attention.

He spied a small man. Though shorter than Sir Kay, he stood out from the mob because of his simple, white, Roman toga, adorned with gold thread hemwork. Clean-shaven and shorthaired, he reminded Peter irresistibly of his brother stationed in Gibraltar.

The man carried himself with regal grace and economy of movement, a natural king. He leaned back against a couch with a red dragon headboard.

Arthur, thought Peter. *If that's not King Arthur, I'll eat a raw rat.*

Arthur earnestly discoursed with a huge, Gallic gentleman, nearly six feet tall. The lanky giant's black hair hung down his back and out of sight behind the table. He listened intently, hands clasped before his face, forefingers pressed against his lower lip. Peter stared, unable to take his eyes from the long-haired man.

The man raised his eyes, met Peter's gaze. For an instant, Peter felt an inexplicable wave of guilt. He recalled every lie, act of brutality, every murder committed for queen and country. The grinning, bloody Sergeant Mulligan, who fell apart that one day in Londonderry, loomed before his mental vision, ghostly finger pointing an accusation at Peter.

Cheeks flushed, Peter turned his face away to avoid the scrutiny. *He knows,* whispered a voice in his head.

A cool hand pressed against his brow. It felt so real, Peter had to touch his own forehead to make sure it was only in his head. He looked back at Long-Hair, tried to meet his gaze but could not.

Through the smoke, the man gazed into Peter's heart, saw the sins and awfulness. Yet he smiled, gestured to an empty couch. Peter approached hesitantly and reclined, copying the other men at the table.

He blinked and shook his head; he was once again Major Peter Smythe, 22-SAS, under arms for queen and country—*or king and country, as it were,* he corrected himself.

"Your Majesty," Peter acknowledged, nodding to Arthur.

"Yes?" inquired the long-haired man.

"I'm sorry?"

"My error; I thought you were addressing me."

"You're unusually polite tonight," said Arthur. "May I introduce your countryman, Merovius Rex, *legatus Augusti provinciae Sicambriae pro praetore.* Merovee, governor of Sicambria." Merovee bowed his head.

"Ah . . . pleased to meet you," said Peter. *Merovius Rex . . . King Merovee. Governor of Sicambria? There's that word again!*

"And Merovee, may I present my own champion, the greatest of my warriors, legate of two legions, consul for the second time, and *tribune* of my personal guard—this is Prince Consul Lancelot of the Languedoc."

Peter's mouth dropped. He gasped involuntarily.

Merovee sighed. "Yes, Artus, I know him well. I fear Lancelot is under a death sentence in Sicambria; he attempted to assassinate me some six years ago. Imperfectly, as you see." He smiled pleasantly. "Of course, I am somewhat elevated in station since then."

Arthur sat back in his chair, nonplussed. He looked from Merovee to Peter *(Lancelot? Lancelot du Lac!).* Arthur's expression plainly asked whether there would be trouble under his roof.

Merovee laughed, extended his hand. "Well met, Lancelot; I forgive your rash act, as our Master taught."

Hesitantly, Peter took the king's hand; it was warm and strong, the hand of a warrior born. He felt an exploratory pressure from the thumb and third finger.

Peter's eyes widened. King Merovee was a Mason.

CHAPTER 10

A CROWD GATHERED AROUND PETER—APPARENTLY NOW "Lancelot"—Arthur, and Merovee. Whispers of "Death sentence" and "assassination" slithered through the room. *Damn it,* thought Peter, squirming, *I'm supposed to be inconspicuous—not the center of intrigue and speculation!*

Peter's respirations increased, and he felt his chest squeeze viselike. He felt a sudden rush, "speedy-jeebies" they called it in his narcotics law enforcement class. Peter half rose, looked wildly about for escape, then realized there was nowhere to go.

He sat hard, felt moist perspiration on his face, the back of his neck. *Something* was inside him, squeezing and kicking, desperately trying to *get out.*

Arthur, or Artus, as Merovee had called him, seemed to thrive on the attention. Prochronous phrases peppered his stilted speech. "Have you recovered from your illness of a few moments past?" he asked.

"Illness?" responded Peter.

"The *morbus terribilis* that caused you to leap from the bench and flee the room, a mere instant after Cei announced Merovee's approach." Arthur smiled; the crowd laughed.

"Perhaps," said King Merovee, "the warrior was offended by the odor of my men, who have ridden unbathed for many days!" The crowd roared again. Peter deduced that Lancelot-baiting was a popular sport at Camelot.

Moans and wolf whistles from the back of the crowd heralded the approach of the most beautiful woman Peter had ever seen. She was a golden angel, Harlow-hair cropped short in a virtual butch. She wore a blue, embroidered dress cut to expose her perfect breasts, with some sort of ugly, purple drapery dangling behind her and looped around the front. Peter's throat constricted, he writhed uncomfortably on the wooden bench.

His heart rate had slowed, not yet normal, and his head cleared somewhat. But the feeling of something or some*one* trapped within his chest grew stronger.

"Gwynhwfyr," said Artus, "pray join us. There is yet brew to drink, spice to smoke."

Peter mentally rolled her name across his tongue. *Guinevere,* he realized. She smiled, passed Arthur, and sat next to Peter. "See any fruit you would like to pluck, Lance?" she asked.

He realized he was staring at her breasts, quickly averted his gaze. "Good ah good ah good evening, Your Highness," Peter stammered.

No one had a right to be so beautiful.

"So formal!" she exclaimed. "Have we not slopped pigs together, as you Sicambrians say? You weren't so stuffy last night!" She laughed like a harp of heaven, and Peter turned brick red.

"Ah," said Artus, pointing a mock-accusing finger at Peter. "Looking to take advantage of Guest-Right, are you? Tell me, Gwynhwfyr . . . is the court gossip true?"

"I cannot answer, gracious lord and husband, until you clarify which gossip concerns you." She smiled innocently. "Do you wonder about length, thickness, or duration?"

Peter choked. The crowd dutifully said *"Oooooh"* in unison.

Arthur chuckled. "I was more interested to know whether young Lancelot here, as the rumor says, *truly* never removes that fish scale of his."

"Your conversation makes a lady grow dizzy," said the princess, fanning herself with an intricately carved, wooden "pie-piece" fan that dangled from her belt. "Pray pass the Arabian spice."

Without waiting, Guinevere leaned across the table to grasp

the water pipe, incidentally rubbing her breasts across Peter's hand. The nipples were ripe strawberries; Peter caught himself staring, stared instead at a harp left unattended near the couch.

Gwynhwfyr inhaled deeply from the hookah, held the smoke, exhaled slowly. "I know not the answer, my husband. There are no scales on the part that interests *me*."

The crowd laughed and applauded, pounding the table and stamping their feet. Peter shrank into himself, took a long pull from a wine mug.

Wrong, wrong, wrong, not the cruise I signed up for! Romans, Masons, Queen Guinevere a drug addict? I need a holiday already! He crossed his legs. *Please God, give her a mark, a blemish, something to turn back these mad desires. . . .*

The honeyed wine was hot but weak, its sweetness nauseous. "Why kinsman," laughed Merovee, "your ears are red as the wine you drink!"

"So, ah, tell me," Peter asked Guinevere, if indeed it was she. "Where did this . . . Arabian hashish come from?"

"Arabian what? Oh, the hemp? From Arabia, I would imagine." She laughed again. Peter flushed in annoyance.

"No," her persisted, "how did *Artus* get hold of it?"

Artus spoke up, answered for his wife. "From my friend al'Sophiate, Sultan of Deh Bid, Qomsheh, and Yazd. He made his fortune selling peppercorns, silk, and hemp-spice throughout Arabia, Armenia, and Judea, and somehow bought his way onto the citizenship rolls. I campaigned with him when I commanded a cohort of the twenty-third Roman Legion, in Jerusalem, where I also met our guest, Merovius Rex. Did he never tell you stories of that campaign? Of course, he was but a governor and legate then."

Arthur, a Roman legionnaire? Campaigns in the Holy Land? Sweat rolled down Lancelot's brow as he envisioned tearing Malory limb from limb. *What mad rabbit hole have I fallen down?*

"I speak little of those days, noble friend," said Merovee. "The loss of my birthright is still painful."

Artus seemed embarrassed. "Damned narrow cut," he whispered. He looked around the crowd, called out, "Where is the boy? Where is Cors Cant Ewin?"

"Here, General." A young man of about nineteen pushed his way through the throng and picked up the harp. He wore a blue robe, bound at the waist by a leather belt with silver rings. He wore no armor whatsoever. The knife that dangled from his belt was meant only for dinner meat. Peter could not tell whether the garment was Roman or Briton, or neither.

"Cors Cant, sing us another tale," begged Artus.

"A bard, then!" exclaimed Merovee. "I have heard much of the bards of Britain. Druid trained? Have you passed the examination at the Druid College?"

"Well, yes and no, Your Highness," hedged the boy.

"Yes and no? I do not understand; which is it to be?" The black-haired king frowned, puzzled.

"You asked two questions, Sire: yes to the first and no to the last."

Again the crowd roared; *easily amused,* thought Peter, ears still buzzing. Merovee himself slapped the table, laughed heartily, without trace of annoyance. Peter was quite taken with the man.

Cors Cant Ewin, thought Peter, *a bard, and young enough not to be suspicious. Even the Connecticut Yank had an inside snitch.* He decided to question the boy at the first opportunity. In the meantime, he surveilled the mythic princess for signs of Selly Corwin.

Cors Cant looked over the crowd, pantomimed drinking from a bottle. Peter followed the boy's look. An auburn-haired girl, older in the eyes but not the years than Cors Cant, scowled and folded her arms. The sleeves of her chemise looped nearly to her knees, swaying in the faint breeze. If she understood his sign language request for a drink, she refused to acknowledge it.

The girl wore none of the finery of Guinevere or the martial elegance of Lancelot himself. But the crook-armed sunface embroidered on her brown and white tunic, which modestly covered her chemise everywhere but sleeves and feet, jumped out at Peter. Did the sun wear a halo, or was that just an oddly shaped ray?

"Anlawdd," implored the boy, made his phantom drink signal more urgent. "I spy a dozen bottles by the columns across the hall," he explained, "but I can't break through and get one!"

"So tell a slave," she retorted.

"It's just a favor—my throat is parched from singing!"

"Cors Cant Ewin, I am a freeborn woman, not a Greek

serving wench, in case you've been driven lunatic by the moonshine and can't understand the difference. Fetch and carry your own bottle."

The embarrassed boy looked to Artus, who gazed back with a bemused expression. The crowd made rude noises, pressed the boy close. He clutched his harp to his chest. "Anlawdd," he pleaded, "you know I can't order the *Dux Bellorum*'s slaves!"

"All right," she grudgingly said, "but don't take this as license to order me to clean your tunics or scrub your floor. I'm bound only to the princess, and her by love ... not annoyance and irritation, which is all that certain other people inspire!" She wheeled and headed toward the open-air section of the hall, where five marble columns reached up to touch the delicate half-roof.

The boy's not attending to her distress, thought Peter. *Bad news; he surely needs a couple of pointers about females.* Peter considered that one of his areas of expertise.

Something else struck Peter about the girl—*Anlawth, was it?* Years of experience questioning suspects and terrorists sounded a warning, like a beeping watch-alarm that he could not shut off: the girl was "political," in the sense of an IRA provisional or an SAS major.

She hid some terrible secret, something dreadful she had done or would do; and it ate at her heart. Anlawth the Betrayer, accused the voice in Peter's head, the voice he never ignored. *I shall keep an eye on you, lass,* he thought, watching her burnt orange hair escape from beneath a white turban as she bobbed and wove toward the wall.

Artus and Merovee began quietly to speak in Latin. Peter listened hard, but their conversations was a bit beyond his seven years of Sunday School Latin.

Now that's odd, he thought; *I had no trouble speaking ancient British and Sicambrian, which I've never heard ... why can't I understand Latin too?* He had no ready answer. *Damn—I want to know what they're saying ... and why they suddenly dropped to a different language.*

After approximately two minutes, the girl returned with a pottery jug. She stood upon a table and whistled shrilly. "Cors Cant!" she cried, slinging the jug overhead like a cricket ball.

The boy lunged, a horrified look on his face. He caught the jug by its neck, while nearly losing control of his harp.

"Anlawdd!" he exclaimed, anguished. He lost his balance, sprawled full length across the table, barely managing to save both harp and jug. This brought another hoot from the mob.

"Next time, exercise your feet, not your tongue, Cors Cant Ewin!" lectured the girl. She tossed her head dismissively; the turban slipped from her head, exposing even more auburn locks and somewhat spoiling the haughty effect. She stormed across the hall like royalty, ducking behind one of the marble columns. Cors Cant's face fell as she left.

History and destiny, Peter thought. He watched the column carefully. As he knew she would, Anlawdd crept back as soon as the song began, watching raptly from behind a great, hanging tapestry.

But whom does she betray?

The tapestry depicted a harpist climbing out of a deep pit into the sun, looking back over his shoulder at a woman who appeared to be falling back. It looked vaguely Greek.

A thought occurred to Peter; he reasoned carefully. *I understood British and Sicambrian immediately, but not Latin . . . perhaps it's* Lancelot *who can't speak Latin?* For the first time since jumping, he began to feel like a rational man again. *Please, God, let there be logical rules!*

Cors Cant was an excellent musician. He plucked an intricate tune and sang a complicated verse simultaneously. *The lad could make a fortune with a Fender Stratocaster,* Peter thought. *Does he speak Latin, perhaps?* Peter glanced surreptitiously around the room for paper and pen, but saw nothing.

Another thought perturbed Peter: did Artus and Merovee shift to Latin precisely *because* Lancelot would not understand? What secrets did King Arthur keep from his own champion?

The boy's song was a complicated story wherein "Artus *Dux Bellorum*" outfoxed an enemy called the Westies. For a wild instant, Peter thought he meant the Chicago gang of the sixties. Then a verse caused Peter to stiffen in recognition:

The general bore upon the frothing flanks of war,
He tore from blackened flames a blazing brand,
And spurred the knaves to dark and bloody waves,
To barren graves, past shore, in Wes' Seax-Land.

West Seax-Land, West-Saxon . . . Wessex?

Peter decided to test his new confidence, reason logically where in England he actually was. Willks's laboratory was twenty miles south of Bristol; how far had he actually shifted geographically?

He listened to the description of the battle, inferred that the Saxon kingdom of Wessex lay directly east.

But where the hell is Wessex? Peter shut his eyes and concentrated. While at Sandhurst, he had read for a test on the wars between Wessex and Mercia. Where Wessex stood was now—or would be in a few centuries—Dorset, Hampshire, Wiltshire, Somerset.

And if they lay to the east, then Camelot must be somewhere in Devon or Avon.

Peter fidgeted as the boy's song went on and on. Cors Cant had sung for a solid forty-five minutes. Peter wondered how he managed to keep the throng breathless throughout. They hung on every word, stayed silent even during lengthy instrumental codas.

After defeating the "Westies," Artus spent many minutes judging their generals. If the song was to be believed, some thirty different persons were judged. Each got between three and fifteen verses of punishment, ranging from being drawn and quartered to six months without the option.

After this marathon star chamber proceeding, Artus, undoubtedly fatigued from all the gavel-banging, journeyed northward to soak in the old Roman baths at Aquae Sulis. *Also known as Bath,* Peter deduced. This provided him with his second clue. He mentally called up a map and sifted through the towns south of Bath.

One name jumped out in a blaze of cognition: Glastonbury. As a boy, Peter always thought Glastonbury Tor was the ruins of Camelot. It was certainly ancient enough; some of the ruins dated from Jesus's time, preceding Arthur by half a millenium!

It was a sobering thought. Peter imagined King Arthur being shrouded in the mists of antiquity . . . yet he lived as long after the birth of Christ as Peter lived after the War of the Roses.

He settled back, found an unexpected well of patience for Cors Cant's endless epic. He took a long drink from the mulled wine, discovered it grew on him as the evening passed.

Still he brooded: *From Bristol to Glastonbury . . . do miles matter in a matter of centuries?* Peter's head swirled. Blundell had said he would find himself in the "nearest" mind, not by geography, but by personality. *Good Lord, it's lucky I didn't end up in a soldier on the Irish frontier! But where did Selly land? And what in Mary's name did she do to half create a world where cities, people, perhaps all England ceased to exist?*

He watched Guinevere through slitted eyes as she prattled away. She teased the boy, tried to distract him from his harp. Behind the tapestry, the autumn-haired girl, Anlawdd, glowered darts at Artus's wife. Anlawdd was not pleased at the attention the princess gave Cors Cant.

Peter studied Guinevere, Gwynhwfyr, tried to ignore the tightness in his pants. *Could she be—? No, impossible. When I found myself in Lancelot's body, I still had my own mind, my own personality.* Guinevere was too bubbly; not empty-headed, but emphatically not politically oriented. How could such innocence hide the soul of a Provie terrorist? Peter glanced at her breasts, quickly away. He crossed Gwynhwfyr off the suspect list.

Okay, my fairy-fey, then where do *you hide? Do you know me yet, realize I've come after you?*

Words drifted through Peter's mind, words from a song he had first heard a quarter century ago, a millenium and a half from now. They throbbed in his head like a migraine: *soul of a woman, soul of a woman, soul of a woman.*

He had listened to the song over and over in 1969, when he was eighteen. It was a difficult year. Peter was in open rebellion against his father, who had decreed that Peter should make the westward pilgrimage to Sandhurst. Peter himself, newly released from a brief stint in army hell, preferred to wander no farther than Hyde Park, Carnaby Street, and the Royal Albert Hall. His father won . . . as always.

Soul of a woman. . . . The words held special meaning; his own sweet colleen, Zenobia Wedgeworth, decided she preferred the company of a lecturer at Oxford. The day Peter saw them arm in arm at the cathedral on a bank holiday, he visited a barber, sold his record collection, and rang up Sandhurst to say "take me, I'm yours."

Peter blinked, shook himself from the reverie. *Damn the hash smoke!* he raged.

Merovee and Artus put their heads together, spoke simply, quietly. Lancelot listened, heard just enough to convince him the conversation was important. *If I can get a transcript, maybe the kid can translate, if he knows Latin.*

He felt for his pocket, jamming his fingers before he realized he had no pocket. He fumbled through the pouch: nothing that remotely resembled paper or pencil.

He turned to the man at his left. "Excuse me," he rumbled, "do you have any paper or, uh, quill and ink?"

The man stared for a moment, mouth parted. Then he clutched his belly, laughed like a loon. "Good one, Lancelot!" he said and slapped Peter on the shoulder.

"Yeah that was pretty good, heh-heh," said Peter lamely. *Damn! I would have to land in the body of an illiterate! Now what?*

Again, he felt a wave of dizziness as he thought of the real, displaced Lancelot. Again, pressure built like a champagne bottle just before the cork pops. He gritted his teeth, bearing down hard as he would have in a high-G turn in aerial combat. The pressure eased. For a moment, his head pounded as it did when a pilot woke from a blackout. The pain ebbed.

Artus and Merovee still talked; Lancelot still had no paper, no pen, no ink.

There was only one course of action: he would have to close his eyes, listen so hard it hurt, and memorize everything that he could. At a more private moment, he could write it down, then find somebody to translate. Perhaps Cors Cant.

He laid his head down, opened his ears, and pretended to pass out.

CHAPTER 11

CORS CANT EWIN PLAYED A MELANCHOLY VERSION OF THE fourth great battle of Caer Lludd-Dun. His heart was heavy behind the strings. Anlawdd had refused to stay and listen. Perhaps she tired of his pursuit.

Can't she tell how much I love her? Apparently not; she lost no opportunity to speak a harsh word or laugh at his lovestruck humiliation.

Blood on the stones! he thought; *I know I look ridiculous. I can't help it . . . whenever you're near, my tongue rolls into a seashell and my legs become limp as seaweed.*

At last he finished. Half the table had found partners and lay locked in amorous embrace. Half were well into wine or spice. The third half snored loudly.

Lancelot had collapsed into his bowl of fig soup. Only a slave boy's timely intervention saved him from ignominious drowning. Artus and Merovee huddled, spoke in conspiratorial whispers, a map between them.

Gwynhwyfr commanded he "strike a dancing tune." Cors Cant responded absently with an ancient tune from western Eire. It began languid as a highland stream, soon frothed like the River CuChulainn. On two occasions, once while sober, the princess had said it was her favorite.

She stood, swayed to the music, let her robe and chemise fall to the floor. Naked save for a gilt net sewn with jewels, she danced to the center of the hall where five long tables outlined a center pentagon. She wove a complicated web, spun deosil and widdershins, an intricate pattern that looked like enchantment to Cors Cant.

Did Anlawdd stitch that dress for you? Cors Cant wondered. He glanced at Gwynhwyfr's naked, glistening body, wet with ecstasy and exertion, then quickly looked away, lest Anlawdd see his desire. *I don't want her, I don't want her,* he insisted, praying it was true. *Not her! I want my own fire-goddess, my blood-dipped seamstress, my very own Anlawdd!*

A small crowd of citizens and a few freedmen and women circled the princess. They cast off their shoes, danced barefoot on the wooden floor. Some joined Gwynhwyfr in dancing skyclad.

The half-moon burst from behind a cloud, shone high through the open roof. Dawn would come soon. In the sudden white, Anlawdd appeared from nowhere and joined the circle. Cors Cant's heart leapt in anticipation; alas, she kept her clothes on, all but her sandals. She wore the Apollo tunic, or the "Lugh" tunic, as she preferred to call it, and a long shirt beneath that covered all. In the moonlight and candle glow, the tunic looked brown and white, rather than its true, bright colors.

For weeks, Cors Cant had tried to get close to her; but she wore impenetrable armor beneath her chemise. Some force held her back from letting him in—perhaps her faith, perhaps something more sinister.

For a moment, his eyes watered; then he blinked them clear. Anlawdd could not man the wall forever. Soon or late, she must throw open the gate.

Cors Cant longed to join her in the whirling ritual. But the dancers swayed to his tune, and music was the lion's share of the cantrip, as Æsop the Greek would say.

At last, Gwynhwfyr noticed the others' exhaustion. She spun faster yet, two revolutions to each beat, then suddenly became a petrified statute, as if she had seen a Gorgon. The bard found a trapdoor to end the song on cue, let his harp ring into silence. He flexed his fingers to ease the stiff pain. The dancers collapsed to the floor, all but the princess herself.

She returned to her couch, breathing heavily, but remarkably fresh. Sweat rolled down her slick, nearly nude body, reflected between the pearls and copper buttons of her mesh chemise.

Slaves approached, rubbed her down with cool oil. Cors Cant began to respond to the sight, uncomfortably aware that Anlawdd had risen to her knees to watch him. He struggled not to imagine himself as the slave boy.

Cors Cant laid his harp in his lap, silently cursing the goddess Aphrodite, who had carved Gwynhwfyr's body from equal parts sunlight and wild cherries. The wind in her wake blew frenzied love, the scent of passionate beasts in fertile fields. She stared directly at the bard.

He shifted, but her eyes did not follow; in truth, she stared right through him. He glanced over his shoulder, saw the object of her attention was besotted Lancelot instead.

Gwynhwfyr rose, walked stiff-legged around the table, grabbed a handful of the Sicambrian's hair, and yanked his head upright. She kissed him on the mouth with passion, and he struggled in her grasp.

She furled herself around her champion like a windless banner. She stroked his back, moaned with pleasure.

The boy looked for Bedwyr. The giant watched the embrace, smiling indulgently. *Hypocrite!* thought the bard, pressing his harp closer.

Gwynhwfyr ground her pelvis into Lancelot's. The Sicambrian's eyes widened.

Cors Cant leapt up, unable to contain himself any longer, and ran blindly from the table. He stumbled, found himself on his knees, nose-to-nose with Anlawdd.

"Anlawdd," he gasped, "can you not find it in your heart to lend me a moment of precious love?"

She did not change expression. "I don't understand what you think love has to do with it," she said. "Not unless you call the coupling of horses, swine, and dogs *love,* for that's all you want from me."

"Anlawdd, that's not true! What I beg is nothing less than sacrifice to Bacchus or Aphrodite, or Rhiannon. It's a holy worship, the cross into the rose, and it makes the fields fertile!"

"Not to mention seamstresses." Anlawdd's eyes shifted. She would not look at Cors Cant.

He gritted his teeth, struggled against visions of Anlawdd dressed as Gwynhwfyr was, writhing in the spiral dance. "But Anlawdd," he whispered, "my need is so *huge!"* He held his breath, desperately hoping the princess's love dance had worked its magic. "Please!" he begged, "let us away to quiet room, to sacrifice in peace."

Anlawdd stared, mouth open in astonishment. She glanced back at Gwynhwfyr, pressed lips together angrily. "Why now, Cors Cant? Did *that woman* stir your passion so? Honestly, I don't know why you don't just jump her in the stables, instead of pursuing me like a lost puppy!"

Cors Cant caught and held her elusive eyes, trying to grin roguishly. "Anlawdd, beauteous mistress of the needle—"

"And don't *Anlawdd-beauteous-mistress* me, Cors Cant Ewin! Those bardic tricks may work on slave girls and kitchen wenches, but not on a prin—not on a freeborn seamstress from Harlech!"

She sat on her haunches, hands on knees. One wild hair curled from under her turban to cross her face.

He lowered his eyes, abandoning roguishness in favor of pity. "It's true she inflamed my passions. But I burn only for you, nevertheless. How can you deny me so cruelly, when the princess herself leads the worship of Venus in the Fields every year, and holds a *saturnalia* the month after next? Will you make me wait two months? Will you deny me even then, even for the good of the crops?"

She bit her lip, glanced again toward the princess of fertility. "I . . . I don't know, Cors Cant Ewin. I know boys have a harder time controlling . . . I mean, if you absolutely *must* . . . Oh, I don't even know what I mean!" She folded her arms across her chest, clearly upset.

"I . . . I guess we can give it a try. I guess," she said, unconvincingly. "But something feels dreadful wrong, like I'm in a wheelless chariot being dragged by a runaway horse."

She stood, gestured with pale eyes toward the southeast courtyard. Cors Cant followed, heart pounding so he could hardly hear the music. *At last, at last!* Anlawdd's steps were leaden, however, and she trembled slightly, though she firmly set her jaw.

She slipped between the bare columns, led the boy toward the stair that led up to the apartments used by Gwynhwfyr's ladies-in-waiting, where Anlawdd lived.

CHAPTER 12

I WASN'T QUITE SURE HOW I HAD GOTTEN MYSELF INTO THIS mulligatawny—I didn't even know for sure what young ladies *did* in their chambers with young boys! Though we embraced the old religion in Harlech, it was a tepid, Romanized version, simply substituting "the Lady" for Mithras, or for the Christ, if you prefer, though I don't see much the difference. To the Harlech nobles, including my father, religion was like a pickled, salted plum: you call it a joyous treat, but in fact it makes your lips pucker up like a fish, and you'd not want more than one at a time.

We had none of the joyous abandon of the princess's *saturnalias!* I could never fling myself at the feet of every guest as she is rumored to do, though of course I don't stick to the walls like a fly and watch when she entertains, since I have many other things I would rather do—sharpen my axe, spy on sundry Saxons, That Boy, and my target, count my fingers and toes to make sure they're all still there after a few weeks in Camlann.

We mounted the stair, That Boy and I, and I confess my dainty, royal feet were as leaden as the hooves of Calumphus, Father's ancient war-horse, who's more fitted to draw an ale wagon than charge into battle.

I sneaked a glance at That Boy. He wasn't bad-looking at all, at all; not quite as tall as I, but still lithe and surefooted, though that may change when we're married and the slaves cook my best recipes, so we each put on thirty pounds of affluence. His long, brown hair was wavy as the shaggy mane of a native pony, the way I always wished mine was, rather than straight and flat like an Arabian mare's, and it framed a face that flickered between eager expectancy and nervous fret. I was pleased to note I wasn't the only trepidatious person on the stair.

I couldn't see his eyes, but I knew them to be hazel, crackling with light when the sun shone or lanterns flared, splintering into a myriad separate colors, like sunlight through a watery window, or at least those colors for which we've a name, since I'd seen them many times before.

But what was happening? Could I compromise my mission with selfish love? I felt like a character in a Greek song, betraying her duty for love of a young boy, and of course I remembered what always happened when love beat duty: misery and destruction, the wrath of the gods, then straight to hell with Judas and Sisyphus and that lot!

I felt the rough, uneven stair upon my feet, light-sandaled in the Roman fashion, and swayed with dizziness as we neared the top so I had to clutch at That Boy's arm like an old crone too deep in her cups, though I hadn't drunk a drop, nor a small horn at most!

His bardic arms supported me, no mean feat since I could probably crack his riblets with a bear hug, and led me toward Gwynhwfyr's apartment.

The real reason I faltered, however, would have frozen the marrow in his bones, and I wished upon myself all ilk of plague, pox, and misfortune that I hadn't the soul of a warrior, enough courage to tell him *why I had come to Caer Camlann.*

The words rose and lodged in my throat like dried bread that you swallow whole.

"Cors Cant," I began; he waited, tilting his head to the side like a bird, and my heart pounded like Geoffanon on his anvil. "Cors Cant Ewin," I tried again, but this time the blood beat and rattled in my ears like all the pots and pans of Caer Camlann tumbling down the chimney.

"Yes?" he asked, no doubt fearing I remembered an urgent appointment.

"Nay, 'tis nothing," said I, "just a momentary thought, like a mouse you spot in the room, but which scurries under the door before you can sight it proper and pounce upon it."

"Are you sure you want to do this?" he asked, and I wouldn't swear that his voice didn't betray at least *some* hope that I would say "No, I'm not sure," which of course I was not.

But can a girl be blamed for pride? Unsure I might be, bees buzzing in my stomach and thought-mice scrambling about my feet, but to such a question there is but one answer: "Of course I'm certain, Cors Cant Ewin! Do you take me for one of your giddy court maids, who press you away with one hand even while they beckon with the other?"—or words to the same effect, for I can't remember everything just as it was.

But is That Boy sure he wants to share himself with a plotting assassin? asked my conscience. I had no answer, so I said nothing, like a soldier.

The old stories were true, I discovered: how could I possibly raise my dagger, carry out my mission, when the one I would kill was so much the father to Cors—to That Boy, whom I knew even then I might someday love? How could cold, proud duty fail to fall before love's hot blood?

But I was not just a court–to–court girl! I knew who I was, who my own father was, and I knew the duty of war.

I closed my eyes, and That Boy brushed the hair from my brow; the turban was a mistake—it fit the princess but not her seamstress. I felt a phantom dagger in my hand, knew when the moment came I could raise it and strike, boy or no boy.

Alas, I knew too that the blow would end *three* lives, not one: for when Cors Cant looked up from the bloody wound and saw the fell hand of the murderess, his love would parch like a mud puddle in the Arabian sands, leaving him nothing more than a shade summoned from Hades to speak empty prophecy; and this obliteration would take my own soul with it, and all from one strike of a sliver of steel!

We were *damned to hell,* all three of us: Anlawdd to wither from guilt, Cors Cant to crumble from betrayal . . . and Artus *Dux Bellorum* to be struck down in a pool of gore by the maiden of his own, dear wife.

Ah, it was an eternal, crimson triangle that Sophocles would rightly cheer!

I allowed That Boy to draw me inside my lady's chamber, has warm palm burning my own icy fingers. I could neither plant my heels nor charge ahead, a war-horse confused by too light a touch of her rider's knees.

I crossed the threshold into darkness—Chapel Perilous as the Builders say—with tears on my cheek and springy legs that barely supported the weight of guilt.

CHAPTER 13

PETER WOKE TO A MOUTHFUL OF FRENCH KISS. A SWEET TONGUE swirled his own, groped toward the back of his throat. He responded unthinkingly. *Such a dream! But when did I doze off?*

He opened his eyes, saw Gwynhwfyr fitted around him like a cheap suit of armor, scented with sex and spice. He froze; it was no dream.

Sitting astride him, she ground her pelvis into his lap, moaning. Peter thrust forward savagely. The crowd cheered and he woke fully, realized he was the center of a very large bit of attention.

A hundred hungry eyes watched the two of them. Gwynhwfyr loved it, becoming louder and wilder as the audience clapped. Daunted, Peter tried to halt; but her sex-scent so overwhelmed some part of him that his body continued, unconcerned who watched or whistled.

Some part—some piece—something inside me pushing, driving, uncaring—

He fumbled for his tunic, pulled it up to expose his underbreeches. Then he seized control back from the alien presence: *Good God, what am I doing? Guinevere and Lancelot, their love brought down a king!*

He abruptly realized who and what he was. He shoved her away with his hands while his hips still thrust mindlessly.

"No! Not with—" His words vanished, sucked from his mouth by Gwynhwfyr's next passionate kiss.

Head turned to the side, Peter caught a glimpse of Cei, who made frantic chopping motions with his hand. Peter summoned the will to push the queen from his lap and stagger to his feet.

He stalked toward the rear of the hall, slaves melting from his path like bowling pins. He looked back once, saw Artus standing in the circle of lamplight, watching him leave with a polite, sharklike grimace.

"Mary and Joseph!" breathed Peter, gripping a table. He finally regained control, beat down the warring spirit. He could almost visualize the fiend within his head, a huge, brutal, cunning brute, king in his own right, barbarous and lusting. He had never felt such a thing inside himself before. He knew what—who it was: Lancelot of the Languedoc, the *real* Lancelot.

Got to get out of here, got to find the boy and pump him, I mean question him, find that bitch Selly and bring her back!

He stood straight, forgetting Gwynhwfyr for the moment, and a queasy thought flitted through his head. *Bring Selly Corwin back? How in God's name am I supposed to get either of us back? Jesus!*

She must know, he prayed; would a careful girl like Selly have gone without knowing the way back?

Maybe. She was Provisional IRA, prepared for any sacrifice.

"And I'm a soldier," he said, half-aloud. He hardened his face. "If I can't bring her back, I can bloody well stop her from doing whatever it was she did." Peter thought of the ghostly forest world, empty of human civilization—or at least English civilization—and shuddered. The worst part was, it was seductive . . . a world of peace, with neither population nor pollution.

He remembered his plan to write the Latin down for translation. Alas, much of it had fled when he dozed. Some remained, however, and he urgently needed to copy it down before he forgot it, too.

He wandered among the darkened tables, bumping into shadowy furniture while searching for writing utensils. At last, where Kay and his friend had been sitting, Lancelot found an abandoned game with stones, a map of squares, and oddly marked dice. Next to the board was a quill and ink and a scrap of parchment with a running score written in Roman numerals. It seemed that some people, at least, *could* read and write.

He looked quickly to make sure no one watched, then grabbed the page and flipped it over, furiously scribbled the few phrases that still stuck in his mind. But when he finished, they did not look quite right. *Damn, must have mangled them more than I thought.* He shook his head, continued toward the kitchen in search of the boy.

CHAPTER 14

ANLAWDD TOOK CORS CANT'S HAND GINGERLY, LED HIM UP THE stairs, into the room she shared with two other ladies. Anlawdd's roommates were gone; even Gwynhwfyr's slaves were at the feast, to serve her. Anlawdd and Cors Cant were quite alone.

The girl unfastened her belt, hesitated a moment, then squeezed her eyes shut and dropped her outer tunic.

The shirt clung to her body, outlined small breasts, strong thighs. Cors Cant breathed heavily, wondering again why he found her so compelling.

Body as white as ocean foam, bushy hair red-dark as wine.

But was that not also true of half the ladies of the court? Why Anlawdd? What did she mean that the others did not?

"Why me?" she asked. He jumped guiltily.

"I . . . I don't know, fire hair."

"Auburn," she corrected. "Cors Cant Ewin, you've chased me like a hound on a deer. Now I'm standing her practically nak—na—nearly unclad, save for a shirt, and now *you're* trembling like a frightened baby buck!"

She opened her eyes, blinked rapidly. *Are those tears?* wondered the bard. *Why does she stare at my sandals?*

Anlawdd's voice softened, from desire or from fear. "I don't understand, Cors Cant. I . . . I don't know what I'm doing here, or why I'm taking my clothes off. And I don't know why I'm babbling either, not falling into your arms like a lover, or slapping you and running away, or . . ."

She stamped her foot. "Oh! it's like trying to walk two hounds who want to go in opposite directions!" She shifted her gaze from his sandals to the top of his head.

Cors Cant fumbled with the knots in his leine, but all his pulling and tremble-handed twisting could not unhook the ends.

"Anlawdd, I don't know the answers. I'm not a full Druid yet. I only know I love you. No one else." He shrugged, unable to explain any better.

"So?" she asked, "what is love?"

"Who are you now? Socrates? Love means we can be together. Always."

"You're talking about marriage, Cors Cant. Not love. That's the Roman in you."

"Marriage used to be for love alone," said the bard. "Look at the goddess Rhiannon and Pwyll, prince of Dyfed . . . she gave up her godhead for love of a mortal man." *What are you, a Philadelphia philosopher?* he wanted to ask. *Is this fascinating discussion absolutely necessary at this moment?*

Anlawdd finally shifted her gaze to Cors Cant's nose, pretending to look him in the eyes. "That's a fey tale, Cors Cant Ewin. You know what marriage is! It's a contract, like corralling my prize sow with your red-ribbon boar and hoping for piglets. What has that, or *this,* to do with love?" She caught at her chemise, as if to draw it tighter about her body.

The bard's fingers picked nervelessly at the Gordian knot,

which grew more tangled with every heartbeat. "How civilized," he muttered. "Now who's being Roman?"

"I am who I am," said Anlawdd coldly. "I'm not . . . I might not be the girl you think I am."

Something in her tone of voice caught at Cors Cant, chilled his stomach. "Then who are you?"

"Maybe your worst nightmare. Maybe closer to blood than auburn. I'm a girl and her shadow sewn together like a black-armored knight."

She waited, clutching the fabric. "Cors Cant, I could have tailored half the tunics in Gwynhwyfr's closet waiting for you! Honestly, aren't you going to *do* anything? I'm freezing wearing nothing like this, and I don't even know if I want to, or would let you if I did! But you're the man, you're supposed to make the decision, *carpe diem*, as you'd probably say, instead of . . . why, it's like the hounds leaving it up to the vixen whether she wants them to chase her or not!"

She looked far from eager. She watched the curtained doorway as if praying for an interruption. *But then why doesn't she just tell me to go, or put her tunic back on?* He hesitated, unable to move forward or back. He knew exactly what she meant about walking two hounds.

No. I'm going to be a proper Roman, bold and fearless, and take what's mine by right! Carpe diem! He yanked the still-tied leine over his head. But a treacherous leather thong caught on his throat. Gurgling and writhing, he dislodged it after a struggle. The bard stood before his inamorata wearing only his breeches, stretched a trembling hand to stroke her cheek.

Anlawdd closed her eyes, moved forward a step, but turned her head away. She spread her arms, screwed her face up. "Do it now," she said, flat-voiced. "Lift it, don't tear it. It's borrowed from the princess."

Her body shook. Her skin was clammy. Cors Cant asked, "Are you a . . . a virgin?" *Please, gods and goddesses, not the both of us! What if I, well . . . what if I miss?*

"No, of course not!" she said, face and shoulders as red as her hair. "What a silly question, Cors Cant, you know we Harlech seamstresses have h-h-hundreds of lovers!" She opened her eyes, seemed to breathe slowly, deliberately. Her pupils were tiny, pale green dots in oceans of white. "Should a temple not be worshiped in? Should the assassin not sink the knife in the k-king?" Her smile flickered, faded to a neutral expression.

That's a weird way of describing love, thought Cors Cant.

He stepped forward, gingerly touched her pale breasts through the sheer cloth. Her nipples stood hard and inviting beneath the diaphanous chemise. A single lamp cast erotic, jumping shadows in all the right places. Anlawdd stiffened, held her breath, still trembling violently.

After a long moment, Cors Cant shook his head, lowered his hands to his sides. "No, my love," he whispered hoarsely. "I only want to give what you're truly willing to receive."

She exhaled slowly, bit her lip. A smile of relief cracked the corners of her mouth, metamorphosed quickly into . . . annoyance?

"Cors Cant Ewin! How dare you take a girl to the brink, then coolly cast her aside! It's like cooking the meat, um, the feast then not e-eat—not serving it." But her voice betrayed a grateful tone.

He watched the breasts rise and fall, wondered whether he would ever again see them so free, feel their firmness beneath his gentle hands. How would he know when the chemise should finally fall?

She clasped her hands behind her back. "I guess there's a time and a place," she whispered gravely.

"So, um, what do we do now?"

She hesitated long enough finally to look him in the eyes, then look back to the window, the half-moon, the fog-shrouded stars. "I don't know."

"Will we ever . . . ?" She did not move, and Cors Cant started over. "When *is* the right time, right place?"

"I don't know. But it's wrong just yet. There's too much I don't know, and I'm not happy not knowing things. I don't even know how *I* feel, let alone you."

"I love you," he protested, tried to look as sincere as humanly possible.

"So you say."

"I do!" he protested, wounded. *An interesting question,* spoke the Druid within him; *would Myrddin even bless such a marriage?* Freeborn she was, but a seamstress still . . . not a Druid, not an artist. Not even rich.

"My heart didn't tell me that," she answered sadly, "for I

shook like old Uncle Leary, the morning after the night before. Not yet."

"But your beauty . . . ! Skin white as ocean foam, hair red
as fire reflected in a still-water lake!"

"My hair is auburn," she corrected again, angrily. "Don't
you have eyes for anything above my breasts? And you'll not
sway me with lines of foolish Druid verse! You think a girl
just melts into your arms because you compare her to lakes
and oceans and other geographies? Pah!"

The fire was back in her eyes, and she snapped her fingers.
"There's a lot more under my turban than under my shirt, you
know, and by Jesus, Mary, and Medb, it'll be a hot swim in
the Sea of Eire before I ever offer to *you* again!" She pointed
melodramatically toward the doorway, like a Greek actor
doing a bad turn as the goddess Juno.

Stunned by her sudden about-turn, Cors Cant slunk across
the room, crumbled leine in hand. As he pulled the curtain
wide, he glanced back, saw her confused, tormented face, no
surer than his; and beneath the torment, some desire? A little
bit? He shook his head, scuttled out into the corridor.

"Seamstresses!" he exclaimed, just loud enough for her to
hear. Then he clumped back down the stairs.

He returned to his room, thought of Anlawdd in her sheer
chemise as he lay on the mat and relieved his aching soul.
But the act hardly satisfied and left behind no physical evidence. He covered his face and wept, silent and frustrated.

At last, feeling hungry (having eaten only his pastry) Cors
Cant rose, skirted the *triclinium* and slipped directly into the
kitchen, desiring to speak to no one. He hoped to bolt himself
into a dark room with a plate full of Morgawse's honey afters
and eat them, one after another, until the hurt went away.

As he ghosted through the curtain, he bumped into a mountain and stopped cold. Prince Legate Lancelot hulked in the
doorway.

"Bard," demanded the champion, "you speak Latin?"

He was so agitated, his affected accent had nearly vanished.
The boy smelled lust on Lancelot, a lust named Gwynhwfyr.

Cors Cant was too frightened to try to duck the question.
"Yes, *Tribune,* you well know I speak all languages of song.
Latin and Greek both, as well as—"

"Come with me, son, I've got a translator's job for you."

A meaty hand propelled him back through the curtain, back up the very stairs he had just descended. Terrified, he prayed they would not run into Anlawdd.

They mounted to the first landing, turned away from her room, and pushed through another doorway at the end of the hall.

Where in Hades are we? the boy wondered. Clearly an austere soldier's apartment, hung with swords, axes, pieces of armor. The plaster on the walls was heavily scored and notched by blades of all sizes. A tangle of spears leaned against the far corner, and Cors Cant finally recognized the blue and black colors of the Languedoc.

One chair and a single stool filled the room, along with the shattered remnants of a table. Lancelot let the bard loose and sat in the chair, one leg across the other in an uncomfortable-looking position.

Cors Cant bowed his head as he spoke; when the *tribune* took on one of his moods, it was best to remember all respect due his rank.

"*Imperator,*" he asked, "what do you wish translated into Latin?"

"Back to front, son," said the Sicambrian. "I've written down the Latin. Tell me what it means."

Cors Cant looked sharply at him. *Written down the Latin? Whom does he think to fool? I've seen him struggle to sound out his own name on a scabbard!* But now was not the time to quibble.

"I'll read it to you," continued the prince.

"Read away, Sire, but I can't promise results, not knowing how well you heard the words of a foreign tongue." It was a legitimate concern; in all the years at Camlann, Lancelot had refused to learn Latin, much to Artus's annoyance.

Lancelot snorted, worked his mouth around the first phrase. "*Pax restituenda est, quod cumulo pretiosus, prius cum terra sub barbatulum unguiculus bisulcus torqueat.*"

Cors Cant drew back, mouth parted. "But that's not even proper Latin!" he cried.

"Blast it, I may have gotten a few words wrong ... translate it anyway!" Lancelot, scratching his unshaven face, glanced down at the paper again. *Did I not know better,* thought Cors Cant, *I'd swear he was actually* reading!

The bard rubbed his own chin, still smooth from yesterday's shave. "If you say so, Prince. It *sort of* means 'Peace must be restored, because I am extravagant and pile it up, since first the little cloven hoof twists under one wearing a billy-goat beard.' "

"What?" thundered the Sicambrian. He threw his feet down, knocking a cup of wine to the floor. Cors Cant stared at the spreading stain, trying not to imagine a slightly darker stain of red, if the prince got mad enough.

"I told you it wasn't proper Latin, Sire!" pleaded the boy. "Let me see that paper, maybe I can make sense of it."

Cors Cant plucked the page from Lancelot's reluctant hand, puzzled over the garbled text. If Lancelot did not write it (a given), then who in the world had? Whoever it was could have benefited from a long, quiet study of Virgil.

Yet, when he sounded out the garbled words in his head, he realized with a start that the gibberish *sounded* like other words, words that made sense. It was almost a game ... I-love-you becomes olive-view, *unguiculus bisulcus* could be—*ungulis bisulcis?* cloven hooves?

"Wait," said the bard, "maybe I *can* decipher this. Could the person who wrote—who dictated to you have possibly meant . . ." He sounded out a revised version haltingly. *"Pax restituenda est—quocumque pretio—priusquam terra sub barbarorum—ungulis bisulcis—torreat?"*

"I guess so," Lancelot looked blank. He kicked at the wine puddle and frowned.

Cors Cant continued quickly. "That means, um, Peace must be restored, whatever the cost, ere the land wither beneath the cloven hooves of barbarians. It makes sense, lord, though I do not know the sense of it."

"Mind not the whys! Just tell me what they said."

"They?"

Lancelot did not answer. Cors Cant stumbled through the next phrase. *"Tribune,* as ah as you have written it, it says *Pax? Immolatium culmus. Legumen iustitiae, non regero saccum dotare, morose homines regressi sunt. Tumeo inde Pachyn Oedipus capitulum."*

"Which means?"

"Translated as best I can, this means Peace? A thatch of burnt offerings. Men have crabbily driven back the greenbean of justice, and I'm not carrying that sack back here to give it away. Thence I, Oedipus, inflate Pachys the penis-head."

"God's teeth!" swore the Sicambrian. Lancelot stood, pulled a handcloth from the top of the desk. As Cors Cant watched in horror, the champion prince of Camlann stooped and mopped at the spilled wine.

Turning quickly back to the puzzle to avoid staring at the prince debasing himself, the bard corrected the passage into something resembling actual Latin. "I'll bet it was supposed to be *Pax? Immo etiam—cultus. Legi et . . .* yes, *iustitiae,* that's right. *Non regi . . .* ho, this is an impossible piece. Wait, the next two—hah! *sacerdotique,* sure as I'm from Londinium. *Sacerdotique mores . . . hominum regendi sunt. Tum deinde—pacem adipisci potueris."*

"Well?"

"That's it."

"What does it *mean,* boy?"

"Oh, give me a moment. Um . . . Peace? Civilization, rather. Justice and law, not kings and priests, must govern Man's conduct. Then you might get peace. Mind you, General, this is a *very* loose translation. I could be guessing the wrong right words."

He braved a glance at Lancelot. The Sicambrian was still acting like a household slave.

"You win," said the prince, exasperated. "From now on, just read what it should be."

"Thank you, Prince." Cors Cant stared for some time at the next line, finally puzzled it out. "This one is harder, but I think it's supposed to be *Concedo. Consilium tuum firmum ad probandum est, instrumenta ponuntur. Digitus ad mortem meretricis scribendam libratur. Nonne subscribes?* I'd translate that as I yield. Your basic plan is sound, the apparatus set in place. The finger is poised to write the whore's demise. You'll sign?"

"Sign what?"

"No, uh, *nonne subscribes* means 'you'll sign.' "

Lancelot grunted, motioned him to continue.

"Ah . . ." the boy paused, moved his lips, then nodded when he got the sense. *"Brevi tempore. Verba nostra nobis diligenter commentanda sunt. Donec Ierusalem restituetur templumque reficietur, plani conveniemus.* Soon. We must

study our words with care. Until Jerusalem is restored and the
temple rebuilt, we meet on the level."

Lancelot gasped. "Does *menda mille rotare* mean 'we part
on the square'?"

"Well, no. It's more like 'a thousand blemishes whirl
about.' "

"Bloody hell, you know what I mean! What it's supposed
to mean, does it mean what I meant?"

Cors Cant clicked his teeth, studied the parchment. Lancelot had finished performing his slave's task. "What you wrote
was *'menda mea rotunda,'* which is probably supposed to be
'mensa mea rotunda,' my table is round. *Mensa Mea
rotunda—est non quadrata—sed autem de fine—ultimo—
consentimus.* My table is round, not square. But we agree on
the ultimate goal. See? There is a square in there somewhere.
You were right, my prince."

The phrase sounded suspiciously like a code of some sort.
The Sicambrian nodded, as if familiar with it.

"And the last," said Lancelot, *"et in arcadia ego."*

"And in Arcadia I," translated the bard. "It means nothing,
just a fragment. Not even a sentence. And in Arcadia, I *what?"*

Lancelot nodded. "Thank you, Cors. You look troubled.
What's wrong?"

Cors Cant blinked at the sudden change in subject. "Troubled?" he repeated.

"Relax. Everything will work out. I know all about it."

The bard sucked in his breath. Word traveled so quickly
through Caer Camlann! "You . . . heard about Anlawdd? Already?"

Lancelot nodded. "There are no secrets in castles, eh? So
when is the blessed event?"

"Event? Alack, probably never!"

"Never?" Lancelot looked confused.

"Sure and I'll never get Myrddin or Artus to arrange a marriage between a Druid and a seamstress," sighed Cors Cant.

"Marriage? Is it truly necessary to marry to have love?"

The bard shook his head, astonished at how perspica-
ciously the prince had divined the essential conflict. "Sire,
you must possess some of the magic of the Blood Royal
yourself. You reach right into my soul and find the question.
Rem acu tetigisti, as they say."

"They?"

"Rome."

"Will Anlawdd consent to bed-warming without marriage?"

"Sure and she would, but that's not the question. Will she consent to *love* without marriage? Is she willing to love one too far above her station to ever marry? And how do we stay together when she must hop at the beck and call of her mistress?"

Lancelot grunted, tugged his mustache. "Son," he said, "as a bard, you've got your finger on the pulse of . . . of Caer Camlann. I'd like your opinions on a few matters."

"You want *my* opinion, *Imperator?*"

"Yes, your opinion as bard. You'll answer as a bard, you swear?"

As a bard! "Ask me anything, Prince Lancelot of the Languedoc! Upon my bardic oath, I'll answer as knowledge permits."

The Sicambrian smiled, put a finger to his mouth, shushing. "Tell me everything," he asked, "of Arthur and Merovee, and what scheme they are cooking up between them. I would like to know what that Si—Sicambrian cockerel is plotting."

Cors Cant's heart leapt up his throat.

Gods of Rome—he swore me to secrecy! Cors Cant felt the blood rush to his face. *What did I think, he wanted the name of a beautiful court princess? That he wanted to know whether Gwynhwfyr took arsenic to pale her cheeks? I'm a fool!*

He leapt to his feet, torn now by a thousand walking hounds dragging him every direction on the earth. *Fool! useless half-a-bard! Now what—do I tell Lancelot, a foreign prince, what's in my master's heart? Or tell him nothing and violate my bardic oath?*

Cors Cant sat quietly against the desk. Lancelot reminded him unnecessarily. "You swore an oath to tell me, son. Don't make a liar out of yourself."

Liar or betrayer. What a wonderful choice. For a moment, he wished Anlawdd were present. Then he was desperately glad she was *not.* Could even a seamstress love a man as witless as he?

The Sicambrian stood silently. Cors Cant tried to speak, but the words caught in his throat.

Without honor, he thought in Myrddin's voice, *a bard is*

nothing more than a fancy tale-singer. Then Artus's own voice spoke like falling within his mind: *if not true to yourself, you cannot be true to me.*

Cors Cant hung his head, numb as a dying man. "I'll . . . I'll tell you what you ask, Sire."

There was no other choice. By his own tongue had the bard condemned himself.

CHAPTER 15

"I ALREADY KNOW WHAT ARTUS WANTS," SAID PETER. "BUT why Merovee, of all people?" An old copper's trick, pretend you already know, need only confirmation. In fact, Peter knew nothing about anything.

"Of course Merovee!" protested the boy. "The Long-Hair controls Sicambria as Artus controls Britain, and both were schooled in Rome herself. Both fear the long night that surely follows Roman withdrawal."

Romans? thought Peter; *what the hell does King Arthur have to do with the flipping Romans?* Cors Cant continued. "Besides, Merovee is of the *Blood Royal* . . . you know what *that* means."

"Yes, yes, get to the point, boy." Peter was tantalized by the phrase. Surely the *Blood Royal* meant more than simple royalty, else why would it cut such ice with a lad in the court of Arthur himself?

He hoped the boy would drop a few more hints, but for the moment chose not to press the issue. Interrogation was an art, and Peter did not even have the proper artist's tools; without access to arrest, isolation, fear of punishment, sleep deprivation, the calumny of criminality itself, he had to rely on finesse.

"Well," continued Cors Cant uncertainly, "I know not for certain, but . . . does that not suggest the scheme to you?"

"I'd hear it from your own lips, *Cor'can, how that beast Merovius leads himself our general into Roman vices!*"

Lancelot—*Peter*—gasped, clamped his mouth shut. Whose words had torn so suddenly from his throat? *Not mine, I don't even know Merovee!* It was a ghastly feeling; for a moment, someone or something *outside* had taken over Peter's voice.

Cors Cant continued warily, seeming not to notice the outburst. "I believe Merovee and Artus seek to band together to restore the *Pax Romana* to the Western lands, under their own hands, without pollution from that new Roman church."

It took all of Peter's self-control not to leap to his feet. The Roman Empire restored, ruled by King Arthur and a Frenchman! It was insane . . . and it had certainly never happened, not in Peter's past.

A terrible thought occurred to him: had he and Selly *already* changed history by journeying back in time?

He controlled his breath, hoped the bard was oblivious to his mental state. "What stands in their way? Why such secrecy?"

Cors Cant watched Peter narrowly, considering his answer. He seemed on edge and sharp-toned, as if he had just had an unpleasant encounter and wished he could withdraw and lick his wounds.

"*Imperator* Lancelot, do you feel well? Will you be well enough to fight on tomorrow's morrow? The *Saxons* stand in the way, here and across the sea! The same barbarians who destroyed the glory of Rome in the first place aren't likely to cheer its return!"

"Saxons destroyed Rome?"

"Saxons, Jutes, Huns, they're all badgers in a bag."

"But of course," said Peter, he hoped smoothly. "I meant which Saxons in particular are the greatest danger?" *Keep talking, son; you're doing fine.*

Pressure began to build inside Peter again, like an inflating life raft in his gut. Suddenly, a burst of what he knew was Sicambrian exploded out: "*they should all be skinned, Saxon and Roman alike, with their hound fathers, pig mothers, and whore sisters begotten upon diseased slaves by purple-arsed Huns and rat-buggering Visigoths!*"

Cors Cant blanched, then flushed with embarrassment. The boy obviously spoke Sicambrian as well.

He sat down on the stool, drew up his knees. He stared out

the window into darkness, paid Peter only half a mind. *Jesus,* thought Peter, *what's become of my self-control?* A very unpleasant suspicion formed in Peter's mind that the blustery Lancelot was starting to break loose. Peter flushed when he remembered that, according to Blundell's explanation, Lancelot was the "nearest" personality to Peter himself.

Blundell, Willks, no one knew what happened to the original personality of the host body. Peter had the uncomfortable feeling he had begun to find out. Lancelot wanted to regain control of his own body.

Cors Cant answered, still distracted by a memory. "I, ah, fear it is Cutha, son of Caedwin himself, come not to try his skill against yours, but his eyes instead, spying our defenses. For a subsequent attack."

"Did you tell Arth . . . Artus, Cors?"

"Sooner tell a fire-haired wench that she loves a boy despite herself."

"What?" Peter shook his head, tried to parse the analogy.

Cors Cant came back to himself. "I suggested to the *Pan-Draconis* that we fall upon the unwashed swine, cut him down before he crosses the threshold! But Artus commanded a truce. Said it would be illegal to slay Cutha under the peace flag."

Cors Cant chewed his fingernail, brushed his long, brown hair from his eyes. He fidgets, noticed Peter; *nervous, self-conscious.*

"Imperator," said the boy quietly, hesitantly, "could you not arrange to—slay him in the contest? Swing the axe overhard, accidentally pierce his armor? All have seen your might, all would swear you were just carried away by battle lust."

Peter sat back, pursed his lips. Even in this age of fable, chivalry, and romance, was it normal to talk so casually of killing a man because of his race? Especially a race Peter himself shared.

"Of course," the boy quickly amended, "once I take the marshal's staff, I can do nothing to help you. I can't violate my office, much as it galls my Cymric heart."

Peter smiled faintly. *A moment past he tried to arrange a murder . . . now it's Marquis of Queensbury rules.* "I promise nothing," said Peter, "save that whatever I do, I do for Britain. Please mention this talk to no one. Official business, don'tcha know."

Cors Cant stood uncertainly, looked toward the curtain, back at "Lancelot."

"Come on, son," said Peter. "Let's go find that lady friend of yours."

"Anlawdd? But she said it would be a hot swim in the Sea of—"

"You believed her? Babe in the woods, she's a woman! They're all fickle, like the wind."

"They are?" The boy seemed dubious.

"Like the wind."

"Anlawdd isn't. She means what she says. I think."

"Never. Believe me, boy, if it's one thing I know, it's women. Soul of a woman, and all that."

Cors Cant raised his brows. "Soul of a woman. Did you make that up?"

"No, I heard it from—from a bard in a far off land."

"Sicambria?"

"Farther."

"Is there more?"

Peter thought for a moment, sang the entire first verse. It sounded wrong, of course, since it was written in a language a millenium in the future.

The bard looked dissatisfied, considered the verse with detached professionalism. "I think I can work it into . . ." He stood still as a rock, head nodding almost imperceptibly. "Listen, how does this sound?

> *Late have you come, empty shall ever go,*
> *The soul of your clever lover shall ever know*
> *The empty soul of a woman, created below.*

"Hm, well. Almost," mused Cors Cant. "I'm trying to fit it into *Orpheus,* as Hades talks to him in the underworld, bargaining for the life of Eurydice. What do you think?"

The boy sounded so earnest, so proud, that Peter had no heart to tell him it stank. "It's certainly a verse," he compromised. "No question." *Sorry, son, Robert Plant has nothing to fear.*

Cors Cant smiled, took it as thumbs-up. "Do you really think Anlawdd will see me again?"

Peter smiled. "Not unless we see her first. Let's get tracking." He put his hand on Cors Cant's shoulder, steered him through the curtain, down the stair.

They had almost reached the ground floor when a fat man with a wild beard and calculating face rounded the spiral. All three halted, averting a head-on.

"Lancelot, Cors Cant," mumbled the blimp, as if taking inventory. He wore a shapeless black and grey robe, puffed at the sleeves as no one else's clothing had been. A ratty, old tree branch was thrust through his wide, white leather belt. His beard stuck out in all directions, worse than Willks's on the latter's worst day.

"Mer-then," said the boy, bowed deeply.

"I sought you, Lancelot," said the fat man. "The king sent me. He inquires of your health."

Peter's heart jumped. Could "Mer-then" be *Merlin*, the Camelot Magician? "My health is perfect, Merthen," he said, warily. Exactly what powers might the "great enchanter" wield?

Bloodthirsty killer, but yes! raged the alien voice in Peter's head. This time, he caught the words in time, bottled them up inside his throat. For several seconds, Peter fought Lancelot for control, finally pushing the belligerent warrior's soul down, deep into his hindbrain.

When Peter opened his eyes, he saw that the old man had taken a step back down the stairs. The magician's eyebrow shrubbery bobbed up and down, then lowered fearsomely. "Why did you leave table so suddenly? I was concerned you'd a brain fever."

"Well—" Peter thought furiously, "when nature summons, men must obey," he explained. "And I don't remember seeing you there, anyway."

"All right; *Artus* was concerned. He asked after you." His smirk gave Peter the uncomfortable feeling he was unbefooled. "Perhaps your constitution suffers from the island mist. Would you feel more at home in the sunny fields and mountains of Sicambria?"

A wall of animosity sprang up between them. This "Merthen," he decided, would cheerfully sell Arthur and England up the Thames for thirty pieces of silver.

"I *like* the gloom of this island," said Peter. "Suits my disposition well this moment, old fraud." He felt Cors Cant stiffen, move away from him. With Lancelot's senses, better than his own had been, he smelled fear in the boy. But his own trepidation faded; Merthen-Merlin was nothing but a blustery humbug, easily brushed aside.

"Yes, I heard of your flight from fancy this evening," sneered the old man. "Try a love philter from Fey Morgawse. 'Tis said she'd lift the *spirit* of any man who's still a man, General."

Peter bore down hard on the writhing spirit of Lancelot, which threatened to burst forth in murderous rage. He took firm hold of Cors Cant's arm and shoved past the sad old charlatan. Myrddin pressed back against the wall to avoid them.

Just before they disappeared around a corner, Myrddin called out. "If you journey to Morgawse, you'll need this." He raised his hand, showed it was empty, and closed it into a fist. When he opened his hand, three silver coins graced his palm. "The harlot comes not for free."

Peter snorted. *Parlor sleights! This is the great enchanter?* He shook his head and continued downstairs to the great hall, fighting Lancelot with every step.

CHAPTER 16

I SAT BENEATH THE STARS IN THE *TRICLINIUM,* TRYING TO COOL MY blood from my last encounter with That Boy, That irritating, frustrating, *infuriating* Boy!

All I wanted him to do was be a warrior for once, to know what he wanted and to take it! Was that too much to beg? Must I decide all questions for the both of us?

'Tis a foundation of sand upon which to start a marriage, sure. I won't be yanked around like a dog on a rope, but then again, I want a lover—not a child's kite that I must launch every time and only runs as far as the tether I choose to give it!

"It's not going to work out," I said aloud, uncaring whether anyone heard.

There was nobody around, anyway; the table I sat upon

was meatless and smokeless, thus unoccupied. Those few remaining revelers crowded around Merovee, blinking their tired, drunken eyes and roaring in beery approval at everything said by anyone of quality, lest a jest pass unnoticed.

I had no choice. I was a warrior, and *I had my duty.* Artus must die, and soon—and before that, any love I might hold in my heart for That Boy . . . not that I admitted I loved him, of course; but I knew I had to slay the nonexistent love I didn't really hold in my heart for That Boy who so vexed me anyway, and whom I neither thought about nor talked to.

Over and over I saw his face as it would be when he saw the *Dux Bellorum*'s body: his red cheeks would pale, turn white as bone, and his eyes would widen in shock and betrayal.

Would I stand like a moon-touched fool, babbling some crazy story about how I mistook the *Pan-Draconis* for a thief in the dark—or perhaps for my bloody brother, may his soul rot forever in hell as his body putrifies on earth? Or would I have the courage to say "I murdered God, Cors Cant Ewin, and if you have the slightest shred of loyalty to Britain, you'll slay me as I stand for such *hubris?*"

I buried my face in my hands. I honestly did not know what I would do, and I'd never felt that way before in my life.

Unbidden, a scheme began to flower in my brain. I would play the assassin, yet cravenly escape with my young life, perhaps even elude detection by That Boy and live a lie with him, though sure and his Druid eyes and magical nose would soon ferret out my guilt, smelling the blood on my hands, perhaps.

If I could but goad the ever-seething Lancelot to erupt in fury during the upcoming tourney against that bastard Saxon Cutha and kill the Saxon pig—for all know the Sicambrian knight's legendary temper, falling into berserker rage in battle—then I could undoubtedly murder Artus and cast the finger of suspicion on Cutha's guards, who might have killed the *Dux Bellorum* out of revenge for their master's death at the hands of Artus's second-in-command.

I ground my teeth; apparently, Anlawdd of Harlech had a real flair for assassination. And here I thought I was highborn and perhaps a warrior—I felt like a Roman priest who suddenly discovered a gift for inspired lovemaking . . . it's nice to find new talents, but couldn't it have been *anything* else?

The practical side of my soul spoke up, pointing out that as it was my duty to kill Artus, so it was my duty to escape detection, for if I were caught, the repercussions against Harlech and my father would be so savage it would undo all the effect of killing Artus in the first place! Harlech would no more be free than we are now, for Lancelot, Cei, and especially his bloody brother Bedwyr would raze the city, putting to the torch anything that survived the onslaught of blood and steel.

The thought of beloved Harlech burned to ashes, her citizens slain in the streets, so horrified me that for a moment I almost forgot the silver lining ... that at least my cursed brother Canastyr Canllaw would die as well. But I resolved to implement the plan and save Harlech anyway, trusting to God and Rhiannon suitably to punish Canastyr in hell after I slew him, as God might someday give me the opportunity to do.

CHAPTER 17

THEY DISCOVERED ANLAWDD FAR AWAY FROM THE CROWD, IN the open-air section of the feast hall. She sat cross-legged on a table, leaning her back against a pillar. She looked perfectly miserable.

She had changed clothes into a man's breeches, boots, and tunic, the dress Cors Cant had seen her wear when not at formal functions. A long dagger was stuck in her belt, and her unbound hair fell across back and shoulders like a fall of autumn leaves.

She watched Cors Cant as he approached, her face open and vulnerable for a moment. The boy's breath caught in his throat, full of hope. Then Anlawdd's brows furrowed.

"Cors Cant Ewin, I am absolutely not speaking to you! And how dare you walk off like that without even a word?"

"But—but *I didn't!*" It was no use; she had only paused to draw breath. Sooner interrupt an October rain.

"And without even introducing me to King Merovee,

though you *know* I haven't met anyone so grand since I arrived. I was going to give you a warning for your *Dux Bellorum,* but I can't since I'm not speaking to you. So I'll have to tell General Lancelot instead, *if* you will show the bare minimum of politeness and introduce us, for of course I've never met him, either."

Cors Cant's head swam trying to make sense of her diatribe. *I wish she wouldn't say "bare,"* he winced. "Lancelot of the Languedoc, *Imperator,* Consul, and Legate of two legions, this is Anlawdd of Harlech, seamstress to Princess Gwynhwyfr. Harlech is in Cantref Gwynedd, to the north, in the kingdom of Cymru."

"On the coast," added Anlawdd. She extended her arm in a Roman salute. After some hesitation, Lancelot responded.

"What's the warning?" demanded Cors Cant. Anlawdd ignored him, turned to Lancelot.

"You know, if *certain people* kept their ears open instead of their mouths, they might hear interesting pieces of intelligence, such as a drunken Saxon talking to a scullery maid he was trying to ride in the kitchen about an upcoming match between Lancelot and Cutha the Saxon."

Lancelot leaned forward, cocked an ear attentively. Anlawdd continued. "He said that the real reason Cutha fights you is to gauge Caer Camlann's strength, and he intends to slay you if he can. In the heat of the match, you understand."

Cors Cant gasped, grabbed Anlawdd by her arm, and spun her around. "But why didn't you tell us earlier? Surely you realize what a blow that would be to Artus!" Her arm was strong as iron, an odd attribute for a seamstress.

She tensed, then relaxed, but fixed him with her stare. "Cors Cant Ewin, take your hand *off* me! You had your chance earlier, but your sincerity was somewhat lacking. Though I'm certain," she sniffed, "that you were perfectly sincere with yourself, later."

Cors Cant clenched his teeth. The accusation cut like a blade, especially being true.

"Anlawdd, Lancelot is our greatest general!"

"You're right," said Anlawdd meditatively. "Probably, Cutha intends to poison him. You know how those Saxons are. If I were you," she said, turning back to Lancelot, "I wouldn't drink any potions anyone gives you, not even if he says it's a magical philter of courage."

"I take your warning seriously," Lancelot replied with a courteous nod. Anlawdd watched him, eyes agleam, and Cors Cant felt a stab of jealousy for the Sicambrian rake.

"Does the Saxon come with many men?" asked Lancelot.

"He's expected to bring thirty warriors," said Cors Cant, trying to watch both Anlawdd and Lancelot simultaneously, "an honor guard. Artus permitted this—the *Dux Bellorum* expects you to win and wants the Saxons to learn a lesson about British might."

"Personally," declared the seamstress, "I think Artus has been driven mad from drinking tainted wine, or from listening to that barbarian sister of his."

"Anlawdd!"

"In any case, if thumping Cutha is supposed to make an impression," she continued, "imagine the impression you'd make by running him through!" Anlawdd flourished her hand grandly. Cors Cant yelped and grabbed his eye, whipped by her finger.

"Are you all right?" she asked.

"I'm fine," he lied, blinking.

"Let me see." She steadied his face, pried his eyelids open, and inspected his eye.

She actually cares! he realized. "Look, Anlawdd, about what happened upstairs. I'm sorry . . ." he took a deep breath. "I'm sorry I ran off so fast. I apologize. I know you're probably frustrated that we couldn't—"

"Frustrated? *Me?* Cors Cant Ewin, I'm sure I don't know *what* you're talking about! Good-bye. And don't forget I'm ignoring you. And not speaking to you, either."

She hopped off the table, stalked away with a lithe, muscular grace that had haunted the boy since she first arrived at Camlann two months ago. Cors Cant thought he saw the specter of a smile before her face was lost in the flash of her hair. She vanished into the kitchen, brushing past a serving boy as if he were invisible.

"Lancelot," he asked in despair, when she had gone, "what am I doing wrong?"

"Not a thing, son."

"Then why does she . . . ?"

"Soul of a woman, Cors."

Cors Cant looked at Artus's table, far across the hall. The *Dux Bellorum* was still deep in conversation with Merovee. The king was well called *Caesar,* "hairy man," for his black hair overflowed his head and cascaded down his back.

An Amazonian woman approached Lancelot from the opposite corner of the *triclinium.* She was almost as tall as the Sicambrian, and bore more scars than he. "Lady Morgawse summons you," she said in a gravelly voice.

"Where is she?" asked the Sicambrian.

"Where *is* she?" exclaimed Cors Cant. "In her apartments, of course!"

"Oh," said the Sicambrian smoothly, "you mean she's left the hall? I didn't notice."

Cors Cant looked at him speculatively. That was the second or third time that Lancelot seemed not to know what should have been second nature, after so many years at Camlann. *Why did he choose today to drop his "Dumb Sicambrian" act? And why become the "Forgetful Sicambrian" instead?*

The bard made to accompany Lancelot, but the general stopped him. "Cors Cant, mind if I field this conversation single-handedly?"

"You want me to . . . ?"

Lancelot gestured for the boy to scoot off.

Cors Cant looked wistfully kitchenwards, where Anlawdd had vanished a few minutes earlier. "I think I'll get a bite to eat," he mused.

CHAPTER 18

MARK BLUNDELL WATCHED THE DC READOUT, STRAINING TO concentrate on only the "real" timeline. Something was anomalous, the field was drawing ten percent more power than it ought.

He clicked the mouse pointer on the Control Center icon, opened the Circuits menu. For an instant he hesitated, wondering which of the thirty-one major integrated circuit paths might be causing the problem.

So peaceful. So calm. He heard the birds at last, saw them flit from tree to tree. Once, he thought he saw a pair of horsemen ride past, distant, carrying an odd machinelike device between them. But his attention was torn away by Willks, and when he looked back, they were gone (if they ever were).

"Damn, no time," he muttered, opened each circuit monitor in turn, and scanned them as quickly as he could, hoping for something to jump out at him.

"Tighten the field focus," yelled Hamilton from across the basement.

Don't look at the PET scan monitor, watch what you're doing. Don't look at the PET scan! Mark spared a glance at the PET scan. Even from fifteen feet away, he could see the consciousness field oscillating larger and smaller twice each second.

"Jake," shouted Willks, "how's it look now?"

"Oscillations, two point one Hertz."

Tweet-tweet.

"Now?"

"Oscillations."

Twitter, chirp.

"Blast it, how about *now?*"

"Oscillations. Mark, what's with the power?"

Blundell jumped, turned back to his console. It took him a moment to focus his brain; when he did, he saw the power overplay had leapt to 143 percent of normal. "Heavy overplay!" he shouted. Then he smelled the tang of ozone.

"Cut it! Cut it!" he shouted. Wisps of smoke curled from the coils, nearly invisible against the grey walls of the basement.

"Belay that!" shouted Hamilton. "He's too far; if we cut power now, he's severed."

Mark continued clicking through the circuit monitors. At last he discovered the anomaly, localized it to one part of one chip. "Jesus, there's microcurrent leakage on 23. It's in the chip. We can't do anything about it except replace the chip."

Replace the chip . . . easy to say, a solid day to perform.

Mark stood slowly, stared at the doughnut. The glow was brighter than it should have been. Smythe's body curled and jerked convulsively as stray electrical impulses coursed along his central nervous system, driven by a hellacious magnetic field no longer properly contained. Even Selly twitched.

"Jacob," pleaded Blundell, "pity's sake, bring him back if you can. He's dying in there." Hamilton turned his face away, lips pressed tight. It was an impossible request, and Blundell knew it.

"Mark," said Willks, more gently than he had ever spoken before. "Mark, he might still have made it. Into the body. Won't know until we power down in three minutes."

"If we can," whispered Blundell.

"We can power down."

"The damned machine is cooking itself! There's smoke— look at it!"

"Mark!" Blundell turned to face the old man. Willks's cheeks were white as the winter snows. "Mark, we *can't* stop in the middle. You know that!"

Blundell nodded. He glanced back at the console. The power overplay had crept up to 151 percent, but no higher. At some point, the chips themselves would begin to fry. But that point was quite a bit higher than the current power level.

Assuming it doesn't shoot up again, he thought, clenching his fists. *So quiet. No time machine, no Roundhaven. No traffic. No M-5 or roundabouts. Is that really so bad? But what in God's name did she* do?

"Tighten the field," quietly suggested Hamilton, "if you can."

"Radius nought," said Willks. "There's nothing more we can do. Our young commando rests entirely within the arms of Schrödinger's wave equations. Hope the old Kraut knew what he was doing when he wrote them."

They stood quietly for the next three minutes, staring at the doughnut as the blue glow slowly subsided.

CHAPTER 19

PETER WATCHED THE BOY RUSH TOWARD THE KITCHEN. *DIDN'T that red-haired girl vanish that way?* he wondered, dismissed the thought. *I'm here to track a terrorist, not meddle in the love life of a kid fifteen hundred years dead.*

Morgawse ... Peter quickly replayed Thomas Malory's epic in his head: Queen Margawse, who slept with Arthur and bore the foul Mordred, the bastard who ultimately murdered Arthur and destroyed Camelot.

He followed the Amazon to Morgawse, prepared himself to face the fell queen with a calm facade he did not really feel. She was as high on his list of suspects as Guinevere was low; according to legend, Morgawse had every character trait he remembered of Selly Corwin.

Besides, with each new person he met, there was another chance he would make a crucial mistake and be discovered as an imposter. *So much to remember,* thought Peter, *so many ways to cock it up.*

The huge warrior woman led him out the back of the *triclinium,* across a manicured courtyard of browning grass and heather with a central grove of aspen, their shivering leaves beginning to turn. The Amazon cut left through trimmed hedges, ignoring the well-marked cobblestone path, and led Peter through a line of decorative, marble columns into a three-story annex. Like the other apartment wing, the walls were white concrete with inlaid mosaics and painted sigils.

Morgawse's apartments were on the first floor, guarded by more of the powerful-looking Amazons. Peter smiled faintly and wondered what point the queen was trying to prove. *I could drop any one of them in twenty seconds,* he thought. *She ought to invest in a platoon of legionnaires instead.*

Morgawse sat in a high-backed, wicker chair, surrounded by several nude women, who knelt, heads bowed. The queen watched him like a goddess watching her high priest approach. Her salt-and-pepper hair hung to her waist, braided in dozens of snakelike tendrils, "corn rows," a millenium and a half ahead of their time. It must have taken hours.

She's vain, he thought. *Maybe I can charm and flatter her.* It was worth a shot. Her son Mordred was the most likely ally for an IRA terrorist to pick up; Peter would have to keep an eye on the both of them.

He realized he was actually keeping an eye on the nude women . . . slaves? He stared the queen in the face to prevent his gaze from straying.

"Well met, gentle Lancelot," she greeted him, faintly sarcastic smile lowering the temperature of the conversation.

"Well met," Peter repeated. "The woman told me you wanted to see me."

Morgawse's mouth twitched, did not quite smile. "Your accent has improved markedly since the moon rose tonight," she observed. "Perhaps your *sensus* follows your *cogitatio?*"

Cogitatio? His thinking? What did sensus *mean?* "My mind feels particularly sharp today, Queen Marg—Morgawse." Peter made another mental note: *relearn everybody's name!* Malory was an untrustworthy tour guide.

"Has your mind come to its *sensus* about your upcoming match with Cutha of Wessex?"

"Some. I'm sure I can beat him; I hear he's—"

Morgawse dismissed the question with an annoyed wave. "I care nothing for your strategies and tactics, Lancelot, as I've told you before. Consider instead the *stakes and consequences;* I hope you are not so thick-skulled as to plot to *kill* the filthy Saxon . . . are you?"

Ignore the witch, kill the pig! commanded Lancelot's brutal voice in Peter's head. It was so clear, he had to stop himself from looking around to see who spoke. Disconcerted, Peter phased out for a moment to suppress the angry thoughts, missed the next thing the queen said.

"Are you listening, you Sicambrian lout? I told you, leave Cutha alive. *Do not kill him.* Have it?"

He started, remembered Anlawdd's admonition a few moments before. "Why? What happens if he dies?"

Morgawse's eyes widened, as if he had just relieved himself in the picnic basket. "Lancelot, Lancelot, how many times need I walk you through it? Cutha is an emissary from Caedwin, under Roman safe-passage, as well as our own guest-law. What do you *think*—if that's the word I want—would happen if you spit him in our very courtyard?"

"All right. No spitting."

"No decapitations, amputations, punctures, maimings, or eviscerations. Swear it, Legate."

Peter licked his fingers and made a cross upon his heart.

Morgawse looked dubious. "Is that an obscure Sicambrian oathtaking rite?"

"If you like," said Peter.

"Forget it. Swear like a *Roman*, you barbarous hound."

Like a Roman? How did Romans swear? "I swear by Jupiter—"

She spoke in clipped, pained syllables. "Take your hand from behind your back and put it on your testicles *properly*. Now swear, by Mithras and Sol Invictus. And don't even *think* of breaking such an oath, lest that part of you in your hand wither like rotten fruit!"

Reluctantly, worried that it was some trick on Selly's part to expose him, Lancelot put his hand between his legs and gingerly held one testicle between thumb and middle finger. "I sw-sw-swear by Misrath and Saul Invictus that I won't kill Cutha!" He spit the oath as quickly as possible, dropped his reproductive gland as if it had come alive like the Monkey's Paw.

He attempted a charming smile, surreptitiously wiping his hand on the back of his breeches. "Well well well well well, Morgawse, it's time for you to do me a favor in return, what?"

"A favor?" She raised her eyebrows, tilted her head slightly. "What *kind* of a favor?"

You wouldn't mind if I put a tail on your son Mordred the murderer, would you? Oh yes, jolly good. . . .

"I, uh . . . I'd like to get together with you. Later." He smiled roguishly, did his best Errol Flynn imitation. *Later, when I can interrogate you a bit, test for the Selly Corwin factor.*

Without changing expression, she managed to look pained. "Oh. I suspected it would come to that. It always does with you, doesn't it? Must you always be the conquering general?"

She absently toyed with her long, black and grey hair, stifled deep anger beneath an impassive mask. "Agreed, Lancelot; *after* the combat, in your room at midnight. Do it quickly, if it must be done."

Do Morgawse and Lancelot already have a relationship? Something sounded wrong, but he played his part up, afraid to back out at this point, lest he break character. The roguish charm bit worked on Gwynhwyfr, why not Morgawse?

"Never quickly," he retorted, "always measured and satisfying." He winked and bowed, took his leave toward the stairs.

It was not until he half crossed the room that he realized what actually happened: Morgawse had not offered herself because he *seduced* her. She offered her bed as bargain for him not to kill Cutha. Apparently, this was not uncommon for the brutish Lancelot.

I am champion. I seize what I see! exulted the buried voice, giving Peter a splitting headache.

He stopped, aghast, almost turned back and recanted the assignation. But that would draw even more attention. *That's ... that's nothing less than prostitution!*

Peter winced at a sudden pain in his groin. He thought for a moment, decided he would manage to have a sudden battle wound that would prevent such a performance.

Another thought occurred. *Joseph and Mary, what if I don't need to fake it? I could actually be wounded or killed! And if I were, what would happen to my body back home?* It was an uncomfortable speculation; Blundell had never discussed the possibility.

Peter realized he had exited the annex and passed through the aspen courtyard without even noticing it, and had reentered the *triclinium*.

The party had wound down. Men and women were sprawled around the feasting hall in various states of undress. The candles sputtered one by one, plunging the hall deeper into darkness. Only those few candles around Artus and Merovee were replaced. The two still conversed in hushed tones, oblivious.

Peter suddenly felt weary, as if he had marched a day and a half without rest. He skirted the edge of the hall, near the openair columns, and found the stairs. He climbed them to the second floor, found the room where he had first awakened, threw himself down on a mat without even drawing the curtain-door.

The end of Day-One, he thought, then drifted asleep, dreaming of machine gun–wielding IRA knights on horseback.

CHAPTER 20

ANLAWDD WAS NOT IN THE KITCHEN, *TRICLINIUM,* OR ANYWHERE Cors Cant could find. He wandered dejectedly for a time, then settled down on the front steps as the frenzied *saturnalia* unraveled.

He buried his face in his hands, imagining the wild, blood-haired goddess at his back. A voice, almost her own, argued harshly in his head: *Auburn, not red! Cors Cant Ewin, how do you expect to become a full bard if you can't observe the simplest*—he almost felt her fingers gently touch the nape of his neck, nearly felt arms encircle his body.

The wooden floor creaked behind him. He stiffened, held his breath, and slowly turned to look.

King Merovee stood politely, waiting for the boy to invite him farther. Cors Cant fumbled to his feet, gestured for the king to sit.

"Let us both sit," said Merovee as if speaking to an equal. He pulled a long-stemmed, clay pipe from his pocket, filled it with the Persian hemp, and lit a taper from a lantern on the nearest column. He spent some time lighting the pipe.

Cors Cant breathed the smoke that curled from King Merovee's bowl. The king smoked in silence a few moments, during which the boy began to see with true bardic vision. He noticed fascinating, barely visible geometric patterns woven into Merovee's tunic: interlinked triangles that formed six-pointed stars. Queerly, the stars seemed to rotate slowly, betimes even crawled across the king's garments like a cohort of ants.

Cors Cant breathed deeply, *in, one-two-three; out, four . . .*

and five. Soon, he noticed the strange geometry everywhere, in the columns, the carved wooden railings, even the stars.

"Cors Cant," said Merovee at last, "you look weighted down, like Atlas bearing the heavens on his shoulders. How could you have so many troubles at your age?"

"I never realized," said the bard, "how stars they were. I mean I never realized how starlike they were. Were. Were they always so perfectly formaled?"

Merovee smiled, offered the white clay pipe to Cors Cant. The bard hesitated, remembering Myrddin's admonition ("slack-jawed, dead-eyed wastrels, scoundrels, the Roman disease, idlers with more money than honor, lawyers, philosophers, not worth a single, silver *milliarensi!*"); then, trusting the Long-Haired King, he inhaled deeply, choking on the thick smoke.

Such bizarre behavior, breathing smoke. By nature, we run from smoke and choke on its acrid burn. Astonishing how quickly the nobly born took to it when the Pan-Draconis *introduced it.*

Come to think of it, they didn't begin to adopt the rest of Artus's modern ways until he first introduced this marvelous Persian invention. Could they possibly be related, or is that an example of what the orators call post hoc, ergo propter hoc, *the fallacy of believing that one fact following another must have been caused by the first? Why have I never wondered about all this before?*

Cors Cant blinked, realized he had sat for quite a long time in utter silence, analyzing the habits of his betters. "I wrote a song about Atlas once," he said quickly, remembering nought of what the king said but his reference to the giant. "He got tired of carrying the heavens one day and dropped them. We each had to carry our own piece of sky."

"May I hear it some time?"

"But it's not canonical."

Merovee raised a questioning eyebrow.

"I mean it's not part of accepted bard lore," explained Cors Cant. "It's not in the proper style, or anything. There are no great heroes, no edifying moral at the end. Not even a one-eyed giant. In fact, it's more what you'd hear in a wineshop, sung by a drunken bawd strumming a lyre." He sank his head onto his arms. "That's what they keep telling me . . . my songs are just *wrong.*" The words tasted bitter, but there they sat.

"Do you want to know something? So are the songs of my own court bard. I make him sing them anyway."

"He does? Songs that . . . cast doubt upon the rule of his own king?"

Merovee laughed, and relit his pipe. "Doubt! The man thinks I'm a mindless child betimes! That's why he's still my court bard after eight years. I value his view because it's unique." The king's pipe glowed like a signal fire. "Fear not your own songs, Cors Cant; Artus is wider and deeper than you think."

He smoked in silence, seeing his own geometric figures, then continued. "You're not weighed down by seditious songs; it's more than that. What's *her* name?"

"W-who?" gasped Cors Cant.

"The woman whose step you heard in my boots."

The boy's stomach lurched. He edged away. "Then it's true!" he declared. "You *are* half-god and look into men's hearts as we look into a book!"

"They say I'm half-fish, not half-god. But I'm not half-witted, and your thoughts are easy enough to guess. Especially after an illuminating conversation I just had with my host's wife, who has a certain, auburn-haired, talkative seamstress who has developed a sudden annoyance with, as she quaintly puts it, 'the entire bardic race and a certain bard in particular who sha'n't be named.' "

"Oh." Embarrassed, Cors Cant drew his knees up, thankful for the darkness that hid a flushed face. "Sire, you color it thus too?"

"It?"

"Her hair. You said auburn, Sire. It's red, isn't it?"

Merovee considered a moment. "Child, what color does *she* call it?"

"Hm. Your fishy half is the fish of wisdom, Sire."

"Some say."

Cors Cant shook his head. "There's something else she's hiding. Faith, but I know it's the key, but damn me if I can put a needle on it, Your Majesty."

Merovee smiled, stretched his long legs and rested them upon a stone dragon. "Tell you true, Cors Cant Ewin; don't expect her to come to you, because she *won't*. They have the edge, women do, and they're not about to give it up."

"So what should I do? Track her down? Then what?"

"Beg, flatter, promise; above all, intrigue her."

"With what? There's nothing intriguing about me!"

Merovee tilted his head back, his long, black hair forming a lion's mane on the ground. Apart from the hair, he looked even more Aquiline than Artus.

He is more Roman, remembered Cors Cant; Governor Merovee had been chosen king of Sicambria and the Languedoc people by the Flavian Emperor Valentinianus himself, as the Roman legions withdrew forever from the West. The bard caught a persistent flea, tried to crush it between his fingernails. *Time for another bath,* he decided.

"Nothing beguiling about a court bard?" chuckled the king, shifting so his ceremonial mail tinkled like handfuls of seashells. "Did you not just tell me of songs so heretical you dared not sing them to Artus? Sing them to Anlawdd! Should be intrigue enough for any lass. And while you're at it, Bard, work in a verse about her *auburn* hair."

Cors Cant smiled, impressed by the scheme. The weird geometries faded; he was about to beg the king for another puff when Merovee continued. "Now tell me the *real* problem, my child. The one hidden deep, even from yourself."

Suddenly uneasy, Cors Cant stood, walked out of the torchlight. Merovee's eyes pricked his back like a sewing needle. "I don't know what you mean, Sire," he lied. The words hung in the air like the Persian smoke, obscured and illuminated at the same time. *It's not a lie—I don't know!*

"Confession is good for the soul," said the king so softly Cors Cant was not sure he even spoke it aloud.

Another voice spoke, this time assuredly in Cors Cant's head. His own inner voice, or . . . ?

Forty days He spent in the desert, seeking the answer. Forty nights He fasted, waiting to see which path to take. Would it be wand or sword? Cors Cant shook his head. They were definitely not Druidic thoughts!

"I . . . I cannot confess yet, Caesar; I know too little."

"You know the question. Tell me that, at least."

He chose the sword and damned us all, for what use is rea-

son without intuition? Heaven must be found before 'tis subjugated. Reason alone never made a god!

Frightened, Cors Cant clapped hands over ears. *Out, out, out of my head!* he screamed at the voice. The night air became stale, fouled by superficial greed, lust, vainglory. *Camlann, leasaim! What are we all now but a pack of African jackals, sure, living by picking the bones of dead deeds a hundred years and more ago? Leave me alone, Whisperers!*

Unable to keep silent, he abruptly blurted out his real fear: "There's—there's—there's something wrong with Lancelot! He's a different man. I sense ... no, that's stupid. I'm no Druid or sibyl to see the future!"

The sword, or cross, was both beginning and end. The wand He had already rejected. The heart, or grail, He pulled from His own body to show us. Thirty coins He forced upon the chosen betrayer. Sword, wand, cup, and coin; He held them all, but never together at once.

He, too, shrank from the vision. But it burst upon him like dreams upon the sleepless.

Cors Cant leaned forward, attempting to escape his own head. "He's dying, Artus is dying ... *Merovee, help him!*" The *Pan-Draconis* lay on his deathbed, stared into the face of brutal Brutus, his slayer, and Messalina, the faceless wife. For a moment, Cors Cant could see nothing but the vision, death in a flapping tent. A camel poked its nose under the tent flap, bulged against the wall. An Ægyptian camel, stolen by a fisher king from ancient Cai-Ro.

She stood over the *Dux Bellorum*, an auburn wench with a knife ... but he blinked she—*she* was gone, though the rest of the vision remained, fading like the afterimage of the sun when you look away.

Merovee smoked silently. At last, he spoke, musing. "By what right do you task me with saving Artus? Perhaps his chariot has arrived, Cors Cant Ewin. Perhaps Camlann needs to lose its dragon to find its heart. To do nothing is to do...."

He noisily cleared his throat. "No, pay no mind what I just said. Prophecies belong to the land of Might-Be. Weep not, perhaps there is still time to divert this one."

Without knowing how he knew, Cors Cant knew the king spoke but a half-truth.

CHAPTER 21

*T*WO GIANTS BATTLED ACROSS A TWISTED LANDSCAPE OF FOLDS AND *valleys. A bearded thug caught his lobster in a death hug. The crustacean switched its mandibles open and closed, danced a complicated lobster quadrille.*

"I am the stronger!" boasted Shaggy Polymorphous, perversely cracking the lobster's back. But it was Sergeant MacMick, his sad eyes clouding, body torn by the blast and redder than any lobsterback. Pull yourself together man, pleaded Pater Smite. The sad-eyed Mike leaned his head back, back, crack to tore apart from the force of the blessed opened to show his still-pimping heart.

Created a door. And through the door, bloody as a newborn babe, burst Laughs-a-lot of the Languid Dock! dripping! blackclad, wild ravenshair explodes like paddy bums a drooping axe in his feist teeth long like a pan-dragon. And there is blood in his eye, and there is blood in his heart, the blood of an eagle taken for lunch and darkness belched back.

Peter lurched awake to a Chinese gong. It repeated, thunder of a huge sheet of metal being thumped by a large, blunt instrument. *The sort of blunt instrument that Lord Wimsey was always finding embedded in the victim's skull,* he thought dazedly.

His head throbbed. A most terrible dream faded from his memory before he could look at it in daylight. He sat up, shivered in the chill air. *The filth, the Roman swine that infest Camlann with their—*

Peter gasped, doubled over. He had never felt such an urgent need to urinate. He would burst!

Panicked, he stared wildly for a container, anything to relieve himself into. "Bedpan!" he gasped. No, not a bedpan ... what did they call it? "Chamber pot, under the bed!"

Peter lunged for the side of the mat, realized there was no "underneath." He staggered to his feet, hobbled around the room twice, sweating profusely. At last, he noticed a tall, straight vase containing old, dried flowers. He yanked the stems from the vase, fumbled at his tunic. He barely managed to raise it in time to avoid splashing himself.

At last he sighed loudly, the vase nearly full with yesterday's ale and wine. He glanced at the curtain-door, discovered a low shelf containing a filled washbasin and an empty chamber pot.

The walls were unfamiliar, prisonlike. No, they were comfortable, old friends! He rubbed his eyes, washed his face in the icy basin. *So civilized, so modern, these Roman knights, not at all what I ex—*

Peter still felt tipsy. *Good King Jesus, what do they put in that wine? I was only supposed to fake a drunk.*

It's the buggering pig Romans polluting our souls with decadent laws and lascivious demigods. . . .

Stop it! He covered his ears and squeezed hard, and the voice diminished in volume. But it was still there, angrily denouncing Romans and Saxons with colorful phrases.

Quickly, feeling slightly ashamed, Peter emptied the vase into the chamber pot. He rinsed the vase with the remains of the wash water, spilling it out the window and replacing the dead flowers.

He inspected the room, and his eyes focused on a number of spears or javelins in the corner. He frowned, remembering the impending joust. *God's sacred heart. So tomorrow's the day I die.* He leaned over and put his head between his knees, trying to quell the raging storm inside his head.

So what'll happen? I'll fight, I'll get killed, and probably wind up back in Willks's cellar. Selly Corwin will have a free hand; she'll murder Arthur or burn down Camelot or whatever she's planning, change history, and all of England will disappear.

If the entire village was replaced by a virgin forest in Selly's timeline, it was clear that England, too, was gone—else the burgeoning demands of an industrial nation would have long ago sacrificed the wood to houses, farms, and factories. Selly had done—or would do—*something* that caused Peter Smythe's England never to exist.

A loud snore caught Peter's attention from behind the curtain, out in the hall. The *closed curtain,* he realized, almost positive he had left it open the night before.

He drew the dirk he had never bothered removing the night before and yanked the heavy canvas aside. Behind it was a young man, perhaps twenty-one years, curled in a foetal position around the door hole. His sandy hair was slicked straight back and stank of bacon grease. His tunic and breeches seemed more like those worn by Merovee's men than Artus's. He smelled as if bathing were a foreign concept. *Surely not one of the Roman set,* thought Peter.

The lad choked on a loud snore, staggered to his feet, awake in seconds. *Jesus, God, love to have him on sentry duty,* admired Peter. "Why are you snoring outside my room, boy?" he demanded.

"Lancelot, is't truly *you?*" The lad spoke with such pie-faced awe that Smythe felt the least he could do was bless him.

"Last time I checked. Who the hell are you?" It was clear from the boy's tone they had never met.

"You know me not, but you know my mother, the Lady Morgawse. My name is—"

Peter interrupted him with an upraised hand. "Mordred . . . is that your name?"

The young man's eyebrows shot up to his hairline. "You've *heard* of me?"

"Your fame precedes you, Mordred. And I have met your mother." Peter's mind worked furiously. It was Mordred who engineered Arthur's death, set Lancelot up with Guinevere, and forced a war. A natural ally for Selly Corwin. *Well you won't get away with it this time, you bloody greaser.*

Mordred held his wide-brimmed, very un-Roman hat awkwardly, shuffled his feet. "Prince? Sire?"

"Yes?"

The boy lapsed into silence, then spoke again. "Sicambrian lord?"

"*Yes?*" Peter was growing tired of the banter. He desperately needed information, time, a drink.

"Prince, my father King Morg suggested I come to you, the greatest warrior in both islands. I—I want to learn to fight, to command troops in battle."

Taken aback, Peter scrutinized the lad. He was compact

and lithe, a little taller than Lancelot. Mordred was achingly beautiful, a marble statue of Apollo. Peter was instantly repelled, unconsciously reached down to adjust his tunic. Fast on his feet as Mordred might be, you could never trust the "pretty boys."

"Haven't you already received training in the, um, manly arts?" stalled Peter.

"My education has not been neglected! I speak Latin and some Greek, play chess, know the sacraments and sacrifices of all the religions of the Big Island. I know horse, lance, axe, and I can fire from the saddle as Artus teaches. But lord, I know nothing of fighting. *Real* fighting. And how am I to govern when my father dies if I've not served as a general in the legions?"

A good lad. Trust him. Use him. . . . Peter shook his head, trying to rid his mind of Lancelot's oily voice.

Mordred swallowed nervously, continued. "King Morg my father told me to offer myself first as a captain of centuries."

Peter observed him without expression. According to Malory, Mordred was the illegitimate son of Arthur by Margawse, Arthur's half sister. So who was this "King Morg"?

"First, a surprise exam," said Peter. "How many soldiers in a century?"

"Tradition says a hundred," answered Mordred, proud of his knowledge, "but Artus prefers sixty-five to seventy-five, with twenty cavalry."

"Why?"

"I . . . I do not know, my prince."

The centuries are short, as is the gladius *sword.* It was Lancelot's thought, not Peter's, but welcome this time. *Strike fast, many blows spread out, keep the Saxon swine off balance!* Peter pursed his lips; for the first time, he realized there might be an advantage in having two souls behind one pair of eyes.

He asked another question, probing. "How many legions does Arthur command?"

"Five, Sire."

"How many legions do I command?"

"Two, Sire."

"Two of the same five?"

"Yes, Sire."

"How can we both command the same two legions?"

Mordred started to answer, but no words formed. He struggled for several moments, finally gave up. "I do not know, Sire." Clearly, the concept of chain of command was alien to the lad. He was probably telling the truth about not having campaigned.

"So you want to be a captain of centuries, Mordred."

"Yes, Sire!"

"How many centuries do you expect to command?"

Mordred took a breath, recited an obviously memorized force breakdown. "The captain commands a cohort of from four to seven centuries."

Peter did a quick mental calculation. *Between 260 and 525 men; the lad wants to be an instant colonel!* He studied Mordred; another thought occurred. Mordred had said he knew horse and lance. *Maybe I can get him to show me how to joust, give me half a fighting chance against the Saxon.*

Peter smiled as sincerely as he could fake. "King Morg had a good idea. All right, I'll take you on as a *brevet* captain of centuries, the precise slot to be determined later. Your first lesson starts immediately." His head gave a sudden lurch and Peter hastily amended, "I mean, in about an hour. We'll go out to the woods and joust a bit."

"An hour, lord?" asked the boy. He looked confused. "Sire, which hour?"

Peter glanced at his naked wrist, realized he had no watch and covered the *faux pas* by plucking imaginary lint. "What time is it now?"

"The second chime just rang, Sire."

"Chime?"

"Yes Sire. The second *cymbalum*. Did you not hear?"

Peter glanced at the window. It was early morning, still brightening. Eight o'clock? "How do they know when to ring the next sim—cymbal—the next chime, Mordred?"

"Why, they burn a two-hour candle, I suppose."

"Then burn *half* of a two-hour candle, lad. Come along, try to stay ahead of the eight ball."

"The what ball, Sire?"

Peter realized he had no idea what accoutrements were needed for a joust. "As you leave, take my gear with you." He nodded his head at the jumble of armor and weapons in the corner.

Mordred looked askance. "I'll fetch you a slave, Sire."

The thought made Peter shiver; *they take it so casually, the whole barbaric lot!* "Mordred, a warrior must sometimes carry his *own* gear. It's a sacred duty. So get my stuff and meet me at the gate in one hour."

"Yes, Sire," sighed the young man. "Sire?"

"Yes?" asked Peter wearily.

"Not to show disrespect, Prince, but I do prefer *Medraut*, the Sicambrian pronunciation, because of my father."

Peter nodded and waved Medraut away, sat down with head in hands. *Perhaps in an hour the room will stop spinning,* he prayed.

CHAPTER 22

OH MY GOD, MY GODDESS, WHAT WAS I TO DO? I PACED IN THE Court of Flowing Water, circling round and round the fountain, silently begging Rhiannon to cast off her stony silence and spring to life ... that is, if it were Rhiannon and not some Greek or Roman intruder.

I was torn in every direction, like a prisoner about to be drawn and quartered, which I can assure you is a most unpleasant way to spend one's execution: my duty to my father conflicted directly upon my relationship, whatever it was, with That Boy, which ran counter to all the teachings of the Builders and Uncle Leary, who seemed in the opposite camp from the Builder, King Merovee of Sicambria! But I suppose I better start more beginning-wards, or not even I will understand who stood where.

Near enough sixty days ago, I stood in my father's hall, proud that at last he had recognized me as a warrior—better, as his daughter—but still mystified whether my first warrior's task was worthy of a warrior's honor.

Father slowly walked back and forth before his great, green

chair with the flower of our house, his hands clasped behind his back so he wouldn't constantly rub his aching knuckles. He walked as straight as he could, but his face was hard with the pain, his finger joints swollen huge and aching with every change in the weather.

"Anlawdd," he said, "I've a charge for you."

"I know my duty," I said warily, for I did not yet know what he wanted; usually it was something trivial and demeaning, leading me to believe he had forgotten I was as much his daughter as cursed Canastyr Canllaw the "hundred-handed" was his son.

He paralyzed me with a glance, his sea green eyes chill and brittle, challenging me to obedience. "This task is no entertainment for visitors or blessing the dedication of another statue of me. No, my daughter, I think you'll actually *like* this charge."

He gestured me forward. Still wary, for Father *never* called me "my daughter," at least not unless he wanted me to clean the Augean stables or scrape the barnacles off Harlech Tower. Reluctantly, I stepped within a whisper as he cleared his throat like thunder. "When I lived here as a boy," he lectured, "Harlech was a free state, beholden to no sovereign save her own prince. But today, wherever I look, from the snows of the northern mountain to the southern forest, from sunset sea to the plains, what do I see?"

I waited, not realizing he wanted an answer until he frowned at me, irritated. I blinked. "You see Rome, Father," I offered.

"Rome!" he bellowed, nearly bursting my eardrums from the noise. "This Artehe 'War-Leader' is the death of us!"

He took a deep breath, looking slyly left and right. "Like that bastard Vortigern before him, this *foreigner* takes my hand, extended in friendship, and claps the shackle upon it. We cannot ride, but *Artus* must hear about it! We cannot ship, but *Caer Camlann* must approve the shipment!"

Father paused, waited for me to object, for I most often do when he begins to rant. But this time, I agreed wholeheartedly. For six years, ever since Cei campaigned in our Cantref to drive out the Jutes and incidentally bring Harlech to heel in the *Dux Bellorum's* "security arrangement," we had been no more free than crusty old King Morg with his wife, Queen Morgawse, held hostage in Camlann itself.

I knew as well as my father what Artus really wanted: nothing less than the entire Big Island of Prydain clutched in an iron grip! Thus, the *Dux Bellorum* cast his legions to all four corners to chivvy the rest of Prydain into acknowledging his sovereignty over us all.

Father spoke again, seeing I had nothing to interrupt with: "Then what are we to do, daughter? What is Harlech to do? How do we drive the invader from our midst, with his legions and cohorts?"

The question was easy, having but one answer. "We must make common cause with my uncle," I said, "your brother-by-marriage, Archking Leary of Eire."

It was the only logical course. Uncle Leary was a crafty old coot, his beard so long they said he threw it across all fifty rafters in his great hall when he sat down to meat, though I always wondered how he could eat with his beard stretched awkwardly across the ceiling like that.

But Father started at the suggestion as if I had just spoken the name of the skull-faced lord of the shadow realm, for whom naming is the same as summoning. "Leary? Leary?" he said, nervously tugging at his throbbing joints. "Now where have I heard that name before, eh? Heh-heh." He shook his head. "Forget your blasphemous uncle; he's not to be trusted, for did he not give leave for the Roman Patrick to come cry his foreign god in Eire? He has not your best interest at heart, Anlawdd—nay, nor the interests of Harlech."

"Well," I pointed out, "he *is* king of Eire, which must occupy most of his attention."

"No, Anlawdd my daughter; Harlech must handle our own affairs, else we are no freer than we are just now."

I nodded; the old man was actually making sense, which was as astonishing as if a bear had wandered out of the woods, sat down, and begun reciting Virgil.

"Against my wish," he continued, "you were trained to arms, just as your brother, my beloved son."

I allowed no visible reaction at the mention of Canastyr, for Father might possibly not know what the "hundred-handed" had done so many years ago, when we were both young and slept in the same room, just after Mother died. But I think Father *did* know.

"I would have wished you to grow up a proper lady, Anlawdd. But I acted under orders—ah, that is, at the suggestion of my brother whom I shall not name, though you know the one I mean." He glanced fearfully to the west, toward Eire.

Uncle Leary and I had always enjoyed a peculiar relationship, for he could deny me nothing. He would make suggestions, but I would always refuse, instead wheedling him to see things my way. But somehow, I never quite caught how, I ended up doing as he asked and thinking myself terribly clever. Leary had some faerie magic about him, I suppose.

When he smiled, his entire face cracked wide, particularly his sky blue eyes, and he never seemed to notice hardship or misfortune: true enough, when he stubbed his toe against a rock, it turned up fairy gold—his bad luck always spilled over into good, and it profited one to stand near Leary when the clouds burst or the earth shook.

Leary often threatened that if I were not his niece as he was my uncle, he would marry me himself; and it was he who somehow talked Father into having the sergeant train me to arms ... though I never did figure whether I talked old Leary into granting, or he tricked me into asking.

"Am I boring you?" Father asked, startling me out of my reverie.

I blinked like a hound caught nose in the cupboard when you suddenly open the larder door. "No, Father," I lied, "I was thinking about what you said about Artus."

"That's good," he said, sitting on the green chair, spindly fingers gripping the carved lion armrests like a pair of giant, white spiders, "for your task concerns that most noble *Dux Bellorum.*"

Now I was truly intrigued: my charge concerned Artus, and it mattered that I was trained in the use of weapons ... was I to be sent to Camlann as a hostage? It made no sense, but my heart leapt like a startled hare at the prospect of adventure.

"Send me, Father," I cried, "for there is none who can serve you and Harlech better than the city's first daughter!"

He smiled, rather too catlike. "You must journey to Caer Camlann," he said, "and take service under this Roman War-Leader. He will grow to trust you, and you must never let him know who you really are ... for one dark night when all are asleep, and you are allowed the run of his snake pit *Caer Camlann,* then I charge you by your utmost loyalty to me and to Harlech to creep into his bedchamber and *slay the despot!"*

I said nothing, only stared with my mouth opening and closing. I was a warrior, willing to fight and die for the prince, for Harlech! But commit a night-black *murder,* and to kill my own host, yet? To creep like an assassin into his very marital chamber and plunge a dagger into his sleep-shut eye? My insides squeezed up inside of me and rolled around as if they had come detached from my rib cage, and evil humors flowed freely up and down my spine.

So many emotions! I knew the job was deadly danger, which thrilled and frightened me both; I knew it was an irrevocable act of treason and war, which compelled and repelled with equal vigor.

I slept not an hour that night, so anxious was I. Hie me to Camlann to slay the sleeping *Dux Bellorum!* The bards would sing of me for ages, and all Harlech would raise up a statue to me. Posthumously, of course.

I was under no illusions; I knew I would likely not survive the quest. I really didn't mind speeding to the next world if, by severing the tyrant's neck, I could sever the chains that bound my city as well.

Artus was no king or emperor whose rule devolved to his family upon his death; he was nothing but a leader, a general—like Galba, who seized the empire after mad Nero's destruction. Killing Artus would be like removing the keystone from a Roman arch: the whole edifice of Camlann would tumble to the ground, freeing Harlech and the rest of Prydain from the *Dux Bellorum's* dreams of empire.

Alas, I owed fealty to more than one master.

I shared a secret with Uncle Leary that not even Father would ever know.

Four years earlier, when I was but a girl of sixteen, Uncle Leary initiated me into a group he called the Builders of the Temple. I can't tell about the initiation, but I confronted much inside me I never knew existed . . . and remembered aloud what Canastyr had done ten years earlier, though I had never forgotten it to my silent self.

The Builders sought to transform mankind by God's law into gods ourselves. They taught me much secret, occult learning of which it is not lawful to speak, or at least that's what I had to promise, though most of it seemed more silly than sacred.

"You *can't* reveal the secrets to the uninitiated," chuckled Uncle Leary many times, "for those who have not learned the secrets through some form of initiation will hear your words as a confused babble, as if you spoke them in the language of birds and fish." That's one of Leary's greatest problems: he's forever using similes and metaphorical images, like a heavy-handed Greek tragedian.

"The Builder's oath," he added, "is self-enforcing."

I would hope they don't enforce the oaths themselves! One that I swore, as soon as I was initiated, was to do no harm to a fellow Builder, upon pain of having my eyes torn out and crushed, my nose cut off, my hands bound behind my back, hookwinked and hanged from a bridge at midnight, with a brick in one pocket and ashes in the other to weight down my soul and prevent it flying to heaven (not that Saint Petrus or the Mother would admit the soul of an oathbreaker anyway).

My throat squeezed as I remembered what I had heard at a Builder meeting from a brother: I heard the rumor that *Artus himself* was the master of a distant Builder Temple down south in Camlann.

If this were so, I was damned to hell whichever door I opened! I must either defy my father, in which case I could forget about any charge more honorable than the fate Rhiannon suffered—carrying houseguests up the hill on her back like a horse—else I could obey my father, thus defying my oath as a Builder and losing the respect of Uncle Leary forever, which would be worse than all the horrors of oathbreaking I mentioned above.

I sat the whole night on the floor of my room before the embers of the fire, sleep a mocking memory, holding my dagger and gently stroking the steel with my finger. In the morning, I tried to rise but found my legs had cramped. I still had no answer . . . but at least I knew I didn't have to decide today. It would take much time to journey south across the Severn to Camlann, time to take service with Artus, time to gain his trust. Perhaps in those weeks, I could discover the answer to my query . . . which might teach me my decision.

I thought to dress as a comfortable merchant's boy, not the

daughter of a knight or senator; thus I cast aside breastplate and greaves, helmet and lance, wearing only a boiled-leather cuirass as a citizen might wear and carrying my ax and knife. Atop this mildest armor I wore a tunic of sunlight yellow, the image of Nuada Silverhand embroidered upon the breast . . . a present I sewed for my uncle, which I then borrowed back from him more or less permanently. I took a hood of white fleece, both for warmth against the fall breeze and to hide my long tresses, then pressed a miller's cap on top of everything; the headgear had a hidden skullcap of beaten iron, which might save my life if I could get a brigand to strike me politely on the very top of my pointy head, rather than at my face, throat, arms, legs, belly, chest, or back.

Before sunup, I stalked bleary-eyed out of my apartment and down the narrow, winding stair that led to the west gate, stumbling in the blackness, for the torches had of course sputtered out at midnight or a little past.

As I found the bottom landing, where the unadorned stone shone dully in the grey, predawn light shining through vertical slits and murder holes, I heard a step behind me.

I spun, axe up. My brother stepped from the shadows, a crooked, sneering grin on his lips.

I stepped back, my axe-arm falling nervelessly to my side. Canastyr always froze the blood in my veins, like the breath from the lord of Anufyn, the shadow realm. The closer he came, the younger I grew, until he stood but an arm's length away and I was a little girl of six again, just the age I was when he—when we slept in the same bedroom.

"Oh where are you going, sweet sister of mine, without your most loving brother? And dressed down as a peasant, I see!" He reached out his fingers, but I recoiled from his touch as I would from the kiss of a snake. "You should wear only diaphanous silk and white ermine," he added, voice dropping to nearly a whisper.

I shivered, though I was not cold; in fact, heat flushed my face, and I knew he could see my fright and humiliation.

"Leave off, earthworm," I said, though my voice trembled as I wished it had not.

He let his breath out slowly at the hated name; he and I were the only two who knew *why* I called him that.

He struck without warning, right hand swinging up at my

face with something clutched in his fist. He had not actually struck at me for two years—I must truly have rattled him!

If the word and my bold front startled him into an injudicious attack, my response must have knocked all the steam loose from his veins, since I had spent the last two years profitably training under Sergeant Pwyll ap Cun.

Without taking time to think, I bent at the waist, ducking beneath his clumsy blow; at the same time, I lashed out with my own left fist, lunging forward to belt him directly below the sternum, upon his diaphragm.

Canastyr the "hundred-handed" folded like a Roman fan, fell heavily to his knees, gasping for air. I o'erleapt him, darting for the door. There I paused, unable to resist a glance back to see if I perhaps had hit him hard enough to kill him.

He had climbed back to his feet, clutched the empty lantern hook to stay upright. "I'll see—you again," he gasped, "and make—you eat—both word and blow!"

"I'll see *you* again," I promised, exulting; "and when we meet, they'll call you not earthworm but *girl-boy!*" I raised my axe, realizing that at last I was free of his touch, free of his hateful presence that kept me six years old for eleven years. I was away, gone from Harlech, gone adventuring as a warrior maid, like Macha the Battle-Goddess Herself, or Minerva!

But as I pulled the massive, ironbound pinewood door ajar and dashed out into the streets, I knew we both had prophesied true: Canastyr Canllaw the "hundred-handed" would not let me escape so easily.

We would meet again, and soon.

I strolled to the stables, trying not to attract attention; no one penetrated my disguise, or if one did, he kept his opinions politely to himself. There I bribed the ostler to shut his gaping mouth and fetch my favorite roan mare, Merillwyn, not a native pony, but a true Roman draft horse, big enough for war and trained by Uncle Leary's own captain of horses, before the archking gave her to me.

I took my time riding, not pressing the old girl and dismounting every pair of hours to walk beside her or let her graze. I was in no hurry to bump into the *Dux Bellorum* and find out whether I would be damned to hell for oathbreaking or merely slain for plotting homicide.

I crossed the great Severn far east, where there were many

fords not yet swollen by autumn floods and grass was plentiful. I had brought money with me—not enough to arouse suspicion, should I be captured by bandits, for I could afford to be robbed but not to be held hostage—and I paid my lodgings each night at inns, farmhouses, or Roman hostels that were still in operation, though the eagles had withdrawn a half century ago.

At last, when I was but a single day outside of Camlann, I saw ahead of me a row of four white tents set against the leeward side of a faerie hill or burial mound. An ensign stirred in the desultory breeze, the full nine yards: a silver fish caught against a white background. Above the flag, the pole itself was capped by an eagle of Rome and a golden plaque bearing the mark "MRPP," which my faint Latin suggested might signify *Merovius Rex Pro Praetore.*

I had run into the encampment of Merovee, once governor, now king of Sicambria. I reined in Merillwyn, confused and startled: what was Merovee, founder of the Builders, doing in Prydain?

Merovee was the only man who seemed to awe even Uncle Leary himself. I don't know how far Leary trusted the Sicambrian—possibly no farther than he could throw him, which was surely less a distance than he could throw his own beard. But he owed him fealty, as did all of us Builders of the Temple, not only as founder but for being half-fish.

I thought for many long moments, deciding whether loyalty meant actively seeking out instruction. Then I shrugged, decided it was like an oath of truth: you're required to answer only the truth, but you're not required to answer every question you happen to hear!

I skirted the encampment, giving Merovee such a wide berth that I nearly circled Camlann itself, and entered the city at dawn a day and a night later.

I found a good stable run by a huge, fat butterball named Joff, short for Geoffanon, no doubt, and put Merillwyn up in a pair of stalls with strict instructions for oats, carrots, apples, and hay as a last resort, and I do *not* spoil her rotten, whatever Uncle Leary may say.

Then I hied up to the palace, which was grander than anything in the world: stadium, baths attached, fountains and four-story buildings! The town was fine, with a coliseum under renovation, three stages, and more baths for people like me—or at least, like the seamstress I decided to become (I could pass for a miller's son on the road, but such a disguise would be harder to maintain in the baths, I reckoned). I demonstrated my talent for none other than Princess Gwynhwfyr herself, wife of Artus, and she was captivated by my brilliance ... either that, or she was desperate, not having had any seamstress at all since old Biddy Tangwen ran off with Oll the Stableboy, whom the other household contractors called the "Horse-Long Boy"—and I do *not* want to know *why* they called him that!—and he being but half her age.

Thus, several weeks later, I found myself pacing round and round the fountain of Rhiannon (unless it was Diana) in the Court of Flowing Waters, trying to put That Boy out of my mind, which was already full enough with thoughts of Artus, Merovee (who had finally entered Camlann after his avatar smoothed the diplomatic way), my father, my vile brother, and bloody murder.

At last I could stand it no longer; oath or no oath, I saw no moral imperative forcing me viciously to squelch my own needs and desires. Even a warrior must needs be a woman, betimes!

I resolved that if he managed not to irritate me *too* much in the next hour or two, I would take a deep breath, pray to the Lady, and actually ask That Boy out for a pleasant ride—or rather, allow him to ask me, for of course I'm not speaking to him yet. And damn all fools to hell who say I've gone soft in my advanced age!

CHAPTER 23

PETER WANDERED THE ROOM, FUTILELY LOOKING FOR A MIRROR before he remembered there was none. Nor shaving cream. *So now what? If I'm going to be skewered by Mordred, I'd prefer to look and feel my best. What does one use to scrape the face?*

Stone, thought Lance in answer to the question. *Roman stone. Shaving stone.*

Shaving stone? Now that the Sicambrian brought it to his mind, Peter vaguely remembered something about the Romans shaving with pumice stones. It was a ghastly thought. He fished through the pouch he had deposited on the bed table, found the thin, white stone.

Jumping Jesus! I guess I have to try, at least. Peter hesitated, wondering whether to wet his face or leave it dry. "I've never shaved with a bleedin' rock before." He shuddered at the image it provoked: a bloody, dripping, pumice stone, and a pair of what used to be cheeks. He wet his face with the tepid water in the washbasin.

One side of the stone was flat; the other side fit his hand reasonably well. He gritted his teeth, scraped it across his flesh. *No wonder they're all so scarred,* he thought morosely.

The pain was not as great as he feared, and oddly enough, it did seem to give a rough, unfinished shave.

When Peter finished, he sponged off as much blood as he could with a linen "towel" he found next to the empty basin. He sat slowly and carefully on the bed. The headache was nearly gone; he wanted it to stay gone.

He examined the bed table, found nothing worthwhile. No locked drawers or secret compartments. Apparently it was decorative, or for tea and crumpets.

Peter spilled the coins out of his pouch and examined them. There were four silver and eleven copper. The silver coins were each stamped "IMPERATOR CONSTANTINIVS PIVS PRINCEPS" on obverse and "NOVVS DENARIVS" on reverse, while the copper read "GENIVS POPVLI ROMANI."

The word *denarius* struck a chord. Apparently, the silver coins were new *denariuses,* or *denarii,* and had been issued by Emperor Constantine, or in his memory. Peter could not remember when Constantine had reigned. He had presided over the Council of Nicaea; that much Peter remembered from Sunday School. That meant a century or more prior to A.D. 450.

He pulled the folded paper from his pouch, ruled off the

Latin text, and sharpened the sliver of charcoal with the paring knife. *Investigation Log,* he wrote below the rule.

Morgawse if that's how you spell it high on the list, right temperament for Selly. Too obvious?

anlawth impulsive where selly cool. Could be cover—no I don't think so, draws too much attention. she does have the red hair, I don't know if that means anything. Don't trust her shes too deep.

guinevere gwynivear

Peter paused. Gwynhwfyr's image filled his mind, Gwynhwfyr dancing naked as a faerie queen, calling them all to dance with her. . . .

He crossed his legs, scribbled the rest of her entry.

guinevere gwynivear—no too innocent open, Selly is hard and calculating she could never lead a dance like gwinhuver did. Shes pure, I wish circumstances were different I'd very much like to get to know her better. He quickly crossed the last line out, stood and brushed himself off.

He sat down again. To the right of his first entry he made a short table.

Real name	Malory name
Artus	Arthur
Kay	Kay
Beduere	Bedivere
Gwynhuver	Guinevere
Merovay	?
Cors Cant	?
Anlawth	?
Morgawse	Margawse
Merthin	Merlin
Maydrow	Mordred
Lancelot	Launcelot du Lac

He stared at the list, memorized it as best he could. *I do not want to stumble again,* he thought.

The light indicated nearly an hour had passed. He hid the journal inside his chemise—*can't let it be discovered,* he thought—then exited the room.

Peter prowled the corridor, stiff as a fusilier on parade.

He navigated the stairs, careful to keep his head on an even keel.

The great hall looked completely different in morning light. Gone was the vast abyss, gone the thousand-foot-high ceiling, the magical, starlit chamber, the still, torch-burnt air. In reality, the great hall was smallish, stuffed with lumpy couches packed so tight they left barely enough room to swing a cat or heave a brick. Mythic oppression was replaced by squalor, filth, and the stale odor of old hash smoke.

A score of rough-clad boys and girls—slaves, no doubt— scurried about the hall, cleaning. Peter steeled himself, snarled at them to get out of his way. They obeyed without a thought.

The limp, odorous, snoring bodies turned his stomach. *King Arthur's noble knights of the table round, defenders of England!* Peter averted his eyes from a nearly naked woman, sprawled facedown across an anonymous chum, both intoxicated comatose.

He stepped over a dozen prone Sicambrians and was startled to see King Merovee wide-awake, seated in silence at Arthur's table. He watched Peter approach, raised his cup in salutation.

"Well met. You're up early, Prince."

"Well met, Your Highness. Are you up early or late?"

Merovee looked at a hatch-marked candle, nearly guttering out in its holder. The wax ran down one side only; Merovee had found a breezy spot. The king shook his head. "Late, I'm afraid. I've been thinking."

"About?"

"You. Among other things. Why do I not know you, Lancelot?"

Peter drew back. The enigmatic Merovee peered with obsidian eyes. *Half-god—or did he say half-fish? Can't remember.* From Merovee's tone, Peter realized Lancelot and the king must once have been close. "People change, Majesty. I've been a long time at Camelot."

Eyebrows raised languidly. "Perhaps. Don't let me detain you. From accounts of Cutha's skill, you need all the practice you can get." The king rose, stalked toward the doorway that led to the aspen courtyard. Peter bowed as he'd seen others do, continued toward the front door. A thought nagged at his hindbrain, suddenly burst into consciousness.

I'm wearing no arms or armor ... how the hell did he know I was going out to practice swordfighting?

Peter turned back, but Merovee had vanished. *No, it's obvious. Simple deduction, that's all. He must have talked to Medraut as he passed through. Surely the kid bragged about combat practice with Lancelot the Invincible!* Peter chopped the air, dismissed the fright from his mind. *Had to be. No other explanation. I think.*

He purposefully strode to the massive, oaken door, shoved it wide.

He blinked in the sudden, brilliant sun. Pale, wispy clouds dotted the empty sky, a Magritte blue sky, not brown. A gentle, rust-and-olive-colored hill sloped from Caer Camlann seaward toward a large, sprawling village below. A briny salt breeze blew from the west, bore the cries of merchants hawking bread and autumn apples.

I'll bet even the Thames is potable, he thought, swallowing a knot from his throat. Peter turned slowly in the crisp, brown, brittle grass, evaluated the site from a defensive point of view.

The ground was clear-cut from the villa for five hundred yards, where the first town buildings began. Easy shooting from second-floor windows or murderholes in the wall. A charging army would be hedgehogged before crossing half the distance, the survivors winded before they touched the first stone.

Medraut was nowhere to be seen. *Been at least an hour,* Peter thought. Perhaps there was more than one gate? He studied the villa itself.

Not much, he thought. Disappointed, he walked around the buildings that composed Camelot. Scarcely bigger than Wilmhurst, his own public school, Camlann could not include more than a hundred cramped nook-rooms, such as his own. Hardly imposing to a man who had seen Edinburgh, the Kremlin, Windsor Castle.

The complex was L-shaped, two sections fitting together: the dining hall, or *triclinium,* and the three-story section that contained his own apartment.

But there must be more, thought Peter. Margawse's apartments were in a separate building, behind and to the left of the *triclinium.*

The walls were white concrete, decorated with murals of godlike men and women. Peter walked a bit farther clockwise, looking for the "Margawse" wing. Caer Camlann was definitely more extensive than it first appeared.

As he rounded the apartments, he saw two newer buildings attached to the rear of the feast hall, their construction seeming from a more recent era (the joints fitted more precisely; the arches showed the first, faint intimations of a point, as in Gothic cathedrals). The new buildings were arms that extended away from the sea and the town below. The nearest one was undoubtedly the building to which the Amazon had led him.

Over the top of the new buildings, Peter saw a huge, wide-angled A-frame roof, painted brick red. The tops of thin, reddish marble columns stretched down from the roof, vanishing behind the arms. The columns were decorative, clearly too delicate to be structural.

The four buildings completed a square: the *triclinium,* two arms of apartments, and the large, red-columned hall at the back.

"Jesus," he muttered, "this place is bigger than I thought."

All of the roofs seemed to be the same, layers of reddish, overlapping tile to keep out the weather. *I'll hike around the whole fortress—castle, really. Eventually I ought to find that bastard Medraut.* Besides, he thought, it gave him an excuse to case the castle.

From Peter's vantage point at the top of the hill, the town buildings were grouped like soldiers in rank and file. The streets were all straight, dividing Camlann into a grid.

Approximately two thousand buildings, he estimated; the closest third were surrounded entirely by a square, raised-earth mound-wall. Guessing at least four or five people per building, Peter estimated the population of Camlann to be ten thousand. Smaller than Rome or London—*what did that boy call it, Londinium?*—but big for the sticks of Britain. He retraced his steps, past the front of the *triclinium,* to circumambulate the villa counterclockwise.

A grumble of four buildings poked out gracelessly from the "square." They seemed the newest of all, added by an architect who did not believe in matching the earlier construction. The "new wing" fronted on a huge, oval-shaped dirt field.

A graceful, curved colonnade separated the field from the villa itself. Shaded boxes jutting out from the building indicated that it was specifically built for watching some sort of event in the field.

The field was ringed by a track. As Peter walked across it, he saw numerous wheel tracks. *Chariot races?* he wondered as he cut between the columns of the colonnade and found himself in an unexpected garden. *Gladiatorial contests?*

To his right, behind tall hedges, he saw another field, this one long and narrow. He had no idea what it was used for. He wove his way among the roses of the garden, discovered another set of buildings behind the square and the extra apartments he had already identified. He noticed an odd phenomenon: although the design of the villa as a whole was asymmetrical, there was always an underlying symmetry to whichever part of the house could be seen from any one vantage point. Even the ghastly, modern architecture near the chariot field followed this dictum.

Peter passed the midpoint of the narrow field and found Medraut. The boy stood in the center of the sunken rectangle holding two horses, loaded with gear.

Medraut saw Peter, leapt to his feet. "Sire! I beg forgiveness, I assumed you meant the stadium gate."

Peter shrugged, unconcerned. "You got a spot picked out for practice?"

Medraut answered slowly as if he suspected a trick. "Well, I had thought the tournament stadium would do." He gestured at the long, narrow field that flanked the southeast side of the villa.

Oops. I can't bloody well have the entire house overlooking my bumbling, left-footed swordplay! Axeplay, whatever. Start dancing, find someplace more private.

Peter shook his head. "Medraut, do you think you'll only be attacked on tournament grounds and drill fields? Think that *maybe* you *might* want to occasionally practice a real-world scenario?" Peter let an edge creep into his voice.

Medraut shuffled his feet. "Well, I guess so. Is this— modern? Is this how you do it in Sicambria?"

Peter raised his brows, surprised. Had they *never* heard of war games, maneuvers, situation training? *Perhaps there's hope for Artus yet, if I can train him quickly enough.*

Peter strode to the pile of weapons and armor. It was

smaller than he expected: mail, but no breastplates, greaves, or vambraces. Metal bands to surround the midriff. A leather cap, metal-banded. There were a few six- or seven-foot javelins without tips and a pair of edge-guarded axes. Two rectangular, curved shields looked heavy and uncomfortable. Peter looked in vain for the Roman-style *gladius* swords, short thrusting weapons that punched through armor like rifle rounds through a "bulletproof" vest.

He watched the young man closely. Medraut pulled the mail over his head, put his arms up, and jumped up and down a few times. It fell smoothly across his shoulders, not seeming as difficult as Peter had imagined. By copying the boy's motions, he assembled the pile of armor about his body with little trouble. The metal bands circled his chest and abdomen, secured by leather straps. Each man had to strap in the other.

Medraut apologized hesitantly. "I assumed you didn't want the breastplate, Sire. It's so valuable."

"Good thinking," said Peter.

The leather stank, the armor pinched uncomfortably, and Peter wished for the light, molded flak suits of the SAS. At last he stood, armored and accoutred. He approached one of the stallions. It was huge, broad-shouldered, a draft horse with a temper. It watched him malevolently.

He took hold of the bridle, and Medraut cleared his throat. "Sire," asked the boy, worried, "should we not each mount out *own* steeds?"

Whoops! Peter shot Medraut a withering stare, smoothly bent and pretended to inspect the saddle girth. "Nine out of ten riders unhorsed . . ." he tugged on the strap. "Right here, always check it twice." *Gee, it sounds convincing,* he thought; *Wonder if it's true?* The only thing Peter knew about horses was that they had four legs and left surprises for unwary hikers.

"All right, bring me ah . . ." Peter reached blindly for the other draft horse, snapped his fingers.

"Eponimius, Sire?"

"—my horse. Will you?" Medraut seized the enormous Eponimius by the bridle, dragged him to Peter. The war-horse first dug in his hooves, then bucked eagerly when he recognized Peter's scent. Medraut's steed tried to bite Peter's hand as the boy approached.

Peter took the reins from Medraut, stared Eponimius in the eye to plumb the depths of his horsey soul, as a horse-riding girlfriend once told him to do, though he had no idea why. The stallion stared dully back, unable to penetrate the disguise. Medraut loaded a pair of javelins and an axe into slots in Eponimius's saddle.

Peter realize he had not the slightest idea how to fight from horseback. He gingerly probed the closed-off part of his mind, hoping to let just enough Lancelot out of mental prison to access his body-memory for mounted combat techniques.

He *touched* the Sicambrian, was rewarded by an image of Lancelot riding Eponimius, javelin in the right hand, shield in the left, guiding the war-horse by knee pressure. He clamped the psychic lid shut before Lancelot could escape.

He circled to Eponimius's left flank, plucking images one at a time from Lance's jealous, reluctant consciousness, too quickly for the barbarian warrior to break free. It was dangerous work; Peter felt that if he once yielded control, he might find himself imprisoned and the original Lancelot back in control.

Would I even be able to return, then? he worried. If his mind was not his own, could he make contact? Or would he be stuck forever in the Dark Ages?

He finally arrived at his horse, discovered there were no stirrups. The saddle itself resembled neither an English saddle nor an American "wild-West" saddle. Long ridges burst from the sides where his legs should dangle. A high back forced the rider too far forward.

At least the damned thing has reins. But how the bloody hell do you get into it? Medraut was already mounted, waiting agitatedly; Peter had missed the chance to see how the lad did it. He sat nearly on the horse's shoulders, legs tucked back and locked along the underside of the ridges. The reins hung untouched. Medraut turned his horse left and right without using his hands or the reins, cantered across the grassy plain. His shield was held low, in a resting position.

Did Roman officers actually fight hand-to-hand? Peter could not remember. In any event, Artus may be Roman-trained, but he seemed to have some innovations of his own: flinging javelins from horseback, for example, if Medraut's boasting could be trusted. The Romans generally left horseback fighting to their barbarian archers.

Damn, I guess there's no option but to vault into the bloody saddle, armor and all.

He placed his right hand on Eponimius's rump, left clutching a grip on the front of the saddle. He firmly visualized the Sandhurst pommel horse and leapt, scissored his legs to either side of the stallion's back.

Eponimius snorted and shimmied sideways. Peter fell across the saddle, head on one side and legs on the other. He tried to squirm into position, but Eponimius chose that moment to do a little dance, spinning rapidly clockwise three or four times, almost throwing Peter from the saddle.

At last, the champion of Caer Camlann managed to throw himself forward and swing his leg across the saddle. Eponimius gave a halfhearted kick and finally settled down as Peter hooked his legs under the ridges.

Medraut was laughing. Peter glared at him like a drill sergeant staring down a cadet.

"Sorry, my Prince," said Medraut. "Tales are told about how much Eponimius dislikes being mounted, but I didn't realize the vehemence with which he expressed himself!"

"As you were, *temporary* Captain."

Peter imitated Medraut's posture, realized the high-backed saddle with leg locks was considerably less stable than a normal saddle with stirrups. Eponimius responded instantly to a leg press on either side, turning away from the pressure.

Medraut did not hold the reins in his hands, so Peter followed the young man's lead. Peter leaned forward, and Eponimius broke into a run. When he leaned back, the stallion slowed. Without the reins, both Peter's hands were free.

He reached down, plucked the shield from its mount, and slid it over his left forearm. It was smaller than he expected, and did not look at all like the shields in *Ivanhoe*.

With his right hand, he drew an edge-guarded, top-heavy battle-axe, swung it a few times experimentally. He almost fell from his perch. It was easy to strike downward, but hard to pull back up.

He replaced the axe and shield, turned back toward Medraut. With little work, he maneuvered next to him. Eponimius seemed to know what he wanted, responded almost before he gave the signal.

"Sire," asked Medraut, "did you, perhaps, revel a bit too hard last eve?" He sounded honestly concerned, not sarcastic.

Peter did not respond, gestured toward a forest about a half mile distant. "Take us to a clearing in there, son," he said.

They walked their horses to the first trees. Medraut pulled slightly ahead and wove westward toward a path. Another ten minutes brought them to a wide, circular sward. A marble fountain without flowing water decorated one end. Caer Camlann was invisible behind a stand of nearly bare oaks hung with huge clumps of mistletoe. Peter pronounced the site ideal.

They pulled steel caps over their heads, unfastened shields, and slid them into position. Medraut cantered to the far end of the sward, turned to face Peter, javelin in hand.

The boy raised the weapon in a salute, which Peter copied. The champion urged Eponimius into a charge, ready to take his lumps.

CHAPTER 24

CORS CANT STOOD AT HIS OWN WINDOW, SHIVERING IN THE CHILL breeze that blew across field and farm, city and castle. It raised fish scales on his bare skin. The sunrise blinded him with red and yellow, magnified by bright water sparkles from the east wing fountain. It reminded him of Anlawdd's hair.

"How do I win you, my love?"

In Cors Cant's imagination, she stood behind him, ran gossamer fingers down his spine. *I'm not a prize to be carried off by the throw of a pair of amber dice! Honestly, I don't know who is more the brute—Cutha, who takes women by force, or a certain young boy from Londinium who practices tricks and strategems upon innocent waiting-maids!*

He turned, hoping to see her, dreading being seen. Anlawdd's *animus* stood between Cors Cant and the crook-

brass mirror. A translucent phantasm of a girl, and through it
he saw his own reflection: short and stocky, almost graceful,
but never a fighter. What did half-a-bard have to offer, besides nine and ten years of a sheltered life?

Well, continued the voluble shade, *you could offer me love,
if that's not too much of a conceptual leap, Cors Cant Ewin.*
The imagined voice was so real, he jumped guiltily.

"Why the hell does everyone speak inside my head anymore?" he demanded.

*Hmp. I'm not everyone, and I'm not speaking to you, re-
member? Just offering suggestions for any court bards who
happen to be listening. Find me if you want, and I'll let you
apologize.*

No, merely the east wind ruffling a gauzy curtain. A
cloudy mirror reflected bent specters of his heart. "All right,
I'll apologize, Anlawdd. I'm *sorry* you're stuck up, arrogant,
and a tease! Happy?"

A laugh from the door startled him. He gasped, turned too
quickly, and stumbled.

Anlawdd stood in the doorway, this time real as the pig
droppings that speckled her boots. "Why Cors Cant! You *do*
have wit after all, at least when talking to an empty room!"

"I wasn't . . . I mean I didn't—"

"I came to ask you—I mean tell you to ask *me* to go riding
with you, and also to offer you a chance to apologize, but I'll
accept that last apology as genuine. So all that remains is the
horse question. Well?"

"Y-yes! I'd love to go riding with you! Where are we going? How can you get away, anyway?" Cors Cant suddenly
realized the terrible flaw in the plan. "Anlawdd, I haven't any
horse!"

She held up her hand, ticked off fingers as she answered
his questions. "To a secret place; because Princess Gwynhwfyr gave me the day free when I told her why; we'll rent
you one; and I stepped in it on my way to the privy. Now,
I don't want to be critical, and I don't know what the rules
are for court bards, but you'll probably want to throw some
clothes on—at least for comfort's sake. Will midday be soon
enough for you?"

Stunned to silence, Cors Cant merely nodded. He realized
to his horror that he was clad only in a thin nightshirt.

"Good. South gate. Not the one by the stadium, the other one. I'll liberate a lunch, if Cook's still passed out from the revel. I do hope you'll bring an appetite."

He suddenly noticed a very familiar stain on her otherwise spotless boots. "But how did you get pig droppings on your—?"

Not listening, Anlawdd turned with regal dignity, the effort marred only by a slight giggle. She vanished, leaving Cors Cant breathless and confused.

"I ... I love you," he said, long after she had left.

CHAPTER 25

THE GLOW HAD NOT FULLY SUBSIDED FROM THE WIRE MESH PLAT-form when Mark Blundell ran forward, ducked under the mass of electromagnetic netting, and got his arms underneath Peter's and locked across his chest. Three minutes exactly had elapsed since they had initiated the field, the barest time interval, no safety factor.

God help us we're early, prayed Blundell.

The world tilted forty-five degrees from the plane of Blundell's ecliptic. He braced his heels and heaved, but it seemed that Brother Smythe was nailed to the floor.

Or perhaps Mark was just losing strength from the residual field. Outside the webbing, a strange group of people gestured, shouting silently. The laboratory scene faded, along with the pseudoforest.

He strained again, this time managed to move Peter slightly.

What felt almost like a blow to his head knocked him backward. He turned a nearly complete flip on the way down, at least according to his inner ear. Blinked again, was Mark Blundell in the basement lab again.

With a final jerk, he staggered out of the field focus, Peter Smythe in tow. Some force resisted, as if he pushed through a wall of molasses, electromagnetic fields tugging at his molecular structure.

He strained to drag Peter backward, finally popping through a phantom tree that grew between the doughnut coils and the basement floor. The forest timeline had returned, more corporeal, more real with every moment.

Mark's skin burned painfully from passing through the field boundary.

He sat down, trying to catch his breath. Hamilton slid Peter's empty body next to Selly's. Mark leaned back, watched disinterested, uncomprehending at old Willks, wild white hair sticking out like the *Long-Haired King*. Willks directed a spray of white foam from a red cylinder onto the coil generation box, which crackled with merry flames.

Who the hell is the Long-Haired King? Blundell's brain finally rebooted. "Christ, it's on fire!" he shouted.

"Oh, you're back with us?" rumbled Willks, putting the fire extinguisher back on the floor. "A more accurate observation would be, *'Christ, it used to be on fire.'* "

Jacob Hamilton strolled through a deadfall of branches without interacting. He knelt next to Smythe, felt his pulse, and listened to his respirations. Blundell cleared his throat, not wanting to disturb him. "Is . . . he going to be all right? Jacob?"

"Don't know," said Hamilton without looking up. "Just a medic, not a doctor. Pulse is weak and thready, respirations shallow. Temperature way up. If I didn't already know what was wrong, I'd say he needs a doctor."

"Well let's call for an ambulance!" Mark shouted before realizing his mistake. The mind-to-brain uplink was local; the body could not be removed more than about twenty feet from the coils. "All right, let's bring the doctor here."

Hamilton shook his head. "Can't do anything. The connection between Major Smythe's brain and his mind is partially severed. Explain that to a Brighton intern."

"Severed?" Blundell's skin felt clammy. If the connection were completely severed, Peter could never be pulled back into his body. The body would either die, or fall into a persistent vegetative state—"cabbaging," as Hamilton called it.

"Not quite cut," said a subdued Jacob. "Not all the way through, Mark. Look." Jacob Hamilton nodded toward the PET scan monitor: Blundell saw the tiny, brilliant white tear-

drop that indicated a consciousness connection; it was de-
formed, the tail shriveled like a carrot peeling. A small window in the upper left corner of the monitor showed the other
teardrop, Selly's consciousness, on a smaller scale. Unlike
Peter's, hers was fully formed and smooth.

The doorbell rang. After a moment, Wilson, the butler, appeared at the head of the stairs.

"Colonel Cooper, Strategic Air Services," he announced.

Every eye in the room turned toward the fat, uniformed
man descending the stairs. Cooper surveyed the tableau.
"What in God's blue heaven is going *on* here?" he demanded.

There was an uncomfortable silence. Finally, Willks coughed.
"You *would* insist upon an explanation, wouldn't you?"

CHAPTER 26

MEDRAUT HURLED HIS POINTLESS JAVELIN, CONNECTED HARD
against Peter's shoulder. Peter reeled in the saddle. He
barely righted himself, sorely wished for a nice pair of stirrups. At the far end of the run he leaned back in the saddle,
and Eponimius halted and turned. His own throw had sailed
over Medraut's head.

Peter's heart beat wildly, and his shoulder was numb. Boxing at Sandhurst told him what he had done wrong—he had
not "punched out" with his shield against Medraut's javelin,
instead letting it sail past unmolested. He visualized a real
javelin, buried deep in his chest like a bullet—falling—
Eponimius trampling him underfoot. *Forget it! Do your duty!
Forget Londonderry, where the car—*

They charged once more, hurled their last remaining sticks
at each other. Peter missed wide, but at least he managed to
intercept Medraut's deadly throw with his shield.

Medraut continued his pass, stopping his horse at the edge
of the clearing. He quickly dismounted, axe and shield in

hand. Peter did the same at the other end. They would continue the fight on foot.

Medraut sprinted forward eagerly. This time Peter let his mind go on holiday, allowing Lancelot's body to react as it "remembered." Risky, but if Peter continued to try to take charge, he would be munching grass.

Medraut swung his axe. Peter jerked his left fist toward the haft of Medraut's axe to catch the blow on the edge of his tiny shield. He dangled his own axe, then windmilled it over his head, blindsided Medraut.

The lad ducked forward. Peter lost his balance trying to follow, and toppled face forward into the grass. His face gouged a nice divot out of the soil, as he predicted.

He climbed shakily to all fours, then to his feet. "G-good, you already know the basics," he complimented, spitting out dirt.

"Prince Lancelot, can we please progress to something a bit more complex? I'm not ungrateful, but I've already had *some* training."

"Quite right. Testing your, um, level of expertise. Let's continue."

They circled warily. Peter discovered that far from being unwieldy, as he first thought, the axe was well balanced and quick, even for fighting on foot. Swinging sideways rather than striking down, the center of mass was high enough for real reach, low enough for fast recovery.

The shield gave him trouble until he ignored it, pretended it was nothing but his arm. When Peter blocked the "punch" of Medraut's blow, the shield knocked the boy's axe aside.

With two swift blows Peter took the fight to Medraut. The boy's face lost its earnest desire to please, shifted to intense concentration. He was *busy*. Medraut swung too hard, too high. Peter ducked, old training resurfacing from fifteen hundred years hence.

He dug a foot into the sod, whirled 360 degrees to land a bootheel on the boy's temple, a perfect spin-kick. Medraut, his skullcap, and his axe parted company. The boy staggered, fell heavily.

Thank God we weren't wearing full helms! thought Peter.

He fought an impulse to rush to the prone body and take his pulse, another to raise the axe high and bury it in Medraut's skull. Swallowing the urge to greater violence, he stiffened and drove the savage Lancelot deep, deep within once more.

Medraut moaned, climbed laboriously to hands and knees, and shook his head. He picked up his helm, fingered the dent across the right temple.

"Sire, I . . ." He shook his head again, tried to blink the sparks from his eyes. "Sire, what the Hades did you *hit* me with?"

"My right boot, Captain. Do you want to see it again?"

"No! I mean no, Sire. Your boot? But that's impossible!" Medraut stared at the dent. "On . . . on second thought, it were a wondrous blow, Prince Lancelot." He stood unsteadily, eyes still unfocused.

"I think I've had—had enough for today. Sire." He almost left without his axe until Peter pointed it out. Medraut made no attempt to mount. He led his horse back toward Caer Camlann.

Bloody damn, thought Peter, pleased with himself for the first time since landing in the pages of Malory. *Maybe I shouldn't worry too much about Cutha?*

He flexed his arm, marveling at Lancelot's powerful muscles and delicate balance, honed by a lifetime of brutal axework, dozens of campaigns. *And yes, Miss Selly bloody Corwin, you too are going to get one* hell *of a nasty surprise! Soon as I sort you out from the chaff.*

Peter sheathed his axe, retrieved their javelins, and mounted Eponimius as gracelessly as the last time. He rode back toward the villa.

CHAPTER 27

AFRAID TO WASTE A MOMENT OF HIS PROMISED TIME WITH Anlawdd, Cors Cant rushed to dress. Remembering her mania regarding cleanliness, he washed three times and made sure there were no stray pig droppings. Beneath his arms he spread scented paraffin, lifted from Cei's room when the porter last addressed the Senate.

Cors Cant raced to the south gate (not the stadium gate) by third chime, but Anlawdd herself did not arrive until noon.

She wore happier colors than at the feast. Her tunic was off-white, nearly a cream color. A speck of a seafoam green chemise peeked out from beneath it. Yet this modesty was contradicted by the bottom of the tunic, cut short in the style of her wild, Celtic people, exposing strong, shapely legs, burned slightly pink. The pig droppings were gone.

Neither Celt nor Roman, marveled the bard, heart aching. Three small forest green dragons spotted her tunic. She was richly dressed for a seamstress, worthy of the equestrian class or a magistrate's sister.

Gods, I wonder if she "borrowed" the clothes from Gwynhwfyr? Cors Cant looked quickly left and right, assuring himself that no one was close enough to see her clothing and report her.

"Ready?" she asked sprightly. Cors Cant nodded, still worried about her tunic.

"I have something for you," she continued. "A present. A sacrament, actually." She pulled a tiny jar from her bag, uncorked it. She extracted something that looked like dried meat and put it in his hand. He stared at it, realized it was an unknown mushroom.

The bard sniffed. No odor. "Do I eat it?"

"As if it were my flesh," she said with a mystery smile.

He started to put it in his mouth, but she stopped him with a hand on his arm. "Do you trust me?"

"I do," he answered quickly. Too quickly.

"Caterpillars turn to butterflies," she said, releasing his arm. "That's their magic. Tadpoles turn to frogs. But we people have to swallow our magic before making our transformations. Just bear that in mind, Cors Cant Ewin, bard-in-training."

He waited a long time. His stomach tightened; the implication was clear: it was a potion he held in his hand, a chewable cantrip. How much did he *really* trust her?

She watched, impassive, giving no clue to her thoughts. *Foolish bard,* he accused himself, *so frightful of knowledge!*

Did Gwydion hesitate before tasting the potion of speech and understanding?

He jammed the dried mushroom in his mouth, chewed as best he could. It tasted like leather, grew bitter with his saliva. He swallowed and nearly gagged.

Leaning forward, Anlawdd kissed his forehead quickly, a sisterly peck. "Let's go get the horses," she suggested.

They walked across the *circus maximus,* down the hill, and intersected Via Flavius Valentinianus, a graded road which had been Via Vortigernus until twenty years before, when Vortigern brought Saxon mercenaries to Kent and turned the world upside down.

Even streets tell stories, mused Cors Cant. Anlawdd put her hand on his shoulder. He gasped at her touch, and she laughed. *Where is my mind? Anlawdd's legs are worth a myriad dead Vortigerns, he and his funeral pyre a twelvemonth cold!*

They passed through a whitewashed, undecorated north gate, the Triumph Gate, and entered Camlann proper. The sun reflected from the white concrete, dazzling Cors Cant Ewin.

In his years at Caer Camlann, the bard had managed to avoid most areas of the city itself, preferring only the palace, the baths, and the library. Myrddin did not encourage students to sample city life.

Now Anlawdd walked him along streets he had walked but not traveled, past shops he had noted but never noticed. She held his hand, pointed out each building, and told its story. Cors Cant stared in amazement at the Camlann he had never seen.

"Look!" she cried, amazed. "See how each *insula* or city square is crossed by many winding paths, traces of ancient roads from long before you built these arrow-straight, Roman monstrosities!" She spoke as if she, too, saw it for the first time. "Now I do admit I admire roads that never turn aside for minor impediments like mountains or oceans, but surely you see how *these* roads hug and caress the curves of Rhiannon's earth? That's worth something at least, if I'm not wrong, and I'm never wrong, Cors Cant.

"You've been to the baths, I'm sure," she asked. "The real ones, not the private baths in the villa."

"Yes, of course. It's where I met Brigantia."

"In the *baths?*" Anlawdd did not sound offended, just incredulous.

"No, just outside." Cei had once told him women were intrigued by another woman's intrigue. Cors Cant had mooned after the older Brigantia for three weeks, playing love songs under her window, until her brothers ran him off.

"Hmp. Well, the less said about *her,* the better," sniffed Anlawdd. "She's not here now, is she? Then attend to me for a change. Did you ever wonder at this unmarked building next to the baths?"

"Um . . . no." He stared at the smooth, unpainted, concrete walls. It was clearly a public work but displayed no clue of its function.

"It's the main pump for the plumbing. If you don't pay your rates, that's where they shut you off."

"Rates?"

"Water rates. Oh, forgive me, I forgot. You've always lived in Caer Camlann, and Artus isn't likely to shut off his own water!"

"You have to pay for water?"

She rolled her eyes in amused disgust, towed him along Via Valentinianus, then ducked onto a smaller street. He caught a sign painted on an apartment building: Vicus Ætheopae, Street of Ethiopians. The apartments looked deserted.

Soon they skirted the back of a very large, curved building. "Do you know what this is?" asked Anlawdd. "You've been here a hundred times, I'm sure."

"Um . . . oh! It's the amphitheater, isn't it?" He had never seen the back. Artus and his court always entered from Via Romulus in the front.

"Good!" She squeezed his hand, and he felt warm sunlight, though the sky was streaked with clouds. She chattered: "I watched a pantomime here last week. I saw you with Myrddin in Artus's box, but they don't let seamstresses into the consul seats, so I stayed where I was. This is the slaves' entrance, actually."

"Anlawdd, I could have gotten you in!"

"You could?"

"Artus dotes on bards. He grants any minor boon we seek."

"Well, you could have told me! There I was, sweating in the sun among smelly fishmongers and drunken teamsters, and all the time I could have been eating apples and drinking wine with the *Dux Bellorum!*"

"Well how was I to know you were there?"

"Some people could have used their eyes, Cors Cant Ewin."

They turned into an alley that reeked of urine accumulated for years. He gagged, pinched his nose shut. "Serves you right," she observed, still annoyed.

The alley debouched onto one of the Roman roads that divided the city into *insulae,* which the unimaginative Britons called the "blocks," just as in Rome itself. Anlawdd continued the tour, leading eventually, he supposed, to a public stable where they could rent horses, or perhaps a chariot, if it were not too dear.

The sun found another hole in the clouds. Brilliant, whitewashed apartments flashed like Apollo's chariot. From the glare, the bard barely picked out painted lions and eagles, intricate designs of tile and crushed rock.

One street was wide enough for four chariots, the next so narrow he stretched his arms and brushed rough, unfinished walls on both sides. "Where is this?" he asked.

"Via Bonadomina, the oldest street in Caer Camlann. Cors Cant, haven't you lived here all your life?"

"No," he admitted, "I grew up in Londinium, Lludd-Dun you would say. That was where the magical head of Blessed Bran was buried, after the seven survivors of the Eire-land war feasted seven years in your own town of Harlech, followed by eighty years in Gwales."

"I do know my own history, Cors Cant."

"So we're connected, don't you see? They feasted in your birth town, then buried the head in mine. Mystically, that means we're the same—"

"Why did you leave Lludd-Dun?"

"My family was . . ." Cors Cant quickly stopped himself. This was not the proper note to strike in this tune. "Well, suffice to say the Saxons came. Horsa's men, backed by that bastard Vortigern." Defender, hero, he turned the world upside down, brought the butchering Saxons in to . . .

Anlawdd spoke quietly, without looking up. "I have no cause to love Vortigern. We lived under his rule until ten years ago, when the *Pan-Draconis* returned from Rome. He did . . . I don't even like to think about what Vortigern did."

"That was a long time ago," continued Cors Cant. "I met

Lancelot then, and Artus. Lancelot was legate of the legions that recaptured Londinium."

Anlawdd spoke as if Cors Cant were not even there. "I, um, ran away shortly after my—shortly after Prince Gormant retook the throne. I've not been back."

The bard's memory of the sacking of Londinium was vivid red. It burned bright before his eyes, like the white walls would burn at sunset. He shaded his eyes, turned away from the light. "I had nowhere else to go. I came here with Myrddin and the *Dux Bellorum* to become a bard."

"So we're both exiles from ourselves. Strangers in barbarous Arcadia." She touched the back of his hand, a slight brush of her fingers. But it was deliberate. Again, Cors Cant stiffened as if stuck by a needle. "That's an even closer connection than Bran's Blessed Head, wouldn't you say, Court Bard? Let's turn here. Before you even ask, this street has no name, and is *not* one of the oldest in Camlann."

The lane she indicated was not even officially a street. The residents along it had simply cleared vegetation, tossed stones along the side, and raked the soil smooth. The bard became fascinated by the scrunching sound his boots made on the crusty dirt, dried but still untouched from the rains of yesterday's yestereve. Anlawdd's doeskin boots, barely taller than her ankles (and clean), were nearly silent.

A small stream trickled through a wide, rock-strewn riverbed, cutting their path. It washed across the smaller, British streets, but when it came to a Roman road, it dived beneath through sewer holes, lapping pleasantly.

Cors Cant became lost in its laughter. Fragments of a song suggested themselves. He tried to remember where he had heard it.

Gods, it's hot. During spring and summer, the stream became a river, Bran's Tears, and filled the wide bed. He wiped sweat from his face, swiveling his head left and right to stare curiously at the buildings as Anlawdd pointed them out.

"The bright red shop made of mud and plaster is a kitchen owned by Matthew ben Duvid of Judea. He joined the army and fought all over the world, Algiers to Athens to Constantinople ... well, perhaps 'fought' is too strong a word, since he's a cook and didn't kill anybody so far as I know, though if you've ever tasted his *anas fluvialis cum eliquamen cerasum,* which he claims comes directly from Apicius, you might wonder how the troops survived. Matthew's kitchen is a wonderful place to eat, if you're coinless, hungry, and not too particular."

Cors Cant sniffed; they were not cooking. *Of course,* he realized. *It's Saturn's Day, the Judean sabbath.*

"Oh, and across the road is a tanner and cobbler who makes wonderful riding boots, Sean Greasaf from Eire. The cream-colored cottage with the fake Ægyptian glyphs next to the white engineers' office."

"They're not fake," said the bard dreamily. "The sequence doesn't mean anything, but they are real Ægyptian glyphs."

"You know that?"

"Um-hm."

"Really? I wonder where he got the designs?" Hot in the sun, she drew her hair back and tied it behind her neck with a ribbon from inside her shirt.

"Red as the fire of Prometheus is your hair," he sallied, ever hopeful. "Scarlet plumage, like the Bird of Paradise. . . ."

"It's *auburn,* Cors Cant Ewin. Isn't poor observation a disadvantage in your profession? Next to Sean is Thermos the Greek's Chemistry, which is where I got the you-know-what that you ate. He has cold eyes, like a marble statue brought to life, and sends chills up my back when he appears suddenly without a noise and asks you what you want in his shop. I always jump five feet and bang my head against his roof when he does that."

The Chemistry was unpainted, left the original reddish brown of dried mud. From the street, Cors Cant stared through the doorway. He saw walls blackened with smoke, lined with shelf upon shelf of bottles, jars, bowls of powder, human skulls.

An ancient skeleton missing its left arm was propped behind a desk in a lifelike pose. Anlawdd gestured with her hand, and the skeleton jerked upright.

Cors Cant nearly jumped out of his skin. He blinked and stared. The skeleton resolved itself into a wizened old man, at least fifty or fifty-five years old. Thermos's cadaverous pallor and sunken cheeks had produced the illusion of bare bones. He brought his left arm from behind his back, where he had been scratching between his shoulder blades.

Shuddering with nameless dread, the boy hurried along the street behind Anlawdd. Something about Thermos bothered him out of all proportion.

"I can't believe you've lived here for years, yet never even seen the city within a city!" She watched the boy, waited for an answer.

"Well, I'm a bard of the tower, not of the town," he explained feebly, as if that answered all charges.

"Well for goodness' sake, I'm a seamstress to Gwynhwfyr, which involves *many* more duties than barding about at feasts and games, and *I've* explored Camlann from Senate to faerie mounds to *circus maximus,* a hundred byways like this one in the few weeks I've been here. Sometimes I think bards have no curiosity about the world they live in, none at all! Do you sit in a warm *tepidarium* all day and compose lays about Trojan heroes?"

Cors Cant cringed, unable to marshal his thoughts to rebut her argument. *It's because she's right, you ass,* he told himself. He suddenly stopped, struck by the blueness of the Camlann sky; he stared directly upward in astonishment.

Anlawdd stumbled into him. "What in the three worlds are you *looking* at, Cors Cant?"

"I . . . I never noticed how sky it was before," he breathed. *How sky it was?* "I mean, I never noticed . . ." He trailed off, unable to translate the brilliant revelation into mere words. Behind him, Anlawdd chuckled knowingly, and gently pushed him onward.

She threaded between huts and shops, merchants and soldiers, pigs, sheep, and slaves, around the occasional Roman-designed building, saluting the unexpected senator or knight, and wound by a spacious track of circumambulation back to an ancient, round house of dried mud, plastered and painted bright blue and green, interlaced with complex knotwork designs. Behind the house was a corral containing four horses, the gate tied by a leather thong.

There were no windows: the commoner the folk, the less Roman and more British they were. Anlawdd took him by the hand to the door and pounded on the wooden frame.

A huge, burly man with a black beard and leather apron yanked the curtain aside. Cors Cant stared. The man's beard was so long he actually tucked it into his belt.

"Don't want any," he grumped, started to leave.

"Joff!" snapped Anlawdd, stamping the ground. "Have you forgotten my Merillwyn so quickly?"

"Your what?" interrupted Cors Cant.

The giant stared, combed his hair back with one leather-gauntleted hand. "Oh, you. You want her?"

"And another, if you can spare one."

"Warbred?"

"Don't be a silly! We're not riding to war, just a country picnic. See?" Anlawdd held up her bag as if the man could see inside it. *Well at least he ought to smell the lunch,* thought Cors Cant. The odor of pork roast was quite strong.

"Hm. Right, one horse to rent, one day, three *milliarensi.*"

Anlawdd nodded. "Pay the man," she said to Cors Cant.

"Me?"

"Cors Cant, would you rather trot beside me while I ride?"

The boy fished into his pouch, found his entire treasure of five coins and extracted three. Three coins it had taken weeks to cajole from the Camlann crowds!

The man studied the silvery pieces. "Constantine?" he asked, hopefully.

"Well . . . almost," lied the boy. "Magnus Maximus, Macsen Wledig, I'm told." In truth, the coins were probably local counterfeits. Imperial mints rarely misspelled the emperor's name as "Mixamus." Joff grunted and shoved the coins into his shirt without further examination. *Probably can't read anyway,* thought Cors Cant.

Joff led them around the hut to the corral and pointed at a shaggy, gentle-looking pony, native rather than imported.

"All right for you," declared Anlawdd. She untied the gate, stepped gingerly to a larger, shorthaired horse, a vicious-looking mare.

She stared it down. It nickered and nuzzled her cheek. As Cors Cant watched, the horse wavered for a moment, flickered like a blown candle flame. He shook his head; the vision cleared, but his stomach slithered and twisted, snakelike.

Joff disappeared, reemerged from the hut with two saddles. "One millie for yours," he said to Cors Cant.

"Another one?" The boy's heart dropped.

"Don't you listen to him!" interjected Anlawdd. "Tack comes with the horse, everyone knows that!"

"Fine," said the horseman, "then *you* strap it." He threw both saddles down in the mud, stormed away. The equipment was jumbled into one large pile.

"Cors Cant, you do know how to saddle a horse, don't you? Joff doesn't have any slaves. If you need help I can—"

"I think I can manage," he sniffed. It took very little work. His rented pony was docile enough and not too tall. Even so, Anlawdd finished long before he did. He tried not to let it bother him when she recinched his girth. *Why am I suddenly so shirt-tempered? I mean short-tempered . . . .*

He hopped onto the pony, slid forward, and locked his legs. Anlawdd mounted in a single, smooth leap, as though equestrian-born, though her horse stood at least eighteen hands. "Are you ready for travel, Cors Cant Ewin? It's not far."

"Lead on, Auburnious One! I'm at your service."

"How gallant. Are you stable?"

Odd she would ask. He felt wobbly, if truth were told. Instead, he smiled and nodded.

She smiled back, used her own mare to nudge his shaggy pony into a walk. As she passed, he saw a wicked battle-axe sheathed by her side, but he said nothing. There was no law against women carrying axes, though it was an odd adornment for a seamstress.

They walked the horses past the last, outlying house, as old-fashioned and Celtic as could be. They followed Via Camlann west for half a league, then Anlawdd cut off onto a winding hillpath. The high-built palace was quickly lost behind groves of barren oak, ash, aspen, and linden.

Cors Cant stayed behind Her, struck dumb by Her beauty. He watched Her muscles flex beneath Her tunic, stared longingly at Her bare legs, as She coaxed or patted the mare. Anlawdd's hair flowed behind like the autumn leaves surrounding them, just turning for fall. Pulling alongside, he discovered he could glimpse Her right breast through the tunic's armhole with every flutter of the chemise. He slid a bit farther forward in the saddle.

Anlawdd looked back, caught his eye. She smiled for an instant, neither imperious nor commanding, just happy. Cors Cant's chest swelled with pride that a woman like *Her* would ask him to ride!

"What's your horse's name?" he asked.

"I told you once."

"When? You did not!" *Heresy—thou shalt not contradict the Lady thy goddess. . . .*

"Learning to listen is the first lesson," She said, maddeningly. "Does the name *Merillwyn* pluck a chord?"

"No." *Yes.*

"Never heard it before?"

"Never." *Mayhap—did I? did she?*

"As you wish. Hi!"

She leaned forward across Merillwyn's neck, urged the mare into a gallop. Cors Cant shook his reins, *hi'ed* and *g'yupped* until his own rental finally sped to a fast canter, apparently its top speed.

The words were conciliatory, but Cors Cant was sure he detected faint mockery. *Had* She told him? He ducked under a low-hung clump of mistletoe. The name did sound slightly familiar.

She slowed to a walk, far from Camlann's spying eyes. Eventually, the bard caught Her, like Rhiannon, by calling *Anlawdd! Anlawdd!* until She relented and slowed Her pace. "I love a good run," She said. Cors Cant waited for more, but She rode in silence.

The path wound through the forest. Holly and mistletoe graced the branches, hung like old men's beards. Thorns and thistles lined the well-kept road, and Cors Cant smelled new-mown hay, though no farm was in sight.

"Roses, heather bells, sage, and strawberries, can't you see them, Cors Cant Ewin? Or smell them? Of course, they're not here now, but in a summer past or to come they'd be thick as the snow in winter, drench your nose like spring rains drench your tunic. Of course it is, don't be melodramatic."

"Is it safe to travel so far west?" he asked, more to continue the conversation than out of fear.

"Because of Saxons? Of course it is, as I just said if you'd been listening. Don't be dramatic. They're back East, in Wessex. Branwen's grace, I journeyed all the way to Camlann from Harlech on my own when I ran away from my father. I think I can protect you as well as I protected myself."

"I don't need protection! Anyway, I'm the man—I'm supposed to protect *you.*"

Anlawdd chuckled. "As you wish . . . Centurion." *So what*

does a seamstress want with a war axe? he wondered, again finding no answer. Cors Cant carried a knife that might skin a deer, but it would never peel an armored Saxon. He scanned the branches for Saxons waiting to spring upon their heads.

Perhaps an axe to chop a tree, Cors Cant. He jumped— had She actually spoken, or had he imagined an imaginary answer to his imaginary question?

He felt queer—heart pounding, skin clammy. Every sound started him, the gentlest breeze an all-dragon's breath. He jumped in the saddle, said "What? what?" Anlawdd watched him enigmatically. She had said nothing but smiled like Livia, wife of the divine Augustus.

They rode almost a league in silence. Cors Cant heard the *lap-lap* of a nearby stream, dancing between tangled root and gnarled bole. The fish whispered lies and flattery on the breeze.

Anlawdd spoke quietly, voice gentle as river water. "Cors Cant . . . this is a difficult question to ask, and I'll certainly understand if you don't want to answer. I mean I won't take offense, knowing how you feel about Artus, *Pan-Draconis, Dux Bellorum,* et cetera."

The boy nudged his pony closer to Anlawdd. Merillwyn jerked her head, baring teeth at the intruder. Anlawdd calmly seized the reins, brought her under control. "Lancelot is the most beloved, and I don't want to cast aspersions. But haven't you noticed something queer about him lately? I mean since yesterday. He doesn't seem . . . doesn't seem himself, like a girl after her first blood."

The sky blued, bluer than the deepest azure of Myrddin's watery eyes. "A stranger in Arcadia," whispered the boy.

"What's the expression I'm looking for, that describes Lancelot perfectly?" She turned suddenly in the saddle, face a mask of concern. *"What* did you say? Where did you hear that phrase, a stranger in Arcadia? And why are you answering before I ask the question?"

"From you, dear one."

"Me! I've never used it in my life."

"Like Myrddin," recited Cors Cant, "who once pondered what it would be like to live backwards."

"Wait, which question are you answering now? Or haven't I asked it yet?"

"From grave to womb, losing wisdom as he gains strength,

looking ahead to a frightening, backward crawl up his mother's vagina."

"Back to Lancelot. Do you think it's because of Merovius? I heard a rumor Lancelot once tried to kill him, though I wouldn't class the rumormonger as the most reputable source. Out of the merest idle curiosity, where did you hear about *Arcadia,* by the way?" Her last question sounded too casual by half.

"Hm. Your rumormonger spoke truth. Merovee told us himself. He didn't seem upset about the attempt. And it's classical, a kingdom in the middle of the ancient Greek lands of Peloponnesus. Sent an army to the Trojan War. Lancelot and I were just discussing Arcadia, I'm not sure why."

"Yes, well Merovee's a queer piglet too. Always gives me the most uncomfortable feeling I'm a scroll he's slowly unrolling, reading every line!"

"Always? You've met him before?"

"Yes, well, let's not get into it. No, *this* Arcadia is in Sicambria. But if you get lost in Sicambria, you can end up in Alban, so they say, which doesn't seem reasonable to me, since you'd have to stumble across the Channel without wetting your britches."

Cors Cant laughed at the picture. "You have a way with words for a stitching maid!" She smiled, and rainbows sparkled up and down Her hair. *Is it that wrinkled mushroom potion taking hold?*

"What, Bard, do you think I've spent *all* my days sewing other people's tunics?"

"I guess I never thought about it before. What *did* you do in Harlech? Why did you leave? And why cross so many leagues alone, without brother or husband?"

Anlawdd sighed, placed Her hands on Merillwyn's rump, and leaned back. "I don't know what I should tell you, Cors Cant Ewin. I don't . . . now don't take this the wrong way, but I really don't know you well enough yet."

She smiled at the memory. "Before I can answer your questions, I'd have to love you, or at least be *in love* with you, which is different. I haven't reached that act of the play yet, sorry to say."

Seeing his crestfallen face, She hastened to add, "But don't give up hope! There's every possibility that I *will* love you someday, or at least it's not out of the question. Or at least I can't positively rule it out of order."

They rode in silence. Cors Cant was consumed—*Anlawdd, faerie queen of Camlann!* He nerved himself to reach out, touch Her gently, but had not quite courage enough. His arms shrank to mere cabbages of their former selves.

"A hidden glen," she mused.

"Where do we ride?" he asked, hoping She would not notice his arms.

"To a hidden glen, where a cave sheltered me the night before I found Camlann."

"You stayed the night in the wild, so close to the villa?"

"Now think rationally, Cors Cant Ewin; how did *I* know how close I was? Besides, what's wrong with sleeping in a state of nature? I ride here sometimes even now to sleep naked against the cool, mossy tree trunks, feel Mother Rhiannon's tiny fingers caress me. I thought it would be a perfect place for us to get to know each other better, or at least for me to get to know *you.*"

"Anlawdd! Do you mean it?" Involuntarily, he grabbed Her arm. She did not pull away. *And I have arms again!* he exulted.

"I certainly hope you don't plan on frustrating me again, Cors Cant, because it's the most irritating thing I can think of, to get all excited and anxious and then be popped like a soap bubble pricked by a needle. It's like getting up early for Yule and finding no presents by the log!"

"Me? But it was *you* who didn't want . . ."

She closed Her eyes, Her ears. He *thought* he saw the same need and love as he felt himself. Then his perception shifted, and She just toyed with him. He sighed, irresolute. "Well I didn't hear anything," he griped.

Suddenly, Anlawdd stiffened, looked suspiciously at the woods around them. "Did you hear something? I didn't hear anything. . . ." After a moment, She added "There—I didn't hear it again. There's something wrong."

Anlawdd drew Her axe (though no tree stood near enough to chop), rested it across Her Merillwyn's neck. She eyed the bracken and thickly wooded hillocks suspiciously.

A strange horse whinnied.

It emerged from behind a stand of trees, a war-horse ridden by a short, powerful bandit wearing Jutic cloth and mail.

Blackness exuded from his mailed bulk, a cloud of ink expanding in a pool. He moved directly in front of them on the road, a hundred paces away.

Cors Cant heard another noise behind them. Two more well-armed men blocked escape toward Camlann. Anlawdd ignored them, attention riveted upon the man in front, almost as if She recognized him as some long-lost brother.

Her face was whiter than normal—*if he's a brother, he's not her favorite,* thought the bard.

The bandit grinned crookedly, a scrubbed and richly clad Barbary ape, then raised his double-bladed axe in mocking salute. He spoke Irish, a bastardized version from the far north. Cors Cant knew the language, for he had studied a year at the Druid College in Dun Laoghaire.

"Well, well, well! Fortuitous we meet on such a lovely day, *Princess Anlawdd.* Boys, give a greet and merry-meet to Sis and her new slave!"

CHAPTER 28

TERRIFIED, CORS CANT FUMBLED FOR HIS SUPPER KNIFE. HE looked at Anlawdd.

Anlawdd? A princess? She sat astride Merillwyn, regal as Artus himself. Unarmored, she curled her lip at the rider, let her ax hang toward the ground in full view. She carried no bow, no javelin, nothing to use without dismounting.

"Canastyr," she hissed, then continued, speaking the same peculiar Irish dialect. "So the earthworm turneth. What are you doing here? Does your father know you're out?"

"I came for *you,* my heart." A calculating coldness in Canastyr's voice made Cors Cant shiver, breath catching in his throat. Canastyr was no courtier, come to tempt his love away by sweet pastry and zephyr words. The young man continued.

"My limitless love for you drew me hither—that, and a

charge from Father to see how you fared in your quest. Er, you *do* remember the quest, don't you?" Canastyr curled his lip in what only the most charitable could call a smile. "Or have you forgotten so quickly, in the arms of your new eunuch, how it feels to be split by a great blade? Perhaps you need reminding."

Anlawdd stiffened, fury dancing just below her skin like a myriad burrowing insects. Cors Cant sat frozen; he knew some memory had flickered between his seamstress and this Canastyr—her brother?—but it was a signal sent to her ears alone.

"Canastyr," she said, voice sharp as a needle, "you make three errors: first, you followed me to Caer Camlann; that was your first."

She nudged Merillwyn forward, approached Canastyr briskly. Far to the south, low thunder grumbled like the bulls of CuChulainn of Eire. Clouds gathered, black and grey. *Soon the land will be drenched,* thought the boy, shaking, *and I can't even work up a spit.*

The other two horsemen, also dressed as Jutes (and more Jutic or Saxon by the color of their hair, like dirty straw), rode up and seized Cors Cant's pony. A huge, dirty warrior grabbed the bard's hair, yanked his head back to expose his throat. Cors Cant felt sharp metal press against his windpipe, and he dropped his own puny kitchen knife to the ground.

Queer bursts of light like sudden suns plagued his vision, sparkled at the tunnel edge of his eyes. His heart pounding thunder crackles, the pulse beat in Cors Cant's head, forcing tiny, inaudible moans up his throat. The iron blade pressed against his throat pulse, sharp as the tooth of the *Pan-Draconis.* The bandit's odor gagged the boy. He stared at his princess, goddess, his Anlawdd, begged her silently to run, flee, abandon him and fly back to Camlann, Artus, safety. The damnable lightbursts swarmed across his entire vision now.

"Then," said Anlawdd, "you showed yourself to me. That was your second grievous error, earthworm." She nearly dragged the tip of her axe in the dirt. She drew even with the Norther, smiled, and spit on his banded mail brigandine.

Unperturbed, he let the spittle drip down his chest, might not even have noticed. "Yes, daughter of my mother . . . a good, hard lesson. I shall be your teacher again; and this

time, your little recital shall have an audience. Ho! Won't that
be stimulating?"

But Anlawdd had not stopped. She slow-walked Merillwyn
past Canastyr. He turned his stallion against Merillwyn's side,
puzzled.

Without even dismounting, Anlawdd suddenly snapped her
axe straight up, sliced deeply between his horse's hind legs.

The stallion screamed, bucked wildly. Canastyr held his
position for a moment, then was flung wide by his agonized
mount. He fell heavily to knees and elbows.

Merillwyn skittered away from the bucking stallion.
Canastyr's Arabian mount, mad with agony from Anlawdd's
blow between its legs, found a target for its fury crawling on
the ground. It savagely trampled its owner, stunning Canastyr
despite his thick, Jutic armor. He crawled a short distance,
then collapsed, holding his head and moaning. Blood poured
from beneath his hands.

"Daughter of Rhia—!" gasped Cors Cant, turning away
from the gory sight. He clenched his teeth, fighting back nausea. The bard barely noticed the other two men charge past
him toward Anlawdd.

An instant too late, Cors Cant rallied and lunged at empty
air where one had passed.

Terrified, he urged his reluctant, rented pony after them.
"Anlawdd, I'll save—watch out!"

Seeing the danger, Anlawdd leaned far to her right.
Merillwyn swerved so quickly in response that both men
overshot her. *"Stop!"* she barked, pointing at Cors Cant. Startled, he leaned back. His horse obediently skidded to a halt.
Why did I obey? he thought, confused. *They'll kill her!*

More flashes, lightning on a black night. Cors Cant's aware-
ness drifted, fixated upon Anlawdd as she cut behind twisting
Jutes, Eirelanders, Saxons, whatever they were—red tresses *(Auburn!)* streaming behind like Bedwyr's banners, tunic flashing
forest green and cream, like Merovee's cloak of innocence.

The three combatants fought on horseback, as if they had
never heard of dismounting. Miraculously, both the men and
Anlawdd herself stayed in their saddles.

Cors Cant fell across his mount's powerful neck, struggling
to free himself from horrific, magical visions and Anlawdd's
sorcerous command. *Damn—damned mushroom she poitioned*

me! poisoned me withie! He could not think straight, or even follow the battle. Each battlefield flash across his eyes illuminated a different scene, as if he spun in the saddle and saw a different fight each instant.

Anlawdd rose to her knees, wind whipping her short tunic away from her powerful thighs and buttocks, held aloft a bloody axe like Athena, Macha, and Queen Boudicca rolled together in a pastry. She screamed—*"Artus! Merovius, Arcadia!"*

—flash—

Directly she passed the taller man, she snapped her arm in a semicircle, battered his right arm. He spun, face white as her robe. He leaned back as if reclining on a meal couch, rolled off his horse and thudded against the sword.

—flash—

The third man, fat and bald, pointed sword and javelin like talismans. He neither advanced nor retreated, but seemed dumbstruck that such a blow could be struck from the back of a horse.

A frog loudly mocked the bard, croaked *what (rrrabbit!) manner o'hero are ye? Rrabbit-HUP! Savor! Save'er!* The bard squeezed his eyes, shut out the horrors, and urged his terrified pony forward into the fray.

—flash—

With eyes shut the sprackles were worse, a myriad splashing across closed lids like fiery rain.

Hooves pounded. Cors Cant opened one eye.

—flash flash—

The panicked assailant wheeled his horse, tried to flee back the way he came, past the blood-spattered Sarmatian Amazon.

Anlawdd was out of position, but she kneed her horse forward anyway. The two mares drove into each other nearly headlong. Both horses fell, spilling Anlawdd and the brigand to the ground.

—thousand eruptions of lightning snowflecks—

He rose, tried to flee again. Anlawdd lunged, grabbed his shoulder, spun him to face her. He dropped his javelin, useless at such a range, and swung a short, thick sword at her unprotected breast.

Cors Cant flung himself from his pony, cracked a knee on the hard ground.

She deflected the blow with her axe hilt, but took a cut to

her chest anyway. She stepped back, apparently startled, and stumbled to the ground.

Eyes wide, white with terror, the bandit lunged at the momentarily helpless girl.

"No!" cried the bard in terror.

Upon the instant, Cors Cant was *there,* between blow and breast. He somehow traversed Euclid's straight line from alpha to beta without crossing the intervening distance.

As lightning bolts that touch ground begin and end at the same time, so Cors Cant was all points along his path at once, from the dusty Roman road, prone, with an agonized knee, to the space between the murderer's sword and Anlawdd's heart, putting the lie to Greek geometry.

The bard crashed into the bandit from behind, coiling around the larger foe like a snake, hampering the man's sword arm.

What now? what do I do? Cors Cant had no legionnaire training, nothing to prepare him for armed combat!

Do what? Be a hero, rrrabbit! The toad again, begging King Log to transmute into King Stork.

—flash—

The assailant grappled behind his back for Cors Cant, armor restricting his movement like a turtle unable to snap behind its own shell.

—lightning and thunder together—

A hammer blow staggered the boy. He fell back, massive, armored brigand atop him. The man groaned, clutched at his belly.

Cors Cant squirmed from under the body, shaking and sobbing. He stared at the draining corpse, unable to close his eyes or even look away. Jutic iron had not stopped the bandit's own javelin.

Cors Cant looked up. Across the grassy knoll, sunlight caught in her hair, Anlawdd *(princess?)* stood over the still groaning Canastyr, an enormous dagger in her hand.

"And your third error—brother dearest—was a mere technical violation, though costly. You thought me as entranced by my own voice as you are by yours . . . thus looked for no strike until I had finished my speech."

She squatted over Canastyr, lowering her voice. He did not

seem to notice her. "And now, son of my father, I shall make good my promise the last time we met."

Anlawdd pressed her knife between Canastyr's thighs. Cors Cant could not tear his horrified gaze from the blade.

But Canastyr lay limp, head slowly rotating back and forth, oblivious to the threat; in a moment, even this slight motion ceased.

She poked at his groin with the knife, but he did not move: Cors Cant realized that Canastyr was already dead, struck down early in the battle by his own, poorly trained, pain-maddened beast.

Anlawdd realized the truth in the same instant. *"NO!"* she screamed, voice rising finally to crack in falsetto. She raised the blade, reversed it, and plunged it with both hands into the already lifeless corpse. She jumped up, backed away in terror, pulling at her crimson-splattered auburn locks and screaming like a *bean-sidhe*.

"Earthworm! Earthworm! Even now you cheat me—even *yet* you die unpunished! O Lord, my God, will *no one* help the widow's daughter?" Princess Anlawdd sank to the ground cross-legged, covered her eyes, and wept bitterly for a thousand years.

Hearing his love's anguish, long-suppressed nausea welled up Cors Cant's throat. He staggered away, fell against a thornbush and dry-heaved, ignoring the sharp thorns. He had eaten nothing that day but Anlawdd's mushroom; nothing came out.

The sparkles overwhelmed him, the worst lightning storm he had ever seen, all behind his own eyes. A timeless period passed; when he came back from the light, the sun had moved visibly across the sky, and Anlawdd no longer sat where she had before. Limp and dizzy, Cors Cant wiped away tears.

A gentle hand touched the nape of his neck. Anlawdd leaned close, her scent overwhelming him. She touched her lips to his ear.

"I would not have had this happen . . . not today! You must try to put this out of your mind, at least for now." She sounded strangely urgent. She put her arm around him, held tight even as he crouched on hands and knees. Sweat rolled down his throat and chest, turned his skin clammy. He felt her heart pounding, faster than a galloping horse, and she shook.

"I-I-I've never s-seen ..." Cors Cant stopped, took five deep breaths, prayed for the sunbursts to subside. Anlawdd silently waited. "Never seen killing so close," he finished; Cors Cant stopped, overwhelmed by a vivid vision of his father being shot in the head by Vortigern's archer, his mother hacked at like a butchered animal, his sister ...

Anlawdd, Canastyr, the screaming, kicking horse. *How much is fear, how much is that damned fungus?* His head spun, he could not find his balance. The world groaned, trees dripped hot blood, as if a skybound all-dragon, a *Pan-Draconis,* had burst asunder and rained life upon them. Birds of prey gathered, thousands of eagles ready to peck the dragon flesh, pick clean the bones like Carthaginian ruins.

Anlawdd stroked his hair, pressed her face against his. Her breath warmed his neck. "I needed you open, Cors Cant. I had to give it to you. I didn't know this was going to happen! Forgive me. It doesn't have to be a horror, but you have to work back to me. Walk away from the blood and death, for I've something wonderful to show you. Really!"

For an instant, he thought she would kiss him. Her breath grew shallow, skin flushed warm. *My princess,* thought Cors Cant. *Would that I were a prince, so we could love!* Anlawdd's face was green, ears pointed like the Gentry, the Fey. *Who are you?* he thought.

No more than you. No less than He. Did she speak, or was it the recurrent voice in Cors Cant's head?

Himself, he almost turned and kissed her. But he discovered his own fear, embarrassment ... *A princess love a half-bard? What self-delusion is this?*

Cors Cant bowed his head to touch the dirt; then he rose, eyes averted from the butchered bodies. "Whither now, m-my lady?" he whispered. His legs buckled, but she caught him. Balance was still off. *And pray why do Jutirish bridegrooms or brigands or whatever all crowd about shouting your name with hosannas as they murder you, riddle me that, oh principessa?*

"Our destination hasn't changed, Cors Cant. They sha'n't spoil this for me. For us! I want to show you my secret place, open a secret, special door between us that nobody else knows about. A place for us, when we need a place."

The insects chose that moment to begin chirping and buzzing again. The bard looked ahead, eyes high to avoid the shapeless lump ahead of them on the road. The forest thinned; tall, brown grass stretched toward the setting moon's bright half-disk, like fingers waving, gesturing them on in friendship.

"Did you know you can see the moon in the daytime?" he asked.

"What? Where?" Anlawdd looked skyward, and Cors Cant pointed it out to her in the clear, blue void. "Llyr, I never saw that before! Can you always? I don't see how I could have missed it, unless you magicked it into existence just this minute." She sounded so sincere, but the corners of her mouth twitched, suppressing a smile.

"I'm not Myrddin," said the bard. "When the moon is half-full, it rises at noon or midnight. Near the horizon, you can see it."

"Why that's positively amazing, Cors Cant Ewin, Druid astrologer. I don't know how many times I've looked at the sky for—for however long I've looked at the sky. And you know how Saxons are." He could detect no sarcasm in her words, yet—

"Um—Anlawdd, why did they, you know, try to kill you?"

"You know how Saxons are. They'll attack their own mothers, the lazy, dirty, motherless hounds."

"Jutes," he corrected, staring at the dirty, white moon. It opened both eyes, lolled a grey tongue at him. He blinked, the vision passed. "Anlawdd, does that mushroom you fed me cause visions?"

She took his hand, squeezed it. "Sometimes. It lets you see inside, if you really want to get specific. Give me a few moments to take care of the mess, then let's mount," she ordered.

"Anlawdd . . . why did they speak your name as they attacked?"

"Let me take care of the mess. Did I already say that? Then we'll go." Clearly, she was going to evade and sidestep.

"As you command . . ." Cors Cant was about to add *Princess,* but stopped himself. *Does she even know that I speak Irish? Is she really a princess in disguise?* The boy, deciding not to press the issue, let the sentence trail off unfinished.

Anlawdd lugged the bodies into heavy undergrowth, searched two of them for money; she avoided touching the one she called Canastyr as much as she could. The others had between them a single *solidus,* a *double-denarius,* and three *denarii.* Anlawdd dumped the coins in her own purse, and the bard did not object.

When Anlawdd had finished, Cors Cant soothed his pony and mounted. Anlawdd's Merillwyn seemed unperturbed. *I won't forget,* promised the bard; *I won't let you forget, either. They called your name, you called his, and then they tried to kill us both!*

Or did they? Now Cors Cant was not sure. Had not Anlawdd struck the first blow? Perhaps the only killing intent was hers, which would make her a . . .

No! They were Jutes. Not as bad as Saxons, but Jutes kill every day and twice on holidays; they kill their own mothers! She had to do it, or we'd both be lying where they now lie.

The lead stallion was grievously wounded, but had managed to run away. The mount that Merillwyn had rammed was just now getting to its feet.

It whinnied and cantered away, limping on its left foreleg.

"Leave the third horse as well," said Anlawdd; "we have no need for her, unless you plan to ride a Saxon saddle—or Jutic, I should say."

Cors Cant looked at the horse, which stared back warily. Then he struggled onto the back of his own shaggy pony.

"On our way," she said. Her face had lost the innocence of morning, now clouded and overcast.

She turned in the saddle, added "Oh, and Cors Cant; the next time I tell you to stop, you had better pretend you just saw one of those Gorgons you're always singing about." She smiled sharp edges and cut glass.

Anlawdd clucked to Merillwyn and trotted west, Cors Cant in tow.

CHAPTER 29

COLONEL COOPER BENT OVER THE PRONE BODY OF PETER Smythe, trying hard to keep an expressionless, military face. He was not very successful. *Hard to look military,* thought Mark Blundell, *when you're waist-high in a thornbush.* Of course, the bush did not exist for Cooper.

"God," said the Colonel. Blundell wondered whether is was a prayer or an accusation.

"He's not dead, sir," said Jacob Hamilton, nervously.

"I can tell, boy."

Willks bustled forward. "Selly's over here. She's okay, she's just, well, *empty.*" It was as good an explanation as any, but Cooper took it badly, glared at the senior scientist.

"My best bloody man is lying on a concrete slab, brains scrambled, and you say the woman that did it is 'all right, just bloody empty'?" He struggled to his feet, hyperventilating; Cooper was a big man. "Not enough, Mister. Give me a few choruses, and I want them canonical."

"Choruses?"

"You'll sing me 'John Barleycorn,' Willks. What the hell happened? *Where is Major Smythe?"*

Mark interjected smoothly; he had been born to diplomacy. "Colonel, sir, technically Selly did *nothing* to Major Smythe. It was his own act of bravery that cased this, um, condition."

Cooper found a chair and fell into it. His face went grey for a moment, then began to redden. Soon it was florid; Cooper was not a well man.

"Sir," asked Hamilton. "I think I should check your blood pressure."

Cooper waved his hand distractedly. "Tell me again ... what made Smythe think she was IRA?"

Mark continued. "Apparently, Selly made a reference to the 23-something, and Peter said that meant ... well, that she'd penetrated his cover. Rather."

"Steady-on," whispered Cooper. To whom? Blundell could not tell; perhaps Cooper exhorted himself.

"22-SAS," said Jacob Hamilton. He stood by the PET scan monitor, watching Peter's consciousness uplink. It was steady, but far too small.

"That," said Cooper, "goes no farther than this room. Do I make myself clear, gentlemen? Let's say he has seen action in the war against terrorism, and there are some who would be only too eager to finish the job that this Conway girl started."

"Corwin," said Blundell. "Won't breathe a word, Colonel."

"All right, now, that's all right then. All right, we've got to get ahead of the power curve here. All right, here's what we'll do. Wait, did you try to bring him back? That's the first order of business."

Willks answered curtly, cutting off Blundell's smooth assurance. "Of course we tried to bring him back! What do you take us for ... soldiers? We can add two and two!"

Cooper raised his brows. "Now see here, Professor, I'm just trying to bring a little order and coherence to—"

"Trying to take over that project, that's what you're doing!"

"All right! So you already tried to bring Peter back. So why isn't he back?"

This time Mark got an answer in before the hotheaded Willks. "Well, sir, there was a bit of a foul-up, I'm afraid. See, the damned machine's gotten quite a workout, sending two consciousnesses within such a short period of time. Well, it sort of blew out a fuse, you might say. Burnt out a microcircuit."

"Bollocks," declared the colonel.

"Sorry?"

"I said bollocks, and I meant bollocks! So now it's broken, what?"

"Worse. The particular circuit that incended—"

"Burnt," explained Hamilton.

"... controlled the total energy output, damped the field, so to speak. It allowed the field to overpower some of the wiring and short-circuit, and the field contacted Peter's calves as he cogniported."

"Cog . . . ?"

"Transported his cognitive presence. The long and the short of it, sir, is that Smythe's CNS—"

"Central nervous system."

"His central nervous system took quite a jolt. It's like uncontrolled ECT, and he's in a sort of a coma."

"Electro-Convulsive Therapy," said Hamilton. "Shock treatment. Like wiring electrodes on your scalp and—"

"I know what electroshock therapy is!" shouted Cooper, face beet red again. "Are you saying you can't bring him back?"

Hamilton stood up and faced Cooper without flinching. "I'm saying if we try, we might kill him. Sir."

Cooper leaned forward, elbows on knees, for a few moments. *Trying to be coldly rational,* thought Mark, *but he's scared to death.*

"Hamilton, we might just have to take that risk."

"I'm not prepared to do so, sir."

"Assuming this isn't all road apples, pardon my French, then we've got a bloody catastrophe here." Cooper sat up and looked Willks directly in the eye. The Colonel seemed to have recovered from the initial shock. "I'm a military man, and all I know about physics is what I learned at university. But I do know a few damned trustworthy men, brainy chaps, and they tell me this might be *on the level.*"

His eyes flicked briefly to Blundell, who jumped. *Is that meant to be a signal? Is the Colonel a brother in the craft?*

"It's real, Cooper," said Willks. "He's really back there, A.D. 450. They both are. I've no idea how conscious or cognizant they are, but they're there. I'd stake my beard on it." He pointed at the PET monitors, as if that proved his point. They did, of course, but Cooper could not possibly understand that.

"Then we've got a bleeding catastrophe, Willks. We've got an IRA op, someone who knows a lot more than she ought, romping through English history with a . . . an SAS major who's had a few problems after . . . after Londonderry. I don't like it, gentlemen. I don't like this verse at all, and neither will Roundhaven."

Roundhaven, thought Blundell. *In fact, I ought to give old Bill a call. I think we may need him, soon.*

Jacob shook his head. "No, sir, I can't do it. It's just like killing him, sir."

Cooper began to get angry again. "Look, who's in charge here?"

"I am," declared Willks, voice sharp and definite.

"You? Well, we'll jolly well see about that, won't we? This is a Ministry project. You're not at Oxford! This is Ministry money you're spending here."

"Colonel? Henry?" Cooper and Willks turned to look at Blundell, neither in a mood to listen. "A compromise, gentlemen . . . Colonel, we can't do anything now anyway. Machine's down. Can't do anything until it's up and fixed, right?"

"I suppose."

"Should be twenty-four hours. Meanwhile, let's wait and see if Peter stabilizes. And anyway, give him a shot at the Selly Corwin thing, try to figure out what she's up to back there."

"How long did you say until the machine can be fired up?"

"Twenty-four hours, sir."

"Damned convenient time that, if you ask me."

"It's an estimate, sir; minimum safe cooling period."

Willks cleared his throat. "I guess we can reevaluate in a day or so."

"Twenty-four hours," insisted Cooper. "I can use the time to check this Conroy lass, see what she's on about."

"Corwin," corrected Hamilton.

CHAPTER 30

PETER CAUGHT MEDRAUT HALFWAY BACK TO CAMELOT, dismounted to walk alongside the young warrior. "You could actually do me a favor, Medraut," said Peter.

"Sire? I mean, I can? I should be most pleased, My Prince." He still sounded shaky.

"I've been concentrating so much on this bloody joust—"

"This bloody what?"

"Um, tournament. Concentrating so much I haven't paid much attention to the court gossip."

"You mean the contest with Cutha? Sire, all know that Prince Lancelot *never* pays attention to court gossip."

Peter nudged Medraut in the ribs. The boy winced, grabbed his head to steady it. "I like to encourage that belief," said the champion. "But I do like to hear what's happening, now and again. Specifically, anybody new at the court lately, say in the last month or so?"

"New?" repeated Medraut, rubbing his temple gingerly. "Well, Mother and I just arrived a fortnight ago. We were visiting Morg for Lughnasade. Cei just returned from the Wessex front. Oh, and Merovius Rex, of course, but of course you know that."

"Any new women pop in, ah, arrive lately?" Sweat rolled down Peter's face. He reached up to touch his helm, yanked burned fingers away. *Hot sun, iron helm, duhhh. . . .*

"In the court? Nay, *that* I'd have definitely noticed, Sire." Medraut's disappointed expression convinced Peter he was not lying.

So if she's here, she appeared in the body of a court regular.

They passed under the outer gate, and Peter wondered once again about Morgawse, Medraut's mother. "Medraut, stable the horses, will you? Oh, and is, um, Morgawse in? I'd like to have a quick chat with her."

"I'll check, Sire. Will you be in the *triclinium?*"

Peter nodded. It was the only room besides his own that he could find.

The gong rang again. *Has it been two hours already?* wondered Peter.

"Good noon, Sire," said Medraut, saluting, "and thank you for an interesting demonstration." Peter lifted a hand in response as the young man turned toward the stables.

After the bright sky and gentle wind of the clearing, the villa seemed unbearably dank and stale, dungeonlike. Even the open roof did not help, as clouds rolled across the sun, darkening the skylight.

The gloomy banqueting hall was abuzz with activity. Knights and ladies, serving wenches, kings, military commanders, nobles, consuls, and senators had roused themselves, bustled about on mysterious errands. The hall was nearly deserted. Yet King Merovee was in exactly the same position Peter had last seen him, propped against a couch smoking a long-stemmed, clay pipe.

Again, Peter's nose told him it was not tobacco the king smoked.

Perhaps he had moved, however, for the pipe was red, not white, and a broken white pipe lay on the table before him.

Merovee watched him with eyes too knowing, smile too forgiving. Uncomfortable, Peter shifted his gaze. He felt a sudden pressure he could not deny. His face reddened as he realized the utter necessity of finding a washroom immediately.

But where?

He certainly could not waltz up to the nearest slave and demand to be led to a washroom! How could he possibly explain not knowing where it is already? Odds were that at least once in his life, Lancelot had used a privy.

Peter stared frantically about the hall, hoping for a visual clue, an alternative to sprinting up the stairs to his own chamber and chamber pot. Besides, he needed more than liquid relief.

Walking gingerly, Peter edged toward the garden door. If utter worst came to utter worst, perhaps he could find a big bush outside.

Considering how civilized these Roman knights were, it occurred to Peter that defecating in the bushes might be considered a *faux pas,* even for Lancelot.

A serving girl—*slave* girl, he corrected himself—brushed past carrying a tray full of suspicious-looking lumps with grey butter on them.

"Ah," stalled Peter, looking over the proffered sweetmeats warily, "what are they?" He studied the slave girl's face. It seemed very dark for a Briton.

"Each is a different bread made with apples and other fruits," she answered.

"You know who I am?" The girl nodded, eyes wide. "What is your name?"

"I am Radiance," she answered shyly.

Peter chewed his lip, wondered whether Radiance the slave girl would think it strange if Lancelot of the Languedoc asked after a washroom, or whatever they called it: privy, he decided. At once, a plan leapt fully formed like Minerva from Peter's head.

"Well, Radiance, have you seen a herd of pigs wandering through here? Because there's the devil's own mess in the main, ah, privy!"

"Yes, sir. A mess, sir? I'll clean it at once, sir!"

"Almost slipped and broke my crown, Radiance. Wouldn't have done, what with the tournament tomorrow, what?"

"Which privy, sir? I'll fetch the mop, sir!"

"Never mind the bloody mop! I want to show you this mess ... you might need two or three mops!" He pursed his lips; the last had not come out quite right. "Hurry, the main, downstairs privy! Move!"

Radiance almost dropped her tray on the floor. She deflected it over a table and bolted across the hall. Peter followed with the most dignified haste he could manage without an accident.

They crossed the hall, ducked around the stairs into a fairly large room. As he reached the room, he almost barreled into the slave girl, who stared in confusion at the spotless floor.

"Great Caesar's ghost!" exclaimed Peter, "looks like we're too late ... they've already cleaned it!"

Radiance lowered her brows and glowered at Peter. "If ye'll not be needing me then, sir ... ?" Peter shook his head, a bit too nervously. She shot him another dagger look and huffed away.

"What was that all about, Lance?" asked a familiar voice. It was Cei. He sat on a long bench built into one wall. It took Peter a moment to realize there were holes cut at regular intervals along the bench, and Cei sat atop one of them, his tunic hiked up and breeches dropped. He held a scroll in his hands.

Peter looked about helplessly until he realized there were no enclosed stalls. Sighing, he approached the hole farthest from Cei, arranged his garments, and sat.

The smell was not as bad as he had feared. *Perhaps there are servants—slaves—who hose down the by-products? Speaking of the unspeakable, to where do they drop?*

"Lance? Who cleaned what up?"

"Eh? Oh, sorry Cei. I, ah, thought there was a mess here. Somebody told me ..."

"Who told you?"

"What the hell difference does it make? He was obviously drunk!"

"I want to know who's spreading rumors about my staff, that's why." Cei snarled convincingly, then broke into a smile. "Really, Lance, you know I take pride in my duties as porter. Held the job for eight months now." He returned to his scroll, chuckling every few lines.

Peter decided to probe a bit. He had to find out more about the alliance between Artus and Merovee, discover whether Selly Corwin had already changed history.

He leaned forward, elbows on knees. "Talk to me," he said. *I'm obviously his commander; let's see what kind of report I can drag out of him.*

"What's to say?" Cei shrugged his shoulders, set down the scroll.

"You know our task," snapped Peter. "How close are we?"

Cei raised his brows in shock. He scanned the room carefully, assuring himself they were alone. He reached within his tunic, extracted a deck of hand-painted, leather, Tarot cards.

"It's Bedwyr's fault," said Cei, conspiratorially. "We can't get to any of the king's inner circle. Not just fealty, something more . . . well, *you* know what they say about the Long-Hair."

Get to them? Peter's head spun. Obviously, Cei, Bedwyr, and Lancelot had formed some sort of conspiracy that was attempting to work its way into the inner circle of King Merovee, the "Long-Hair." But why? Were they trying to save the alliance, or break it up?

When in doubt, bluff it out. Peter turned a level, drill sergeant's gaze on Cei. The man's face reddened, and he spoke through clenched teeth: "Gold won't do it, lord. They're fanatics! Can't be reasoned with."

They who? Merovee's men? "A fanatic can never be convinced," quoted Peter, "but only converted." Who said that? He could not remember. Somebody from another life, long ago. Long to come. "If you can't bribe them or convince them, try *turning* them. Converting one of them with rhetoric. A young one. Think now; if you wanted to turn one of the inner circle, what would you say?"

Cei paused a long moment. "That's the problem, Prince. What Sicambrian would *not* cheer the defeat of Saxony, the restoration of the peace of Rome? You should know, more than anyone. There is no anti-Roman movement in the continent to work with, as there always has been here."

Holy mother of God, thought Peter. *I'm a traitor, working against Artus and Merovee to break up their alliance!* Then another thought brushed the first aside: *Of course I have to break up the alliance. It never bloody happened! There was no alliance; Rome fell . . . and Arthur died. What was I thinking?*

"The real problem," Cei continued, "is the *Blood Royal.* They say he's half-god."

"I thought he was half-fish," mumbled Peter.

"The Blood Royal," repeated Cei, rolling the phrase across his tongue. He absently shuffled his Tarot deck, handling the cards expertly. "What the hell does *that* mean? So he's a king. Kings have been betrayed a thousand times before."

Peter felt pulled in two directions: on the left, he could not allow history to be changed. But on the right, he was a loyal man—for queen and country. How could he betray both at one blow?

"By the way, Lancelot. We . . . we have *it.*"

Have what? From the tone of Cei's voice, "it" was something dreadfully important. And clearly "Lancelot" should already know what "it" was.

"What did it cost?" he asked. *Keep the conversation going, let him spill it all on his own.*

"A life. A soul. Isn't much, Lance. But it'll do the job."

"Any chance of, um, cocking up?"

Cei shrugged, fiddled with his cards. He would not look Peter in the eyes. "We'll stash it in your room later. Seems safest."

Excellent! So long as it isn't a—a—a bomb. . . .

Peter's head veered wildly; for a moment, he was back in Londonderry, all wrapped up in his man O'Riordin. The room was red, the street was red, blood streaked the ceiling, the sky, the tiny air holes, the stars.

Blood blood blood blood—the words began like a gallop in his head, screamed louder with every pulse beat. Soon he was riding, bloody axe in hand, trampling fallen, butchered bodies and exulting in a wild war wind, howling a song that was ancient when Romulus suckled the wolf's teat.

Lancelot! Lancelot of the Languedoc! Saxonbane, blood of a thousand devils!

Blood!

Peter gasped, hugged his knees. He slowed his breathing, pushed the barbarous Sicambrian back into the hindbrain, the reptile brain, where Peter's own atavistic savagery found a home.

"Are you all right, sir?"

Peter nodded quickly, not trusting himself to speak. He was finished. He should rise, return to the *triclinium* to await Medraut with Morgawse's invitation to speak with her again. He should rise.

"I'll tell you a secret," said Cei, quieter yet. "Even *Artus* is afraid of Merovee. You may be the *Dux Bellorum*'s favorite, but I've known him longer than anyone. He's begged advice from Myrddin, Morgawse, even the young bard."

"Cors Cant?"

"This unholy alliance is killing him, draining his manhood."

"Cors Cant's?"

"I've never known him like this . . . Sire. For the first time in eleven years . . ."

"Yes?"

"I begin to regret my oath. To serve the *Dux Bellorum*. Artus, the consul, the Senate. To bring my army entirely under *his* control."

"Artus's?"

"I was a prince. Technically, I suppose I'm king now. My father stood with Vortigern. Well, you know. I brought a legion to Camlann to march against Vortigern under dragon and eagle.

"But Lancelot . . . there is no reason they cannot march again beneath the golden boar of Cei, King of Clwyd—if you track my drift. Of course, Bedwyr and his knights will go wherever I go. And if we were joined by your two legions of black and silver . . . Well, who could stand against us? Please just keep it in mind, Sire. The *Pan-Draconis* is neither prince nor priest and has no army of his own."

Peter said nothing. He understood. Artus's men were drifting, frightened by the *Dux Bellorum*'s obsession with the revivified Empire, *Pax Britannicus*. The empire that never was.

Peter found a pile of rags, used one, and threw it into a bucket.

"Tell me about Cors Cant," he said.

"He's the fool, that boy. But you ever notice where the Fool falls in the Ægyptian deck?" Cei riffled his Tarot cards.

Peter shook his head; he never went in for ESP, astrology,

any sort of woo-woo. Strictly a here-and-now man, though he was aware that the Tarot held a deep significance for Masons.

"It's the *first* trump," said Cei, spreading his hand wide. The Fool was faceup on the bottom. "The Fool steps into the abyss. But it's also the *last* trump, right after the World. Cycle starts and ends with the Fool."

Cei slowly turned the cards over, then upturned the top card. It was the Fool again. Peter jumped; he had not seen Cei move it.

"Well, continue your efforts," said Peter. He wondered what those efforts might be, but prudence dictated he shut up. He rose, adjusted his clothing, and departed from the privy. Cei picked up the scroll again as Peter left; this time the porter did not laugh.

Something about Merovee that scares even Artus. Peter looked at his hand, remembered the subtle pressure of thumb and third finger; *Merovius Roi . . . King Merovee . . . Merovee the Mason. . . .*

Merovee who probably read the Tarot. But did that make Cei a Mason? And what exactly was it Cei and Bedwyr "got?" And after they stash it in my room, is it going to bite me on the arse?

Peter strode through the *triclinium*, looking for Medraut. The boy was nowhere visible, so Peter sat at a central table. Suddenly remembering he had had no breakfast, he picked up a knife. He attacked the remains of a pork roast, wolfed a huge slice of artery-clogging, burnt pig. Selly, Artus, plots and plans, pots and pans, they all rattled around his head like Baba Yaga gnashing her iron teeth.

Deep in thought, he did not notice Myrddin, the court humbug, until the annoying greybeard cleared his throat.

"Ho, Lancelot. What were you doing with that young blackguard, Mordred?"

Peter glared at Myrddin. "I do as I please, with whomever I please. What business is it of yours?"

Myrddin seemed about to say something rude, but swallowed it down. "You are the right hand of Artus. How can you be seen with a traitor such as Mordred? Know you not whose son he claims to be?"

Despite his dislike for the old fraud, Peter felt a pang of guilt. According to Malory, Mordred was alleged to be the illegitimate son of Arthur by Margawse, his half sister . . . but Peter alone knew that Mordred would indeed turn traitor and kill his father!

"He's just a boy, for Christ's sake," mumbled Peter. Myrddin seemed taken aback at the vehemence of his words. He looked the Sicambrian up and down.

"A boy who is his mother's son, Tribune."

At once the pieces fell together. Mordred was the son of Morgawse . . . it would be so simple for her—for Selly—to poison the boy's mind, turn it against Artus. Malory put the blame for Arthur's death squarely at the feet of Morgan le Fey. But was Morgan "Morgawse"? Then who was *Margawse?* Or were they the same person, split in two by centuries of myth and storytelling?

Nice theory, thought Peter's skeptical side; *now how about a shred of evidence? This is assumption piled on guessing.*

"Myrddin," he said, "the only thing I hate worse than an honest traitor is a talebearer. Why don't you leave, before I forget you're a priest?"

Myrddin's eyebrows shot skyward comically. He back-pedaled, putting his hands up in a combination soothing, warding-off gesture. "Just a word to the wise, friend Lancelot. Medraut owes allegience *only to his mother."*

And Morg, whispered Lancelot's barbaric voice, *Morg sellsword, friend of Saxons!*

"What do you expect me to do?" demanded Peter. "Cut his head off during dinner? Might cause a ruckus, don't you think?"

"Well," grumped the sorcerer, "can't make an omelet without cracking a few eggs." He chewed his mustache and looked offended.

Peter blinked, amazed at how old some expressions were. "Well, I have no intention of cracking any eggs today. Nor of continuing this conversation. Your opinions have been noted. Now go off and worship a bleedin' tree, or something."

Myrddin stood, brushed himself imperiously, and stomped off toward the stairs.

CHAPTER 31

GREYBEARDED CLOUDS, THE *HUNDRED* GREATEST LEERY FACES, rolled like pepper curls. Black bottoms full of rain swam across the southern sky. Blue-black slants—heavy rain drenched South Saxony, forty leagues distant.

Anlawdd and Cors Cant skirted the cloud cover, outrode wind and rumor. They leapt the river, ducked beneath tree branches that grasped and clutched. Anlawdd decided they were far enough from the ambush to be safe.

Danger past, Cors Cant shook in retroactive terror, gripping his reins hard enough to cut deep folds into his palms. He feared not so much for himself—but he might have lost She Who Made the Sky Blue and the Grass Green! Anlawdd could have been cloven by a Jutic war axe.

They circled a black pond whose wind-driven waves lapped against a cliff nearly as tall as a house. It was a single, massive boulder, sod-covered on the leeward side, washed clean and white on the windward, beginning an arm's span above the waterline. As summer fed into autumn, the water level remained low; this would change when the rains began.

A great ash tree grew hard against the rock; Anlawdd led him thither, reined up next to the tree.

Cors Cant sneaked a glance at her as they dismounted. She pretended not to notice. Try as he might, he could not stop seeing her with a crown on her head, bloody axe in hand. The mushroom had his brain in a death grip.

What did they want? what would have happened? Had her axe not fallen, would we be dead at their hands? Or is my feathery love a madwoman, a fowl murderess? He pushed the thoughts down hard. Some thoughts were not to be thought. Myrddin would understand, he who knew tomorrow's morrow.

Anlawdd straightened her tunic, pulled her hair back in a horsetail. Sunlight shone through overarching branches, spotted the auburn with fiery, gold stripes. He watched her, peeking through the armholes of her tunic and chemise, where he could just barely see her white, perfect breast with its cherry nipple. He tried to feel honest lust instead of the sick and morbid fancies that plagued his mind since the encounter with Canastyr and his bandits.

"Cors Cant Ewin, will you *stop* staring at me as if I'd grown another head, and follow me into here?"

"Anlawdd, what did they want? How did they know we'd be upon the road?"

The princess-seamstress skirted the pond, her own image reflected darkly in the water; she walked up to the ash and touched the bark gently. "Because they were following us," she said, voice soft as the ripples in the pond.

"You saw them?"

"No."

"Heard them?"

She shook her head. "I saw nor heard nothing, Cors Cant, and that worries me. That's like sitting in a chair and not noticing it's gone. I have must have been . . ." She glanced at him and frowned. "Distracted," she concluded.

The great rock, blue above and white below, was covered by brown, hairy moss. Anlawdd put both arms around the tree and hugged it.

"Um," began Cors Cant, "are-are-are you one of the Gentry? Fey, as they say Morgawse is?" Everything was confused, blue grass, green sky. Anlawdd's mushroom muddled his thoughts. Rainbows danced around her head, and Cors Cant could not stop his tongue from rattling. "For if you are fey, t'would explain much—how you knew to bring an axe along, and how to fight—if you were a dryad queen."

She lowered orange brows for a moment, then shook her head, laughing. "I'm as human as you, Cors Cant, if a bit more polite! I'm not lusting after this tree, if that's what you're worried about; just squirming around it, which is what you should be doing, by the way. Come on, follow!"

With Cors Cant's heightened senses, he heard a faint edge in her voice, realized Anlawdd (*Princess* Anlawdd?) was much more upset by the Saxon encounter than she was letting on.

As she spoke, she squeezed between the tree and the rock and disappeared. After a moment's hesitation, Cors Cant followed.

Behind the tree he discovered a thin, black crack in the boulder, into which he squirmed. He was not as thin as Anlawdd and found it a tight fit. He gasped as he stepped into a frigid stream that flowed from the crack into the pond beyond.

The crack became a narrow tunnel that split the stone into halves, invisible behind the ash tree whose roots had doubtless caused the crack. For a moment, Cors Cant panicked, almost dashed back out again. Then he heard Anlawdd's voice ahead of him, ghostly and detached. *Like the shades Orpheus met in Pluto's realm,* he thought, panting.

"Cors Cant, are you coming, or did you get stuck? Perhaps you should consider eating a bit less? My father is always stuffing—"

"No, I'm fine," he lied, voice shaky. He pushed forward, splashing in the icy stream. The crack narrowed, and for a terrified moment, he thought he *would* get stuck. Then the boulder ended, the crack debouching into a natural cave.

The floor vanished, and he fell to his left against the wall, which tilted, becoming a new floor at knee-level. After another long squirm, Cors Cant found himself in a black cavern, chill with stale, motionless air.

For an instant, he thought he was in a great, drippy bath, a moist *frigidarium* with leaky plumbing. Then he blinked, and it was only a natural cave once more. His heart pounded unnaturally fast, and he had a sudden terror that he would faint.

Cors Cant opened his mouth to call to Anlawdd, but she whispered first. "Quiet and listen . . . not a sound, Cors Cant."

He stood quiet, listened to the faint burble of a sluggish, underground stream and his matching pulse. As his eyes slowly adjusted to the gloom, he saw faint patches of illumination from moss along the bank of the stream, which bisected the cave floor.

"Are you ready?" Anlawdd asked, voice thick and hushed.

He nodded, realized she could not see him, answered "ready." For what? He heard a creak, as if a tiny door opened, and his stomach lurched.

He saw flickers of movement all around them. *What is it?*

What are they? Faeries? He dared not ask aloud, lest they hear and disapprove. *Is it magic? Is she really a princess? Am I going to die? Was Canastyr going to kill us or throw a saturnalia?* The bard clapped hands over ears, swayed as his balance rolled slowly forward and back, Anlawdd's cantrip in full control.

She struck a spark into a wad of tinder, blew it alight, and lit a candle. Cors Cant gasped, stared at a riot of crystal suns that reflected back like jeweled eyes. *Into the Light . . .*

"Into this temple your path now wends from now on we're your only friends . . ." Who spoke? *Who was that?*

Crystals blazed from every wall, all the colors of Iris's Woof, and some colors Cors Cant had never imagined. Red spattered like blood, blue sheened like deepest ice *(or the eyes of an Irish assassin now dead, did he mean to kill or throw us a feast, bards and heroes and kings and red drippy Jutic axes in the back. . . .)*

Black veins branched and twisted among the jeweled cavern walls, outlined brilliant, star-shaped figures, trapped souls of demigods, like the glass windows in Myrddin's crystal chamber, where light and shadow danced without candles. The boy stared, struck mute by the sight. For once, so too was Anlawdd.

She stepped close, put a gentle hand on his shoulder. They stared together.

The walls were windows into an infinity of possible worlds. Each sparkling jewel caught the reflection of all other jewels, formed an interconnected net of light, strung like strands of a fisher king's cast. What matter that they were not truly precious stones, merely crystals grown wild in the ancient caverns? The beauty ripped at Cors Cant's gut like a deep wound.

The stream flowed through the cavern, widening from a handsbreadth down a fist-high "waterfall" to produce the burble.

Anlawdd spoke at last. "What happened in my room . . . well, I don't want it to happen that way again. You know that."

Cors Cant lowered his eyes, afraid to hear the rest of her words. "Sorry, My Princess."

"Next time it has to be—I mean if there *is* a next time . . . well, I was in my cups, and you were drunk on music and the need of men, and I felt sorry for you. I want next time, if there is a next time, to be *right,* Cors Cant. Look, see the water? It's cool and refreshing, and you can drink from it without tasting limestone. But when it reaches the pond outside it becomes black and corrupt."

He nodded. *What is she getting at? Is she just nervous? Did she take some of her own cantrip?* Anlawdd continued, almost babbling. "Take your boot off, feel how cool it is. Really, Cors Cant, you can't touch the water with your boots on!"

My boots are unboiled, he thought; indeed, he had "touched" the stream all the way through the tunnel, his boots not being proof against water.

But he was compelled to obey; her leathery potion had robbed him of resistance. He bent to his right boot.

"No," she said, "the other one is easier." Obediently, he pulled his left boot off and dropped it, dipped his foot in the cold water. He shivered, yanked it out again. The water burned like ice.

He looked at Anlawdd, and her face flushed. She licked dry lips and continued. "This place always brings out the solemnity in me. How serious are you, about your path? About *us,* I mean?"

The boy thought a long time while Anlawdd waited, silent. *Are you the sword that I pick up in the desert? Or are you the wand of intuition? Once chosen, I can't unchoose—this I know!*

"I wish I knew," he said finally. "My warp is woven to find out, I guess."

"Do you trust me, Cors Cant Ewin?"

"I trust you," he whispered. *Are you my cup, dare I slake my sword within you?*

"With your life?" He nodded, she asked again: "With your *hands?*"

His hands! The hands of a harpist, a bard. What did she plot against his hands?

Through tricks and traps and breaks and bends, initiation never ends. Remember . . . we're your only friends!

His voice cracked, but again he found himself saying "I triss . . . I trust you." *Courage! That's what you are, my love, my princess, my goddess . . . courage, the pentacle of valor!*

"Then you must come with me now."

"Where?"

She grinned; her teeth were sharp and pointed, like a dog's. *Gods, I hope it is just the cantrip, please let it be!* he pleaded silently.

"To Arcadia," she answered.

She set the candle on the ground, where it cast horrific shadows up her face. Now she even looked like a shade from Hades. She reached both hands to hold his head. "In service to the Light, to Isis, to Mary, to Diana we labored long to build the Temple of the Sun," she intoned. "We are the Builders of the Temple. We studied these heavenly gems, drew links between the stones of the earth and the stars on their crystal spheres."

"I don't understand," whispered Cors Cant. He grew frightened. Anlawdd's words seemed older than she, older than Artus, perhaps older than the soil beneath Caer Camlann itself. *I just want* you, *not illumination!* But he could not say it aloud.

Cats rats got his tongue, words unspoken silent hung.

She let go his head, slowly circled around behind him, still talking. He could no longer see her, and the voice sounded queer, different.

"What is an apprentice initiate? He seeks experience, being but an apprentice. Yet he is initiated into the mysteries of Man's inner being. *He is a candidate for soul knowledge.* This you must know from Myrddin and the Druids, do you not?"

"Where did you learn these words, a candidate for soul knowledge? That is a Druid mystery not given to others!"

> *Wherever did she learn those words,*
> *From cats or rats or beasts or birds?*
> *How deep within the temple heart*
> *You stand and play your ancient part!*

"How many roads lead to Rome?" she asked.

He shivered, far from home. "All of them." Cors Cant desperately wanted to turn and face her, see if it was still Anlawdd behind him. Her voice sounded distorted, mutated. *Is she still she?*

What else could Anlawdd ever be? Her voice intoned from such a height.

"How many paths still lead to Light?"

He almost answered, realized the only answer was silence.

"Cors Cant Ewin, it's clear this illumination is more than you can handle. Bend you down, snuff out the candle!"

He hesitated, bent awkwardly, and inhaled sharply. A cuff on the back of his neck threw him to the ground. "Never quench one element with another, lest your anger them both, Bard! Use your fingers, not your breath."

Lest you court your lady's death. . . .

He reached out and snuffed the candle, plunging them into total darkness.

"Stand up straight." Anlawdd's voice grew queerer, thicker. It was not *her* voice. Cors Cant trembled at its majesty, for he realized whose voice it be.

"THIS IS THE TEMPLE, BUILT FOR KING SOLOMON AS IT SAYS IN THE HEBREWS' WRITING."

The boy stood, creeps iced up and down his back.

Her voice, not her voice, spoke directly into his ear. He jumped; she had not moved, he could swear.

"LET THE TALKER SLEEP. LISTEN, DO NOT WANDER AWAY, CORS CANT EWIN! KING SOLOMON IS SOL, THE SUN, AND OUR TEMPLE IS THE ARCHING SKY OF NUIT. AS ABOVE, SO BELOW. SOL IS FATHER OF US ALL, LUNA IS MOTHER. EACH OF THE SEVEN PLANETS IS CONTAINED WITHIN US, ALL PARTS OF ONE SOUL. DO YOU UNDERSTAND?"

Something, perhaps the cantrip, opened his mind to her words. Each one bit deep as a snake, injecting meaning into his heart. "I . . . *do* understand," he marveled.

From farther behind him:

"ALL HAVE ATTAINED THEIR HEIGHT IN THE SOUTH."

From his left:

"ALL HAVE SET IN THE WEST."

Back widdershins, behind him now, all the way around to the right:

"ALL HAVE RISEN IN THE EAST."

She completed the circuit, stood directly before Cors Cant. Yet she made no mention of the North, where she stood.

"RAISE YOUR LEFT HAND," commanded Macha-Diana-Anlawdd.

Cors Cant did so, steady and unafraid. Her palm gently pressed against his; for an instant, her lips brushed his own in a kiss full of promise and the future.

"VENUS, LOVE, GUARDS THE DOOR BETWEEN SLEEP AND WAK-
ING," she whispered, stepped back again.

She made a sharp rap, and the boy jumped as it was answered almost immediately from behind him. *Someone else is
in here!* Now he did tremble. Anlawdd he trusted; but who
was this other?

"DOES THE CANDIDATE COME OF HIS OWN FREE WILL?" she
asked.

He paused a moment. Was he supposed to answer? Hesitat-
ingly, he said "I do. I mean, he does."

"WHAT DID IT SIGNIFY WHEN THE CANDIDATE CRAWLED
THROUGH THE NARROW PASSAGEWAY INTO THIS TEMPLE?"

Cors Cant waited a long moment. This question was crucial, he knew from the tone of her voice. But his head spun
like a frightened, confused newborn babe. *Blast that bloody
fungus! I can't think can't plan can't . . .*

*A newborn pup, birthed and free, swims between the sky
and sea!*

"He was born. Born again," croaked the bard. He blinked.
Where had that answer come from? His own throat, but
surely not his own mind!

"WHY IS YOUR LEFT FOOT BARE?"

"You told me to take my boot off!"

"AND YOU BLINDLY FOLLOW AUTHORITY! CAN YOU NOT SEE
HOW ABSURD YOU LOOK?"

Or was that second tap merely an echo? he wondered. "I
can't see *anything*," he said, annoyed and shaking with the
effort. "It's dark!"

"NO ONE CAN SEE IN THE DARK," Anlawdd retorted.

Again, Cors Cant shivered, as if a foot had brushed his
deathsite.

Something touched me . . . it was cold, sharp. A blade; it
pushed his leine aside, pressed directly against the flesh
above his heart, just left of his sternum.

"IN WHOM . . . DO YOU TRUST?" asked the voice; the first two
words were carefully enunciated, the last three added as an
afterthought. Two, then three.

"I trust—" he began, gasped as the knife jabbed sharply
forward, nearly pierced his skin!

"I trust—" Again the warning pressure. Cors Cant's mind
went blank, he could not think what to say next. *If I guess*

wrong, will she actually kill me? Likely. Her last words were deadly serious, and since she spoke them, he had never heard her so silent.

So who the hell do *I trust? Myrddin?* Rivers flowed beneath the old Druid's surface, currents the boy would never fathom. Trust the Druid? Sooner trust a whirlwind!

Artus, too, concealed a complex tapestry of motive behind the smooth, white, Roman linen. And now Lancelot was so changed, so alien.

And nobody *understands Gwynhyfyr!*

I trust Anlawdd. Yes. Yes, but—

"I trust y—"

He choked off the reply, too hasty by half, and realized to his horror that *he did not!* No matter what his feelings, or how she made his soul leap, she was *another,* a separate person. He could never truly be sure of how *she* felt.

Thus everyone, even Anlawdd, was ultimately an enigma.

He knew the answer to her question. It was probably not the answer she wanted to hear. *So this is it? Here I die, run through in a smelly cave by a red-haired goddess seized in the drama of ritual!*

His chest throbbed where the point pressed deep, deeper. A thin trickle—blood or sweat?—rolled down his belly. *Well damn her,* he thought savagely, *then let her kill me! I'm a bard, and blast it I'm going to speak the truth for once, whatever the cost!*

"I . . . I trust only *myself!*" he shouted, defiant to the last.

"THEN LET THE CANDIDATE TAKE THE FIRST STEP FORWARD, INTO THE LIGHT."

The knife did not waver, still pressed hard against his breast.

If he took even a single step forward, the boy realized, she would either have to pull the knife back, or he would run *himself* through.

But the defiant streak still burned strong. Without a second thought, he strode forward with his bare left foot. Anlawdd drew back the knife as he advanced. He stumbled a bit; the ground he stepped onto was slightly higher than where he stood.

Silence. He drew his right boot even with his left foot, waited for an eternity, shaking with retroactive terror. How close had he come? Would Anlawdd have *really murdered him* in this hidden place had he answered incorrectly? At last, he heard the most welcome sound he could imagine: a spark being struck from flint.

In a moment, she had the candle relit. He stood on the tiny ledge which made the miniature waterfall, a natural stone step. The fiery princess had pulled her tunic so as to bare her own left breast. She looked powerful, Amazon warrior rather than princess. Candlelight reflected from her eyes like cold stars, her face held the gravity of Merovee himself. Relief flooded him like cool rain falling from the southern clouds.

He swayed as she spoke. The words pierced his brain and heart like needles, there to lodge forever.

"Water," she said, indicating the stream. "Fire, earth." She nodded at the candle, the ground. "Control the breath. Air is always the key. You are ultimately responsible for *everything that ever happens to you.* Trust no one but the divine within *you.* And now, Cors Cant Ewin, you are a Builder. Welcome." She pointed to the stream. "The river is our mother, and we must render unto Mother that which is Mother's. Which in this instance, in case you couldn't figure out the symbolism, means toss the rest of your money into the stream."

He smiled, then bit his lip. She sounded like Anlawdd again, no longer a possessed witch. *Sure hope she lets me pick it back up again,* he fretted.

He reached for his pouch, panicked when he found it missing. "I . . . I must have dropped it," he stammered.

Anlawdd frowned, seemed almost black in the flickerlight of the single candle. "Cors Cant, I don't know what is considered proper where you come from, but here we *honor* our Mother! Throw those silly, old Constantines into the stream."

"Anlawdd, I'm not telling a story! My pouch is gone, with all my money." A thought occurred to the bard. "Look, I hate to ask you, but do *you* have a coin? You could give it to me, and I'll throw it into the stream. Then I can fetch it out again and give it back."

"NO!" she screamed. The vehemence startled him, and he flinched. Her voice was agonized, desperate. "Wisdom can *never* be bought! It must always be freely asked for, and *freely given.* That is the Law of Solomon."

She paused, smiled faintly. "Oh, I believe you dropped this on the way in, Cors Cant Ewin." She reached behind her back, pulled out his pouch, which she had tucked in her belt. She tossed it to him.

Hands trembling, he pulled his two remaining silver eagles out, dropped them into the stream. One missed, and he nudged it in with his bare foot.

"Why, Master Bard," she said, "I'm sure it's clean by now. You can take it back." He crouched and retrieved the coins, feeling the perfect fool.

"There is one last initiation," she added, holding her knife up. "You *must* trust only yourself," she repeated. "But you can *choose* to trust another with your own free will. Do you choose to trust me?"

This time he did not answer instantly. He thought about it carefully. *I see us intertwined. Our lives touch in so many places! If I ever trust anybody ... I will trust Anlawdd.* "Yes," he said, slowly but truthfully.

"With your life?"

"I already did."

"With your hands?"

He lowered his head, looked at his feet. She was right. They did look comical, one boot off and one boot on. "Yes," he said.

She set the candle on the ground, then turned the edge of the knife toward herself. Clenching her teeth, the girl pressed it against her left palm and slowly sliced her hand open.

Black blood streamed down her palm and wrist, dripped from elbow into water. She panted but did not cry out, handed the blade to Cors Cant. "Don't cut too deep. You still want to be able to play that harp of yours." Her voice sounded steady, but again he caught a tiny waver. *Mary and Rhiannon, someday give me control like hers!*

He held the shaking knife against his own palm, nerved himself to make the cut. *You can't do it!* screamed his brain. He pressed his lips together, furious at his cowardice.

Anlawdd blinked a tear from her eye, said nothing. But he understood how much her hand hurt. Quickly, before he could think better of it, Cors Cant sliced his palm shallowly.

For an instant he felt nothing; then the pain struck, and he bit his knife hand hard to keep down a yelp.

She seized his left hand with hers. Palm to palm, their

blood mingled, black as night in the candlelight. She intertwined her fingers with his and gripped tight.

Anlawdd took the knife from Cors Cant with her other hand and dropped it beside them. She held his right hand as if shaking hands, but pressed noticeably harder with thumb and third finger.

The bard reciprocated, guessing that was the correct response. For the first time, Anlawdd smiled, looked down at the knife. "It would be so easy . . . too easy. I won't jump the sword with you today, Cors Cant Ewin. Today you're my *brother Builder,* which makes me your sister, you know. We might someday become lovers, or maybe stay brother and sister, and I honestly don't know which."

She stopped to inhale, then continued. "I hereby give you permission to *try to win me,* which is better than getting me out of pity for a few moments among the needles and spools of thread, if you think about it. We meet on the level, and part on the square. Never turn your back on the widow's son, Cors Cant."

"Who's the widow's son?" he asked.

"Never answer that question save to another Builder, whom you will know by the sign I've just given you. Then, *tell* him that the widow's son is Hiram Abiff." She enunciated the words carefully, and Cors Cant grew suspicious.

"That I'll tell him," he said, "I'll tell him so. But truly, *is* Hiram Abiff the widow's son, or do I just say that he is?"

Anlawdd smiled. "Too clever by half is three times a halfwit, Cors Cant Ewin." She squeezed both his hands hard, then let go suddenly. She fumbled in her own pouch for a moment, extracted a long strip of clean cloth. She tore it in half and wrapped her bleeding hand.

Cors Cant did likewise with the other half, while wincing at the sharp, tearing sensation. *I'm going to feel this a long time,* he thought ruefully. He clenched his jaw, worked his left hand. It hurt, but he could still move the fingers.

"The brothers and sisters of the Temple of Sol Invictus thank you, and me especially. I'm glad I showed you my secret place, but we'd better get back." Her voice turned serious, and she lost her smile. "I'll bet there'll be some questions about our Saxon friends back there. I . . . may have acted in haste. But I had my reasons."

"Jutes," corrected Cors Cant a second time.

Anlawdd smiled and snuffed out the candle with thumb and finger. Cors Cant blinked in the instant blackness, felt her brush past him toward the crack. He followed, but she stopped so suddenly he ran into her.

"*What* was that you called me?"

"What? When?"

"Just a bit ago—you called me princess!"

"Whoops." Had the cave been lit, she would have seen his face redden. He shuffled his feet, uncomfortable under her invisible gaze.

"So," she said, "you speak Uncle Leary's tongue. I guessed you might, but hoped for the best."

"Yes, Your Highness." The moment the words left his lips, the boy felt a wall spring up between himself and Anlawdd. He bit his lip, forgot even his throbbing hand. *Princess* Anlawdd.

She felt it too. "Don't ever call me that. Never! Yes it's true, I'm the only daughter of Prince Gormant of Harlech—well, the only *legitimate* child of either sex—well actually, the *only* child, now; but what of it? It doesn't make me any less 'Anlawdd' that I was yesterday, does it?"

She continued, scarcely drawing breath. "And before you start to think that I'm too high-ranked for you, don't even think it! I told you you had a chance to win me, and *I* certainly knew I was a princess, and you weren't, I mean you weren't a prince, when I said that, so it still goes." She lowered her voice, sounding very vulnerable for a moment. "There are no titles in the Temple, Cors Cant."

He backpedaled a step. "All right, all right! I'm sorry, Your—I mean, I'm sorry, Anlawdd."

"Cors," she begged, "please don't tell anyone. I don't want to be sent back to Harlech. Not *now*. I have—a task." She sounded for all the world like an ordinary, young girl, pleading in the dark, though Cors Cant liked not the queer way she said the word "task."

"And besides," she added, "not everyone lives in the temple, *Bard*. For some, titles make all the difference in the world."

He moved closer until he felt her breath on his neck. Her lips were near enough to kiss. He almost did, but she was too easily wounded. It was not *right;* he wanted his next move to be right.

"I will tell no one," he swore.

"I mean it," she whispered. "If word gets about, you won't like the consequences, and neither will I, not a bit."

"No one. I swear!"

Anlawdd broke contact first. "So, Brother Bard, how do you come to know Irish? It's, um, it's not an everyday tongue in Camlann. You know."

The mood was broken. "College," he answered.

"You've been to Rome?" she asked, incredulous. "Or was it Alexandria? Didn't that bishop burn it down?"

"Druid College, back east, in Dun Laoghaire. Taught us Saxon, Greek, and Latin, and the five tongues of the islands, including Irish, though you and Canastyr spoke an odd dialect of it."

"Uncle Leary says we speak like Demonsthenes, except with concrete in our mouths instead of pebbles."

"To be bards, we learned the songs of all the world, Sicambria to Greece to Rome to Mauritania, from the chants of the Sephardim to the blood songs of the Sarmantians. And of course our own songs, whose stark beauty shames the pearls of the empire at the edge of the world."

"Don't you get some sort of *imprimatur* when you graduate, a lyre-license or something?"

His cheeks burned. She had touched on a very delicate subject. *Rem acu tetigisti,* and a sharp needle at that.

"Well actually," he amended, "I didn't, ah, *quite* graduate. I, well, I *almost* passed the bard exam—next year, I swear!"

He felt relief. It was finally out. "In Dun Laoghaire, the Archdruid Cynddylig Cyfarwydd the Guider taught me Greek and Latin letters. Myrddin later showed me how to mark the sounds of our own languages in both. We learned astrology, medicine, natural philosophy, and theology. Did you know the Norsemen worship versions of our gods, like Thor for Taranis? 'Course, the Romans think we worship versions of *their* gods."

She was near enough that he felt her smile in the black dark. "In all your studies, Cors Cant Ewin, did you ever learn the science of alchemy?"

"Alchemy? No, is that not just a myth? Myrddin taught that alchemists try to turn lead into gold!"

Her voice dropped to a conspiratorial whisper. "In the

Temple, I actually did it once. Turned base metal into gold. I think your Myrddin is a bit too *literal* sometimes . . . someday, I'll show you how it's done, I swear. *It's the whole secret of the Builders,* upon which the order is founded, or so Merovee says, according to Archking Leary, and you may as well believe Uncle as anyone. Dun Laoghaire was named after him—or his father, actually."

She brightened again, her voice rising in tone. "Well, don't just stand there like Blodowwedd Maid-of-Flowers! Let's get back to Camlann and make up a tale or two about fighting off the whole Jutic army. See? I got it right this time! It'll be much more interesting than what really happened." She was Anlawdd again, just Anlawdd.

He was beginning to feel himself again as well; the cantrip was finally wearing off. "Right behind you, Sister Autumn," he said, grinning like a goblin.

CHAPTER 32

PETER ROSE AS THE BARD AND HIS SEAMSTRESS SWEPT INTO THE hall, surrounded by soldiers, senators, even slaves. In the hubbub, Peter could make out nothing but the word "murder." Curiously, both Cors Cant and Anlawdd had bandages wrapped around their left hands.

Peter approached quickly, arriving at the same time as Artus. "What did you say about murder?" asked the *Dux Bellorum.*

"Attacked us!" The boy cried. "Three Jutes. They were after . . ." He looked at Anlawdd, who almost imperceptibly shook her head—*he's about to lie through his teeth,* thought Peter. "They tried to kidnap us!"

"Where?" demanded Arthur, furiously. "Cei! Lancelot! Call out a cohort, we'll hunt the dogs down!" He stopped in mid-command as Anlawdd extended her hand, frightened.

"Sir," she said, bowing her head to look at the floor as she spoke, "there really isn't any need to trouble your soldiers. I, um, well I mean Cors Cant chased them away, sir. He was very brave."

Artus stroked his chin, looked from Anlawdd to the boy. *Now* she's *the one lying like a rug,* Peter thought, confused. *So what the hell* did *happen?*

Artus shook his head, perturbed. "An unarmed bard, chase away three Jutes? Cors Cant, I would not like a bard to lie to me. See, Cutha himself has just now entered the hall."

"And *this* is my greeting?" cried a grating, guttural voice. Peter turned to see a tall, muscular Teuton with straw-colored hair, caked with grease and dirt. "Three brothers slain but two days after I arrive!"

That's odd . . . how did he know that? The girl said they'd been chased off—and Cors Cant said it was Jutes, not Saxons.

Cutha pushed his way between Peter and Artus, addressed the *Dux Bellorum.* "You will pay for this, Artehe . . . one way or another, tomorrow morning!" Cutha did an about-face, shoved Peter out of the way, as easily as the Sicambrian might shove the seamstress. Cutha stomped between the columns of the hall, and vanished back outside.

"Slain?" asked Artus. "Now it seems our young bard has slain three Jutic Saxons or Saxon Jutes with a supper knife! I *will* have this sorted out. I won't be bearded in my own hall. Did you kill them?"

Silence reigned. The bard nodded his head, while Anlawdd continued to stare at her feet as if she had just noticed them.

But nobody noticed the Clue of the Omniscient Saxon, thought Peter. No one else in the hall had known the Saxons or Jutes were dead . . . so how did *Cutha* know, if he only just arrived?

Artus continued the interrogation. "Were they Jutes or Saxons?"

"Jutes, I thought, sir, for they wore Jutic armor and dress."

"Did they speak Jutic or Saxon?"

"Ah. . . ." The bard chewed his lip, again looked like he was about to tell a whopper. "It's hard to tell the difference between those two tongues, sir."

Anlawdd gasped, as if she had suddenly discovered the

critical clue in an Agatha Christie novel. She kicked the bard's ankle, squirming and shifting her eyes doorward.

"Consul Artus, may we leave?" asked Cors Cant.

Artus looked from one to the other, clearly noticing Anlawdd's urgency. He nodded. "We *will* speak of this later, in a more appropriate venue." The boy saluted and vanished like a witness at a Londonderry bombing, his bird in tow.

Artus rubbed his bare cheeks, was silent for a long time, nearly a minute. Then he turned to Peter. "That is one furious Saxon, Galahadus my friend, my lance. I hope you've got one of Myrddin's tricks up your sleeve. You may need it tomorrow."

Peter frowned, remembered the feeling of being brushed aside like an annoying child. "Perhaps I do. I think I'll retire to my chamber." *Why did Artus call me "Galahadus"?*

He trooped up the stairs, blank face hiding deep thought. *Gwynhwfyr is too flighty; Morgawse is too worried for the* Dux Bellorum. He shook his head, temporarily crossed both off his list of suspects.

That doesn't leave many. Can't picture that seamstress as a twentieth century Irish terrorist. So who's left? The other ladies of the court . . .

Peter halted in mid step at sudden epiphany: *whoever said Selly had to inhabit the body of a woman?*

"Jumping Jesus and Mary!" he swore. "She could just as easily be a *man* now, damn her!" Angry as his blindness, he yanked aside the curtain to his room.

Cors Cant Ewin sat in the only chair, knees drawn up pensively. "Prince Lancelot," he said, "I need help, fast! I helped you with the translation, didn't I? Please, I beg this boon of you!"

"What boon?" asked Peter, warily.

"It's Anlawdd. Cutha did not lie. The Jutes were slain, but I cannot say how. I cannot lie to the *Pan-Draconis,* yet I cannot tell the truth, either." He looked up, terrified. "Prince Lancelot, what do I do *now?*"

CHAPTER 33

COLONEL COOPER SAT IN SMYTHE'S ROOM, STARING AT THE man's equipment laid carefully on the bed. *No gun. No vest. No medical kit. Peter, Peter, why did you disobey me?*

Nearly twelve of the allotted twenty-four hours had passed. Cooper looked at his watch: 1530. It was time.

He picked up the telephone, dialed an outside line, then a special number known to no other man in Her Majesty's government, not even Roundhaven. He had only called the number three previous times in as many years.

It rang three times. He hung up, repeated the procedure. On the first ring, the receiver was picked up, but nobody spoke.

"Riverrun," he said, "past Eve and Adam's."

"Loved a long the riverrun," answered a voice, thick with an Irish brogue, undoubtedly carefully practiced.

Cooper took a deep breath. He had planned this conversation for many hours, made careful notes. Yet now everything sounded feeble, mewling. He snorted, continued. "An operative. One of yours. We want her stopped."

"We're in a state of war, Colonel. Sure you know men get hurt, get killed."

"This is different. Many innocent lives, English *and* Irish."

"Irish, is it? And since when do the *sassenach* care aboot an Irish life here and yon?"

"Damn you, don't make this harder than it is. I've not abused this line. You know I haven't. I'm asking you to recall an operative before she completes her mission . . . and I'm prepared to offer."

"Sorry, Colonel; the IRA doesna' bargain with terrorists."

"Neither does the 22d. What do you want?"

"It's a woman?" Cooper grunted affirmative. "Ah, I've just the thing. Troina; Troian uiNaill."

"Trina O'Neal?"

"Everybody's own fair sweet colleen, caught in the act, with a hundred pound of Semtex. Now relaxing as a guest of the Crum."

Cooper thought a long time. He remembered the case; it was one he had planned. True, O'Neal had only been convicted of possession with intent, stopped before she could carry out her bloody mission, which surely would have been as brutal as the Londonderry op that had cost Peter Smythe his nerve.

But she was hardly a "fair, sweet colleen." Trina O'Neal was known to be a captain on active duty, implicated in the Carnaby Street Clothier bombing. That had been a bad one.

Cooper closed his eyes, envisioned Selly Conway or Conner or whatever her real name was. He imagined her with a high, conical hat balanced on her head, a diaphanous Mediæval gown, and a wicked knife in her hand, plunging it into . . . whom? Peter Smythe? King Arthur?

Can I possibly buy into this absurd faerie tale? But my God . . . what if it is true. . . .

In the end, no choice. He had to know. "All right, Trina O'Neal." *May God have mercy on my soul.*

"Who's the lass?"

"Selly Corwin," said Cooper without hesitation.

"Nae, tell me her *real* name. Her Irish name."

Cooper chose his words carefully. "So far as I know, Major, that *is* her real name." Corwin's dossier was incredibly skimpy, but it seemed to check out. She had a birth notice, public school, university record, VISA and MasterCard receipts and a Harrods' account.

"Selly? Selly *Corwin?* You're joking, mon."

"Corwin. Call her back, don't let her do this."

There was a long silence. "Give me a minute," said the IRA major at last. Cooper sat still, receiver pressed against his ear not to miss a single utterance. For three telephone calls, three years, he had waited for the major to make a mistake, mumble something that would reveal an ongoing operation. This was the fourth time he was disappointed.

But so is he, thought the colonel. *If I've gotten nothing, neither have I given.* He heard computer keys click as Major

—— consulted a data base program. *God, what I wouldn't give for a copy of that file,* wished Cooper. It was surely encrypted, but perhaps, if they managed to get a code . . .

It took much longer than normal. Minutes ticked past. Cooper felt a single bead of sweat roll down his nose, but he refused to move to wipe it off; the noise of shifting might garble a clue.

"Colonel," said the voice at last, "I regret to announce that the deal's off."

"Can it be that important?"

"Colonel, *I canna locate Selly Corwin.* I know every lass on active duty, but I checked anyway. Colonel, she's not one of ours."

"She's *what?*"

Major —— spoke carefully, trying to hide the worry in his own voice. "If she is on an operation, it is not sanctioned. Not one of ours."

Cooper finally plucked a handkerchief from his pocket, liberally swabbed at his face. His hand shook, scraping the telephone slightly against his growing stubble. "Then . . . whose is she?"

The major chuckled, too Irish by half. "You tell me, Colonel. You English have many enemies. There is another possibility, an' I mention this only to paint a complete picture."

"Which is?"

"She may be working for *no one.* Your Selly Corwin may be an indie, a fanatic. A rogue elephant."

A rogue brogue, Sweet Jesus! An uncontrolled IRA "buff" at King Arthur's round table. Cooper felt stomach acid rise up his gorge, winced as his much-maligned esophagus burned.

She's not working for anyone. She's a lone wolf, irrational, a fanatic! And my God, Peter doesn't know. . . .

"I'm sorry," said Cooper.

"An' Trina?" The voice was too carefully controlled. Cooper's eyebrows raised a fraction.

"I'm sorry," Cooper repeated, hung up the receiver. For many minutes he sat, massaging his temples, trying to swallow the bile back down.

She could do anything.

At least the sanctioned operations followed a coherent pattern. They generally called a warning when they planted a bomb . . . sometimes late, sometimes misleading, but at least *something*. And the IRA had never done in London what the PFLP did in the Athens and Rome airports, deliberately machine-gunning women, children, and elderly tourists to death with the single-minded ferocity of a crusader on a suicidal *jihad*.

But a *rogue*. . . . She could do *anything*.

Before he rose, Cooper rang one more number. The telephone was answered immediately.

"Tracking and Criminal Data Center Corporal Wilson on watch how may I help you sir?"

"This is Colonel Cooper."

"Yes sir. Please authenticate."

Cooper did, then continued. "I want a thorough background check on a provie prisoner in Crumlin Road Gaol, Trina O'Neal. I want to know every man she's slept with since she became an adult, with photos and dossiers. Direct the report to my office, Top Secret." It was worth a try, Perhaps Major ——'s own feelings could betray his identity. Why not?

"Yes sir."

Cooper hung up the telephone.

CHAPTER 34

HO! PERHAPS WE'RE GETTING SOMEWHERE, PERHAPS THE BREAK IN *the case we've been* . . .

"Whoa, slow down," said Peter, hand out. Cors Cant looked confused, and Peter realized the boy had said nothing since his first request for help. "Now what's this about Anlawdd and Saxons? Or was it Jutes?"

Cors Cant stood, paced narrowly, a corralled colt. "She's not what she seems to be, but I can tell you no more, for I have sworn."

Not what she seems to be, hm? "You've sworn not to tell."

"Yes."

"Given your word. Your word is important to you, isn't it?"

"Would it not be?"

Peter paused a beat. Another Celt with fanciful ideas of mystical honor! *Laddie, I can handle a dozen of you.* "Did you also give your word to Artus, swearing to serve the, ah, *Dux Bellorum* and your country? When two oaths conflict, which do you follow?"

Cors Cant stared at the floor, chewing his fingernail. Peter spoke again, the soul of reason: "Cors Cant, I am Artus's chosen champion, commander of his—legions." Legions? that was what Cei had said. "Your oath to Artus is an oath to me. Tell me what you saw."

The bard looked at Peter's feet. His voice was quiet, trembling. "I . . . cannot. She is a sister, I cannot betray her!"

A nun? For a moment, Peter was nonplussed. He felt pressure in his right hand fingers, realized he had pressed his thumb and ring finger together tightly. *Merovee. I shook his hand. He gave me the sign. Whatever they call it, they're bloody Masons.*

On a whim, Peter stepped forward, extended his hand. Cors Cant took it. The boy's eyes widened as Peter pressed with the same two fingers Merovee had used; Cors Cant fumbled the grip in return.

"Tell me," urged Peter, "for the widow's son."

The boy visibly started. "The w-widow's son?" Peter nodded silently. Cors Cant narrowed his eyes, asked, "Who is the widow's son?"

Dilemma . . . how far up the craft was the boy? Peter decided not to chance a level higher than Cors Cant had learned. "Hiram Abiff," he said. "Tell me now, as a brother in the craft."

"Sire! Are you too a Builder?"

"Didn't you recognize the grip?" They broke contact. Peter put both hands behind his back, watched Cors Cant intently.

The bard took a long breath, let it out, resolved. "She slew them, she did. Three of them, horse to horse, with a war axe! One of them she knew, for she called him by name—a Cymric name. She fought like a Briton, not like a Roman, staying in the saddle. I've never seen anything like it!"

Cymric? A Welsh name, then, neither Saxon nor Jute . . .

fascinating. But how did Cutha know, and why did he think they were Saxon?

"Remind me of something, son. Anlawdd is Gwynhwyfr's lady-in-waiting? A *seamstress?"*

"Ah. So that's occurred to you, too."

"Great Caesar's Ghost, a stitching maid killed *three armed men,* on horseback, with a battle-axe?"

The boy nodded eagerly, shuffled his feet. "And she gave me the right to win her! Imagine!"

"Win her? In battle, you mean?"

"Battle? I . . . how could I possibly . . ." Cors Cant's face lost its eager, coltish look. He shifted, glanced over Peter's shoulder. He even seemed to shrink slightly. Peter knew he had struck an open wound.

"What did she tell you exactly?" he asked.

"Well . . ." Cors Cant looked skyward, and Peter could tell he was mentally editing. "She said I had the right to try to win her. And she also said we couldn't—you know—like we were going to in her room. Not until it was *right.* But Sire, how do I know when it's right? What if I guess wrong, and she gets angry?"

"What were the circumstances when she said that? Where were you?"

"I can't tell you. In a secret place of Anlawdd's."

"What was her mental state?"

"Her what?"

Peter gestured helplessly, trying to find fifth century analogs for "mind-set" or *"weltanschauung."* "What had just happened that might affect her thinking?"

"You mean besides just having killed three brigands?"

"Oh. Yes, that might complicate her message."

Peter mentally moved Anlawdd several notches up the suspect list. The IRA could teach a girl a lot about killing, in all its various forms. Whatever else she was, Selly Corwin would be a magnificent scrapper . . . maybe good enough to kill three men, especially if they were Saxon conscripts, demoralized and stunned by the girl's ferocity. *Or Jutes, or Welshmen,* he added.

And why did she not tell the truth in the first place? Why had the men attacked at all, especially when their own prince was about to sign a peace treaty? And why attack a stitching girl?

Unless *these* Saxons did not want a treaty. *Rule number five*, thought Peter, *never assume all your enemies are brothers!*

"Cors Cant," he said, keeping the conversation going, "think logically. She knows you're a bard, not a fighter, so I don't think she meant win her in a battle. You're already the court bard, so you don't need to prove yourself that way. Perhaps by 'win her,' she meant for you to prove, um, that you love her and are willing to marry her."

Cors Cant looked confused. "Love her? Of course I do, but what's that got to do with marriage? The alliance would be unthinkable!"

"Alliance? What alliance could arise from a court bard and a seamstress?"

The boy slapped hand over mouth, literally tried to catch the words and pull them back. *Someday,* thought Peter, *I'll teach you the gentle art of poker.*

It was clear from his reaction that Anlawdd was much more than a lady's lady, somebody important enough for Camlann's court bard to worry about the "alliance." Important enough to rate first-class warrior training. Important enough for a three-man assassination squad ... unless they had planned to kidnap, rather than kill her? Peter filed the datum away, probed a bit deeper with a risky gambit.

"They weren't after you at all, were they, son? They were after Anlawdd."

"Well—"

"It was an ambush. They were waiting for her along the road somewhere. And if Anlawdd got all three of them, that means you didn't kill a single one. Did you?"

"Well—"

"Women are funny about the love stuff. Much as she may realize you're a bard, not a warrior, she wants to know you'll *try*, at least, to be a swashbuckler. A hero, I mean." *Yes, Peter, and what you don't know about women could fill a—*

"But—"

Peter stroked his chin, tried to feel as wise as he looked. "Do something self-sacrificing, Cors Cant. That ought to bring her around. Ah, *protect* her from something. Be a dashing rogue." *Good advice, my dear fellow! It's worked so well for you that you've had twenty-three lady friends in ten years!*

"Well—"

"Son, she's just looking for an excuse to fall in love with you, anyway."

"She is? But how can I protect *her* from anything?" He sounded anguished, urgent. He said "Her" as if it were capitalized.

If she's who I think she might be, it's you who'll need protection, bard.

"There are lots of ways to be selfless," Peter growled. He needed to be alone to ponder this new evidence—and to think of a way to fend off Morgawse, when she showed. He had to get rid of the boy, even if it meant feigning a war wound. If it worked, he could use the same excuse on Morgawse.

"You're a bard, right? Go and compose her a song. Now leave me. My leg burns like fire after that terrible wound I suffered at . . ." He gestured helplessly, as if the name was on the tip of his tongue.

"Mons Badonicus?"

"Mons Badonicus."

"But that was your shoulder, Sire."

"No, that one healed fine. But, um, a surgeon—" yes, he recalled, they did have surgeons then, "a surgeon told me there was a nervous connection between the arm and the leg; ah, betimes my leg aches like a son of a bitch."

"Sounds like nonsense . . . but I haven't studied medicine yet at the Druid College."

Thank God, thought Peter. He made a scuttling gesture toward the door. Cors Cant took the hint.

" 'Pon the morrow, Prince Lancelot. Luck in the lists."

"Thanks."

The boy left. When his footsteps receded down the stairs, the warrior picked out an axe and practiced what he remembered of the strokes that felled Medraut. But his mind ranged a millenium and a half away. *The problem: do I bait the trap with honey or vinegar to catch an Irish spider in her own web?*

CHAPTER 35

J ESUS AND MARY, WHAT A DAY. PRACTICING WITH ANCIENT WEAP-
onry, mapping Caer Camlann, practicing, filching paper (he
ran into a slave and had to pretend he wanted to draw pictures), practicing, steering far away from anyone who might
conceivably know Lancelot well enough to smell a wharf rat,
and mooning after Gwynhwfyr.

Stool tipped back, propped against the cold, unyielding
wall, Peter tried to compose his mind before bed. He wrote
in his investigative log, hawk-watching the door-curtain, wary
of someone entering and discovering him engaged in such
out-of-character literary activity.

*A deep one anlawth, cold in her way but not entirely like
Selly, I think. With my luck shes probably a mason or boy
scout or somesuch, as well! Try handshake*

*But where did she get such battlefield training? Or is the
boy lying? What is Anlawd hiding? and who did she kill on
the road—the Buddha?*

*Point 1, Selly must know we would know where she went.
Readings still visible on machine.*

*So point 2, she must know we'd try to bring her back, and
when that failed someone would come after her. Shes not stupid. she knows it would be me.*

*Concl: Selly Corwin knows I'm coming. Maybe guesses
I'm here.*

*Unless she's not here yet herself? Blundell said timelines
not linear, could be here before her or months after. Turn it
around, she can't know when I'm coming, may not know I'm
already here!*

*Morgawse sees too deeply to be a terrorist. She'd see the
endless cycle of attack revenge counterattack, maybe she'd be a*

Sinn Fein politician, more likely a barrister in modern times. Thinks too much to be a good soldier.

Gwynhwver

He hesitated, tried to imagine sweet Gwynhwfyr with a blade in her hand, cutting the *Dux Bellorum*'s throat as they slept together. Suddenly, the image twisted in his mind. He saw them engaged in passionate sex instead, a copy of the *Kama Sutra* spread-eagled before them, flipping pages in orgasmic fury.

He shuddered, unsure which vision disturbed him more. When Peter finally wrenched his thoughts back to his log, Gwynhwfyr had her left leg hooked over the bedpost, her right hand and foot on the blue dots, while Artus spun the arrow.

Suspricks

SUSPECTS on the male side: Cors Cant, Kay, Bedwer, Medraut, Merovee.

Female suspects: Anlawth, Guinevere. He sighed as he wrote the latter name.

Cross off Cors Cant, hes too much a part of his world. But hes not telling all about Anlawth and the fight with Saxons. Merovee, no. Gut feeling. Won't turn my back to him but he's not Selly Corwin.

Leaves five primary suspects, An Gwyn Kay Bed Med, but it could be someone completely unrelated—hat check girl, window washer.

Peter heard a creak in the hallway. He quickly slid his log inside his chemise, listened intently.

No one. It was the wind. *The end of Day-Two,* he thought. He lay back on the mat, tried desperately not to think of the blond princess and her Kama Sultry dance.

CHAPTER 36

I SQUEEZED THAT BOY'S SHOULDER AS WE LEFT THE PRESENCE OF the *Dux Bellorum*, for he had held up under heavy examination without spilling the badger out of the bag, and a princess must always reward loyalty. Then I said "go," and pointed imperiously, for I needed to be alone to think, and, to be sure, he gave me no argument, perhaps having his own thoughts to order.

I returned to my room in Gwynhwfyr's apartment, drew the curtains, snuffed the candles (with my fingers, of course, minding what I told That Boy in the cave), and sat crosslegged in the dark, thinking of what I had just learned.

First, the only possible way that Cutha could have known so quickly what happened is if there had been *another* Saxon, I should say Jute, besides the two I killed (and Canastyr), one who rode like the wind to Camlann, found Cutha, and broke the bad news.

Or perhaps I *should* say "Saxon," for it was now clear that despite their dress and armor, Canastyr's two accomplices were Saxons, not Jutes—and that raised a sticky can of earthworms.

Of necessity, we in Harlech must occasionally contact Jutes, for the principality of Hrundal's brother, Prince Hrothgar, sits along the southern coast of the Isle of Monapia. (Hrothgar and Hrundal can't stand each other, and either Hrothgar was cast out of Winchester or else he scarpered, a hare's dash ahead of the hounds.)

Jutes are a pain, but in the main they're neutral . . . but Saxons! They're something else entirely, and I really can't say what without using words from their own language.

I sat in my room, wondering what even such an earthworm as Canastyr could do with a pair of Saxons, clearly in contact with Cutha, when suddenly I remembered *where I had seen that bastard,* the son of Caedwin.

I leapt to my feet, stood shivering in the dark with my heart pounding like a fox pursued by hunters . . . *I saw Cutha in my very own father's hall!*

Cutha and one of the men I slew sat in Gormant's own *triclinium,* swilling beer and gorging themselves on honest, Harlech meat; but they were dressed as Britons, not Saxons, or else I would surely have had something to say about it! And so would have Uncle Leary, when I told him.

They were speaking when I entered to ask Father where he had left the royal seal, for I had to approve the new prayers that finally included Pope Leo, though of course he became Bishop of Rome ten years ago. When I entered, Cutha and his Saxon slave fell instantly silent; I didn't think much on it at the time, but I realized now that I would surely have recognized the Saxon accent, even if they were speaking Cymric or Irish.

Were the Jutes in league with the Saxons, as the arms and armor on the Saxons and my brother suggested? It was a horrifying thought, for if they were, then surely my own father, Prince Gormant of Harlech, was involved, for Canastyr never stepped outside without Father's approval!

And he would never step anywhere again.

I thought I saw a faint glow in the corner of my room. I blinked, but it was still there. I began to approach, but at once my heart jumped, then pounded like a Saxon war drum; instead, I backed slowly to the opposite side of the room, though that was still a mere five paces from the incandescence.

It took shape, an anguished, writhing form that vaguely resembled a man, perhaps the soul of a man who died in torment. Before it had half formed, I knew who it was.

I pointed at him: "Haunt me not, Brother! Your blood paints your own hands, not mine!"

Canastyr's shade said nothing, but hissed like the wind across a field of dead grass. In my mind, though, I heard words, spoken not aloud but directly into my brain.

Murder foul corrupt fratricide. . . .

"Your own horse slew you! 'Twas no doing of mine!" It was a feeble evasion, for 'twas my blow that set the mount to madness with the pain; and had Canastyr lived but a few moments before, his blood would indeed have stained my hands more directly.

Murder!

Spectral hands reached toward me, stretched across the distance toward me, toward my breasts. I screamed, pressed back into the corner. "Why? Why would I murder you?" I sobbed, unable to master my fear.

Because—

Because—

"I had no reason! You followed me to Camlann, you *made me do it!*"

Because *YOU LIKED IT.*

Rage swelled within my stomach, and I strode forward, waving my hands. How did he know? How did Canastyr know, even in death, what I feared most—that somehow I had *enjoyed* what he did to me those years ago?

I didn't! I don't think . . . no, I know I didn't!

Still, the thought terrified me, for what if it were true? Did I kill my brother because I wouldn't let him do it to me again, or because I couldn't stand his accusing smirk, his knowing smile that said *I know what you really want, you perverse witch!*

My waving hands fanned away the spectral glow like smoke from a greenwood fire, and I fell to the floor, gasping with relief. Canastyr's shade had fled; but his foul, rotting breath remained: it remained in my mind's ear, whispering his evil accusation.

I knew then I had to leave, had to get out of Camlann as fast as I could, for the foulness and corruption of Rome pressed in against my body, crushing me beneath its perversions and heresies: Artus must die, and die soon, today or tomorrow, if I could bring myself to do it. Of course, when a murderer will stoop to fratricide, can regicide run far behind?

In Rome, anything that wasn't compulsory was forbidden; what wasn't forbidden was soon becoming compulsory. Worse, all roads led to Rome—so they told me, but maybe it was just another Roman lie.

Nothing simple; conspiracies lurked wherever I looked. Oh, how I longed for the good old days of petty kings and princes, when life was simple, when lords and ladies rode the wild hunt through the woods, lived in harmony with all natural things, spoke and walked with the gods as if they were cook and nurse, and gave nary a thought to politics, religion, and the ethics of assassination!

I spit, but the taste of Canastyr would never leave my tongue, his accusation sticking like bitter tree sap that you chew and chew but never manage to swallow or spit out.

I *didn't* want it! How dare he say I did?

I *didn't.*

CHAPTER 37

A PIPE CALLED, LONG AND BLUE ACROSS THE MOOR. *COME TO ME, come/blood for me, blood!* Mist wrapped around the grey drones, the green chanters; bright red melody punctured the misty veil. Sergeant MacBanquo's ghost walked at midnight beneath the ruins of a Londonderry cafe spreading itself over twisty streets and straight, Roman roads. Major Smythe ran in circles, collected pieces of his command in a russet potato basket.

But then the sun rose, and Peter opened his eyes to a painful glare: dawn through the southeast window.

He jerked upright. A piper did stand at the gate, piping in the morning. Peter rose, fumbled for the—for the—for something that should have hung from the bedpost. It was gone, no Ingram Mac-10 machine pistol.

He shook his head, felt a cold, wooden handle in his hand. It was a short, Roman sword, a *gladius,* not a gun. He was Lancelot now, not Peter Smythe. Legate of two Roman legions for Artus *Dux Bellorum. Remember that,* he ordered himself. *Must not let Her spot me before I spot* Her. He smiled, realized he thought of Selly in the same tone of voice that Cors Cant Ewin thought of Anlawdd.

Ah, Day-Three. This is the day I die in the stadium, cheered on by the entire population of Camelot.

He filled his chamber pot, made his toilet, and pondered. Too many mistakes. Too many ways to cock it up; Lancelot, the original, had lived at Caer Camlann for years! How could Major Peter Smythe possibly hope to mimic the man?

The bard's already spotted me, at least knows something's wrong. How can I ...

He closed his eyes, turned his attention inward. He still felt it: a sharp-edged, slithering lump inside his head. Lancelot of the Languedoc, the Sicambrian, general, consul, senator, champion of Camlann and Artus's right hand. Present, *in Peter's own head.* There was knowledge for the taking!

Dare I let him out of the box? Have I a choice?

You will let me out, pig demon!

A truce. I have no wish to be here. Catch me the spy and I'll fly.

No answer. Perhaps Lancelot was thinking it over. Perhaps he still did not understand what was happening. Peter opened his eyes, fell back into Lancelot's body.

Footsteps; three men approached. One pounded on the wall next to the curtain. "Prince Consul, Champion of Camlann, coming down with us to break your fast, Sire?"

"Sure, Cei," answered Peter. "Give me a moment." Cei, Bedwyr, and a third man, still unknown, conversed outside in low tones about Cutha's chances while Peter dressed.

Lancelot's wardrobe was chiefly marked by lack of creativity: all that he possessed were tunics, shirts, skirts or kilts, and breeches in blue, black, blue *and* black. Peter sniffed the clothing, futilely searching for something clean. The Champion had apparently avoided being infected by the dread Roman (and British) disease of bathing.

God and Mary, nos morituri *in dirty underwear....*

Peter selected pants with a distinct cross-weave, almost tartanlike, a light chamois, and a black tunic. Hoping he remembered correctly, he pulled on the same armor he had worn when he arrived. The trembling in his entire body was barely noticeable.

He pulled back the curtain. Cei pushed past into the room followed by a tall, blond teenager.

"All right, what're you planning to use?" asked Cei. He crossed to the pile of weapons, selected the axe Peter had practiced. "Pig killer, *gladius,* shield. What else?"

Peter pulled at his lower lip. He had dreaded this moment. How was he supposed to answer? "Nothing else. Fighting light today."

"No lances?" Cei sounded incredulous.

"Of course lances. I was talking about hand-to-hand."

"Fine," drawled Cei. "Gwyn Galahadus, take the shit to the stables. Armor up Eponimius; make sure that bastard pig-fucker groom brushes him down. If he forgets, I want him flayed."

"Yes, sir!" said the young man. He gathered the apparatus, sneaked an awe-filled glance at Peter. "Mother sends her warmest regards," he said, for Peter's ears only.

Peter nodded. "Thank you, son." *Is this Sir Galahad, my squire? Where did I hear the name Galahadus before?* Peter's ears reddened as he remembered that Malory said Galahad was Lancelot's son.

"Let's go, Prince," said Bedwyr. "Cei, can Myrddin conjure something?"

Cei shook his head as they left the room, headed for the stairs. "Cutha's got his own sorcerers or something, that's what. He said he can't get a thing on him. Damned Druids."

Bedwyr apparently agreed. "Fucking bastard Druids never do anything when you need it. Get rid of 'em is what I say. Cut their tongues out, let honest soldiers run the island. What I say."

Harsh, discordant stress grated in Bedwyr's voice. *He's ready to bite the head off a nail,* Peter thought. He himself was cold with fear. *Ought to get that bleedin' Druid Merlin to stand in for me. He could use his magic to ward off Cutha's axe blows.*

He remembered a scene: long, long ago, fifteen centuries in the future, a Royal Marine gunnery sergeant lined up (would line up) his Loyalist Belfast company. He spoke quietly, unlike their drill instructor: "Your body knows what to do. Trust your body. It's your mind what gets in the way, you lazy Irish hounds. Set a goal, draw a straight line, and tear through anything that bloody gets in your way like a bloody tank." Captain Smythe stood before the men—his first command—and listened closely to his gunny.

All I need do, thought Peter, twelve years later, a millenium and a half earlier, *is draw a line that bisects Cutha the Saxon and follow it right through him. Simple. Oh bloody right, just as simple as Londonderry.* He turned his head, stared intently at the smoothed, painted wall as they trooped downstairs, forced himself *not* to think of bloody Sergeant O'Neill, who was simply everywhere at once.

CHAPTER 38

THE PIPER BLEW A LONG, BRASSY YELLOW NOTE AS PETER stepped into the frosty morning. A crowd of at least six to eight thousand surrounded him, cheered lustily—much of the town and surrounding countryside excepting those too young, too old, too sick. Hands unseen clapped his back, while those in front clenched their fists in support. *Shouldn't I wear a robe and boxing gloves?* he wondered.

Instead, Galahadus had dressed him in a molded metal breastplate, sculpted to resemble Arnold Schwarzenegger's chest, with an assortment of chain mail, iron skullcap, and leather pieces. This time, a mailed hood had been added, which apparently served the function of making the games more exciting by blinding the combatants.

For the moment, Peter carried both hood and cap; it was too hot to wear them just yet.

A tidal mob rushed Peter along through the *triclinium,* counterclockwise around the front of the palace, and through a hedge-maze courtyard to the stadium he had explored earlier.

Bedecked with red and green ribbons, the stadium was a hundred and fifty yards long, but only thirty yards wide, with a sunken floor of moist sod, where yesterday it had been dusty dry. Either it had rained during the night, or Artus had had slaves out watering it with buckets.

White marble columns lined the palace side and half of the opposite side, supporting a roofed grandstand viewing area in which most of the spectators gathered, howling lustily. Gold ribbons sequestered a central box from spectators. More seats circumnavigated the stadium, but thousands had to stand right at the edge of the field to watch the show.

Artus and Gwynhwfyr occupied the center chairs, Myrddin and Cors Cant to their left. The *Dux Bellorum* wore his customary white Roman toga, while the faerie-gamin Gwynhwfyr appeared in gold and mother-of-pearl–trimmed purple drapery that pinned at her left shoulder. Beneath it, Peter saw a tartan tunic.

Cors Cant's knees were drawn up. Pensive and intense, he watched Peter. Merovee sat at Artus's right hand, blue-trousered legs gracefully crossed, hands neatly folded in his lap. He nodded politely when he saw Peter; a flicker of excitement crossed his lips.

Anlawdd stood behind Gwynhwfyr and the bard, draped in a slightly off-white robe with black fur trim. She munched grapes out of a bowl, when she was not offering them to Gwynhwfyr. *Where the hell did they get grapes, for God's sake?* As Peter watched, she peeled one and surreptitiously dropped it down Cors Cant's collar.

The bard jumped, slapped his back. He stared 'round, trying to see who was the culprit; Anlawdd stared into the middle distance, innocent and open-faced.

Gwynhwfyr raised an obsidian black bottle to her lips, chug-a-lugged half. She put it down and belched loudly. A trickle of wine colored her cheek. No one except the old magician Myrddin thought it rude; he rolled his eyes and shook his head, tried to disappear into his voluminous grey robes.

"Lancelot!" shouted a voice in the warrior's ear. He jumped, said "Hunh?" A faint flicker from short-term memory told him he had been called several times.

It was Cei, wicked grin on his face. "Oh, Prince, methinks the Saxons want to know if your spirit's left your body."

"What?"

Cei leaned close, spoke through teeth gritted to a smile. "You're standing there like a damaged cow! Care to do something, like, perhaps join Cutha for the benediction?"

"Whoops. Sorry, just thinking."

"Try not to. You're in Lloegr, not an Athenian philosopher's college."

Cei led him toward the center of the stadium as the crowd

filled available space on the perimeter, yelling, laughing, making book.

Cutha waited impatiently. White-faced, grim-lipped, he glowered at Peter, trembling with fury (or fear?). His own armor was much different from Peter's: heavy on the chain mail, with an iron vest made of banded metal. He, too, used an axe; but it was longer and had no point at the top.

Cors Cant descended to the field and crossed the bare dirt, took by the elbow an incredibly ancient man with a white beard tucked into his belt. "The Archdruid of Camlann," said the boy reverently, "Cynddylig Cyfarwydd the Guider. Myrddin's master." Cors Cant bowed and withdrew. The old man stood calmly until Saxon and Sicambrian were nose-to-nose.

"May the strength of Wotan flow through your arm," said Cynddylig to Cutha, "and the courage of Donner Thunder-Bearer stiffen your resolve to fight to the bitter end."

"Your penis I will tear off and slowly down your throat twist it," promised Cutha under his breath, smiling sharklike at Peter.

Unperturbed, the old man turned. "Accept the wisdom of Rhiannon, the battle strength of the Morrigu Triplet, the ordered mind of the *Dux Bellorum*'s Mithras."

"Kiss me," suggested Peter to Cutha.

"My hand up your anus I will shove, you to your death I shall strangle with your lower intestines that I tear out." Cutha grinned. Alternate teeth were missing, a hideous jack-o'-lantern.

"Accept the holy swastika on your brow," continued the unflappable Cynddylig, "a sign of favor from Donner and Blitzen." The priest dipped his finger in a vial of oil, anointed Cutha's brow.

"Not even Dasher, Prancer, and Vixen can save your arse," said Peter. He stared expressionless at the Saxon.

"You the sworn man of Artehe's wife are," said Cutha. "After you I kill, in front of all her subjects, she will I rape, and upon Artehe himself will I urinate."

Peter began to sweat from the intense heat inside his armor beneath the rising sun.

"Take this necklace of stars, sign of the wisdom of Rhiannon." The Archdruid handed Peter a necklace strung with tiny crystals. "Let it remind your divine horse Eponimius of Our Lady of the Stars, that it may carry its burthen as She carried Hers."

"There's a motley lot of little boys around here, Cutha," responded Peter. "Wouldn't you rather have one of them? That's what your mother said last night, anyway."

"The two of you bring great honor upon this field," said the old man, still pretending he had not heard a word. *Or perhaps he's deaf as a post?* "Go and try your might, one against the other. No horse-stomping, eye-gouging, groin-kicking, or ear-biting. Student of the bardic arts, Cors Cant Ewin, will marshal the fight."

He thumped his staff on the bare, muddy soil, turned and shuffled back to the shaded stand. Cors Cant rushed up to take his arm, then returned to the field after seating the old man, tucking a blanket around him.

Peter and Cutha pressed belly-to-belly, gave each other The Stare. Cei pulled Peter back, while a Saxon retrieved Cutha. Back at the stands, Gwyn led Eponimius next to a boarding stair. Peter stepped up and mounted the horse, a far easier and more graceful method than the pommel-vault. He locked his legs over the ridges, then worked the shield up his left arm, fixing the curved rectangle at a jaunty angle.

Cors Cant raised a wooden staff, shouted *"PAN-DRACONIS, REX ET REGINA, PRINCIPES, MILITES ET DOMINAE, CIVITES, ET CETERI,"* he called. Peter jumped, startled at the volume. "The match is between Cutha the Saxon, second son to Caedwin, King of Wessex, and Lancelot the Sicambrian, Prince of the Languedoc, champion to Artus *Dux Bellorum* and the Island Earth." The crowd roared, incoherent save for howls of "Lance!" and a few smothered shouts of "Cutha!"

Peter was abruptly pulled off balance by a yank on his hair. He turned to behold Gwynhwfyr, standing upon the boarding ramp. She smiled puckishly, grabbed his face, and squirted her tongue down his throat. She entwined her fingers in his black locks.

He grabbed for her own hair, tried to pull her away. But it was too short; he only pushed her head closer.

She tasted of honeyed wine, tangy roses, scented ginger, spiced musk, husky fire, burnt pollen. The burning sun, the stadium, crowd, castle, even Gwynhwfyr herself vanished into the hot, moist kiss. Peter wilted, nearly fell from the saddle.

"A favor," she breathed into his mouth. Her grey, restless eyes darted away and back again, hummingbirds.

"A-a-anything you w-want," he whimpered.

She puzzled a moment, then laughed like a watery dulcimer. "No, stupid—I want to *give you* a favor, not ask one!" She hiked up her tunic and chemise to expose slender, white, perfect thighs. Peter goggled; she wore no undergarments save for a single ribbon of gold and silver thread embroidered on white cloth tied about one creamy thigh.

Gwynhwfyr untied the ribbon, looped the pungent cloth over Peter's incredulous face, tied it at his throat. "Just a sample," she said, then leaned across Eponimius and licked Peter's cheek. "See me after you unseat this unwashed, uncouth thunder worshiper!"

Struck dumb, Peter peeked over his right shoulder, toward the royal box. Artus watched the scene, mouth grim. Merovee pretended great interest in the bowl of grapes. Peter tried to disengage, but Gwynhwfyr wrapped her arms about his waist and grabbed his thigh. "Afters?" she begged again.

"Yes-fine-let-me-go!" said Peter through clenched teeth. She pressed her breasts against his armored chest, leaned her head back in ecstasy. He noticed a faint scar beneath her ear he had not seen before. At last, he reached back and disengaged her hands. He urged Eponimius forward to his spot, next to Cei, who took the reins.

Sweet Jesus and the Virgin, what monster have I created? Cei thumped his breastplate, snickered. " 'At's a bit of all right, hey?"

But Cors Cant was still declaiming about the match. "Cutha of Wessex comes to Camlann direct from the Jutic front near Alban. He fought bravely on the field and killed four Jutes with his own hand! In competition his record is seventeen wins, no losses, one contested decision."

Cors Cant continued his recitations, clearly a memorized spiel. "Lancelot of the Langedoc is champion of Caer Camlann, legate of two legions, tribune and consul. His most recent command was at the third battle of Mons Badonicus, where he caused grievous damage among, um, the Wessex forces." Cors Cant bowed courteously toward Cutha, who hocked and spat. "Senator Lancelot holds a competitive record of twenty-three wins, no losses."

An egg sailed over the heads of the crowd. The boy ducked, but the missile continued way overhead toward the stands.

"Lance!" called Cei. "Cutha favors reverse overhand blows." Peter nodded, hoped to figure out what a reverse overhand blow was before it beheaded him.

Gwynhwyfr jumped up and down until she caught his attention. Clearly, she did not believe in brassieres.

"KICK HIS INNARDS OUT!" screamed the princess of Britain. Peter guiltily poked at the ribbon around his neck as Cei slapped Eponimius's rump. The stallion reared, screamed, and bucked to the middle of the field.

It spun him around several times. Dizzy, Peter pulled the mailed hood over his head. It nearly ripped his ears off going on. He blinked, realized all he could see was metal rings. Tiny flashes of light hinted an outside world. He twisted the hood frontwards again, trying to find the eyeholes, and slapped the cap securely atop his head, hoping it would stay in place.

He groped for a javelin. Eponimius lurched forward, and Peter almost succeeded in unhorsing himself. He thought he heard the crowd roar with laughter, but his own breath was so loud in the metal hood he could not be sure.

The crowd cacophed. Cei shouted something unintelligible. Peter squinted through steel rings, realized Cutha was charging toward him like a locomotive. The Saxon raised his spear, flung it directly at Peter's chest. This javelin had a wicked, sharp tip.

Eponimius saved Peter's life. The horse sensed danger, skittered quickly sideways. Cutha's javelin grazed Peter's shoulder, buried itself a foot in the soft earth.

Spurred to action, Peter leaned forward and Eponimius galloped around the stadium perimeter. He turned when he reached the southwest end, his first javelin still unthrown in his hand. *Is it okay to reserve weapons?* "Marshal" Cors Cant watched but said nothing.

Cutha faced Peter across the field. The Saxon war-horse snorted, pawed the dirt like an impatient bull.

He charged. This time, Peter waited not upon the blow, but charged in turn. He cut to the right, raised his weapon to throwing position. "Viva El Cid!" he cried, added "Die, you bleedin' bastard!" No one could hear him anyway.

Cutha mirrored his position, also raised his javelin. But just before they made contact, the wily Saxon leaned hard left, swerved across the line of the charge to Peter's right.

The Sicambrian stared stupidly, unable to throw without striking his own horse's head. Cutha leaned now to his right and extended his javelin like a pool cue, deftly tapping Peter's breastplate as he passed.

The world rotated sideways. Peter slipped, slipped, finally rolled off Eponimius's port side in slow motion. He struck the dirt headfirst, ploughed a five-foot furrow in the peat.

The field spun sickeningly; Peter gripped it, afraid to let go lest he slide off into the sky. Stunned, face drained of blood, he pushed himself to his knees, grimaced at the pain. Gingerly, he reached up to feel the dent in his helm. The crowd was stunned to silence—*Lancelot unhorsed!*

His skull throbbed. But a fierce, angry voice—his old drill instructor—berated him to his feet. He wobbled, but stood. He felt a weight in his hand, looked down, and saw the axe. *When in God's name did I pick* that *up?* Peter marveled. His shield was nowhere to be seen, one broken leather strap remained buckled around his arm.

Cutha reined in his horse. He curled his lip at Peter. Then he kicked his horse forward with spurless boots, charged the grounded Sicambrian. Peter prepared himself for a death blow. Without a shield, he could only try to dodge out of the way of the viciously barbed javelin.

A white robed figure streaked across the field. In an instant, Cors Cant threw himself between Peter and the charging warhorse. *"HOLD! HOLD!"* screamed the boy.

The crowd roared, but a single woman's voice, Anlawdd's voice, carried above the rest. *"NO! GET OUT OF THE WAY, CORS YOU IDIOT!"*

The boy held his staff above his head, as if he thought it would magically deflect the Saxon's blow. Peter watched the bard's last moments on earth. It was Sergeant MacDougal all over again.

CHAPTER 39

ORS CANT WATCHED CUTHA CLOSE THE DISTANCE, JAVELIN LOW-
ered like a thrusting lance. *I should be terrified,* he thought.
Instead, a calm descended across him, a peaceful shroud. He
held aloft his marshal's staff.

"*Hold,*" he commanded. The Saxon could not possibly
have heard above his own horse's hooves, but Cors Cant
knew he did.

The crowd fell silent. The entirety of Cors Cant's attention
was focused upon Cutha, a wonder the Saxon did not burn
under the gaze. But the bard *knew* that Artus had risen to his
feet behind him, finger outstretched, just as he *knew* Anlawdd
had leapt the rail and was halfway across the field, a lance from
the weapon pile in her hands. Neither could stop the Saxon:
Cors Cant would live or die according to Cutha's temperament.

The Saxon thrust his javelin. The spear plunged straight
toward the boy's breast, but at the last instant, Cutha whipped
it over Cors Cant's shoulder and passed him by, howling a
chilling war cry.

Cutha vanished behind the bard. Cors Cant saw only the
field, the stadium crowd, behind them Caer Camlann rising like
a mountain. His hands began to shake uncontrollably. At last he
forced the muscles to obey, lowered his arms. "Th-that was an
il-illeg . . . unacceptable blow," he explained in a whisper.

He looked behind him. Artus's face was red with anger.
Princess Gwynhwyfr hid her face in her hands, afraid to see
Cors Cant turned into bard-on-a-stick.

Anlawdd pretended the lance had suddenly grown too
heavy for her, "poor, weak woman" that she was. She
dropped it and scuttled back to the stands.

The spell broke. The stunned crowd began to babble and

207

shout. Cors Cant's knees abruptly buckled and he sat heavily
in the dirt. He looked at Anlawdd; she watched, face pale as
a midnight courtyard. Then she forced a disdainful headtoss,
weakly ran a hand through autumn hair.

Cutha galloped around the chariot track. He raised his javelin, hurled it into the dirt at Lancelot's feet. The Saxon dismounted and elaborately drew his axe.

The boy took a deep breath, turned to the champion of
Caer Camlann. "Are you able to continue, my Prince?" His
voice broke, and he cleared his throat.

"Yes, of course," said Lancelot, voice a cold north wind.
"And thank you, bard." He raised his own axe, saluted the
Saxon respectfully.

Cutha did not return the salute. "Yourself from the field remove, Child Bard," he growled. Cors Cant raised his staff to
signal them to continue, ran to the sidelines, close enough to
feel Anlawdd's presence, but far enough to observe her.

Cutha advanced on Lancelot, swung his axe in a double
loop. Lancelot held his stiffly, an awkward tyro. Cutha circled
and struck; the Sicambrian parried, barely.

Cors Cant saw a flicker in his peripheral vision, a man
threw something. Another rotten egg whizzed over the combatants. Again it missed its target; but this time it struck another: Anlawdd.

She gasped as the raw, rotten mess splattered across her
face. The crowd jeered and pointed at her. Cors Cant looked
away, so she would not see that he had seen.

The Saxon struck like thunder, feinted like lightning. Lancelot got his axe in the way of each blow, but that was all.
He launched no counterattack. His defense was clumsy, reac-
tive rather than proactive. Even Cors Cant, with his limited
combat knowledge, could tell that much.

Anlawdd wiped the egg from her face, fixed her eye on the
location whence it had come, and disappeared into the crowd.
She seemed preternaturally calm, as the bard had been when
Cutha charged him. In a moment, even her hair was lost to view.

Lancelot's mirrored breastplate caught the morning sun,
rippled like midnight water. Cors Cant realized the man
moved well, never off balance. But each of Cutha's axe blows
fell as a complete surprise to Lancelot.

White eclipsed silver as Cutha circled, his freshly painted

white mail a stark contrast to the senator's Roman armor. Cutha struck a vicious overhand blow, and suddenly Lancelot was *there–not there.*

The champion spun in a fast circle and Cutha cleaved the air where Lancelot had stood a moment before. The prince was now behind Cutha; Lancelot put his hand on the small of Cutha's back and pushed, sent him sprawling.

Very deliberately, Lancelot raised his axe, whipped it down viciously at Cutha's exposed face. At the last moment, he pulled the blow, and instead drove the axe deep into the dirt.

Cors Cant stared openmouthed. The crowd hushed again. The prone Saxon stared at the axe, then at Artus. "The champion yields!" cried the ecstatic Cutha, scrambling to his feet.

"Ho! Not a word of it!" shouted Lancelot, drawing Cutha's attention back. The prince gestured with both hands: *come get me, Saxon hound!*

Confused, Cutha looked to Cors Cant for a ruling. The boy stepped forward into the ring, turned to Artus. But the *Dux Bellorum* merely smiled, gave him no help. Merovee seemed inordinately amused, as if to say, *it's your call, son; pass it not to another!*

This is ludicrous! thought Cors Cant. *He's unarmed, but* . . . Cors Cant walked slowly to center stadium, all eyes upon him, each ear attuned. He opened his mouth, thought better of the answer.

He stared at the empty-handed Lancelot, the armed Saxon, the axe buried deep in the tournament field. Many men had died on the ground where Cors Cant's feet trod: gladiators, rebellious princes, bereft and lonely lovers, slaves.

What was one more suicide, one more bag of blood and bone?

He spoke loudly, so all could hear. "I will not interfere," ruled Cors Cant. "Lancelot disarmed himself voluntarily. He chose a steep, rocky road; let the chariot roll. Fight!" Suddenly nervous, feeling their eyes, he dashed for the chariot track.

The raging Saxon charged the short distance, chopped downward in an ugly, whistling, full-swung arc. Lancelot moved only slightly, yet it was enough that Cutha cut only the wind. This time, Lancelot turned the same direction as Cutha, grabbed the Saxon's neck and his right wrist, whirled him in a short circle.

Cutha stumbled to his knees. He struggled up, pulled his
axe back for a killing stroke. Lancelot skipped forward, drove
a metal-shod heel into Cutha's solar plexus.

Mail was never meant to stop a blunt blow. Cutha doubled
over, backpedaled out of range. The next time, he approached
warily, axe held high. Lancelot let him get within range, then
dropped and spun on his heel.

His right leg hooked back, swept Cutha's feet from under
him. Cutha floated a moment, thudded to his belly, once-
white armor now stained with black mud, green grass stains.
He crawled to hands and knees.

Lancelot stepped forward, swung his banded, gauntleted
fist in a tight arc, connected squarely. Cutha's head rang like
a *cymbalum,* metal skullcap flew a man length across the stadium. He staggered back, and his knees wobbled, then buckled. He sat abruptly, dropped his axe, and lay back gently.
Cutha struck no more.

The champion of Caer Camlann grabbed a handful of mail,
hauled Cutha to a seated posture. Lancelot pulled his fist back,
aimed a blow to separate the Saxon's teeth from his mouth.

"HOLD!" cried Cors Cant, dashed back onto the field, marshal's staff high. Lancelot kept his fist cocked, looked to Artus.

"Less . . ." hissed Cutha through a mouthful of blood,
"fishnish . . . less us fishnish." He was dazed, clearly unable
to defend himself.

"Consummatum est," proclaimed Artus, soft voice heard
from southwest to northeast. Merovee smiled in agreement,
and Lancelot dropped Cutha to the ground. The Saxon lay on
his back, put a hand to his forehead, feebly pounded the
ground at his side.

Cors Cant raised his staff briefly. "This hero's fight is finished. Lancelot of the Languedoc, champion of Caer
Camlann, consul of the Empire is declared winner." Then he
quickly departed. A dozen Saxons stormed the field, angrily
shouting "Foul! Foul!"

Cors Cant swerved to avoid Morgawse, who swept from
the stands surrounded by her Amazons, face set in grim fury.
The boy looked for Anlawdd but could not see her. He ran
around the chariot track, watching Artus's men quell the riot.
On the villa side of the field, he spotted his love wiping egg
from her face.

"You!" she cried and sputtered incoherently for a moment, a piece of eggshell still stuck in her hair. "You—you—you heroic fool! Foolish hero! I'm not speaking to you ever *again,* rash Cors Cant Ewin!" She stomped away, nose in the air, but stopped after a dozen paces and turned back to finish not speaking to him. "And don't think I was impressed by your courage, either. Men! *I* wouldn't have thrown myself in front of a charging Saxon. And just see if you ever catch *me* allowing an unarmed man to fight an axe-wielding murderer, even though it did turn out for the best, and quite a humiliation for Wessex, too. Caedwin will be hopping! But don't think even *that* will save you from my perpetual silence, you . . . you *babe of the forest!"*

With that, Anlawdd finally made good her threat and stormed away to the villa.

The boy followed, stepped over an unconscious, moaning man with a trampled basket of rotten eggs. "But . . . Anlawdd! Wait, don't—" It was no use; she was gone.

"Anlawdd," whispered Cors Cant to the wind in her wake, "I love you." *Late again,* he chastised; *too late by half.*

Cors Cant looked toward the stand. Lancelot struggled as Gwynhwfyr wrapped around him in a lustful bear hug. Artus watched, unamused.

The boy blinked. For a moment, though Anlawdd's potion was long since worn off, he clearly saw a terrible dream-vision of blood across the *Dux Bellorum*'s chest. It spread rapidly, a mortal blow!

Cors Cant ran across the field, heedless of the remnants of the Saxon mob. He gained the reviewing stand, saw fresh blood on Lancelot's hands. It stained Gwynhwfyr, too; all three were smeared with the stuff.

Then the boy blinked again, and the vision was gone. The linen was white and unstained, Lancelot's hands normal pink as he peeled off his gauntlets.

Cors Cant felt a hole open in his stomach. He turned his back, sat on the stage, knew what the vision meant. *Damn Fate and Her sister Despair!* he thought. *I shall not allow it to happen to Artus* Pan-Draconis!

Another part of him responded immediately. *Foolish talker! There's nothing you can do. You're useless, half-a-*

*bard. Soft hand never dealt harsh blow! Stick to harping and
singing, know your place!*

A gentle voice touched his ear. It was Merovee, who stood
at Cors Cant's side and put a hand on his shoulder, again
spoke as if he had overheard the bard's innermost thoughts.

"These dice were cast long ago," said the king. "Play the
faces you see. Remember, any player can lose, any can win.
Fortuna Diva taunts and teases, but *there are no losers 'til the
game is won.*" He smiled faintly, then stepped back into mystery once more.

CHAPTER 40

GWYNHWFYR ALLOWED PETER TO DISENTANGLE HIMSELF. "THUS
my favor *did* bring you luck," she breathed, licking her lips
suggestively. Peter blushed and pulled his hips away from hers.

"Ah, I don't think we should be so-um-close; it isn't
proper." His cheeks burned as if frostbitten. Gwynhwfyr
caught them, puffed his face like Andy Panda.

"My heart pounds when you thrust yourself into the fray,
Prince."

"Really!" he snapped, shocked to the core. "This simply
isn't the correct time to . . . I mean, here's Artus standing at
your side!"

"Don't be so stiff, Lance. You're such a hard man. Can
you not let formality trickle away?" Her lips betrayed no
trace of a smile, her eye not the flutter of a wink.

He bit his lip. Artus stood three feet away, watching and
listening to the entire exchange between his wife and his
champion, his face unreadable.

Peter squirmed under the scrutiny. Soldier he was, but a
Sandhurst man, not a randy corporal. Playing innuendo and
out the other with a woman in her husband's presence was
simply not done.

Lancelot firmly pushed her away, hard-heartedly turned his head.

Alas, he did no such thing. Somehow, the signal crossed between heart and hands. Instead, he stumbled into her arms. Lip-to-lip, breathing her breath, his eyes dilated as his throat constricted. Gwynhwyfr's coppermelt eyes and pheremonic musk bewitched him.

He tried to protest, could only whimper faintly. She put her mouth to his ear, whispered a husky cantrip:

> *Winter frost comes budding May,*
> *Night to noon, the fires burn*
> *So soon inside your faerie-fey,*
> *'Neath smiling moon, golden day.*

"Are you my faerie-fey, Lancelot of the Languedoc? Do you carry me under the mound, below ground, trapped in your arms for a fortnight of centuries, six months each year?"

He dry-swallowed. Paralyzed, he stared into twin pools of copper until they merged into one brilliant eye, Polyphemus of all women. Ensorcelled, entranced, entrapped, ensnared.

I am not in love.

Entwined in her arms, unable to stop his heart, he kissed her. Her tongue penetrated his mouth, sucked his will like Circe, left only the armored, collapsing husk, a hollow Odysseus.

Gone native! Gone native! screamed half a life of foreign campaigns. Half a sob tore from his throat, a wild beast howled from the trap. *Gnawed his own leg off, he did, but damn me, I am not in,* not *in love!*

He crushed Gwynhwyfr within his arms. Her breasts pressed against his chest, nipples hard beneath the silk and linen chemise. One of her hands slid up his back, grabbed a handful of hair above his neck. Her other hand stroked the side of his leg from thigh to waist.

Ahem.

"Hog ham *hot* hin huvv," murmured Peter, a vague attempt at defiance from the pit of lust, face buried in her throat.

"Ahem." Artus cleared his throat, louder this time.

Reality grabbed Peter by the ears, shook him like a furious headmaster. He leapt from the princess as if she were electrified. "Artus! Ho! Fancy meeting you here—heh heh—hope you enjoyed the fight Your Highness, I mean sir."

Artus leaned close, spoke for Peter's ears only. "Galahadus, do you *really* think this is entirely appropriate?"

"Well . . . well . . ."

"I mean with all these people about. Now, I don't like to interfere in my wife's affairs, but . . . no, this is too much."

"Well . . ."

"Stop saying 'well.' You know the rules, Lance. This is a proper Roman household. Propriety, probity, and discretion are the order of the day. Every day."

"W-well, I didn't mean to—"

"Silence, Majesty, I'm not finished. If you cannot contain your emotional outbursts, I suggest you go on campaign. Immediately." Artus spoke through gritted teeth, as he flicked his eyes toward the crowd. "There are *guests* present. We will put our best face forward." Cutha and the Saxons' heads swiveled back and forth between Artus and Peter like spectators at Wimbledon. They could not hear, but they had eyes.

"Well . . . Ah, what do you mean by campaign?" Peter shrank a bit, fearing he knew exactly what the *Dux Bellorum* meant. The suggestion smacked uncomfortably of Colonel Cooper's "solution" to the Ulster-willies.

"Do you feel alright, Lance? The campaign against the Jutes, man. Up in Gwynedd."

"But I can't go on campaign now!" *Not with an IRA terrorist waiting for the slightest chance to cut your throat!*

"Lancelot," clarified Artus, reasonably, "I'm not asking you to pop over Hadrian's Wall and settle the tribes. Just take a *maniple* of men to Harlech, on the coast, and make a show of force, put the fear of the *Pax Romana* back into their bellies. And perhaps cool your own excitement, hm?

"Prince Gormant of Gwynedd has sent me an urgent message to send you and Cei to Harlech with a few men. A *maniple* was his suggestion; he says there aren't that many Jutes. He says the damned Jutic barbarians tramp his whole cantref as if they owned it, burning fields and towns and making tax collection impossible. We can't very well let foreigners raze the countryside, can we?"

"No sir. Of course not, sir." *Maniple? How many men was*

that? Peter clenched his teeth. *Good God, is that a brigade? a regiment?*

"Good. Off you go in three days."

"My dearest husband," began the princess, too quickly, "you know how I love following the campaign . . . is there any chance—"

"Alas," continued Artus, still speaking to Peter, not his wife, "Gwynhwyfr's household duties prevent her from leaving Caer Camlann for some weeks. Storerooms stand empty, priestly duties pass undone. Her work is cut out for her, as they say."

"As you command." She emphasized the last word harshly, a prisoner unjustly condemned to the dock.

"Upon the third sunrise, Lancelot," said the *Pan-Draconis*.

"Well . . ."

"And stop saying 'well'!"

Peter stared at Gwynhwyfr, tried to batten down his feelings. It was ridiculous, impossible. *I'm not really even here! And I too have my work cut out for me.* Though he said nothing more, he was very worried about what might happen in his absence. What mischief might Selly Corwin get up to with no hound among the sheep?

Maybe she's not even here yet. Maybe she'll land in the body of a slave, or get stuck on campaign along with me. And how many men in a bloody maniple?

The germ of a thought grew in his mind, a plan. It would be better for all concerned if Selly *did* get caught along on the campaign. So why not pack the brigade with every suspect he could, to better the odds? "Artus," he asked gently, "may I pick my own troops?"

Artus nodded. "So long as you don't split cohorts. Take the next two days to drill them on Mars Field. It's been months since Mons Badonicus, since they last fought under the blue and black."

"Aye aye, sir." Peter saluted Roman style and withdrew toward the palace.

All right, clearly a maniple is some part of a cohort, which is what, 360 men? He pushed his way through grumbling Saxons, found Cei at his side. Bedwyr joined them en route.

"Sire, do you realize what this *means?*" demanded Cei, agitated. "We'll be gone twenty days, if a day! The Christ lover Merovee will have three entire weeks alone with Artus!"

"I doubt it," said Peter cryptically. *Not likely. Whatever I may feel about the man, Merovee is still a suspect! He'll stay within sight, or I'll know the reason why.*

"Cei," said Peter, "round my lads up in the courtyard."

"Legionnaires, knights?"

"A maniple."

"Cavalry?"

"Um, surely. Get them here by next chime. Full gear, arms and armor. We're going for a bit of a hike." Suddenly, memory flared. He remembered a diagram in a history of warfare textbook. It showed a cohort, 360 men, as six small squares lined up in two rows of three squares each. If those squares were maniples, they included about sixty men, fewer than a rifle company.

Peter's pleasure was at once eclipsed by a new worry: if Lancelot the Legate normally commanded two entire legions, perhaps ten thousand soldiers, why in the world was Artus sending him out with sixty men?

He shook his head, continued toward the tower. It was a clear rebuke, a snub, sure to be seen as such by every other knight and senator under the *Dux Bellorum*'s command.

Or was Artus trying to *get Lancelot out of the way?* He stopped, stared over the stadium wall at the square, white buildings of the villa itself. Through the colonnade, he saw the edge of a courtyard with a single fountain visible. A chill wind blew mournfully through the columns and arches; shivering, Peter crossed his arms.

It's not entirely impossible, thought Peter slowly, *that Selly is Artus. If so, what would she do? Kill herself merely to deprive England of her greatest legendary king?*

Who was this strange "Artus," and what was to happen out of the sight of Lancelot of the Languedoc?

CHAPTER 41

WORRIED, CORS CANT SHADOWED ANLAWDD'S STEPS TOWARD Caer Camlann. She paralleled the colonnade, then cut through the hedgerow to the main apartments. As the bard approached the door, he saw Centurion Cacamwri in earnest discussion with his brother, a junior officer in the Third Legion. The bruiser Cacamwri still "owed" Cors Cant a hiding, so the boy quickly joined a clump of hostage princes, sons of local chieftains.

They circled the courtyard, laughing and mocking Cutha's defeat, heading toward the *triclinium.* Cors Cant lost Anlawdd, who walked past Cacamwri without a glance.

He disengaged before the hostages entered the villa. An Irish barbarian clutched his sleeve, demanded in his own guttural tongue whether Leary had yet arrived. "No," said Cors Cant, "he has not been seen." He pulled loose and sprinted to a side door in the apartments.

Leary? Ling Leary of Eire approached Camlann? Cors Cant cantered nimbly up the stairs. What grand scheme could have brought together Artus, Merovee, and Leary, High King and archenemy of all that is Roman in Britain?

He shied away from the bannister that overlooked the hall and padded down the corridor to check Princess Gwynhwfyr's room for his warrior-princess-seamstress-sorceress.

Someone else in the hall . . . Cors Cant ducked into an alcove, not wishing to be seen. It was brutal Bedwyr, Cei's hired assassin. The man looked back toward the stairs sneakily, ducked into Lancelot's room. The champion was either unusually silent or not present.

Cors Cant waited. After a long count of a hundred, Bedwyr emerged humming, elaborately casual. He quick-walked

217

down the corridor away from Cors Cant, took the stairs three at a time with his long stride.

For an instant, the bard hesitated. After all, his duty to Artus clearly demanded he investigate this strange occurrence, especially given Lancelot's queer behavior recently. Why should Bedwyr sneak into the champion's room when no one was present?

On the other side of the coin, Lancelot would slay Cors Cant if he caught him rifling his personal effects. The bard wrestled with his conscience for two or three heartbeats, then strolled down the hall, pausing at Lancelot's curtain-door. He looked up and down the corridor, took a deep breath, and pushed through the curtain.

The sunlight nearly blinded him. He squinted, blinking rapidly while his eyes adjusted. At first, the cramped room looked the same as yesterday, when Lancelot had him translate the mangled Latin sentences. The bard stood in the center, silently observed all four quarters, ear cocked for footsteps up the stairs.

As co-Consul with Artus, at least in name, Lancelot could have had any size quarters, even as big as Artus's. Instead, he eschewed the slightest ostentation, scorning tapestries, painted walls, furniture. *Hard-as-a-Lance,* his legions called him, and he drove them like a well-drilled team of chariot horses.

Oddly enough, they *liked* Lancelot. Artus had five other generals, two of them legates, very popular among the citizens of Britain. Yet none inspired such single-minded devotion among the troops as Lancelot.

Once, Myrddin had told Cors Cant, Lancelot faced a numerically superior army from Eire. The champion advanced alone, signaling he wanted to speak with the opposing king.

The armies faced each other beside a lake. Lancelot said nary a word. He simply gestured to the captain of a small unit of legionnaires and pointed at the lake.

Without a word, they marched straight into the water, shields, javelins, breastplates, and all, sinking without a trace.

The Irish army bolted without a single blow struck.

The bard shook himself from his reverie, quickly scanned the room looking for something different. It was then he noticed a new bottle of wine, thick, sugary sediment caked in the bottom. It sat on the desk that had been empty yesterday.

Sediment. Thick sediment crusted the bottle halfway up . . . not even the wretched wine of Gallia Transalpina, or Sicambria, should have had that much sediment!

Heart bruising his rib cage, straining for the sound of approaching Lancelot, Cors Cant worked the cork loose and smelled the liquid. A faint, oily underscent prickled his nose, unlike any wine he had ever smelled. Poisoned? Cors Cant sniffed again, remembered smelling the same odor before, while preparing a concoction for Myrddin.

Nightshade! Is Bedwyr trying to murder Lancelot?

Cors Cant worked the cork back into the bottle. *Perhaps it's for the champion to use, not drink.* But what possible use could Prince Lancelot have for a bottle of poisoned wine?

Just then, Cors Cant heard the sound he had dreaded, a measured boot tramp rattling the stairs. Lancelot, beyond a doubt!

The bard stared wildly—if he bolted, Lancelot might see. But in the bare room, there was no place to hide.

He spied the window. He dashed to the hole, leaned out. From the high third story, it was a long, long way down.

The boots reached the landing, tramped along the corridor toward the room. Dizzy at the thought of dismemberment, Cors Cant took several deep breaths and straddled the oak windowsill. He gripped it with fear-hard, trembling fingers and carefully swung his legs over. He lowered himself, scrabbling frantically for a toehold.

His groping foot found a slim crack in the concrete, barely enough to wedge a corner of his sandal. He dangled from the sill, weight resting on one leg, one foot, one sandal, ultimately upon a single crack in the walls of Caer Camlann.

The curtain swished aside. Lancelot entered the room, cursing vividly.

Cors Cant held his breath. There was no way to explain his presence if discovered. Lancelot would probably gut him before he could spit out a word.

It'd be easier than that, he thought. *All he has to do is pry my fingers loose. Dead bard in the yard, they took it so hard!*

Lancelot stomped up and down his room, barely larger than the boy's own room in the other wing. He paced, five steps up—five back, over and again.

Cors Cant's leg ached. He lowered himself slightly, dangled more than stood. Within moments, his fingers numbed, so he stood straight again.

A cold breeze whipped across the face of the building, plucking like a clumsy hand. His leg spasmed. He squeezed shut his eyes, pressed his lips to stifle a yelp of pain.

Lancelot froze in his paces. For an instant, Cors Cant feared the prince had heard his silent cry. But Lancelot did not approach the window.

The Sicambrian swore by the Roman Christ. Cors Cant forgot his ache, startled by the out-of-character oath. *Lancelot of the Languedoc, cry to Jesus and Mary? He* is *possessed!* thought Cors Cant. Then he heard the distinct sound of a bottle thumping back onto the table.

So, the prince sees the wine and knows it is poisoned. The odor of nightshade is unmistakable, yet he places it casually back on the table. Ergo, Lancelot is not particularly surprised, and it must not have been meant for him. Quod erat demonstrandum.

Cors Cant shivered at the implication. Murder by poison was a coward's act, un-Roman and un-British both. Could the champion's Sicambrian ancestry be creeping from under the thin plastering of civilization?

Lancelot's steps retreated to the door. *Please, Diana Rhiannon, let him leave!* prayed Cors Cant. Lancelot pulled the curtain aside; but rather than leave, he admitted another man, who entered on quiet feet.

"Lancelot, a peculiar situation has developed," said Artus's voice.

Not the Dux Bellorum too! Cors Cant threw his head back in despair—*they'll never leave; I'll hang till I drop!*

Throwing his head back was a mistake. Off balance, he struggled to grab the wooden sill with numb fingers as his foot slipped slowly out of the crack. He was falling ... but *very* slowly. His left hand lost its hold; he teetered precariously on the edge of a sickening drop.

Take the sword.

His foot slid out—

Take hold the sword! The voice in his head, the same voice from his encounter with Merovee. What did it mean, what sword?

Cors Cant looked down. The red courtyard cobbles waited

to gobble him up like chipped dragon's teeth. There was nothing he could do; his death was foretold.

Suddenly, fear vanished. He felt a wrench, realized he was no longer *in* his body, but looked down upon it from a height. *I will die. Someday, maybe even today, this instant.* But he felt only peace, relief at the prospect. At that moment, he saw the sword.

It extended from the sill, hilt first, the point buried in the concrete, as if it were the sword that legend said Artus's father, Urtus, drew from a rock to become king of three realms.

Cors Cant's other hand slipped; he had fallen too far back. The wall was out of reach. He watched curiously from above, wondered whether he would live or die. Crimson cobbles beckoned.

So too did the sword. *Grab hold the sword!* commanded the voice. Outside his body, he heard it as clearly as if Merovee stood at his elbow.

Time crawled, slow as when the heroes sat before Bran's Head, as the decapitated relic spoke of empires past and darkness to come, spoke for a hundred years while the men aged but an evening.

Cors Can stretched forth a spectral hand, *willed* his fleshly arm forward to clutch the hilt of the ghost blade. His left hand, then his right. For many heartbeats he hung, foot miraculously stuck in the crack, two hands on the hilt.

Are you an omen? Is the sword my path, not the harp at all?

A presence behind him, Merovee's animus perhaps, shook its head. The boy felt it. *Look beneath, behind, between. A sword is not always a sword, a cup not always to hold wine. Gold buys more than bread, trees grow tallest in the ocean.*

Cors Cant pulled himself to the wall, the sill. He gripped it tight. The sword faded into a wreath of mist, drifting across his face and chest.

A sick feeling gripped Cors Cant. He fell, wildly uncontrolled. With a crash, he collapsed back into his body, hanging on to the sill only by a Roman miracle.

Now you know, laughed the damnable Merovee-voice, *how easily we may each be tempted to grab hold the sword! Remember this when next you hold your love in your arms.*

The boy pressed his face against cool, solid concrete. Panic flooded back. He trembled at the thought of falling, dashing to a myriad, myriad pieces on jagged, red cobbleteeth. Gradually he became aware of his surroundings. Artus was talking again.

". . . demands to accompany you to Harlech," said the *Dux Bellorum.*

"You cannot be serious! You can *not* be serious! *Cutha?*"

"He says the Jutes are as much his enemy as mine. He desires to see our techniques for repelling the invader."

"But Cutha is a . . . well, I just beat him on the field of honor, and he swore revenge. Do we trust him in a combat?"

"I did not hear him swear revenge. But turn not your back." Artus's voice moved from right to left as he paced the room. Sweat poured down Cors Cant's face, turned clammy in the cold wind.

"Are you looking for something, sir?" asked Lancelot.

"Eh? No, just pacing, Galahadus. Anyway, Cutha swears to you as captain to general," continued Artus, crossing the room again and swishing aside the closet curtain. "If that's not enough, then ponder the fact that there shall be five Saxons, counting Cutha, against forty Camlann soldiers, in our own cantref of Gwynedd. With those odds, not even a berserker rage would tempt Cutha to attack. He's not the suicide sort." This time, Artus's voice was muffled, as if he spoke from inside a desk drawer or closet. "You haven't seen Gwynhwfyr, have you?"

Lancelot spoke slowly, as if distant. "Well, orders are orders. Like I tell my men, three ways to do things, the right way, the wrong way, and the army way. Gwynhwfyr? Not lately."

"I'm glad you understand, Lancelot. I don't like him either. Never trust men who don't bathe! But we have made common cause; time we started acting like it. Now if you'll excuse me. . . ."

Again the *Dux Bellorum*'s voice drifted from one side to the other. Cors Cant shook like a taut line in a strong wind. Not even the reasonable sword would save him if he slipped again.

"Sire, I beg a boon." Lancelot sounded elaborately casual.

"Yes? What do you wish?"

"There are a few people I'd like to take along on the expedition. Give them some experience."

"Oh? Prince Gormant asked for you, Cei, and Bedwyr. Who else?"

"The bard, and his . . ." Cors Cant gasped. Would Lancelot reveal his secret to the world? "And a friend of his," concluded the champion.

"Why the bard?"

"To entertain the troops."

"Hrm. Who will entertain me until Myrddin recovers from his ailment? He says he cannot sing even one song."

"Are there no other bards, sir?"

"Nay. Jugglers, though. I'll have to content myself with watching the young boys drop their balls. Anyone else?"

"Let me see." Lancelot hummed tunelessly for a moment, as if he had not considered other "guests" until that moment. But Cors Cant got the distinct impression that Lancelot had a specific list already planned out. "How about Medraut? And Morgawse—"

"Great Jupiter, Lance, Morgawse? You, ah, have something with her, too?"

"No!" Lancelot sounded guilty, as if caught in bed with a Barbary ape. "Don't need Morgawse, I guess."

"Prince Lancelot, this is not a social visit. Why do you need my princes and courtiers? And my bard?"

The answer was too slick by half. Neatly planned and rehearsed. "Well, Medraut needs experience commanding a few troops, and the bard has begged for an adventure. Something he can write a song about, sing at the next feast, you know."

Cors Cant almost fell from his perch. *Adventure! If this is adventure, give me the baths, a winecup, and . . . well, you-know!* He listened incredulously as Lancelot lied as only a Sicambrian could. "The boy came to me this night, said his lady love told him she could only love a hero. You wouldn't want to ruin his chance for glory, would you, Sire? And of course I need Merovee because of his Sicambrian warriors."

"Oh, now it's Merovee too?" Artus's voice held a knowing smile. "Well, we have completed our talks. And there are certain nighttime liberties that he does not favor, being not quite as civilized as those of us who grew to manhood in Rome herself."

"Liberties?"

"A jest, Consul. Libertius, you've noticed him? Hair like spun gold, will make a fearsome general when he comes of age."

A long, frozen silence. Cors Cant struggled to bring Libertius to mind, could not summon a face.

"Good evening, Artus," said the Sicambrian, voice chilly.

"Fare well on your journey, my friend. Take whomever you want and can persuade to go—with *one* exception. Naturally."

Another long pause. "Naturally," Lancelot agreed. The two seemed to know whom he meant. Neither chose to illuminate Cors Cant.

"Good evening." The curtain swished again. Artus left. After a moment, so too did Lancelot, clumping down the hall in his iron-shod boots.

Great, thought Cors Cant; *now get the hell out of here!* But when he tried to pull himself up, his arms did not respond.

Frightened, he tried again: no response. Fear turned to panic as he thought of slipping to his death for dangling too long!

With terrified urgency, he lunged for the sill. At last, leaden muscles responded. He hooked one cramped elbow over the sill, again stuck, unable to climb backward or forward.

No sword this time, he told himself. Want to live? Get yourself over that sill . . . now!

He stretched his right leg to its fullest, only the toe in the crack now. He maneuvered his body like a deadweight, pushed it just slightly across the sill. Suddenly, his last toehold slipped, feet trod only wind.

The bard clung grimly. With a monumental effort, he wriggled up and over, fell in a heap on the bare floor.

He lay thus for many breaths, cold wood pressed reassuringly against his cheek. Then he labored to his feet. The mystery bottle was gone.

He worked the limp, spasming muscles in arms and legs, hobbled through the curtain into the corridor. The stairs were deadly; he clutched the bannister and staggered down.

Cors Cant finally reached the *triclinium.* Stiff as an old man, he walked back to his room, stepped through the doorway.

Anlawdd waited for him, blinking back tears. "I'm going to be sent back to Harlech," she said, voice emotionless and flat. "Leary's arriving any day now. He knows me, Cors Cant."

CHAPTER 42

"KING LEARY? WHY WOULD THE ARCHKING OF EIRE CARE about a seamstress? Or even a . . ." The bard silenced himself before blurting her secret. Walls, and curtains, had ears.

"He knows me, Cors Cant, which is as much to say he knows the secret that you were about to shout from the rooftops, and I'd h-hardly imagine he'd let me continue to playact as Gwynhwfyr's seamstress! Not without telling you-know-who."

"Who? Oh. Of course." Anlawdd had changed into a black and grey chemise, but no tunic. Red dragons were embroidered around the midriff, the waist pinched by a thin, silver chain. "Didn't I see the Princess Gwynhwfyr wearing that at Lughnasade last?" he asked.

"Who do you think sewed it for her? Well, mended it, at least. Cors Cant, do you think I know nothing but axes and Saxons, horses and wars? I can sew a tunic, follow the hounds, clean and cook a deer, bake a pie, cheat at dice, set sewer taxes, compose a song—well, maybe not as good as yours—cast a love spell (but all women can do that), slop pigs, lie like a bishop, and even stay awake during interminable Senate sessions about whether the general of the army deserves a triumph for beating the third, junior undersecretary to the governor at Londinium at the mock war! And the less said about *him,* the better. But he knows me. Ard-Ri Leary, I mean, not the undersecretary. He's—he's my . . ."

"Your what?" Cors Cant stared with eyes wide. She stopped so abruptly, as if a terrible secret caught in her throat on the way up.

"Cors Cant, do you know *why* I demanded you never tell a soul what I was? It was because of the wall it would build between us, like Hadrian's Wall that keeps those Albion barbarians from ravaging our cities. As soon as I'm known, then it's off to Harlech I'm packed, like a lost treasure sent back to my f-f-father." Her face reddened slightly.

"Harlech," said Cors Cant. He rolled the word on his tongue, tasted Western Sea, thick mead, bitter wine. "Anlawdd, the others may be bound by sword oath to Artus. But I am not. I'm a bard, free to go and come. I can live with you in Harlech, if you wish . . . I'm not planted here like a crop."

She set her face hard. "You don't understand. Besides, Artus needs you.

"Can a dream be right if everything about it feels wrong?" he asked, half-aloud, half to himself.

She shook her head. "I can't begin to count the number of things I've done that were right but hurt like an axe cut, all because of that silly princess tiara. My father always put me in charge of the unpleasant duties—one in particular—keeping the triumphs and gladiatorial contests to himself. We all must walk on the broken cobblestones sometimes, even Merovee. Imagine how he feels when he sees a poor woman dying of fever or leprosy, and he's not allowed to even touch her."

"Touch her what?"

Again she fell silent, looked at her hands as if she'd never seen them before. "Um, never mind. You've problems enough of your own, Cors Cant. Come what may, you *must* stay here. It's your spot."

Cors Cant smiled grimly. For once, he had information that Anlawdd did not already know. "Off the spit and into the fire, Princess. Neither of us shall be here when Leary arrives. Lancelot is taking us both to Harlech, along with an expedition."

"What?" Anlawdd's mouth dropped. "To *Harlech?*"

"I heard him talking to Artus. There's Jutes out there and we're supposed to fight them. I guess. Your father sent word to Artus to send Lancelot, Cei, and Bedwyr to drive away the Jutes. For some reason, the legate wants to bring us, you and me."

"Well you might at least have *told* a girl, instead of letting her ramble on saying things best left unsaid!"

Familiar steps clumped down the hall. A man pounded the wall. Cors Cant peeked out.

Oops. . . . "Ah, Prince Lancelot and milady, Princess Gwynhwfyr," he whispered, still acting as lookout.

Anlawdd cawed like a crow, flew about the room behind

Cors Cant, banging chests. *Probably changing out of Gwyn-hwfyr's dress,* thought the bard, wishing he had the guts to turn around and watch her undress.

Lancelot licked his lips, squeezed tight the princess, Artus's princess.

"Cors Cant," breathed the champion, "the princess and I need a place to—heh heh—to talk." She grinned and Lancelot smirked. They fooled no one.

CHAPTER 43

PETER HAD STALKED DOWNSTAIRS AFTER THE MEETING WITH Artus, mystery bottle in hand. *Wine? Is this the "it" Cei mentioned? Smells peculiar. Is it poisoned? For whom is it meant?*

And what had Artus searched his room for, while he explained about Cutha? His wife, or *it?* Something definitely stank in England's green and pleasant land.

But if Artus had looked for the bottle, whatever it contained, how could he have missed it, sitting like a sore thumb on Peter's table?

Peter never believed the "Purloined Letter" myth. When he searched a room, he began with the most obvious spots and moved outward to increasing levels of subtlety. *Unless Artus didn't know what he sought. . . .*

An even more pressing problem was whether Peter could rely upon Cei and Bedwyr in a firefight. The conversation in the latrine was disturbing. What had Cei said, exactly? There was no reason Lancelot's legions and Bedwyr's cavalry could not march again beneath the golden boar of Cei.

At least, Cei still wanted Lancelot to join him, so there was little chance that Cei or Bedwyr would desert from Peter. But what if they decided to kill Merovee, and claim it was the Saxons? What if they asked Peter to help? Knowing what Peter knew about history, the history that led to England, not an un-inhabited forest, did Peter dare refuse, allow Merovee to live?

There had never been any alliance between Artus and Merovee, never been a "Celtic Roman Empire," or *Pax Britannicus*. Peter pushed thoughts of betrayal far back in his mind, wondering how much of the surge of excitement he felt was from the barbaric Lancelot, still chained in his hindbrain.

At the bottom of the stairs, a hand darted forth, grabbed for his sleeve. He ducked, caught the arm from beneath at the elbow and rose. He had half-drawn his dagger before he realized it was Princess Gwynhwfyr.

He held her arm tight to prevent her falling, then released her. "Princess! You startled me. My apologies, Your Highness."

"My, Lancelot, but you are quick! Can you also take your time, when circumstances favor it?"

"Some quarry begs to be toyed with for hours before the killing stroke." *You idiot!* chastised Peter's propriety. *You've let her draw you into another endless, frustrating flirtation!*

Her clothing was plainer than he had ever seen her wear, simple white linen chemise tied with a plain, white leather belt. She looked almost virginal. Lancelot let a low purr of arousal escape his lips.

No! Peter. I'm Peter Smythe, not Lancelot!

"The Vestal virgin, white purity. Waiting to be soiled?"

"I had meant to wear black and silver, the chemise with the red dragons. But my sewing maid said it needed repairs and took it away. Black and silver for you, for your colors."

"Oh, sweet virgin? I *own* all that clothes itself in my colors." *Mary and Jesus, did I actually say that? Was that me? Or Lancelot?*

He waited for her next remark, to which he would unstoppably respond. Instead she struck a low blow. "I—I want you," she said, face open, vulnerable.

No, Princess, thought Peter gallantly, *it can never be. I feel it too, this magnetic attraction. But our love is Britain's peril!*

"Okay," he said, mouth dry. Blood blood blood, the pounding hooves. He was invincible, invulnerable! That mewling, Roman boy-lover was no obstacle. He could like it, or be whipped back to Rome!

My God, my God, what am I doing? Who is speaking, me or Lancelot?

"Now." She clenched her fists, trembled.

No, my dearest love. I have a terrible vision that our love will drag Artus to his grave. His clever mind gracefully extracted him from the peril. *With the* Dux Bellorum's *death, all of Europe falls into barbarism so deep it lasts a thousand miserable years!*

"Now," he agreed with cracked voice. Somebody's voice—his own? "But where?"

We must resist! I love you dearly, but we must forever remain just friends.

Blood! Pounding hooves, ringing axe blows, the solid feel of an Ingram Mac-10 kicking in his hands as he raked a doorway, waiting for Sergeant McManigle to chuck a grenade into the mob of murderous Jutes and Saxons!

"Not my room," whispered Gwynhwfyr. "Artus has spies among my girls. Nor yours, for he would surely hear." Husky with desire, she suggested, "Perhaps the room of another? Who do you trust, who will do as we beg?"

Just friends. Only friends!

"The . . . the boy!" struggled Peter. Or Lancelot. He was not sure which spoke. "The bard, Cors Cant."

She lowered her lids, glanced sideways. The tilt of her head drove him mad with desire. But why? She was just a woman. He had had hundreds!

"I know him," she said. "He loves Artus."

Peter lowered his eyes. "He will do as I ask. He owes me . . . reciprocity." He looked at Gwynhwfyr. Her eyes tightly shut, jaw muscles clenched. *How much does she, herself, see? Does she know the likely outcome of this mésalliance, and hope to escape the consequences?*

For Peter, it was not a matter of probability. He *knew* what had destroyed Camelot, King Arthur, the Table Round. *Conscious evil,* he condemned himself. *Unoriginal sin!* But he could not stop himself. His need for her could not be denied.

But was the need Peter's, or Lancelot's?

Fate. Destiny. Kismet. Inevitability of history, conservation of reality, Adam Smith's invisible hand. The devil, the invisible college, the secret chiefs, the hidden masters, the hidden variable, the universal constant, the power of love, the mating urge, deoxyribonucleic acid. God, heavenly will, this is willed where what is willed must be, guardian angel, Mama, the

*pointing finger, the handwriting on the wall, duty, obedience
to authority, sociobiology, Stanley Laurel, a fine mess you've
gotten me into!*

Not me. No sir, not my fault.

She held his hand. Peter did not remember her taking it.
They mounted the stairs on fairy feet.

*Animal magnetism. Magnetic personality. Fatal attraction,
blind love, blind stupidity, heart, glands, serotonin and nor-
epinephrine, two souls merging, soulmates, love at first sight,
eyes like liquid pools, irresistibility, passion of the ages, le
petit mort. . . .*

He heard nothing, saw no one. Why could not a crisis in-
tervene? Where was a fire, an invasion when you needed
one? Up another flight, they stood before Cors Cant's room.

*Not my fault, not my responsibility . . . look what you made
me do, Colonel Crapper! The final judge! The author of our
being! The clockwork universe!*

Peter heard soft conversation, the boy and his kitchen lass.
The Sicambrian gripped Gwynhwfyr's hand, pounded on the
wall. Cors Cant peeked out the curtain, looked back and forth
between Peter and Gwynhwfyr.

"Prince Lancelot, and milady, Princess Gwynhwfyr," he
said aloud.

Behind the curtain, Peter heard Anlawdd squawk like a
parrot. Cupboard doors slammed, and something fell heavily.
Anlawdd cursed like a merchant marine.

"Cors Cant," said Peter, barely controlling his voice. "The
princess and I need a place to . . . talk."

The bard understood, poetic intuition. He sighed, closed
the curtain a moment, then opened it.

Anlawdd was wearing a man's cloak, probably Cors
Cant's. It covered her from shoulders to floor. *She's probably
starkers beneath it,* thought Peter, embarrassed. *But blast it,
this is urgent!*

Peter spoke to Cors Cant, lowering his voice. He meant to
sound sincere, but the words came out dripping menace: "Not
a word of this, boy—not a word." The bard gulped and nodded.

Glaring darts at Peter, Anlawdd slithered out the door without letting the cloak unwrap from her body. As she passed, a
hint of a black and grey garment peeked from beneath the
brown cloth. The bard followed, pressing close to his woman.

After a moment, Gwynhwfyr stepped gracefully into the room. She looked frightened. "Lancelot, I've—we've been together many times in my dreams. But it's different now, with the afternoon sun making harsh the colors, laying bare every line and wrinkle.

"This is no simple roll on a straw mat . . . my love. Not another Maypole for my bower. You are the champion of Artus, my husband. When that Saxon rode you down, I thought my temples would burst from the blood! Then when you held me—oh Lady help me, I wished . . . *I wished Artus were dead.*"

"He will be. If we do this." *There, I finally spit it out.*

"We haven't embraced for two years. You know that. He says it's his duties, the empire, but he has time for those *boys* of his. But in his way, he does love me. Oh my love, I'm babbling. Shut me up."

Instead, Peter sat carefully on Cors Cant's sleeping mat. With a sickening certainty, he knew how this conversation would end. And worse, knew that it was truly him, Peter Saul-Paul Smythe, who reached for her hand. Not Lancelot of the Languedoc. *Conscious sin; thus do we willingly ride the road to hell. Boys? What did she mean, those boys of his?* He buried the thought, positive he had misheard.

"I thought we could play the game, Lancelot. Even if we shared a bed, he would not care, so long as we were discreet. So long as I would be there for him when he needs my arms around him. We are close, we love, but we do not . . . you know. But now, I would be there for you before I'd be there for him. And I think he knows."

"He knows," said Peter, voice failing.

She untied the straps at her shoulders, let the perfect, white chemise fall to the floor. She stood before him, naked as Eve, tempting as Lilith. Pale skin, blond hair on her head cropped closer than it was elsewhere. And the scent—it pulled him closer like a leash. He licked his dry lips, wallowed in sinful, horrible thoughts of carnal lust, unconcerned where it might lead.

For queen, or king. For country. He seized her, buried his face in her perfect breasts. "Love me," she commanded, threw him backward onto the mat and fell atop him.

CHAPTER 44

I TOLD THAT BOY TO LEAVE ME, FOR NOW THAT I KNEW FATHER'S bloody plan, my head spun like an autumn leaf falling down a cliff from oak to sea-foam. But he clung to me, still a bit shaken from his stupid heroics in the stadium. Foolish boy! But I was firm, perhaps too harsh, for thoughts raced round and round my head like bees round a honeypot, buzzing for attention, and I couldn't concentrate on our repartee.

I shooed him off with misgivings, tramped the hallway, and climbed up the stairs by impulse. I had never climbed higher than Cors Cant's room, and I was curious to see where the steps led.

The next landing was the third from the ground, where dwelt Artus's legal staff and, oddly enough, his shoemaker. The stairs grew a bit sloppy toward the top, leading me to imagine they had been recently repaired in the modern age, thus were deteriorated compared to the rest of the architecture from the golden age of corrupt Rome. Nay, it made no sense to me, either.

Up there, the walls were lined with tall, thin strips of dark wood, mahogany or dark cedar, and the corridor was so narrow I could raise my elbows and scrape them along both walls at once, not that it was overly exciting to do so.

Three junior students at the law held tiny office-apartments along the outside wall, while the senior lawyers had a pair of deep suites overlooking the inner courtyard. The shoemaker's rooms boasted a magnificent view down the side of the palace into the Court of Flowing Water, where I had anxiously paced a night before. I wish I had known a leather-beater was looking down on the top of my head; I might have chosen a different spot to haunt.

The shoemaker was out, so I skulked around his apartment. I stared uncomprehendingly at boots half-made, leather soles, sandals, and miles and miles of lacing, wondering what I sought; large sheets of untreated cowhide were stacked against one wall, and the floor was thickly heaped with scraps and ends.

The window was open, and a lovely breeze fluttered the bead-strung leather thongs that dangled from the upper sill. I approached the window, closed my eyes, and allowed the Mother's breath to caress my auburn tresses. Then I brushed the danglies aside, blinking in the sunlight.

The sun himself had passed noon and was not visible from the southeastern-facing window overlooking the Court of Flowing Waters. I leaned out, only vaguely nervous that the shoemaker might come home—what would he do, revoke my sandals? But I looked left and gasped.

A wooden ladder ran from the first floor above ground level all the way up to the roof; I could easily reach it by standing on the sill in the shoemaker's room, hanging by one arm, and reaching *way* out with my right hand and foot.

I looked back once over my shoulder; the front door-curtain hung nearly motionless, its thick mass immobile in such a gentle wind. Licking my ruby lips, I daintily mounted the sill, balanced like a pelican, and tugged on the ladder.

It seemed solid. Taking a deep breath, I climbed aboard.

The rungs were spaced a bit too far apart for me, but I managed to climb slowly up to the roof. There I found a wide, flat floor, heavily reinforced, with stacked arrows, catapult masses, and covered cauldrons of cold pitch sitting atop small brick stoves. Four catapults guarded the outer corners of Caer Camlann, as well as a number of ladders leading down the courtyard side. The few ladders I saw on the outside were detachable, and in the event of a siege would be pulled up, I'm sure!

I wandered around the roof along the outside edge, realizing at one point that I stood directly over the *Dux Bellorum*'s own apartment.

In that instant, I had an epiphany: *I knew how I would sneak in and kill him.* All I need do was dangle a rope from the roof, climb down, and hide in his own bedroom while he's elsewhere; when he came home, I would plunge the dagger in his breast or back and kill. . . .

And murder Artus. The *Dux Bellorum.* That Boy's father, in a way of speaking, for he had no other anymore.

I sat down on the rooftop, placed my back against the rough, crenellated wall, and wept for a long time, perhaps an eighth of a candle—I don't know why, exactly.

When he had charged into the stadium, That Boy, and thrown himself between Cutha the scum and Lancelot, my heart had almost frozen in place, which would have meant I was dead myself. I'd never felt that before, a dread so horrific that I was literally paralyzed—well, except for charging onto the field with a lance. Had some unruly urchin set my boots afire, I couldn't have moved to stamp out the flames.

Did that mean I really *did* love him, love That Boy? The thought was profoundly disturbing, not least because it would be so hard for him to touch me with Canastyr's ghost getting in the way.

And murdering Artus would be murdering That Boy's love for me—this I knew. Dishonor, disgrace, death, and destruction of my only salvation: despised love. Not bad for a moment's knifework!

Clearly, my father, Prince Gormant, had made a treaty with the Jutes—and possibly with Caedwin's Saxons—though Father is so foolish he might have been ignorant of Cutha's actual race, thinking him some strange form of Jute: he would first lure Lancelot and Cei to Harlech and prison or butcher them . . . then his only daughter would slay Artus in Camlann itself. Thus would die Artus's dreams of empire, for who could succeed him if neither Lancelot nor Cei be present to command the legions?

Surely the Jutes would have promised Father that Harlech would be free once again—and true, the Romanesque hand of Artus *Dux Bellorum* would be cut off at the wrist.

But was Father actually fool enough to believe that without the legions to hold them in check, Hrothgar and Hrundal would still respect his sovereignty? And even if they would, God knows Caedwin and Cutha would not!

Still, I didn't know why I wept; then it struck me. Father's only son, Prince Canastyr, heir to the throne of Harlech (for even an illegitimate son succeeds before a daughter) was dead, trampled to death by his own horse—or killed by his sister's hand, depending on how you look on it. And today, or tomorrow—for the morrow's morrow was the day we departed for Harlech, thus too late to kill Artus—his only daughter, only child now, would also die.

As I had known all along, there would be no possible way to escape capture after Artus was killed, for the screams of the slaying itself would draw the Praetorian Guard inside the room before his body struck the floor.

Thus would pass Harlech.

Gormant was old and doddering, and I'm sure was no longer capable of siring an heir to the throne; the moment he died undescended, my beloved city would be torn apart like a hart pulled down by ravenous hounds, the generals of our own army, not a one of whom was capable of ruling such a grand city and principality as Harlech! Not that Gormant was any King Leary.

I wept for my lost honor, my lost love, and my lost home; I wept for the blood on my hand that would never fade and the Court of Flowing Waters that soon would run dry.

CHAPTER 45

"TOO BAD I CAN'T TAKE *ALL* OF YOU WITH ME," MUTTERED PEter, staring at his list of suspects. He sat at his desk, reviewed his final list for Artus.

Morgawse would not stir from Camlann. A spider in her web; why leave the center of her power, leave the side of her brother, lover, whatever Artus was?

Gwynhwfyr was right out. The major purpose of Lancelot's expedition, as far as Artus was concerned, was to separate Lancelot from the princess. That left Anlawdd as the sole female he could shanghai.

On the male side, all suspects were definite RSVPs, except for Merovee and perhaps the doddering old wizard Myrddin.

I'll let the boy work on Myrddin, he thought; *but how does the knight force the king across the board?*

Merovee. King Merovee. Merovee the Mason.

If he asked Merovee as a "brother in the craft," for sake of the widow's son, then either the king would respond, or if not, would be propelled to the front of the suspect list. It was a win-win proposition.

Peter trooped down into the great hall and found the king with Artus.

They were discussing logistics of the coming Franco-Celtic Roman Empire, trailed off as he approached. A third man at the table was unknown to Peter. Very large, late fifties. He wore long, white hair and a beard, carried no weapon. He wore an animal skin toga nearly as hairy as the man himself.

"Artus," said Peter, bowing his head. The *Dux Bellorum* returned the acknowledgment. "Your Majesty," said Peter to King Merovee, "I need a word alone with you, if Artus permits."

Artus raised his brows, scratched his five o'clock shadow. "This change is stunning, Lance, but most becoming! You've taken my lectures to heart, and I'm most pleased!" To Merovee, he explained: "A week past, he would have said 'bugger off, Celtique, I mus' speak lone to Mervoee Roi!' He seems to have become a Roman overnight."

The Sicambrian monarch laughed politely at the impersonation. "Countryman," he said to Peter, "you have not met Eire. Prince Lancelot of Languedoc, this is Leary, Archking of Eire."

"Most pleased to make your . . . did you say *Leary?*" concluded Peter, incredulous. An ancestor? Surely not!

Peter took Leary's hand, braced himself for the inevitable, then breathed a sigh of relief when Leary gave no Masonic signs.

"A Christian Mithraic prophet tours the Emerald lands," said the Archking, voice hoarse, unaccented. "I have given him leave to preach throughout Eire. He is one of yours, I believe, Merovee. Calls himself Bishop Patrick."

Merovee hunched over his wine. "No friend of mine, I assure you. He is Pope Leo's boy, a follower of Damasus. One of the Roman Catholic followers of Our Lord, a Paulist. He follows the rock, as I follow the twin."

"The rock? The twin?" Leary looked in puzzlement at Artus.

"Peter is the rock, James is the twin, I believe," said Artus. "If I remember correctly. Rome against Jerusalem, *modus versus substantia*. But I am unlearned in theology, Your Majesties."

Leary pulled at his magnificent, white beard, which flowed down his chest and across the table. "My apologies, Christian. I thought you two would find common ground. I invited him here, in fact."

Artus cleared his throat. "I um do hope there isn't to be a scene. Not with Cutha, Merovee, and Leary gracing my table at once!"

"That has been my rule in Eire. Bring everyone to the table together, let them all say their piece. Let everyone say his piece! I admit, this is not the first time such free speech has gotten me in trouble."

The Long-Hair smiled up at Peter. "If this boy and I can put aside our own political difficulties, surely we can both tolerate a Paulist." Merovee's smile was so full of grace and acceptance that Peter had to fight a desire to seize his hand and kiss his ring.

Artus put a hand on his arm. "Lance, one change. You will take my bard, Cors Cant, to Harlech?" Peter nodded, and the *Dux Bellorum* continued. "Then leave me my Druid, Myrddin. The journey is arduous for such an old man, and I require entertainment here at Camlann."

Damn, thought Peter. But if he had to choose between Cors Cant and Myrddin, the decision was easy: with the boy came the bloody-handed seamstress. With the old mountebank came only grumbling, pomposity, and a weak bladder. "Very well, sir," he agreed reluctantly.

"Now I believe Lancelot wishes to withdraw with his friend from Sicambria," said Artus. He stood politely as Merovee and Peter departed. The latter turned for a lingering, backward glance at King Leary. The archking stroked his beard, grinning like a mischievous leprechaun.

Peter and Merovee threaded between the tables and couches, just beginning to fill with early supper guests. Gilt and grey seemed the fashion of the day, and Peter wondered whether the knights and senators got together at a secret meeting to coordinate dinner dress. The men wore toga-styled tunics, gilt thread picking out patterns in the grey cloth . . . early coats of arms or family crests? random patterns? The women mostly wore longer tunics and chemises that brushed the floor. They wore more colors, but grey and gold were still strong motifs.

Perhaps in honor of King Merovee, thought Peter, as they stopped in a shadow beneath an unlit lantern, well distant from prying ears. Merovee himself wore white, but his men wore grey tunic uniforms. Gold might show honor for a king. Or perhaps for the Archking Leary, if they knew he had arrived.

Peter took Merovee's hand, again pressed the sign. Returning it, Merovee said "Greetings on all three sides of the triangle."

Peter was confused, expecting four sides of a square. But he pressed on. "I beg a favor from a brother in the craft," he said.

Merovee waited.

"For the widow's son," added Peter.

The king smiled, a slow, sardonic tribute. "If it lies within my power *and the scope of the oath,* it is yours."

"Come with me."

Merovee understood immediately, did not seem overjoyed at the prospect. "I am not sure whether I can put aside my business with Artus for a routine patrol in Harlech."

"Artus said your business was finished."

"Hm." The king seemed less sure than the *Dux Bellorum.*

"I had a premonition," Peter lied. He carefully looked at the floor; the most elementary mistake of most liars was to stare intently into the mark's eyes. "I saw Artus lying dead . . . slain by a Sicambrian. I don't believe you are that man— but it is somebody close, perhaps from among your entourage." True enough, though of course the "premonition" (courtesy of Thomas Malory) insisted the "Sicambrian" was Lancelot, not Merovee.

"And if we accompany you against the Jutes, none of us shall be here. And neither will I." The king smiled. "Nor you, Lancelot of Camlann."

Peter looked up, caught and held Merovee's eye. "For the widow's son," he repeated.

"Who is the widow's son?" demanded the king suddenly. Peter's stomach lurched; his mind was blank! Then he abruptly remembered, nights of reading as if for university. He opened his mouth, but changed his mind and asked his own question. "Show me the sign for the proper degree." *It's a test,* he thought, *to see if I'm truly a Mason, or whatever they call it.*

Merovee made a motion that Peter did not catch. After a moment, he gave the correct sign. Peter leaned forward, cupped his hand to Merovee's ear, whispered "Hiram Abiff, king of Tyre, who supplied the wood for King Solomon's temple."

"What happened to the poor fellow?"

"Murdered by the three who would not repent, Jubela, Jubelo, and Jubelum." Peter felt an odd twinge of conscience; even though he knew it was only for cover, his immortal soul experienced a shiver at the closeness of the mortal sin of Masonry, for which excommunication was still the punishment.

The king grunted noncommittally. "We shall go with you, Prince Lancelot," he said. "But my men shall not fight."

"Fair enough," said Peter. He saluted and the king acknowledged, then turned and walked back through the sprawling bodies and filling couches, out the front door of the *triclinium.*

With great satisfaction, Peter put a mental check mark next to Merovee's name on his list. Only Morgawse and Myrddin would remain unattended while Peter was gone.

And Gwynhwfyr.

No, never. It isn't her.

Late that night, Cei knocked on the wall outside Peter's room, entered when invited. He had a ledger, but made no move to show it to Peter; rather, he read from it. *Of course, Lance is illiterate,* thought Peter. His face flushed momentarily at the memory of being laughed at when he asked for a piece of paper.

"Regarding the finances for the expedition," said the porter, "I need your approval for the allocation of money for food, water, a pair of chariots, chartering of a *trireme* from Cardiff with captain, crew, oarsmen, and ten marine troops. The officers have their own horses and slaves, so we needn't pay for any out of our own funds."

"Slaves?" Peter felt a ball of nausea roll through his stomach.

"Perhaps a few kitchen slaves from the household. But personal slaves who die or are damaged are the responsibility of their owners. They shall require food, however."

Peter swallowed. He knew this would eventually come. Cover or no, he simply could not tolerate human slaves in his unit. "No slaves, Cei. None. Neither household nor personal."

Cei withdrew a step, raised his brows.

Peter continued. "It's . . . um—" He sought desperately for a plausible reason. "Loyalty. Their loyalty is uncertain. Heh heh. Never know who's paying them under the table for information."

"Great Gods. Who do you expect to curry and water the knights' horses, cook the food, dress us?" Cei seemed honestly horrified at the prospect of currying his own horse.

"You'll cook your own food or eat it raw, I don't care. But *no slaves.*"

Cei stared for a long time, his dark eyes shut almost to slits, jaw muscles tense. "The time is coming, General. Soon you will have to choose in whose world you live: his, or yours. For today, I shall accept your outlandish, modern ways."

"Why chariots?"

Cei spoke slowly, as if to a retarded child. "Because you and I will get awfully tired jogging behind the horses, dangling from the traces."

Which is exactly what will happen to me if I try to ride one of those contraptions. "Why can't you and I *ride* the horses, like all the other officers?"

Cei grimaced. "Galahad, I've not mounted as cavalry since I commanded a cohort in Africa."

"As generals, we need speed, Cei, not comfort. No chariots."

The porter sighed. "May I continue the accounts?" Peter nodded, and Cei returned to his ledger. "I assume you don't need to hear the actual figures, Sire."

Peter slumped a bit, relieved. No slaves. "You assume wrong, Cei. Read them."

Cei raised his eyebrows momentarily, slickly continued the accounting with barely a perceptible pause. "Rations for forty-nine for perhaps three weeks, including water and vegetables comes to about sixty denarii, perhaps a bit less with the *Dux Bellorum*'s discount."

How strange, that Artus must buy supplies. "This money, it comes from the people?"

"Er, which people would that be, Princeps?"

"The people, the *populi*! The citizens of Britain!"

"Sire, the tax system is quite complex, and I doubt I could explain it in the minutes before the feast begins. Upon each ton of corn, we levy a tax of—"

"Never mind." Peter gestured Cei to continue his financial accounting, but listened with only half an ear.

Of Peter's primary suspects, only two, Merovee and Morgawse, would be likely to have enough money to hire more than a few men.

Logically, Peter could see three situations:

1. Selly could have landed in the body of a slave or servant, which would severely limit her capability for monkey business.
2. She could have landed in the body of an aristocrat, knight, or senator who had little money; in this case, Peter would expect a quick, well-timed strike with no more than a few assailants.
3. Finally, if her lucky stars were strong, she landed in somebody who could afford to raise an army. In the last case, her attack could come politically, as a pitched battle ... that is, assuming Selly's history-changing action was the quick dethroning of Artus.

But *was* that what she had done (or would do)? Would it truly change history to kill Arthur a bit early? His major contribution to English history was his legend.

Then what? Is Selly behind this English-French, revivified Roman Empire? Peter was at a loss. Killing Artus seemed to confirm history, not change it, yet he could not see an IRA operative going back in time just to add to the power of Arthur, first in the long line of kings and queens of Selly's mortal enemy, the same England that she blamed for everything from starvation in Africa to the eventual explosion of the sun into a nova.

He dismissed the speculation. Theorizing in the absence of evidence was the cardinal sin of the investigator, according to Sherlock Holmes, yet another Englishman. No matter what she would do to so change the timeline, or will have already done (Peter's head reeled from the future-past tense), it would be or will have already been much more effective if Selly were rich enough in this age to afford an army ... or at least some pretty serious bribery.

Cei. Cei had an army, a legion, in fact. And Cei was turning the knights against Artus—Lancelot, for one—and expressing open rebellion.

But would an IRA member express such disdain of the Catholic Church? *The Provisional IRA are very strict about their operatives; I doubt like hell they'd allow anyone but a practicing, confessed Catholic on undercover operations,* decided Peter. It was possible Cei's opinions were mere ruse to throw Peter off the scent, but without such feelings, why the animosity toward Artus?

Under the "money criterion," Cors Cant was out of the running, as well as his mysterious girlfriend, probably. *As is Gwynhwfyr,* appended Peter with relief.

That left Artus himself, Cei, Morgawse and Medraut, and Merovee. The finances of peripherals such as Bedwyr and Myrddin were still cyphers.

An unbidden doubt crept into his mind and gnawed the edges of certainty. Did the money criterion exonerate Gwynhwfyr? Or was it possible that she had her own source of funds, separate from her husband's? Was it even a real criterion, or mere sophistry designed to exculpate the woman he—that he liked an awful lot?

"Damn," he muttered.

"Sire?"

"Nothing, Cei. Please continue."

The porter recited the rest of the financial report on the expedition; it was utterly boring, and Peter listened to not a word of it.

CHAPTER 46

BLUNDELL NERVOUSLY WATCHED THE CLOCK READOUT: A MINute, another minute, yet another minute. They passed much too quickly, as if Selly Corwin had rigged all the clocks, too.

This is the forest primeval,
The murmuring pines and the hemlocks. . . .

The forest timeline had solidified as the "real" line faded. They were now equally solid, mixed into an uneasy suspension, like timeline oatmeal.

In three hours, at 0400—undoubtedly bang on the dot—Colonel Cooper would barge into the lab and demand they drag Smythe back by main force.

Peter would likely die. But that would not deter Cooper. He would say "ours is not to reason why," or "it's a far, far better thing," and would bully them into tearing away at Peter's mind.

Murder, plain and simple. Blundell knew the likeliest outcome, knew also he would not be able to resist the florid, commanding colonel. Unless, perhaps, he had an alternative plan.

Mark Blundell checked the clock against his watch. Exactly 1:00 A.M., thirty minutes after his last call. He picked up the receiver, dialed for an outside line, and called Roundhaven's private home number yet again.

On the fifth ring, the phone was answered. "Who did you want?" demanded an annoyed voice, clearly Roundhaven himself.

"Mr. Roundhaven, this is Mark Blundell. Stilton's son? You remember, sir, we worked together on the energy policy speech last March?" Blundell held his breath, counted slowly to fifteen. This was the worst part, waiting to see if William Roundhaven would remember one intern out of thirty—admittedly, the son of a very important Tory contributer.

"Oh. Yes, I think I remember you. Tall chap, glasses, balding?"

"That's me, I'm afraid, sir."

"It's *very* late, Mr., ah, Blundell."

"Yes, sir. I apologize, sir, but this is vital! Are you familiar with the Big Time project?"

A longer pause. Then Mark heard muffled speech through a hand cupped over the mouthpiece. "Stand by a minute, will you, son?"

"Yes, sir, I'll hold." He closed his eyes, inhaled a deep lungful of air half-scented with oak, half with disinfectant.

After two minutes, Mark heard footsteps, the rustle of a paper file. At last, Roundhaven spoke again. "So you are on this project. Congratulations, Mark. How's it going?"

"Well to tell you the truth, sir, we've got a terrible problem just now." Blundell inhaled and exhaled, breathing as he had been taught in the craft. The forest air and crickets calmed him as he told Roundhaven the entire story, from Peter's arrival to Selly's disappearance to Peter's accident. The underminister said nothing, let Mark talk himself out.

"Mark," he said when Blundell ran down, "I cannot order Cooper not to try to bring Peter back. Or any of you. I fund the projects—or more precisely, I determine which projects get funded by the Ministry—but I have no authority to give operational commands to an SAS colonel."

"Yes, sir, I know that. But the Minister . . ."

"Mark, the Minister isn't sure which is farther, the moon or Mars. He thinks rockets can't fly in space because they have nothing to push against. The man wasn't chosen for his scientific knowledge, my boy.

"What do you think he would say if I came at him with this time travel story? Colonel Cooper is a quantum physicist compared to the Minister."

"I, um, expected as much. I have another idea, sir. One that I think you *can* authorize."

Can I really do this? wondered Mark, strangely detached. *Have I the spunk? Must I volunteer, just because my father is Sir Stilton Blundell?*

Blundell continued. "Cooper can decide Major Smythe's fate because he's his commanding officer. But he's not *my* commanding officer. I'm a civilian, never in the service. So he has no authority over me . . . am I correct, sir?"

"So far."

"Then if I decide to use the machine myself, go back in time—say to 450 A.D.—then . . ."

"Then unless Cooper gets the Minister himself to take control of the entire project, there's not a damned thing he can do about it. He can't stop *you*, either." Roundhaven's voice lowered menacingly. "But *I* can. And I will."

"You can't!"

"Of course I can, I own the bloody machine!"

"No, sir, I meant you couldn't, not when you knew what

was at stake. Look, we've isolated the problem that caused the power surge, we're fixing it even as we speak. It will be fine, in good working order before I step within the coils. I'm no martyr! But somebody's got to warn Peter about Selly being a rogue. And somebody's got to tell him to stop resisting, to allow himself to be brought back gently. It's the only way we have even the smallest chance of his surviving.

"Please, sir. He's a . . . he's like a brother to me."

"Mark, your father."

"What about him?"

"He's raised over two hundred thousand pounds for us. He's our most important contributer south of the City. And he's a personal friend of mine. You tell me how, boy, how I can call up Sir Stilton and say excuse me, but we lost your only son somewhere back in the Dark Ages?"

"Yes, let's consider my father, sir. My father served in Korea, in the Choson. He was almost driven into the sea during the retreat. You should remember this; God knows he's told the story often enough.

"Sir, he could have died on that march. Thousands did, even men of his own company. And *I wasn't even born yet.*

"Do you understand what that means, sir? Had he died then, the Blundell line would have come to an abrupt end. But he volunteered in the first place and stayed to the end, because Father was a man of honor. He took seriously his obligations as a gentleman.

"How can his son do less? Do you really think my father would want a son who was afraid to risk his life when there was no other way? For the sake of my father and for Britain, you must let me go!"

Roundhaven snorted. "I remember being your age. God willing, you'll still be alive in twenty years to realize how silly and pretentious you sound."

"Then you'll allow the mission?" Mark was not sure which he would rather hear, yes or no.

"Go, get yourself run through with a sword, if that's your destiny. But I'll tell you, Mark, it's not because of that weepy, patriotic speech you made, which ought to take the Bulwer-Lytton prize for pretentious twaddle."

"No?"

"Not a bit of it." He paused for dramatic effect. "I just decided I'd rather face your father than *you* for the next twenty years." Roundhaven slammed the telephone down.

Mark replaced the cradle, stared at his hand, as if everything were its fault. The room began to shake; it took a moment for him to realize he was the one who was trembling. He forced himself to stand, listen to the forest, then clump down to the lab, dodging translucent trees that no one else could see.

CHAPTER 47

I PACED BACK AND FRO IN THE DARKENED ROOM. TWO FLOORS BELOW, Artus held a farewell *saturnalia*. Everyone attended; the palace was deserted except for the *triclinium*.

'Twas time to strike.

But I could not move, for an ill humor still gripped me around the chest, squeezed my breasts most unpleasantly: *could I really do it?*

Take refuge from thought in action, Uncle Leary always preached. I drew a long, grey cloth from my roll of fabric, cut it a handsbreadth wide for two arm-lengths . . . I would wrap my face and head, letting not a hair peep out, and perhaps no one would see who I was (until I slew the *Dux Bellorum;* I suspected the Praetorian Guard would unravel me when they arrested me for treason).

I carefully wound the cloth, leaving only my eyes uncovered. Though I wound but a single band across my mouth and nose, it stifled me anyhow, and I wheezed like a leaky blacksmith's bellows with every breath.

But could I do it? Would I?

My dagger was Roman, thus shocking in its simplicity: pommel, haft, crossbar, blade. No gilt or jewels adorned the grip, no Ogham runes of power along the blade, calling upon sundry gods and goddesses who might or might not enjoy being included in the party (I don't think Druids actually ask before they scribble the names); no, it was a straight, simple blade for a straightforward job, long enough to bite through Artus's chest and ribs into his heart, from either side.

'Twas the same dagger I used on the lifeless corpse of Canastyr, and for that I was sorry: both for sullying Artus with the earthworm's blood and for allowing a horse's hoof to fulfill my own oath.

I paced and waited, praying the shoemaker was at the revel; I had no desire to kill an innocent craftsman. I prayed That Boy was present as well—may he get drunk, or even fall into Gwynhwfyr's arms for the night! Well, no, maybe not *that;* but I did beg the Virgin that he stay below, not accompany his master upstairs to entertain with a private song.

The moon crawled across the sky, the candle burned past mark after mark. Did they miss me? Surely That Boy would notice I wasn't in evidence; mayhap he thought I was still angry about his shameful heroics in the stadium two days past ... so long as he did not come searching for me! I clenched my fists, hoping that his bardic duties kept him belowstairs.

'Twas the last night, for tomorrow at dawn we were to gather in the stadium under the watchful eye of Prince General Lancelot, ready to march to Harlech to be captured and slaughtered. Even if I survived, I would never get another chance, for after Lancelot, Cei, and Bedwyr were taken, surely Artus would surround himself with troops!

(But it was mere justification on my part, for the truth was my own will wavered, flickered like my candle, which I had to relight twice. Did I not snuff out the *Dux Bellorum*'s life tonight, my fragile resolve would shatter, leaving me to slink cowardly back to Harlech—what was left of her, after the Jutes and Saxons slaked their unnatural thirsts.)

My apartment window fortunately faced the *triclinium* with its open roof; if I had the legs of a grasshopper, I could have leapt from my own room into the midst of the revelry without ruffling my tunic. Thus, I could easily hear the *saturnalia* as the roar wound down. When I judged it neared its end, and Artus might soon be rising to bed, I determined to move.

I suddenly felt a terrible pressure inside me, as if my entire body would burst like an over-huffed air bladder! I wrapped

my arms around myself, hugged tight, and held me together.
Then the force subsided. Lips pressed tight, I boldly swished
the curtain aside, passed through the princess's rooms, and
exited into the hallway.

The hall was empty, so nobody saw me in my strange, Ara-
bic garb: grey tunic and trousers, high boots and gloves, a long
rope looped around my shoulder, and my face wrapped like a
corpse awaiting burial. I walked purposefully to the stairs,
mounted them up to the lawyers' and shoemaker's floor.

I hesitated a moment, fearful that the lawyers, notorious for
their stodgy refusal to partake of revelry—which I guess is
like complaining that eunuchs rarely make use of the harems
they guard—might still be working and see me. I mastered
myself and jogged to the shoemaker's room.

Fortunately, shoemakers aren't like lawyers, and this one
was doubtless down at the farewell feast. I crossed to the
window, stepped onto the sill.

I looked downward and sucked in a breath; in darkness, the
drop had grown to dizzying depths! Keeping my eyes fixed
firmly on the ladder, I stepped across, climbed it to the roof.

I cautiously poked my head over the wall, making sure
there were no watch-standers to thwart my task. I'm not sure
whether I was relieved or disheartened that I was alone . . . if
there *had* been someone, I could have quite legitimately
given up and returned to my room: *sorry, Father, but he was
guarded night and day.*

With a heavy boot tread, I took my final walk across the roof
to the point above Artus's apartment, knowing I would likely
never see safe land again. I looped one end of my rope around
a catapult, appropriately enough, and slung it over the side.

Climbing a rope is much worse than mounting a ladder!
But I managed, somehow swirling enough rope around my
right foot that I could press it against the left and stand
against it. There is supposed to be a way to do it simply and
easily, but it never seems to work when I try it; if I can climb
a rope, it's invariably because of good wishes and skyhooks.

I writhed my way down two levels to the *Dux Bellorum*'s
window, found the sill with questing toes. I nearly lost my
balance and plopped upon the cobbles below, but managed to
hang on and enter the room.

For a moment, the *Dux Bellorum*'s fear of the dark defeated me, for he hung lamps and lanterns in every corner and from each wall, lighting the room to nearly the brilliance of daylight. Gwynhwfyr, princess of night and shade, often railed to her ladies about never being able to get a wink of sleep on those rare occasions she spent the night with her husband.

Bright light might drive away night terrors, but it also makes it overly difficult for assassins, who prefer to hide in deep shadows and black recesses. I hunted a bit frantically, aware that I had coolly cut my time quite short, finally found a closet with a curtain. I slid behind it, dagger drawn, my breath ragged and my heart breathing like pots and pans tumbling down a chimney.

After a long interval, *I fell asleep!* It was hard to avoid it, the *saturnalia* lasted much longer than I thought it would, Artus remaining in the *triclinium* until a scant, few hours before dawn, despite his early-morning duties. I blinked awake, wondering where I was and why I was seated uncomfortably in a closet with a heavy dagger in my hand and a spiderweb wrapped around my face.

Directly I remembered, I realized what awakened me: Artus's voice in the outer hall and bootsteps approaching his rooms. I leapt to my feet, nearly fainting from the sudden change in altitude, and crouched in the closet, trembling with anticipation.

The tyrant would die! Freedom would reign! Alas, I felt more like a spurned lover, less like a martyr with every heartbeat . . . and then the *Dux Bellorum* entered the room.

Through a crack I saw him dismiss his guard to the hall. He was alone. He turned, looked in my direction; I dared not draw back, lest the movement itself betray me.

He walked directly toward me, veering aside at the last moment to wash his face and hands in the basin on the clothes press adjacent to my closet. Then he returned to the center of the room, fell to his knees, and began to pray.

This is it! screamed my brain; that was my chance, while his back was turned, his mind concerned with Jesus and Mary, not a creeping assassin's knife.

The moment was perfect—since he prayed, surely his soul would go straight to heaven when he died! I felt no animosity toward Artus *Dux Bellorum* and was happy to oblige his prospects for immortality by making him a religious martyr guaranteed paradise.

Noiselessly, I slipped from the closet, holding the curtain carefully to prevent it swishing and alerting him. Heel to toe, I rolled each step, agonizingly slowly, as I had been taught when creeping into bowshot of a forest buck.

At last, I stood over Artus *Pan-Draconis,* the all-father, war-leader, *the greatest man in all of Prydein,* thick, Roman dagger in my sweating palm.

I raised my hand, muscles straining: one quick strike like a snakebite and all would be over . . . literally.

I froze.

I tried to force the knife down, plunge it into the tyrant's back, freeing Harlech from his bloody grasp; but some force held me tight, like a hound straining at her leash. *I could not drive That Boy's face from my eyes!*

I lowered my arms, then raised them again, dagger gripped tightly in both hands; but again I could not do it. Artus lived, continued his prayers, unremarking the drama behind his back.

Sweat soaked the cloth across my brow, and I blinked stinging tears from my eyes. He was an old man, set in his ways, trying his best with a limited vision into men's hearts . . . just like Uncle Leary, who is my real father in some sense.

At last, the inchoate thought that had nagged at me for days solidified into a concrete statement: *Artus was to Cors Cant what Leary was to me!*

To assassinate the *Dux Bellorum,* I would need at least four daggers: one for Artus, and the shadow dagger that plunged into Uncle Leary—one for That Boy when his father was murdered all over again, and the last for me, for what life would I have even were I never caught?

I stood straight. The dagger-hand fell limply to my side. I tilted my head back and stared into heaven, uncaring whether Artus heard me and summoned the Praetorian Guard to run me through.

How could you DO this to me! I screamed at Athena, whose sudden gift of "understanding" had just rendered me impotent and cowardly.

A warrior who *thinks twice* may as well be a seamstress!

A warrior acts, she doesn't think; and here I had just committed the original sin; I had thought about it . . . worse, I had thought of my enemy as a man.

Artus still prayed, now aloud, startling me so much I

nearly dropped my knife: "Mary, mother of God, guide the young along righteous paths, that they never mistake holy militancy with conquest of earthly realms; for the Antichrist is ever-ready to tempt the pious with soft-spoken reasons for mortal sin, justified by holy ends."

I dropped my gaze, stared at the floor before me. He had ruined me! An unprotected back, an old man with hands clasped in prayer, silly words that he had probably memorized and never understood himself—yet they had destroyed a warrior, kept her from striking to free her home from foreign domination.

No, I thought, *it wasn't Artus: it was Him. He stopped me. It was That Damned Boy!*

I had thought of That Boy and the pain I would cause him and flinched from my duty, failed at my quest. Thus was the empire redeemed from holy murder by my own, selfish act of personal love.

I was both traitor and heretic.

I heard a hesitant foot approaching the room. Suddenly panicked, I crept backwards, praying that I backed into the closet and not the clothes press.

Artus paused, cocked his ear to listen. The footsteps stopped, and a gentle fist pounded the pine outside the *Dux Bellorum*'s apartment.

"Enter in peace," said he, confident that the guard would not allow an unexpected interruption.

As the wooden door creaked open, I took advantage of the covering noise to turn and slip behind the curtain again.

A young man entered the room, a boy actually: That Boy, Cors Cant Ewin himself. He approached Artus with trepidation, bowed deeply and formally.

"Artus *Dux Bellorum*," he greeted.

"A good night, my bard."

"I arrive as you summoned, sir."

Artus nodded, rose and seated himself on a stool. "I need to know—sit! take a seat, lad; take the bed, it's soft—Cors Cant, you are my bard, sworn to my service and I would hope loyal to me in your heart, as well."

"Oh, yes sir!" That Boy vigorously nodded, shocked the *Dux Bellorum* would even consider that he wasn't.

"Splendid. Then I must know what really happened the day

before yesterday, when you and your friend, what was her name?"

"Anlawdd, sir, seamstress to the princess."

"When you and Anlawdd met the Saxons or Jutes or whatever they were. There are some unanswered questions—beginning with the question of whether they were Saxons or Jutes."

That Boy squirmed, obviously having reached some of the same conclusions I had regarding Jutes who spoke Irish but were called "brothers" by the Saxon Cutha, brother of King Caedwin of Wessex.

Artus jabbed a finger at That Boy. "And don't dance me 'round the Maypole with that nonsense about not being able to tell Jutic from Saxon. I know very well you know the difference, for you were taught by Myrddin, who has been my companion for longer than you've been alive . . . though he does seem a bit distant, lately."

That Boy sat stiff and wooden, face pale in the lamplight. "I truly know not, sir," he said at last, "for they were dressed as Jutes but one spoke Irish."

"Irish? Why Irish? And how did he know you even spoke it?"

I held my breath; this was the perfect opportunity for that little fool to spill all my secrets, leaving me naked before the *Dux Bellorum!*

"Perhaps he knew I trained at Dun Laoghaire, sir. I presume he spoke Irish so the other two wouldn't know what he said; but as they never spoke, I cannot rightly say whether they were Jutic or Saxon. Cutha could be right, sir."

"What did he say?"

"Much I did not understand."

Well, that much was true, or at least I hoped so! For Canastyr had spoken covertly not only of the charge I had just failed to execute but of certain private matters between brother and sister of which it is not lawful to discuss.

"Well, what *did* you understand, Cors Cant?"

"That they meant us no good, sir. There is no question that they followed us from the palace and meant to take us then and there."

"What did you do?"

"Cutha is right, sir; all three are dead."

Artus stroked his clean-shaven chin. "That's another odd

discrepancy, boy; how in the world did you manage to kill three armed men when I know for a fact you have had no training to arms at all, at my personal request?"

I blinked; the *Dux Bellorum* himself had ordered that That Boy never be trained to arms? I wondered why.

That Boy stared, mouth working open and closed; I clenched my teeth—he could not possibly convince Artus, the consummate soldier, that Cors Cant killed the men! For his sake, I hoped he wouldn't even try.

" 'Twas not me, sir," he squeaked at last. "'Twas Anlawdd. She killed them."

"A girl killed all three soldiers?" Artus seemed only slightly less incredulous than if That Boy had insisted a giant appeared over the horizon, pounded the Saxons, and lazily departed.

"Yes, sir. She told me—"

I clamped a hand over my mouth to prevent me screaming for him to shut up!

"She told me she had been trained to militia arms by her father, back in Harlech."

For a long time, Artus stared at That Boy. He did not look convinced. I was furious that the *Dux Bellorum* now knew it was me, not That Boy, who slew the bastards, for it meant my days as Gwynhwfyr's seamstress were over; but that in itself might not be such a bad thing, since I must needs return to Harlech directly and report failure anyway.

And at least he hadn't told Artus who I really was.

"I shall give you benefit of my doubt," he said, "for I have noticed that Anlawdd is stronger and of a more volatile humor than any other seamstress I've met. But I am not satisfied, Cors Cant Ewin . . . and we will explore this subject in more depth when you return from Harlech.

"You say Anlawdd hails from that city: will she return with you, or tarry at her home?"

"I don't know," answered That Boy, and I could tell this time he spoke nought but the truth.

"Come and see me when you return; I want to know more about this Anlawdd from Harlech. I believe Archking Leary's brother-in-law is prince of that city; perhaps either Leary or Gormant can shed some light on the miraculous militia-seamstress."

"Why would the archking of Eire know anything about a militiaman in Harlech?"

"Because there is more to her than meets your eye, boy. You are too much ruled by your passions! I truly wish my generals and retainers would take their example from me: I have my passions, but I keep them to myself and never allow them to interfere with duty. Passions are selfish children, driving you leave when you ought to stay, stay when you should leave, and to buy what you would not own under any circumstance. I should like to see you quell them, especially given the difference in your ranks."

"Yes, sir."

"You may leave. Remember what I said when you return."

"Yes, sir." That Boy stood, bowed, and began to walk toward the door when suddenly it burst open with a thud. Prince Lancelot pounded through, the Praetorian Guard streaming behind, confused and angry but unwilling to interfere with the legate.

"Artus!" shouted Lancelot, glancing only momentarily at That Boy.

"What news, Galahadus? Is there an attack?"

"Maybe an attack on *you,*" answered the general. "When I left the, ah, the *triclinium,* I strolled outside for some night air. I looked back and saw your window, clearly identifiable by the rather intense light that streams from it."

"Yes?" Artus seemed as perplexed as his Guard.

"I noticed a thin, black line bisecting your window. When I came closer, I saw it was a rope dangling from the roof and leading directly to your own apartment, sir."

"A rope!" Artus, Lancelot, That Boy, and the Guard trooped across the room to a window, but saw nothing—of course, for they chose the wrong window!

I realized I had but an instant to act; hesitation would allow them to try the *next* window, find the rope, and cut off my only escape. *Now* that I had decided that my own honor could not countenance striking a man down from behind at his prayers—not to mention what I was beginning to feel for That Boy, damn him—the thought of being caught by Artus or the Guard or *especially* by That Boy was more than I could bear!

I bolted out of the closet toward the correct window. Just then, Cors Cant entered the room and saw me.

We both froze, facing each other. I knew he could not see beneath my mask, and even my hair was fully concealed; but he stared at me as if trying to place my identity anyway, without the fear one would normally expect when a young bard encounters an armed assassin in his lord's apartment at night.

He stared at my dagger. He must have recognized it, but could not quite remember where he had seen it before.

I dropped it on the floor, where it clattered like an alarm bell. Lancelot came running; but when he saw me in the center of the floor, he didn't freeze like That Boy: he charged!

That broke the spell that bound me. I turned and raced toward the window, a scant heartbeat ahead of the champion. He made a dive for me, but just at that moment I dived headfirst out the open window, groping blindly for my rope and praying I hadn't chosen the wrong portal as well.

I don't know how I grabbed it, or how Lancelot missed me. But an instant later, I dangled from the line, feet frantically scrabbling for a toehold. Not daring to undertake the lengthy process of wrapping the rope around my foot, I simply gripped it tight and pushed off and to the left. I swung madly away from the palace; Lancelot lunged at me, missing me by a thread and nearly tumbling out the window himself.

Then I swung in hard and bounced from the wall farther left. When I struck the second time, I sprawled across a windowsill, stared into what surely was *Lancelot's own room!* His furled colors, blue and black, were propped in a corner, and the room looked more like an armory than an apartment.

The curtain was ripped from its rod, and Lancelot charged into the room. He gave a whoop of triumph when he saw me clutching the windowsill, and charged across the room at me again.

This time I pushed straight out from the wall, sliding down the rope. I had no plan; I just wanted to get away from that mad behemoth!

Alas, my rope was not quite long enough to reach the ground.

Just as my head dropped below window-level, I reached the end of my rope, dangled sickeningly for an instant, then dropped to the ground below.

I somehow missed the cobblestones, sprawling full length

in a garden of flowers and mud. I staggered to my feet as the alarm was sounded above. Thinking fast, I unwrapped my face and pulled off my boots, tunic, and pantaloons, leaving me stark naked except for a thin, gauzy chemise that I remembered was nearly as translucent as water. Everybody could see *everything!* But it was preferable to being weighted with stones and cast into the Song Pool, the current punishment for traitors.

I left the incriminating clothing behind, quick-walked around the side of the palace to the Court of Flowing Waters, and washed the mud from my arms and legs. Guards and knights ran about the grounds, shouting, waving their axes, and "catching" each other whenever they rounded a new corner. I glided into the *triclinium,* found a jug of wine, and gargled with it, splashing a bit around my face for good measure. I squawked when I accidently dribbled some on my already-thin chemise, wondered whether I should take it off entirely? My entire skin flushed a deep vermilion with embarrassment as drunken revelers leered at me, staring between my legs, where I was afraid to look—my hair is, well, rather dark, and the chemise was sheer white, and now wet. . . .

I sat at a table away from the crowd with the wine jug, pretending to be asleep.

Lancelot and his soldiers pounded into the room, shook us all awake to ask who had seen what. When he got to me, I slurred my words and pretended barely to understand his questions; that, plus the wine smell allayed his suspicions, though he appraised my body quite frankly, as had the rest of the men and a few women.

It was nearly dawn when he finally let us go; I had barely enough time to rush up to my room, throw on some modest clothes, and prepare myself for the journey.

I dressed with a heart of lead, dreading the thought of facing my father with my failure—and with the death of his son and heir, Canastyr the earthworm.

Neither could I shake the image of That Boy staring at me in Artus's room, as if he could pierce my disguise as easily as the boys in the *triclinium* pierced my chemise.

Oh God, I thought, *please don't let him ever find out it was me. . . .*

CHAPTER 48

THE COMPANY ASSEMBLED IN CAMLANN COURTYARD. THE ENtire cast of suspects was present, except for Gwynhwfyr, Morgawse, Myrddin, and Artus himself. No slaves.

Anlawdd was absent as Leary and Artus bade good-bye to Merovee and Godspeed to Peter, but Cors Cant assured the champion that the princess's seamstress, who apparently slew fully armored men at arms in between yawns, would be along shortly. Female problems, said the bard, and Peter inquired no further.

Anlawdd rode up at the last moment on a large draft horse, moments after the Irish king and the *Dux Bellorum* adjourned to the *triclinium*. Cors Cant cantered beside, uncomfortably, on a shaggy pony. *A horseman you're not, lad,* thought Peter, suppressing a smile.

Peter still silently exulted: *I stopped her!* he thought to himself; Selly had made her attempt in the night, sneaking into Artus's room via a rope dangling from the ceiling; but Peter's quick thinking had foiled her plot.

Alas, she had escaped, and he still did not know what body she inhabited. But no one could take the moment away from Peter Smythe . . . he had saved the *Dux Bellorum*'s life from an IRA terrorist attack!

The bard Cors Cant had trouble keeping up with his sewing maid, who rode a remarkably large horse remarkably well. *All right,* thought Peter, *she rides a horse, carries an axe, and kills men by the dozen.* Any fool could see that Anlawdd was a trained soldier slumming as a seamstress. *Probably a princess,* he decided; *everyone else in this world seems to be.*

He stared at the girl: something seemed decidedly familiar

about the way she moved, as if he had recently seen her in "action" before. He filed the question away for future study; Peter's instincts were never wrong in cases like that.

As Anlawdd worked her feisty beast with a lithe, expert grace, Peter found himself thinking quite unbecoming thoughts. At once it occurred to him that there was no necessary correlation between Selly Corwin's personality and the physical attributes of the body into which she jumped. After all, Peter could as easily have landed in Cors Cant's body as Lancelot's.

Peter reviewed the rest of the troops, tried not to imagine Anlawdd's supple body entwined with his on a sleeping mat.

In addition to the named suspects, there were forty foot soldiers led by Cacamwri, a centurion on horseback. He wore ancient, Roman-style armor, frequently mended and scrupulously polished to mirror brightness.

The mudsloggers wore more traditional metal plates sewn onto leather coats, heavy but cheap. Some had primitive chain mail, some wore nought but leather. Carrying axes, short spears, *gladius* swords, and shields, they did not look the least bit Roman. On the other hand, Peter saw no one resembling Malory's noble knights: no jousting-plate, shining lances, feathered helms, or slitted visors.

The "free-floating officers" wore a disparate mix of gear: Cei and Bedwyr wore Roman breastplates as did Cacamwri; Medraut wore a boiled leather cuirass, mail, and lacquered wood plates. Anlawdd wore some odd sort of tanned leather jacket that fell to her knees in a split skirt, but no mail, bands, plates, or other metal: she was an axe-woman, true, but not built like an American Gladiator. Metal armor would probably pin her to the ground two falls out of three.

The bard, Cors Cant, wore no armor at all. A sword dangled at his side like a stage prop.

Peter himself had risen early and spent two hours trying on various combinations of armor and clothing, ultimately choosing a stiff, black and purple leather cuirass as a compromise between no armor at all and a full, silver breastplate that made him feel like a sardine in a tin. He selected a polished, "Vatican guard" helmet with a Swiss-like, crescent brim and flower-petal ribs across the top, primarily because it looked groovy and impressive enough to carry some command weight. Several severe dents had been carefully hammered out; presumably, Lancelot had actually used it in battle in years past.

Beneath the armor he wore as simple an outfit as he could find: maroon-dyed buckskin trousers and a white linen tunic with an embroidered flowering tree, in case he needed to infiltrate an enemy encampment slumming as a peasant soldier.

Now what in God's name am I going to do with eight officers for forty men? It was worse than the Falklands. *I get it: I command Cei, Cei commands Bedwyr, Bedwyr commands Medraut, Medraut commands Anlawdd, the girl commands Cors Cant, and the bard pipes us into battle. Meanwhile, I command Cacamwri and he commands the troops. A perfect command structure!* Peter shook his head disgustedly.

Merovee's twenty Sicambrians wore fishy scale–armor, perhaps a nod to the king's "fishy" ancestry. Merovee bowed, placed his men under Peter's command, except that they would not fight. The most Peter could extract was a promise that they would jump up and down and rattle their sabers at the Jutes, try to scare them off. If they did not scare, the Britons were on their own.

So I command the Sicambrians, but the Sicambrians will not be commanded. Meanwhile, King Merovee floats alongside and stirs up the anthill.

Cutha trotted his horse into the courtyard, smug as a mouse-catching cat. Four helmetless Saxon bodyguards accompanied him. All wore the same smirk.

Whoops, I forgot. Cutha commands the Saxons, who take orders from no one and nothing. It was Peter's worst command-and-control nightmare come true. SAS strike teams generally consisted of a four- or five-man squad with no insignia or identification, an *einstazgruppe* to root out nests of Irish snakes.

Peter had never captained a military group as unwieldy as this Harlech *maniple*. Worst of all, he realized that Artus's troop configurations were *more* efficient, streamlined versions of the typical British unity of A.D. 450.

Joseph and Mary, why don't we separate the officers and enlisted into two teams and have a bleeding rugby match?

Shouts and tumult; orders barked by noncoms indistinguishable from the soldiers they commanded; tearful good-byes by wives and girlfriends. A wave of homesickness washed Peter. Despite the chill, autumn wind, a core of fire burned from stomach to throat. He squinted, almost saw field packs and Uzis, tanks and Jeeps, the knightly trappings of his own warriors.

"Prince?"

"What?" Cei had said something.

The porter was watching auburn-haired Anlawdd with undisguised disgust. "Sire, what the hell is that girl doing with an axe on a war-horse?"

"Joining the expedition."

"What!" Cei turned sharply in the saddle to stare at the girl. Then he stared back at Peter, lip curled. "If you wanted a bedmate, wouldn't a slave girl have been more discreet—Legate?"

Peter gripped his reins hard enough to press a crease in his palm. "You are being insubordinate. General."

"Isn't she Gwynhwyfr's dressmaker? A bit risky; they do gossip to their mistresses. Let her make dresses."

"She hails from Harlech, according to Cors Cant. She comes along."

Cei closed his eyes, struggled with the idea. Then he slowly raised his gaze and smiled coldly. "Today is not the day for strife, General." He bowed in a courtly fashion, mocking gracious deference. "The *men* are ready to move out, Sire."

Peter nodded, pointed west. "Thataway, march."

The sun rose on the sixth day of Peter's expedition, crawled across the southern sky. They marched raggedly toward the mouth of the Severn, where waited a ship from Cardiff—once a Roman garrison, now the headquarters of Artus's northern army and marine force.

Once on the *trireme*, they would sail through the British Channel, skirt Cardiff and Swansea (or whatever ancestor cities existed in their spots in Artus's day), around the Dyfed peninsula and Pembroke Castle (the spot where it would someday be built, if Peter could thwart Selly Corwin), through Cardigan Bay and into Tremadog Bay, docking at Harlech.

After landing, they would grab mops and pails and swab the land that a millenium and a half later would be Snowdonia National Park.

The troop stopped to rest twice. Peter toyed with the idea of teaching them to march in step, but decided it would take too long, and might conceivably change history. Besides, if one of the suspects really *was* Selly Corwin, it would give him dead away. Perhaps literally.

Patience, lad. Let her make the first mistake. Keep your eyes and attention on the "Suspicious Six."

Centurion Cacamwri, the equivalent of a major or lieutenant colonel, issued marching orders to the four noncoms, who screamed them at the men—exactly as it would still work fifteen centuries hence. Soldiers grumbled, found many excuses to drag their feet. The grizzled sergeants hawked and spit, politely correcting young officers, Medraut especially, when they ordered something particularly stupid. For the most part, the noncoms ignored everyone but Peter, Cei, Bedwyr, and Cacamwri. Under normal circumstances, the last could easily have commanded the entire expedition.

Medraut, Bedwyr, and Cei chattered, ate lunch from horseback, and paid no mind to military discipline. Anlawdd, however, seemed aware that an ambush was always possible. She scanned the hills like a bank-robber's lookout. Peter ordered Cei to keep an eye on her as well; Selly or not, she was dangerous and unpredictable.

He watched her extensively himself, purely for security purposes.

Merovee stuck with his Sicambrians, his absence rebuking Peter for dragging the king along. Cors Cant stayed near his lady fair.

Cutha and the Saxons laughed and cavorted, oblivious to danger. Three times Peter had to send Bedwyr to ride back and tell them to pipe down and stop disturbing the war.

The sun set, night winds blew across the bracken. At last, they arrived at the Severn. The Roman *trireme* was moored to a tiny, rickety dock, a dozen oars sticking out of holes along the side, all pointed up—*shipped,* thought Peter—if that were the right word.

"Shall the officers board?" asked Cei. "We can spend the night there. More comfortable than tents in the mud."

Peter laughed. "We'll all spend the night aboard, Cei! I intend to set sail tonight. Maybe we'll be in Harlech by sunset tomorrow."

Every man within earshot fell silent, stared at Peter in shock.

"Um, you might have a hell of a time explaining that to the captain," said Cors Cant.

"Who is stomping up this very moment," added Anlawdd, "like a Fomorian ogre who's just sat in a cooking fire."

A beet-faced, blustery man in rawhide boots crunched through the dead grass, already shouting and waving his fists, though far out of earshot.

CHAPTER 49

"*WHAT IN THE NAME OF LLYR ARE YOU DOING HERE?*" DEMANDED the captain.

Peter was nonplussed. "Didn't you get the word about the expedition?"

"Of course I did, sink my ass. But you're a day early. D'you expect my crew to row on barely a night's sleep?"

Peter leaned toward Cei, whispered, "We left the day we were supposed to, didn't we?"

"Well," said Cei, "you *did* march us 'Roman speed.' Probably Naw didn't expect us to make it in one day. Hell, *I* didn't expect us to get here in a single day. Figured I'd have time to drill the men a bit more."

"Naw?"

Cei nodded at the red-faced bully, who hocked and spit.

But Artus said Cardiff garrison is just across the river. How much warning do they need? Peter sat straight on his horse again. The lack of stirrups was still a strain on his lumbar. "The troops of Artus *Dux Bellorum* travel like the wind," he said, haughtily.

"Blow the wind out yer ass," retorted Captain Naw. "Two days from Camlann to the river, four days to Harlech. It's been thus for as long as me father's had a beard. What, I suppose you think you'll sleep aboard tonight, and you a day early?"

Peter looked back at his men. They were tired, their mood

bitter, alkali. All day, well into the afternoon, they had marched to the Severn with only occasional breaks. Now they were delayed by an insolent galley captain, his face flushed dark red in the torchlight, as red as Anlawdd's hair.

Stop it! If you must steal another man's woman, you already have Gwynhwfyr.

"Not only are we going to sleep aboard, but your men will begin rowing us to Gwynedd. Tonight."

Naw's mouth opened and closed like a sea bass. "Four days! We start on the morn, sure and arrive on the fourth morn hence!"

"Because if they *don't,*" continued Peter, "I'll have you drawn and quartered and your ship burned in the middle of this wretched river. Sink *that,* Naw."

Naw leaned in on Peter. "I'd not think ye likely to do *that,* by my green beard, seeing as the *Blodewwedd* be the only sea vessel this side of Cardiff. Unless you'd care to swim to Harlech?"

Peter smiled. "All right. I won't burn it. Not today. I will, however, send a message to Artus telling him exactly *why* we were late to Harlech. And whose fault it is when the Jutes burn his cousin's palace to the ground."

The captain scratched under his beard (which was grey, not green). He turned angrily, stormed back to the ship without a glance.

Cei chuckled beside Peter, shook his head. "Gormant is no relation to Artus."

Peter smiled. "Does Naw know that?"

They approached the wharf, where a wicked looking galley, or *trireme,* was tied.

The *Blodewwedd* was nearly a hundred feet long and twenty wide, with two masts. A large turret with a gilt dragon, bright red in the setting sun, poked from the deck just aft of amidships. Scores of black arrows lined the wooden walls of the turret within easy reach, indicating it was used for archers.

"Magnificent," said King Merovee. "Copied from the Imperial galleys that carried the divine Julius to these shores. The sailors row the ship to full speed and ram the enemy. Those bladed spars bound with beaten copper are *falces.* They can strip a ship's rigging with a single blow." Peter took mental notes. Merovee seemed to possess an endless supply of minutiae. Odd that he should choose to mention it to Lancelot, who presumably knew better than Merovee what weapons were available, as if the king knew that *this* Lancelot might be unfamiliar with such knowledge.

"So what do we do with the horses?" asked Peter. Cors Cant stared strangely at him, and Peter realized he had made another *faux pas. Jesus God, it was a perfectly innocent question!* There were no retainers, no stables at the dock.

Then the bard crossed the wooden wharf, his pony's hooves clopping like disconsolate, hollow drums. Ragged sailors in Romanesque armor and animal skins held his pony as he dismounted, led it away to the center of the deck.

"Oh," said Peter. *Well how the bloody hell was I supposed to know they put the bloody horses on the bloody boat!*

Cei rode back from herding his men. "You asked what we're doing with the horses?"

"No, of course not. What kind of fool do you—"

"Don't worry, we're dropping them off across the Severn at Cardiff."

"I knew that."

"Hell, I wouldn't want to ship with them all the way to Harlech, either, Sire! Smelly beasts. Never like boats anyway."

The sailors looked hungrily at the beasts. When a man tried to take Anlawdd's reins, she would not hand them over. She looked first to Cors Cant, then Peter for a lead.

Merovee rode up, put his hand on her shoulder. "Daughter, you cannot ride Merillwyn across the waves! Let the marines take her reins, trust the name of Artus to safeguard your mount. She'll be well treated until we return."

Anlawdd bit her lip, staring imploringly at Merovee. Then she tossed the reins to a marine legionnaire, swung her leg over the horse's neck, and hopped off. She spoke to Merovee under her breath, barely loud enough for even Peter to hear. "You know, I never told you her name was Merillwyn."

"Didn't you?" asked the Long-Hair, eyebrows high.

"No."

"Positive?"

"Yes."

"Well you must have," he concluded, "else how would I

have known?" Merovee smiled enigmatically and handed over his own mount.

As Peter urged his own Eponimius forward, his throat tightened and his stomach rolled. He felt a sudden terror at the foamy, vasty deep, the black River Severn, the fragile, wooden plank over which he must ride. *But this is mad! I've never feared the water before!*

Sensing his fear, the horse skittered uneasily and would not advance. Gritting his teeth, Peter pressed his heels as tightly as he could against the horse's flanks, two hundred pounds of Lancelot versus fifteen hundred pounds of Eponimius.

Finally, the horse bolted up the plank, hard up against Merovee's horse. For no reason he could explain, Peter squeezed his eyes tight until he was on the deck proper. He climbed shakily down from the saddle and leaned against a mast.

I am not afraid of water. I am not afraid of the water! But is Lancelot?

It was not a happy thought. Was the Sicambrian's original personality beginning to possess Peter's mind?

The troops and horses crowded the *Blodewwedd*, piped aboard by a marching tune. The ship barely groaned under the weight, waterline relatively low. *I could have brought a hundred men!* thought Peter. The ship was much larger than it looked from outside.

Waves sloshed against the hull from the current, causing the ship to roll gently. Cutha and his bodyguards complained bitterly. "What courtesy this is? British courtesy! Crushed we are, no amenities befitting our rank given!"

"And only barbaric Britons our mounts to watch," added Cutha. Peter ignored him.

"Make free the lines!" cried Naw, after the sailors stowed the gear and tied down everything in sight. They left the mainsail brailled up as the portside oarsmen pushed against the dock, shoving the galley sideways into the current.

"Galley slaves?" asked Peter, leaning over the deckrail to watch.

"Freemen," corrected the steersman, hand on the till.

"Free?"

"Aye, Sire. They're sailors paid, each and every, free to leave with a month's notice."

"God, why do they stay?" Peter could not keep the incredulity from his voice.

The captain materialized behind Peter. "Because I own this vessel and pay them twice the bloody going rate! Artehe pays well."

Artehe? thought Peter. *Yet another damned name for Arthur.* "You don't call him Artus?"

"Rome left," said Naw succinctly. He turned his back, busied himself with a tangled line.

It took nearly two hours to cast off, cross the Severn, and dock again at Cardiff, the sun long set on Peter's sixth day "in country." Fifty servants (or slaves) waited on the dock to lead the horses away to the garrison stables. Cors Cant took hold of Anlawdd's shoulders, to restrain her from following.

Naw shouted and flapped his arms, and they cast off, drifting back to the center of the river as the oarsmen stroked. The shores on either side slid darkly past, invisible from the channel.

Bedwyr suggested Peter bunk with the rest of the men, so they would see he was one of them, but Peter rejected the plan. He cut Bedwyr's protest off in mid sentence by explaining "I prefer respect to love." When Bedwyr left, Peter added quietly to Cei, "But I'll settle for fear, as Machiavelli—as a great ah Sicambrian philosopher said."

"You've changed," observed the porter. "Time was you used to drink and whore with the best."

Damn that fraternizing Lance. Aloud, he merely said, "We're at war. The rules changed."

Peter took the aft cabin, kept the door shut, and appointed Cei liaison. Soon, the Severn opened wide its mouth and belched forth the *Blodewwedd* into the churning sea.

> *The sea was wet as wet could be,*
> *The sand was dry as dry,*
> *We could not see a cloud because*
> *No cloud was in the sky,*
> *No birds were flying overhead,*
> *There were no birds to fly.*

The *trireme* flung itself through black-dark waves with the abandon of a deranged cetacean, pitching, rolling, yawing with especial glee. Half the Britons clung to the gunwales, mouths set in white mockeries of smiles, begging not to participate in the redundant intake and immediate expulsion of food. The rest huddled amidships, trying to concentrate on dice and bronze *asses,* some sort of low-value coin.

The sailors and marines took the trip indifferently, being more concerned with the supply of wine and sugared mead.

Peter himself loved the sea, the waves, the launch and plummet. His cast iron stomach responded well to periodic agitation. Cors Cant seemed to enjoy it as well, though his inamorata looked distinctly green and lizardlike.

As they left the river a day behind, Peter took to standing astride the castlelike fortification, legs planted wide and firm, staring at the slate grey horizon that merged seamlessly with the sea surface as if he could actually see something worthwhile. He summoned the bard to his side, and in a booming voice said, "A sea chanty! Let it roll, lad."

The bard thought for a moment, solemnly intoned:

> *The rolling, sky black, angry wave,*
> *Casts many a soul to watery grave,*
> *Broken slave and soldier brave,*
> *All fall to Llyr.*

"Um, Cicero?"

"Cors Cant Ewin, My Prince."

Peter fidgeted. He knew what a police investigator would do next: set the suspects on each other, set spies to catch the real spy. But it rankled his military side ... no unit could hold together with every man afraid of his comrade. The Soviets found that out, back when there were Soviets, before they exploded into Russians, Georgians, Uzbeks, Khazaks, and a dozen other blood-enemies.

He sighed, set phase II of the investigation in motion.

"I need eyes, lad," he said to the bard. "I need ears belowdecks. I need a man to watch and listen, especially to remarks anyone may make regarding Cei and Artus." The men would be handpicked, but even Cei might make mistakes. Was Peter, "Lancelot," to be ambushed if not satisfactorily supportive of Cei's coup?

"Eyes and ears," breathed Cors Cant, voice hushed but excited. "A spy! Yes, count me in, Sire!" He murmured quietly to himself; Peter thought he caught something about a widow, but it could have been his imagination and the overabundance of Freemasons in Camelot. Cors Cant motored off.

Cei, when summoned, looked not quite as pale as Anlawdd nor yet as ruddy as Captain Naw. To his porter, Peter suggested, "I am confident in the troops you picked, Cei, but a bit chary of this surplus of knights and officers. Nose around a bit, there's a fellow, and see what you pick up? I'm especially interested in that auburn-haired girl that Cors Cant dragged along. She's not what she seems."

And I saw her somewhere she wasn't meant to be—where, blast it?

"I've noticed," said Cei through clenched teeth, eyeing the heaving deck. "Stitching maid with a battle axe."

Peter shooed him away and sent a sailor for Bedwyr.

"Heard ominous rumblings belowdecks against Prince Cei," he confided. Bedwyr, as unaffected by the sea voyage as Peter himself, snarled and fingered his poniard.

"From who? Give me a name, and he'll feed the sharks!"

"Rumors. Whispers. Lies, spread by ghosts in the ranks."

"Ghosts?" Now Bedwyr peeked uneasily around his mass of black locks, looking for phantasms in the sea mist.

"I mean person or persons unknown. Just keep your ears unstopped, Bedwyr, and report back to me anything you hear of interest regarding me, Cei, or Artus. Especially from that bard. Never did trust harpers." Bedwyr grinned in anticipation and beetled off, rattling and clanking.

To Anlawdd, Peter said, "Tell me about Cors Cant. What exactly is he to you?" He plucked an arrow from one of the ammunition boxes in the castle-fort, twirled it like a drummer spinning his drumstick.

"Friend," squawked the girl, gripping the crenels of the fighting fortress. "More than."

"Lover?"

"Less than." Her eyes crossed, struggled to focus. She seemed curiously reluctant to meet his eyes; but it could have been mere seasickness.

"Like your job? Sewing dresses, embroidering insignia?" Anlawdd nodded weakly, too sick to wonder where the cross-examination led. "Use the axe much for cutting fabric?"

"Hunh?"

Peter tapped her war axe with the arrow. "First you're a seamstress. Then you suddenly show up on a military expedition armed with a weapon of war. In between, there is a mysterious incident where three well-armed Saxons meet their maker in suspicious circumstances, and don't try to tell me that our talented bard laid them low. Any explanations?"

With a great effort, Anlawdd mastered herself. In one moment, she went from seasick girl to cold-eyed conspirator, though still pale as one of Bedwyr's ghosts. "I come from Harlech," she admitted, as if that explained everything from aardvarks to zebras.

"Does Harlech generally double-up soldier and seamstress shifts to save money?"

"It's a small city, My Prince. Hard-pressed. We double up every profession, for we are all soldiers, when pressed."

"So you're a militiaman. Called out in defense of king and country when the barbarians attack?"

"Yes, Sire."

"That's all?"

"Yes, Sire." She nodded convincingly.

Liar, thought Peter. *That's a knightly weapon, a battle-axe, not a militia pike or* gladius. "As you wish, for now." *So why do I let her off the hook?* he wondered.

"C-can I go?" Anlawdd's composure began to crack, will-power fighting a losing battle with seasickness.

"Momentarily. I have, ah, one more question." Uneasiness spread through Peter's gut, as if he sensed the unformed question that was about to burst forth like an unseen bomb. "Since Cors Cant is yet less than a lover, how would you feel about loving a prince?"

Directly he asked the question, Peter regretted it. He half raised his hand, as if trying to grab the words and pull them back.

Anlawdd's eyes widened. She brushed a stray hair from her face. "I . . . I don't know, Prince Lancelot. There is something special between . . ."

You bloody idiot, he berated himself, *there's something special between you and Gwynhwfyr, too!* But the more he stared at Anlawdd's strong arms, wide hips, long, autumn hair, the more he was seized by a mad desire to plant his mouth against her full lips and strip her tunic away, fling her to the deck, and teach her the secrets of love. There was no spirituality, no holy love, as there was (he now admitted) with Artus's wife. Just a driving, animal compulsion to *have* the girl such as he had never felt before.

But was it Peter or Lancelot who possessed him with such brutish urges? Lancelot loved Gwynhwfyr! On that, every authority agreed.

Peter felt a snap in his palm, looked down to see the arrow broken in half. Cheeks red, he flung the pieces overboard, where they floated accusingly on the grey-green swells.

Anlawdd's cheeks matched his own rosy hue. She wrapped her arms around her chest, said "I-I-I have to go below, Sire. Please! May I?" But her face did not seem flushed with embarassment; rather, she bit her lip with a certain haunting hunger. She turned and fled for the ladder, not even waiting to be dismissed.

The wind off the ocean was so cold it burned Peter's lungs. The feeble sun barely warmed his back. *Damn! If this is autumn, what the hell is* winter *like, for Christ's sake?*

Peter leaned against the battlements until he was physically recovered enough to venture below to his cabin, one of only two enclosed areas on the boat. Naw had the other.

He had no opportunity to get lonely. Every couple of hours, one of his spies slunk furtively into the cabin and reported scraps of conversation, dirty looks, or inappropriate laughter. Slowly, Peter pieced together a portrait of the unit, though he learned little of interest about his seafaring suspects.

Like any good military unit, they knew far more about the politics than they ought. They knew of the rift between Cei and Peter, they had uncomfortable, subsonic tremors of the growing rebelliousness of the restive Cei against Artus. And they were confused.

If you're counting on their support, Cei old chum, don't turn your back.

Contrariwise, Peter could not bank on their support for the *Dux Bellorum*, who was, after all, not a real king. Artus was more a soldier-emperor whose power and prestige flowed directly from victory in battle. There had been no battles recently. Soldiers have short memories.

So knight and bishop maneuver for control of the pawns. And the queen—which color does she support? The thought of Gwynhwyfr sent an unexpected shiver of guilt along Peter's neck. What was he doing, flirting with that child-warrior-seamstress when he had a real, flesh and blood princess his for the asking?

Mine? Lancelot's! Or Artus's ... never mine. Peter massaged his temples, wished he were three separate people, each with his own feet and hands.

The *Blodewwedd* made slower headway than he expected. He feared Captain Naw was getting his way after all, slacking his oarsmen to slow the journey. What should have taken no more than a day and a half took nearly three. Part of the problem was that the navigator insisted upon hugging the shore, instead of striking straight across Cardigan Bay, which he called Lleyn's Bend.

"Out of sight of land?" he cried when Peter pointed out that this added another forty miles to the trip, six hours at the pace they set, plus another hour's rest. "They'll gang mutiny an' they not see th' land, be 'sured of its proximity!"

"But the Phoenicians!" protested Peter. "The Polynesians, the Irish reivers!"

"Aye, but we're civilized Britons," countered Captain Naw with exaggerated reason, "not wild, mystic Eirelanders."

"The bleedin' Romans sailed across the Mediterranean. Out of sight of land. Five centuries ago!"

"Och, we're but wild Britons, not scientific, astrological Romans." Naw's face was unfathomable, save for a slight curl to his lip.

Peter gave in, paced the deck. At least the delay gave Cei another half day to train the troops, many of whom were battle virgins. Most of these men had not fought at Mount Badon, or Mons Badonicus, as Cors Cant called it.

Each morning began with the call to colors, a practice the men detested. The piper piped the Bear-King, Artus's "national anthem," so to speak. The men held a Roman salute as the red and gold dragon banner of the *Pan-Draconis* rose up the single mast. They drilled the rest of the day, practiced Roman tactics with British innovations.

Peter watched, fascinated, as Cei paced them. Cei's favorite tactic was for a line of soldiers to lock shields and charge. When their tall, curved rectangles collided with the opposing shields, they raised their shield arms in one movement, pressing the enemy line upward likewise. Thus each man was completely unable to reach the opponent directly before him, and vice versa.

Instead, each turned and "gutted" the enemy *to his right* with *gladius*. To hear Cei tell it, half the enemy line could be slain in the first moments of melee by this unexpected attack.

Peter watched the men rehearse each movement separately, then put them together, first the press and lift, then the press, lift, and stab.

"A pity we cannot train the cavalry as well," sighed Peter.

"Sorry?" Cei stared, puzzled.

"No room on the deck. And the horses are back at Cardiff."

"Sire," began the porter cautiously, "We *are* training the cavalry. Are we not?"

Then Peter noticed Medraut, Anlawdd, Cors Cant, and Bedwyr in line with the rest of the soldiers, as well as Merovee's men, cavalry all.

"In any event," continued Cei suspiciously, "I suspect they all know how to get on and off a horse. So why would we need the brutes on board? When we reach Harlech we can lease horses from Gormant."

Peter's face reddened as he realized that "cavalry tactics" in this age consisted of riding up to the enemy, dismounting, and fighting afoot. No wonder the entire unit stared in confusion!

The wind whipped their red and gold, single-hole, sleeveless tabards like pennants, exposing an explosion of color beneath. Each man wore whatever clothing expressed his inner self, Peter decided, with no attempt at uniformity.

Anlawdd wore a drab olive-and-teal weave that was almost invisible in the constant mist against the sea. Cors Cant, easily recognizable by his clumsy blundering (for he clearly was one of the virgins), swam in a dull peach tunic many sizes too big, whose sleeves hung nearly to the ground and were constantly underfoot. Once, they tripped him.

Medraut wore black and white, perhaps in homage to Lancelot's colors (white instead of silver), while Cei and Bedwyr wore matching white with red and blue trim.

The troops wore everything from tartan weaves to leather pants and rawhide boots. Merovee's men, however, all wore black and white, though of iconoclastic cut and style.

The king himself wore pure white, his full, black hair

hanging straight to the small of his back. He did not train, instead spending each day sitting in the stern, reading.

Cei taught other tactics. In one scenario, the front line locked shields and pressed *down;* then a secondary line of axemen reached over their heads and brained the foe. In each drill, both sides struck full force, but with leather guards along axe edges and wooden caps on *gladius* tips. Bruises were commonplace. Peter admired the realism, but worried the men would be too beaten up by their comrades to be effective on patrol.

At sundown of the third sea day, the end of Peter's ninth day down the rabbit hole, the ship rounded a bend of land into what would be called Termadog Bay in Peter's time. They arrived opposite Harlech just as the sun set behind them, over southern Ireland. A city lookout watching seaward would see only the brilliant, red fire of sunset.

Naw ordered the ship to heave to, and the oarsmen backrowed until the ship floated dead in the water. "Drop anchor," commanded the captain.

"This is preposterous!" blustered Peter. "We're but a mile offshore—let's land tonight."

Captain Naw shook his head, a faint smile flickering across his mouth. The man at the wheel spoke up, smugly. "Canna," he decided. "Reefs. Very dangerous in the dark." He glanced at the captain; Peter swore he almost caught a wink.

"Reefs?" growled Peter. "At Harlech? I don't remember any reefs."

Naw shrugged. "If the helmsman believes in reefs, who am I to disabuse the lad?" He turned his back, stared across the bloody waves.

Peter fumed. *So Captain Naw has his way after all. Four days he swore, and four bloody days it will take, the bastard!* In his head, Peter began to compose a report to Artus, demanding ever harsher measures against the bureaucratic, anal-retentive, foot-dragging captain of the *Blodewwedd.*

The red sun played tricks, painted a river of fire from the *Blodewwedd* to Harlech, touched the city walls with golden flame. Peter sighed. It looked as if a smith had poured molten iron across sea and city.

Suddenly, Anlawdd cried aloud, as she pointed wordlessly

toward the city of her birth, her other hand clutching her white throat.

Peter followed her finger, realized it was no solar illusion: great flames truly engulfed Harlech, stretching like greedy talons toward the twilit sky. Several capsized ships dotted the harbor. Four longboats were drawn up the beach.

It took no military genius to deduce what had happened. Unexpected Jutes had seized the city. Harlech was sacked and gutted.

CHAPTER 50

MARK BLUNDELL PACED, NERVOUSLY. HE LOOKED AT HIS watch: 0230, an hour and a half since he had received authorization from Roundhaven to fling himself back in time after Peter Smythe and Selly Corwin.

Blundell was the only possible link to tell Peter that Selly was acting on her own—not under central command of the IRA; the only person who might be able to persuade Peter to let himself be drawn back gently . . . for the widow's son.

In another hour and a half, Colonel Jackboot would pop down the chimney like Saint Nick, demanding they wrench the major back by hook or crook, by main force, which would probably "solve the problem" by killing him.

So now it's a race. Would the machine be repaired before 0400, Cooper's T-time? If so, and if the Colonel did not get wind of the caper, Mark might have just enough time to squirm between the coils and launch himself. Surely Willks would not rush to wake the Colonel.

Jacob Hamilton squeezed past Blundell, arms entangled in a roil of data cables. Sweat beaded his forehead, but he managed a fast smile. "Think we got it licked, matey. We'll beat the colonel by an hour."

"Thanks, Jacob. No noises from above yet?"

"Hasn't said a word. Hasn't popped down the stairs in six hours. Keep your fingers crossed." The postdoc rushed around the back of the machine, bypassed the faulty circuit board with one that would contain a newly programmed replacement . . . eventually.

That was the bottleneck: Henry Willks was the only man on the team who could code the chip and make it work, the man who had done it the first time. Henry, the man nobody would ever dub "Flash" Willks.

Blundell started to gnaw a knuckle, but restrained himself. He crossed his arms, fumed that his own part was finished and he had nothing to do.

"Mark."

Maybe Selly was right after all. What the hell does any of us know about today's dependence on yesterday? What right do we have?

"Mark," repeated Jacob.

Blundell jumped as Hamilton poked his shoulder. Willks stood behind them both, rubbing sleep from his eyes.

"Finished, I hope," grumbled the old man. "As we'll all be if you bollix this up."

Gingerly, Hamilton took the board from Willks's hands, egg-walked it around the back of the doughnut to the cables, carefully laid out awaiting connection. A husky voice spoke in Mark's ear, Wylie Rosenfeldt: "Five to one the damned edge connectors don't fit." He chuckled, even forced a grin from Blundell.

"All right," called Hamilton, "power up. Anybody smell ozone?"

Blundell hovered above his power console, initiated the start-up program, NFW. As usual, he felt faintly embarrassed at what the initials stood for, another American joke courtesy of Rosenfeldt, the chief programmer.

The lights flickered, somebody cut them. Mark listened to the familiar sounds of the time doughnut powering up: a high-pitched, nearly inaudible whine that made his hair stand on edge; a gentle hum as the circuits warmed; bursts of static and white noise from the monitors as they translated a wide signal into both video and audio components: and beneath all the other sounds, felt rather than heard, the pulse of the timestream itself, caught and twisted sharply by the time field.

The platform glowed bright blue, healthy, beckoning. Mark's stomach fell suddenly, as if he rode an endlessly dropping elevator.

"Power up," he declared when the five "happy faces" appeared in the appropriate windows of his monitor. He wiped his own brow with his sleeve. "Um, hot in here? Nothing's burning, is it?"

"Time seek engaged," said Willks, "give it a few minutes to center on Selly and Smythe, as best it can."

"Selly's PET unchanged. Smythe's . . ." Hamilton paused, stared at the oscillating image. "Hm. I've never seen this before. Damn."

"What?" Mark's voice was too loud. *Must get control . . . control the breathing.*

Hamilton peered close, moved his head back and forth to view from slightly different angles. "Looks like a miniteardrop *within* the normal teardrop of Smythe's consciousness. Like a bleedin' fractal, folds within folds. Don't know what the hell it means. Every few seconds it sort of jumps, expands to fill a quarter to a third of Peter's normal pattern."

Willks coughed. "Maybe we should forget sending anybody else, just try to bring Smythe back?"

"No," stated Blundell firmly. "Last time we tried that we nearly killed Selly. If Peter resists, in his semisevered condition . . . he won't make it." He took a deep breath, closed his eyes for a moment. Then he stared at the glowing platform, the slightly out-of-focus coils. "No, Hank, I've got to go back. No choice."

Blundell wiped his palms dry on his trousers; he approached the platform with firm step and palpitating heart.

"All right, Mark. It's your call."

"Like bloody hell it is!" barked the Voice of Authority from the stairs.

Blundell froze. He did not need to turn to identify Colonel Cooper, who added, "Stand down from that device, Professor Blundell. We've got one and only one task to perform, and you're not a part of it."

Nobody spoke. At last, Hamilton asked the inevitable. "Who tigged you?"

Cooper smiled like Sherlock Holmes. "The lights dimmed and flickered. I figured the game might be afoot."

"Sir," said Blundell, "you don't understand! Unless we send someone to tell Peter to stop resisting—"

"Good work, men, you brought that thing up an hour early. Let's move the major's body into the coils. Gently, there! He's not a sack of potatoes." Cooper edged close to Blundell as the graduate students Conner and Zeblinski wheeled the gurney next to the platform. "No, son, I'm not ignoring you," said Cooper, voice deeper than the ocean floor. "I understand what you're trying to do, and it's damned heroic of you. But the decision has been made, Blundell. And we just don't go around behind the brass's back. Bad form, you know."

Hamilton looked questioningly at Willks, who turned away, waved his hand dismissively. "Shit and fried eggs," muttered Hamilton, as he bent and checked Peter's vital signs. "Okay, lads, shift him over."

They grunted, laid Peter's body among the coils, his skin pallid as the grave in the blue light.

"Set," said Hamilton.

"Power?" asked Willks.

"Go." Blundell clenched his teeth, sat down heavily in his leather chair.

"Chips?"

Mark switched to screen five. "Fine."

"Feedback?"

"Norm," snapped Hamilton. He was not happy.

They continued through the checklist, answering with clipped monosyllables. At last the dreadful moment approached.

"Go, go, and go," said Blundell, reluctantly. Three "happy faces"; the only other alternative was to lie about it.

Like a zombie, Willks double-clicked CALLBACK at the "client" Mac.

The high-pitched whine increased to a scream. Blundell's ears throbbed. A small-minded part of him was pleased to see that Cooper was more sensitive. The colonel clapped hands over ears and winced.

The power jumped offscale, and Mark quickly had to recalibrate. Now ozone did indeed fill the room, so much so that Blundell felt his breath growing short from too little oxygen. The smell was so sharp, his lip curled back.

"Power overplay," he reported. "One seventy one percent."

He shook his head. The circuits would all fry, as they were never designed to drag a man back from the past by main force.

As quickly as he could, he displayed each power screen. This time, there was no microcurrent leakage; Willks had apparently done a bit of redesign work when he rebuilt the board. "No leaks," declared Mark.

Don't look at the PET scan. Watch the power monitor. Don't look at the PET scan. Don't look.

Mark stared at the PET scan, watched the teardrop expand slowly to fill the web pattern. The inner teardrop continued to fluctuate within.

Mark held his breath. The only sound was from the doughnut itself as it strained to retrieve Major Peter Smythe.

"Holding," said Hamilton, voice startlingly loud. He stared at the teardrop, as if carefully inflating a child's balloon with a tire pump. "Holding . . . holding . . . breaking up."

Blundell stared, paralyzed. The interference was faint at first, faintly touching the perimeter of the teardrop with grey. For a moment, Blundell prayed that it would simply fade away, the teardrop continue to expand until it subsumed the entire brain pattern. Then Peter would be back.

A vain hope. Prick the perimeter, and . . . The analogy of the balloon was accurate.

Like an exploding soap bubble in ultraslow motion, the teardrop began to wobble. Curled pieces of pattern "hair" fluttered, turbulence in the timestream that bit and cut at Peter's consciousness like angry, roiling, whitewater rapids.

Never stood a chance. He never stood a chance. The banal thought swirled through Blundell's head, tossed by the same current that shredded Peter's "teardrop" into a Rorschach ink blot.

Mark felt nothing. His hands tingled, could not feel the console keys as he rapidly changed from screen to screen, desperately searching for a technical difficulty that he could fix, and bring Peter back.

There was nothing wrong. *Everything is in perfect working order, sir. No microleaks. No short circuits. No provie spies or Pakistani bombs.*

His ears rang. Looking through the shimmering, hot air over the Crays he saw Hamilton pulling Peter's body from the platform onto the gurney again, feeling his carotid artery, shouting something. For a moment, all was silent.

Then sound rushed back into the room. "CRASH CART!" was what Jacob was yelling. He blew into Peter's mouth, began CPR. "Started resuscitation at 0320," he said, voice cold as the grave.

One two three four five six seven eight nine ten eleven twelve thirteen fourteen fifteen, breath, breath, one two three four five—Mark counted carefully with Jacob, made sure he did not miss a single trick. *Silly, actually. He was a medic in the army. Thirteen fourteen fifteen . . .*

"Cardiac arrest," said Willks, somewhat belatedly.

Cooper was muttering something. Only Blundell was close enough to hear. "Christ, don't go AWOL, Peter."

Breath, breath.

"Call an ambulance," suggested Willks.

"On the way, sir," said Zeblinski, who moved in to relieve Hamilton on the CPR. Jacob attached the leads from the crash cart to Peter's chest.

Breath, breath.

"Four," said Hamilton. "Clear!"

Zelbinski leapt back as lightning struck Peter through the patch leads. His body convulsed. In the PET scan, for an instant the entire pattern rolled counterclockwise.

"Negative conversion," said Hamilton, rubbed his face in his shirt. "Three, four. Clear!" He hit him again with the electrical equivalent of a sledgehammer.

"Did somebody call an ambulance?"

"Negative conversion."

"It's on the way, Professor."

Breath. Breath.

Mark glanced at the PET monitor. It was almost black. The glow that was left resembled the momentary residual flicker on a television screen when it is turned off.

"Drug box." Hamilton snapped his fingers twice, stretched out his hand. His fingernails were impossibly dirty. Blundell saw the box he was reaching for, overcame his paralysis long enough to push it into Jacob's hand.

Hamilton grabbed out a syringe with a ridiculously long needle. "Hold it for a minute, matey," he said to Zeblinski. When the graduate student stopped pumping, Jacob pushed the needle into Peter's chest.

Christ don't go AWOL.

"When did you say the ambulance would get here?" Willks seemed dazed, frightening Blundell. Mark needed somebody in charge, somebody to give orders. Cooper stared sickly and Willks wandered like a madman. Only Hamilton and the other "noncoms" had any idea what to do.

"Neg," said Zeblinski, watching the EKG.

"Give it a minute."

"Negative conversion."

Hamilton tried three more times to jump-start Peter's heart with the crash cart. Whenever he did, the PET monitor flashed for an instant with a standard pattern, faded quickly to black. Faust and Conner switched off performing CPR with Zeblinski.

"0345," said Jacob. The tone of his voice told it all.

"He's not dead," said Blundell.

"Is the ambulance here? Did I hear an ambulance?"

"I'm not a doctor, Mark," said Hamilton. "I can't legally pronounce him dead." Conner paused in the CPR, but Jacob said, "No, keep going. You got a bleedin' appointment?"

Fifteen minutes later, the firemen arrived. Hamilton spoke quietly with them in a corner. Mark caught the phrase "3:45 A.M." Faust was on the CPR, wearily pumping on Peter's chest.

Nobody seemed in much of a hurry. The firemen watched the EKG scope, listened to Peter's chest. Cooper brought them a phone, and they telephoned the emergency ward at the hospital.

Peter's face was grey, the color of long-dead ashes. One eyelid was fully closed, the other open a slit. The eye was dry, no spark behind it. Mark's hand crawled toward Peter's face; he could not stop it. He touched Peter's cheek: it felt like wax.

This is silly. He's not dead. He can't be more than a few minutes dead anyway.

Faust stopped pumping, but did not give Peter the two breaths of life, either. The firemen folded Peter's arms across his chest.

"Let's go, Mark," said Jacob.

The dead body was covered, rolled on the gurney toward the stairs. The firemen folded up the gurney legs and carried Peter upstairs.

"Let's go." Jacob put his arm around Mark's shoulders, led him away toward the stairs.

Blundell spared a glance back at the machine. Zeblinski and Willks were shutting the power down in sequence. Nobody had thought to do it during the crisis. As the blue glow faded to black, Cooper slowly vanished into the shadows of the basement laboratory.

CHAPTER 51

THE *TRIREME* ROSE AND FELL, AND I ROSE AND FELL WITH IT, NOT being a sailor nor having my "sea legs" yet. It was hard to pace nervously on that bucking deck, but I did my best.

Well, I thought, *did he or didn't he?* Had That Boy figured out yet who was the apparition he saw in the *Dux Bellorum*'s apartment that night? The fear had gnawed at me every day of the voyage, eating away at my stomach like Mother's hot spice sausage.

But I had a more pressing—and more dangerous—task: I had to find a way to communicate with the Harlech nightwatch, give them the message to send to Father that Artus was still alive . . . so he'd better drop his plans to kill or capture Lancelot, for his entire scheme had come to nought.

I glanced cautiously back at the bunkhouse; it seemed quiet, and all the running lights of the *trireme* were doused so no one would know we were in the bay. Alas, I would have to shatter that secrecy.

I strolled to the bow as nonchalantly as I could manage. I nodded to the officer of the deck, passed him by; fortunately, he did not ask to look beneath my cloak, for he would have wondered why I carried a small, lit lantern beneath it when all exterior lights were supposed to be black. I was ready to explain that I always did a bit of reading before bed, and even had a scroll with me—a history of the bath in Rome, I believe.

At I reached the bow, I made sure no one watched, then ducked beneath the line that led to the bowsprit ram, lowered myself over the side to a reinforcing railing just above the waterline, and wedged my arm into the ram brace. I had no idea in the world how I would get back up to the deck; but at least I was unlikely to be spotted, either.

I stood as steadily as I could, with the swells washing over my feet whenever we dropped into a trough, and opened my lantern to send a short beam landwards.

There was no response. I repeated my action, opening the lantern for a moment and closing it smartly. Upon the third try, I finally saw an answering flash.

Using the signal code of the Harlech nightwatch, I sent a message:

"Anlawdd. Message to Gormant. Mission."

"Ready for message," the watch signaled.

"Failed. *Dux Bellorum* alive. Repeat. *Dux Bellorum* alive. Canastyr dead."

There was a long moment of darkness. At last, they responded: "Is Lancelot aboard?"

"Yes."

"Cei?"

"Yes."

"Do your ships pose threat to Harlech navy?"

"One ship, Roman *trireme*. Marines. Knights. Merovee, Sicambrians."

"Number?"

"Fifty plus ten marines." I hesitated, then beamed my own question. "What happened?"

They waited a long time before responding, and I grew worried. "Fire accidental," they said at last. "Not as bad as it looks."

I stared, not understanding how they could possibly say that. The fire clearly engulfed nearly the entire city!

"What should I do?" I asked. "Mission failed, Artus alive." I added, just in case they had missed it the first time.

"Come in," they responded.

"What is Gormant's mood? Will he kill because of failure? Canastyr, Artus."

They beamed a quick response: "Canastyr, Gormant forgives you. Kill Artus later."

I blinked, not realizing at first what they had just said. Then revelation struck me.

It was possible they might have missed the earlier signal

that Canastyr was dead . . . but how could they possibly have thought *Canastyr* had been sent to kill Artus?

Either the watchman knew the plot, or he did not . . . if he did not, then he would have said nothing—but if he *did* know, he would have known that it was me, Anlawdd, sent to kill the *Dux Bellorum!*

Suddenly terrified, I cast my lantern into the ocean, where it hissed into blackness and sank immediately.

The only good explanation for the weird lapse was that *I wasn't signaling to the Harlech watch,* not the ones set by my father to watch for my return with news of Artus.

And if I weren't signaling to the watch . . . then I was probably signaling to the same Jutes who had sacked my city . . . or to their Saxon allies.

My unknown conversationalist tried several more times to contact me, finally gave up. Then I saw a frightening sight: far to the south, *another* lantern flared in a complex code I didn't understand. It kept pausing, during which time undoubtedly somebody else aboard the *Blodewwedd* sent his own signals.

For a long moment, I stared into the black waves. It truly was "wine-dark," but perhaps "blood-dark" would be more appropriate.

I had failed again . . . first, I had allowed my passion to interfere with duty; now I had stupidly made assumptions and jeopardized everyone's life, even That Boy's.

I stared at the waves, wondered what it would be like simply to let go, fall forward into the icy sea, and sink beneath the surface, down, down. . . .

I have never before been as close to falling on my sword as I was then, staring at the ruins of my home, a chill creeping up and down my spine as I realized I had just been chatting with the murderers who slew it, and had given them critical information.

I leaned down, lowered my hand. The water washed across it, and for some reason, I thought of King Merovee, whom they call half-fish.

I heard a voice in my head. I don't know whether he spoke to me, or whether I was simply mad and hearing demons.

Why do you think it's warmer down there than up here, daughter?

"I've done the best I know how," I said, "and nothing has worked. I'm not a warrior, not a man, not a girl. I'm surely no princess. I cause nothing but pain and misery to everyone I meet."

You're a Builder; that is something.

"I've even failed at that. Would a Builder have been afraid to carry out his duty?"

What is duty? Do you really know? Does any of us? Learn to do better!

"I can't learn!"

"Then jump." The last was spoken aloud, or so it seemed, and I was so startled I lost my footing. My feet slipped from the railing as if they had been kicked by someone behind me, and I fell into the water.

Only my clutching hand saved me, for I managed to grab a line that looped down from the ram to the bow. I swallowed water, pulled myself up sputtering.

Frantic, I struggled up the line, hand over hand, but something held me, dragged me back toward a watery grave!

I surged against it, finally ripping myself from its grasp. I shinned up the rope faster than I had ever climbed a rope before, finally reaching the deck and heaving myself up and over with a single tug.

I sat heavily, panting, coughing, and dripping water like an overturned bucket.

My my, said the mocking voice, *it seems you aren't quite ready to cast yourself upon your sword yet . . . are you?*

I scowled, salt water pouring down my face from my drenched and dripping hair. *You sure have a startling way to make a point,* I thought.

Startling or not, however, the point was made. My self-pity had washed away into the ocean. Louder than all other thoughts, one echoed from ear to ear: a warrior fixes the problem—*not* the blame.

I raised my eyes to heaven, still angry at Athena (or was it Discordia?) for how she went about bestowing wisdom . . . you'd think there'd be a better way, or at least a drier one!

"All right," I gasped, "I get the message."

I stood, shivering in the chilly air, and stormed back amidships to find a spot to hole up for the night. The officer of the deck first saluted, then stared at my soaked clothes and wringing-wet hair.

"Haven't you ever seen a girl take a bath before?" I snarled at him, and disappeared quickly, before he could ask questions.

Damn That Boy!

CHAPTER 52

CORS CANT EWIN DOZED FITFULLY IN THE BARRACKS, CURLED UP like a melon slice, arm cast protectively about his harp. He shivered in the chill. The rolling deck, the clamor of arms and armor outside the low-roofed shelter kept him from sleep. Even the faint sounds from the burning city distracted him, sounding nearly like screams.

He had gingerly suggested Anlawdd might find his arm a comfortable pillow, but she interrupted, waved away his offer: "Cors Cant Ewin, look what they're doing to my city—*my* city! I can't imagine what Lancelot is thinking, why he doesn't just order the attack right now, and damn the darkness! It's like watching a vicious cat tease a poor mouse, while you stand behind a door, unable to liberate the poor thing! I'm quite positive I won't sleep a wink all night, imagining what I'm going to do to King Hrundal when I get my hands around his throat! Now what were you saying, Cors Cant?" She thoughtlessly poked holes in the furled sail with her dagger, annoyed that Captain Naw had told her that wives and mistresses weren't allowed on deck during wartime.

"Um, nothing, Your Hi—I mean, Anlawdd." She was not listening anyway.

That was long before; he had no idea where Anlawdd had wandered since. Cors Cant shivered in the common quarters that housed sailors, marines, and Lancelot's troops, all crammed together like herring barreled for market. The room smelled of pitch and urine, spilled wine and scores of unwashed bodies.

The bard seized a high plank for his bed; no one else wanted it anyway, fearing the fall. It was barely wide enough for his slender self, kit, and harp.

He picked the instrument up, leaned it onto his chest, and plucked softly, trying not to disturb the marines. Only after a moment did he realize he played "The Making of Blodewwedd."

> *A thousand blooms of oak and broom,*
> *Purple and yellow and white,*
> *A grove complete of meadow sweet,*
> *Woven in gold sunlight.*
> *Does Math exhale the living breath*
> *To maketh Blodewwedd . . .*

Blodewwedd was a "flower-woman," made as a wife for Lleu Llaw Gyffes, the "skillful-handed, fair-haired one," whose mother Arianrhod cursed him: he could have no name until she gave him one, no arms until she armed him, and no wife of any people on the earth. She was tricked into giving him a name and arms, then Math the sorcerer assembled Blodewwedd from plants and flowers.

Blodewwedd eventually fell in love with someone else and betrayed Lleu; would this expedition betray Artus? Try as he might, Cors Cant could not shake the feeling of impending disaster. He shook his head, changed to a more sprightly tune, as much to warm flesh as to raise spirits.

Almost immediately, a boot flew across the common and crashed against the wall above his head. "Leave off torturing the cat, boy!" growled a nasal voice with a Manx accent.

If I knew who it was, Cors Cant grumped, *I'd be tempted to tell Lancelot I'd heard you plotting, next time I see him.* An empty threat, the bard would never abuse his trust. *But some would; I wonder who the prince has set to spy upon* me?

Lancelot ducked inside the crew hold, flanked by Cei, and called the company together. Most sat up groggily, but Cors Cant was grateful for the interruption to his own morbid thoughts.

"We're going to get wet, boys," said the Sicambrian general. "Two hours before dawn, we drive straight into Harlech harbor. The marines roll over the side, swim to the docks. We'll try to get you as close as possible.

"When you hit the wharf, cut empty boats adrift, if you can. Scout the Jutic numbers, then move north like hell. Merovee's heavy infantry will beach a mile north to wait for the marines. If it looks feasible, we'll take the port and hold it while the *Blodewwedd* returns to the Cardiff garrison. Maybe we can hold on for the legions."

"What if it *doesn't* look feasible?" It was Medraut. Morgawse's son did a good job of concealing his fear, but his voice cracked slightly.

Lancelot shrugged. "Then we'll return to Cardiff ourselves, and hope the Jutes don't land reinforcements in the next week. Sleep now," Lancelot told the warriors. "We'll attack, ah, one candle before dawn."

The sailors busied themselves, raced fore and aft like Artus's African monkeys to ready grappling hooks, boarding ramps, balls of pitch to set ablaze and catapult at the foe— just in case, insisted the captain.

Inside the cabin, Cors Cant groaned, rolled onto his stomach, and nearly crushed his harp. He locked arms across ears but could not block out the noise of impending battle. When he closed his eyes, the deck rolled and spun like a plate on a juggler's rod.

He reached out a hand to touch the sword he had liberated from the siege supplies in the *lalarium* of Caer Camlann the night before they left. *Won't Anlawdd be surprised to see me account for myself in battle!* False cheer: his hand shook, almost as cold as the iron blade.

A few hours later, he gave up feigning sleep. He stood, tucked the sword in his belt, wrapped a blanket around his shoulders. The bard hesitated, then tucked the harp beneath the blanket, swung down and walked the deck in search of Anlawdd.

He needed advice, comfort. As he walked, he plucked a tune, more verses from the morbid tale of Blodewwedd, muffled by the blanket so only he could hear it. He sang in a whisper.

> *Make me a bath upon the bank,*
> *Roof it with branches sere.*
> *A foot in the tub, on billy goat's flank,*

> *Struck by a year-forged spear.*
> *Nor house, nor horse, nor 'pon the plain*
> *Shall Lleu Llaw Gyffes be slain.*

Beneath the archers' turret, Cei leaned on the rail, watching the dull red conflagration on shore. No Anlawdd in sight.

The porter heard Cors Cant approach. "Can't sleep, Bard? Me neither. Always scares the shit out of me, watching everything making ready."

"You're scared, General?" The railing was a black shadow against black clouds. Cors Cant groped for it, stood next to Cei, craned his neck seeking auburn hair that probably looked brown as everyone else's in the moonlight.

"If you weren't scared," said Cei, "I wouldn't want you in *my* command. I don't like berserkers. They're like Hannibal's elephants, perfect weapons 'til they turn on you."

"Hannibal ... Hannibal and his elephants. I memorized most of that lay. He conquered Rome."

"He almost did. Came across the Alps, north of Rome."

"But I never understood the elephant parts. What are they, huge horses? They're animals of some sort, I got that much."

"Artus says an elephant is four tree trunks, a wall, a snake, and a rope sewn together, and it's close enough, boy. I saw a real elephant once, in Rome. Tall as a house, a huge, grey beast with a nose like a curling snake. Five armored men can ride atop, and the monster itself can kick an army apart."

"Blood of Mars! We should get some. Are they expensive?"

> *She's made him a bath upon the bank,*
> *Roofed it with branches sere.*
> *"The goat I have brought, and here is his flank,*
> *Stand on it now if you dare!"*
> *As Lleu stands, a foot upon each,*
> *A poisoned spear his side does breech.*

Cei laughed, a rare occurrence. "They're wild, temperamental monsters! Can't tell friend from foe, wouldn't care if they could. A panicked elephant kicks your *own* army apart, as Hannibal discovered. Stick to men. At least treachery is easier to predict than madness."

Cors Cant tried to imagine an elephant; the image was both

frightening and silly. "I never get to go anywhere or see anything," he complained.

"Is this your first campaign?" Cors Cant nodded glumly. "Do you go as bard or soldier? Do you have a weapon?"

Proudly, the boy showed Cei the sword.

"Macha's tits, who gave you that? You must have an enemy. We keep that trash in case of a seige!" He tapped on the railing. "Here, boy, strike you this Jute before he cuts your throat."

Cors Cant hesitated. Where was Captain Naw? Would he mind having his deck rail cut apart? The crew were not watching, so Cors Cant drew back his arm and swung the sword at the bolted wood.

His arm jarred as if struck by a quarterstaff. With an awful, raspy snap, the blade split toward the tip, and the point spun into the choppy sea. As Cors Cant gingerly raised the remaining piece, he felt the blade rattle back and forth within the hilt. Obviously, either the tang was shattered or the wood that held it was split.

He sucked in a breath, stared at the useless shard of metal. The rail was slightly chipped, barely noticeable.

"Here, take one of these." Cei squatted, untied the lock on a black and grey trunk, identical to a dozen others lashed to different parts of the deck. It contained four swords and three axes.

He hesitated, drew a *gladius,* and handed it to Cors Cant. It was heavier, but far better balanced than the one at the boy's side.

It looked familiar. With a sharp gasp, he realized it perfectly resembled the phantom sword whose image outside Lancelot's window had saved him from a gruesome death. He gently laid his harp on the deck, threw the remaining piece of his old sword over the side, and balanced the new one in his hand. "A sword for Gwydion, or Aeneas!"

"Hah! Don't fool yourself. It's good, but not great. Standard issue to infantrymen, and it'll do for an untrained bard. You might want to get one of the sergeants to show you a bit about swordplay before the morning, if you think it will make any difference. Myself, I'd just advise you to stick close to Prince Lancelot and forget about fighting.

"Don't worry about sleep," continued Camlann's porter. "Return to the hut and lie quietly without moving until we rouse you. You'll be almost as rested."

At that moment, Cacamwri approached. Cors Cant grabbed his harp, faded quickly into the darkness before the hated centurion could see him.

The bard continued his circumnavigation to the bow, near the dragon ram. But he met Merovius Rex, not Anlawdd.

"Your Majesty," exclaimed the bard, "look what Cei gave me." He held out the new sword, but the king looked only at the harp, shook his head. "A sword won't give you courage," said the king. "I know it all too well. Courage comes from the *cup.*"

"The cup?"

"The sword gives valor in battle, useless without the cup of spirit, sympathy. True courage is the combination." Merovee took the bard's hand in his own, held him face-to-face, eyes locked.

"What are you . . ." Cors Cant's question trickled into the ocean, unasked.

Unable to turn his gaze, he fell into Merovee's eyes, deep wells below the valley. Deeper into black, past the red of war, the blue of art, the green of worship, past color itself to brilliant white.

Cors Cant fell back, yet he never struck the deck, long though he fell. He was a bird, wings frozen in flight; a dragon endlessly arcing backward toward a ground ever distant. He was aware of his body, several bodies far upon the horizon, lost in mist upon water. But *he* was not among them.

He stood, then, within a room, white on white. Grey fog rolled through the window hole, blowing moonlight before it; but no moon peeked through. The circular room was divided into Euclidean segments of arc by geometric lines of no thickness. At the apex was a body wrapped in a shroud of purest silver.

As Cors Cant watched, fascinated and horrified, the body burst into flame. But the flame did not consume.

In his vision, the bard approached unafraid, and reached for a burning corner of the winding sheet. Black words charred the cloth, which was otherwise untouched by the flames. *Et In Arcadia Ego*—"And In Arcadia I." Merovee's meaningless words, as "transcribed" by Lancelot (who could neither read nor write).

"They still mean nothing!" cried Cors Cant. What signified

Arcadia, a rude and barbarous land full of savages whose only classical contribution was that King Agapenor sent an Arcadian army to the Trojan War on Mycenaean ships?

Oddly, the bright, colorless room reminded Cors Cant of the bright, rainbow glitter of Anlawdd's cave when she lit the candle, brought him *into the light.* He looked down, saw a shallow stream running across the floor; it was not there before. His bare, left foot stood in the water.

He felt again the cool, soothing underground river, exactly as he had in the crystal cave. *And beneath me flows silent water.*

An underground stream was a classical, Pythagorean allusion to a secret passed from generation to generation, or a secret bloodline. But how did the Long-Haired King, the auburn-haired princess, and the almost-bard interlink? What secret, what bloodline, had passed from hand to hand leading back from *someone* to ... to the widow's son, who was *said* to be Hiram Abiff, but only in months ending in a Y?

The letters floated up, peeled off the silver shroud of flames: *ET IN ARCADIA EGO.* Slowly they rotated, began to move into a new stellar configuration, an anagram floating black and charred in the air:

I TEGO AR—

Afraid in his dream, though he knew not why, Cors Cant shuddered, quickly covered his eyes before he could see the rest. When he dared peek, the letters had vanished.

He crept forward, compelled. His fingers touched the miraculous cloth, prepared to yank it free, reveal the face of the corpse.

Then rough hands seized his shoulders, whipped him back to front. Anlawdd held him in his dream, inspected him with a worried look.

She, too, was dressed in white, her robe trimmed with silver. A silver crown weighed down upon her head, a bloody axe dangled at her belt. "Cors Cant Ewin, *what* are you doing in *my* dream? I'm asleep on the deck, resting before the war, and suddenly here you are in my private head, rather rudely, I might add! With a sword! This simply isn't your war, you should know that by now. But men will be boys, I suppose, and the boys have to play soldier now and again.

"By the way," she continued, "I have something for you, a present, you might consider it." She turned a hand palm up; it held a tiny vial of brown liquid, a potion like that she had given him before his initiation. "If you're ever alone in the womb of the Mother, sore wounded and afraid of dark Arcadia, this may bring you to the light."

She put the cold glass thimble in his hand; it was labeled *drink me*. "Now forget the sword and go back to your harp!" she commanded, tossed her hair in a very Anlawddian fashion. "Leave the battles to me, who was, after all, born to it." She snapped her fingers imperiously, then rustled her robe most princessly. Cors Cant blinked, and found himself awake again, still in Merovee's grasp.

The bard was filled with the deep certainty that the burning, shrouded corpse was *not* his own. Nor Anlawdd's. The cloth and the corpse were half-Saxon, half-British.

The king looked at Cors Cant, seemed to sense that the bard had just seen a vision. "It may be music that fills your cup, but I think not. Seek instead an ocean of love," said Merovee, gray eyes almost clear, framed by his long, black hair. "Promise me this: when you find her, stay by her, *let her guard you from harm*: that is her task in this life, that's why I sent her to you."

"You sent her?"

"She is one of mine. She *knows* me. Let her fill your cup. But not until you find her, and her alone."

"But ... if she doesn't want me?"

Merovee said nothing, but took Cors Cant's hand. He made the sign Anlawdd had taught the bard. "Stay by her, or she may be lost. Two are one together, but nothing apart."

Cors Cant returned the sign, clumsily. *Merovee! I should have guessed ... who else is a Builder? Myrddin? Lancelot? Surely not Artus....* "I promise," he said sincerely.

"You are more important to our children's children than all the rest of us combined." He smiled, tiny wrinkles at the corner of his mouth betraying a much greater age than he seemed. "Though I confess I do not know why. Yet. You have a task yet to perform, a secret to pass that flows deep underground."

He squeezed Cors Cant's shoulder, faded into night's black to join his Sicambrians. For an instant Cors Cant thought he saw a golden flicker in Merovee's hair, as if it, too, were on fire. Then the king disappeared. The bard continued his quest around the rolling deck.

Across the bow, past the ram that rose to seek the starless

sky, then plummeted into the inky ocean as the *Blodewwedd* pitched fore and back, he spied a cloaked and hooded figure crouched against the rail. It held something bulky shrouded under the cloak, something that glowed.

Cors Cant approached, curious. Who else was restless on this red-lit night? It was not Anlawdd. At the scrape of his boot on the deck, the figure turned, a metal clank coming from the cloaked object. It was Cutha the Saxon.

"Meistersinger," said the hooded man, "how it goes?" Polite words, cold smile; but he spoke a bit too quickly, as if surprised with his hand in the butter dish.

"Have you seen . . ." the boy trailed off, strangely reluctant to speak her name aloud.

"Your stitching maid soldier? By the stern she will be found, by the catapult at the stern." Cutha shifted his weight. A slight trail of smoke escaped his cloak, and Cors Cant whiffed tallow.

"What are you doing?" The bard's brows furrowed. "What's under there? A candle?"

Silence, a crooked grin. Cutha reached beneath the cloth, produced a fetish lantern to Taranis Thunderer, or "Donner" as Cutha called him. "A religious people we are, boy," said the Saxon. "Superstition? Perhaps. I pray, for strength and courage." Cutha's voice softened. "Away my fears I drive." Cors Cant felt a flash of kinship.

First Cei, now the Saxon! Maybe I'm not such a coward after all. "I didn't mean to intrude, Prince Cutha."

The Saxon stepped close. Cors Cant recoiled from the odor of unwashed sweat and grime—*hydrophobic Saxons!* "Boy," admitted Cutha, "more than that it is. Please . . . by fear and respect I rule. Nothing do I fear, my men think. You won't tell?" The man's blue eyes beseeched.

Seems everybody's trusting me with their secrets. Not sure I like it. With a resigned air, Cors Cant promised: "If you insist. I'll tell no one I saw you here."

"Your debt," whispered Cutha, turned back to the rail, stared at the distant city fires. They cut a red trail like moonshadow along the water. The Saxon bowed his head. His hood fell across his face of its own accord.

Embarrassed, Cors Cant continued quickly toward the stern. When he had nearly circumnavigated the deck, he found Anlawdd. Had he started out in the opposite direction, he would have found her directly.

She sat cross-legged in an alley crack between the catapult and Naw's cabin, yawning as if she had just awakened. Cors Cant waited, but she made no sign she saw him. He squirmed into the crack, harp balanced on his knees.

As his eyes traveled from sky to city, the red-dark night solidified into rolling, black smoke that swept inland. The shadow between catapult and cabin caught no light whatever. Only Anlawdd's eyes reflected the moon, the Harlech fire.

Cors Cant smelled lightning, the hairs on the nape of his neck stood straight. The power scent which emanated from the princess frightened him with its intensity. She spoke abruptly, and he jumped, banging his head against the catapult strut.

"Cors Cant Ewin, no matter what may happen I want you to promise me something, that is if you meant all those things you said about your feelings toward me. Did you?"

He nodded, realized she could not see him. "Yes."

"Well I certainly hope so, since otherwise extracting a promise from you would be like pulling weeds and ordering them not to grow back."

She looked at him; he *felt* it. "Cors Cant," she begged, "promise you'll believe me about being a princess, no matter what anybody else says."

Anybody? Says? "I promise," he said, but his voice held a questioning tone. Three promises! Cors Cant squirmed, remembering the Curse of Pryderi: *three oaths a day, and faith betray.*

"Well, one oath for another, my mother always said, and I don't want to hear anything about how you never even met my mother. For my part, I promise you won't be slain in the battle if I can help it, though if you insist upon committing suicide with that bright new sword of yours, there's not much I can do. Are you determined to die gloriously?"

"No! I don't want to die at all, either well or poorly! But how did you know about the sword?"

"I must have seen it before you sat down. Mustn't I have? Then it's a deal."

"Deal." Almost, Cors Cant asked Anlawdd something, but he was not sure what. He opened his mouth, remained silent. Once more he began a question, changed his mind.

"Whatever you're trying to say, spit it out!" demanded Anlawdd.

He gasped. "How did you hear the thought in my mind? Can you see in this dark? Do you have the *sight?*"

"Cors Can Ewin, you sucked in two giant lungfuls of air and puffed them out. You're either trying to work up the courage to say something, or you're blowing up a sheep's bladder."

"Oh. Anlawdd, I—look, it's not a secret. No matter what you promise, one of us might die tomorrow. I . . . I wish you would allow me . . . Princess, I'm only a bard, but could I kiss you?"

He waited, eyes squeezed shut. Silence reigned. Finally, Anlawdd spoke, voice full. "Cors Cant, I—I can't. Not yet. I don't know how I feel. I only know we'll either spend a life together, or break and never see each other again. I *cannot* kiss you just for friendship's sake; I wish I could. It would fill a great space within me."

A lump in the bard's throat swelled until he could not swallow. "I understand," he croaked.

"Do you? Well *I* don't," she said bitterly. "I've always been light and easy. This is heavy, like a sponge full of water. Go," she ordered. But she caught hold of his arm to prevent him leaving.

"Tarry," she said, gripping his arm so hard he gasped in pain. Anlawdd sat silent for many long heartbeats; then Cors Cant *listened* and heard a strange sound: it took him a moment to realize she was weeping.

"I have a tale," she said at last, "about a snake and a girl. Uncle Leary told me this story.

"The girl was created by God and set in a garden, told she could eat anything and everything except one fruit, from a tree called the Tree of Understanding—and one other fruit, from a tree called the Tree of Eternity.

" 'If you eat from the Tree of Understanding,' said God, 'you'll understand right and wrong, and how far you fall short of how you always pictured yourself. You'll realize how much you have to learn, how little you really know. You'll become wise and understanding, like me—like God—and you wouldn't want *that,* would you?'

"Because the girl was still ignorant, like a horse who

doesn't know the halter isn't really tied to the stall, for she hadn't eaten the fruit yet, so she said 'I'll not eat, God; I'll obey your commandment, for I want to keep dreaming my fancies about being a warrior-maid.' And she went about her life, avoiding the Tree of Understanding."

"Anlawdd! That's a blasphemy to the Christian God ... maybe you'd better not—He's supposed to be fairly touchy on the subject."

"But a snake walked up to her—they had legs back then, you know—and he asked how a warrior could walk through life with her eyes closed, like a sleepwalker. In her soul, she might be pure as driven snow, or black as an unlit cave ... but how could she live her life *without knowing?* And the stupid, ignorant girl thought about understanding and seeing herself and becoming like God, and she grew jealous of all the adventure that her brother saw.

"She decided to journey out of her father's house, across the garden to the Tree of Understanding. She plucked a fruit and took a healthy bite; it was the snake's fault anyway."

"What did she see?" asked the bard, feeling sudden fear, though he did not know why.

"Her eyes opened," intoned Anlawdd. "She woke up. She found out she wasn't a warrior at all—just a frightened, little girl who hated her brother for what he'd done to her, what he'd made her think was *her* fault—and who would have done *anything* to get away from him and her father, who knew and did nothing. She found out that her hand faltered at the critical moment and her brain faltered when there was no excuse at all.

"Cors, she found out the mask wouldn't fit anymore, as if her head had shrunk three sizes."

An idea began to form in Cors Cant's head; his unease coalesced into pure terror, for suddenly he knew what she was about to confess. "Anlawdd," he whispered, "don't tell—"

"Yes, bard ... it was me you chased from the *Dux Bellorum*'s room. I crept there to slay him, like an assassin." She let go his arm, and he yanked it back as if her flesh was icy, its touch simultaneously freezing and burning. "Cors Cant," she said, drained and emotionless at last, "you've given your heart to a murderer."

"Canastyr ... ? The man you slew—"

"He was my brother. He—*touched* me, long ago, in a way you'll never understand, I pray to Jesus and the Goddess Mary. Father sent him to make sure I killed Artus."

"Lord," said the boy, stunned. "I wish you had never told me this ... Princess Anlawdd."

She spoke almost too softly for him to hear. "I chose the path that led to the abyss; thank Mary, a little dog yapped at my heels, like in those picture cards Cei has, and warned me one step before I plunged over.

"Now I choose the path out. And my first rule is No More Secrets!" Anlawdd turned, and the moon reflected redly in her eyes, making them glow. Without knowing why, as he was not particularly religious and not Christian fully in any event, Cors Cant Ewin crossed himself.

"Now you know who I am," she declared. "Now you know what I'm capable of doing, and where I falter and lose courage. *Caveat emptor!*

"I once charged you with winning me ... now, my bard, it is I who must win *you*. I must win you back, and in that fight may I truly find my calling as a warrior.

"I don't have many weapons, but one that I discovered at last that I *do* have is truth: never again will I listen when God says not to eat from the Tree of Understanding. From now on, I follow the snake, though he was cursed to crawl on his belly for his audacity in opening my eyes ... rather like what happened to Prometheus in that Greek history you like to sing betimes."

She sniffed. Cors Cant said nothing; he hugged his knees as he tried to banish the image of Anlawdd standing over the *Dux Bellorum,* dagger in hand, ready to end Britain's life. He felt uncomfortable, aware that the world was redeemed from her act of murder only by her potential love for the bard ... and that was a fundamentally wrong reason for a man such as Artus to live or die, an empire like Prydein to rise or fall!

Was the world truly so fragile?

She spoke again after a silence. "I think it'll be a long, hard road back to the garden, if I can even find it again. But that's where the Tree of Eternity grows, and now that I have the beginnings of understanding, I think I'm ready to seek that other fruit."

She reached out, squeezed his ankle. "You can't talk to me now. There is too much you would say that you'd regret later, but putting words back in your mouth is like . . . well, it's like trying to put the wine back in the jar after you've shattered it on the cobblestones, if you know what I mean. Best not to drop it in the first place."

He nodded, though she could never see it in the darkness. He rose, suddenly felt a compulsion to speak anyway, despite her admonition. "I know my heart."

"Do you?"

"I pray you find yours, *whichever* way it beats."

Cors Cant slid out of the alley to the main deck. He looked back; no eyes reflected.

Her invisible voice drifted from the crack. "Look for me before you storm the walls, Orpheus, but don't look back. I made a promise, you know."

Heart aching but oddly expectant, the bard returned to his high plank in the cabin, lay back and closed his eyes. *I only have to lie here and pretend to sleep,* he thought; *Cei said it was nearly just as good. Just pretend. . . .*

Eurydice touched him gently from behind, shade-hands pinched cold and angry, plucked like nails in a board. A queer sort of Hades, full of Saxons and fat, bearded men who covered their nakedness with smooth, wet flippers. Eurydice stood over Artus with a dagger. . . .

The world rocked, a storm, an earthshake! Cors Cant's eyes flew open. He leapt to his feet.

He smelled the cold chill of near dawn, saw the pink eastern sky. Foot-Captain Hir Eiddyl passed to the next soldier, planted a foot on his shoulder, and shook him awake. The foot-captain's twin brother, Hir Amren, following behind, gestured Cors Cant to silence.

The bard pulled on his boots soldierwards, wrapped his harp carefully in many layers of oiled cloth. *Perhaps I should leave it on the boat?* His head said yes, but his hands continued to wrap. He tied a cord around it, looped it around his neck, and ran on deck, sword in hand.

Anlawdd said—she crept into his room and nearly . . . Cors Cant crushed the thought beneath his heel; this was not the day to think on it. He needed more time, an hour, a day; the Tree of Eternity.

The trumps were silent as tombs; the soldiers stood on the deck, eagerly wetting their lips, tasting salt. The only sound was the click and sweep of the oars as the *Blodewwedd* charged the unsuspecting Jutes. The attack began.

CHAPTER 53

I DON'T KNOW WHY I TOLD HIM. I TRIED TO STOP THE WORDS, but they flowed out, and I realized when I had finished that I had finally done right.

At last, I felt clean again.

I knew I had probably lost him anyway, despite sparing the *Dux Bellorum;* That Boy—Cors Cant, I should say—would drift away from me, heartbroken and betrayed, like the snake cursed to crawl on his belly for the sin of bringing enlightenment. When Merovee found out, as I would surely confess, he would cast me out of the Builders, and Leary would take my axe away and give me a mop and broom.

But God save me, *I had my honor back.*

Did it matter? Did such a little thing as honesty and honor matter in the modern age, when men fought in squares, locked shields and struck the man to their right instead of their own opponent?

Did one tiny, barely used soul matter, when my birth city burned like Hell from the fires of her own *hubris,* her own damning pride to think she could cheat and murder her way to freedom?

Could it possibly matter that I finally felt clean again?

It mattered. Oh God, did it matter!

I closed my eyes, listened to the click-clack-click as the left and right oarbanks kissed the ocean swells, shoving us forward into the ambush I knew awaited us. Behind my eyelids, I saw His face, felt His touch on my brow, soothing me and telling me it mattered, oh God.

Behind closed eyes, I saw Arcadia at last: cool, shady grass and happy, bright rivers. Maybe I could become a shoemaker and sew leather all day, kicking through piles of scraps and ends to walk from bench to window then back to bed. Such peace; such solitude! I'd not stab anything but cowhide and my axe would chop nothing but firewood for the long, winter nights.

And in Arcadia, I . . .

The sun rose, warmed my face. I opened my eyes, blinking in the light. No Arcadia; not yet. Still on the *Blodewwedd*, driving to the attack against a city full of bloody Jutes, Saxons, my father, and other betrayers of Harlech. Maybe I'd wake up and find it was all a dream, even Canastyr and what he did to me.

I smiled; what the hell, the fruit of understanding still tasted sweet on my lips.

Watch for the spellbinding conclusion in Part II of ARTHUR WAR LORD, coming out in September 1994.